THE MUSICIAN
AND THE
MONSTER

MEGAN VAN DYKE

Edited by Heather McCorkle.

Cover designed by MiblArt.

Interior character art by Lulybot.

Interior chapter art by Megan Van Dyke.

For questions or permissions contact: authormeganvandyke@gmail.com

www.authormeganvandyke.com

CHAPTER 1

CERIDWEN

MUSIC SAYS THINGS WORDS never can.

I love you. I miss you. I'm sorry I killed you.

Ceridwen Kinsley sat on the roof of her family's house, as she often did, playing music into the night. This place would never truly be home. That title was reserved for their country home, or rather, former country home—the one where she'd grown up. But it was never the same after Mother died. Nothing was.

Ceridwen pulled her shawl tightly around her shoulders—a poor defense against the approaching winter and even less against the ache in her heart. Time passed, but the pain of loss lingered on, especially given the role she played in that tragedy.

The cool metal of the flute pressed against her lips as she played her fourth song of the night, the mournful notes ringing clear from her perch atop the city house. Every night Ceridwen played for her mother, as she had before her father's ruined finances forced them to this small city of no consequence. The half-crumbling house in the old part of the city was all they could afford, and sometimes even that seemed like a stretch.

She longed to play for others, but no one would pay to hear the flute. Not in the backwater city of Teneboure in the far north of Castamar. Nor did her father consider it a proper occupation for a young woman despite their need for money.

Even so, music spoke the truths she dared not say aloud, and this little token of song, something her mother had dearly loved, was the best apology Ceridwen could offer her in the beyond. A familiar, hollow ache radiated in her chest. *Can she even hear me there?*

Some nights Ceridwen felt her presence, her eyes on her. A tingle across the cheek. A shiver down her spine. The slightest hint of a reply on the breeze. It was enough. It didn't matter if people talked about the young woman who played her flute on the roof.

Dim light glowed from the gas lamps lining the streets in the wealthy southern district of the city. A glowing façade, like the fine clothes its people wore to hide their shallow hearts. Even if its residents hadn't gossiped about Mother's passing, they surely commented about where the family resided in the old district, with its aged buildings and lack of more modern conveniences. They were one step away from paupers, and everyone knew it.

Ceridwen's gaze wandered north toward the grand old manor—the view she preferred—where it loomed on a rise at the edge of the city, a handful of blocks from the house. Few lights glowed in the gray towers, the only sign anyone lived there. Deliveries were left at the gates, no balls graced its high halls, and few servants ever came or went. Lord Winterbourne valued his privacy, or so people said. It was the gossip of choice for over a month after he arrived in the city last winter. Whatever went on beyond its stone walls proved an enigma, one that drew her attention often as she played.

A familiar clack of wood—the gate to the little yard closing down below—interrupted her song. Ceridwen's brows furrowed as she picked up the tune again. None of her family would be out this late. Few people were at this hour.

The family goat gave a loud bleat. A chilly breeze brought another sound—a voice, a stranger in the yard. Ceridwen's breath hitched as she lowered her flute and strained her ears. On shaking knees, she edged toward the low railing.

Nell bleated again. Wood groaned.

"Quiet, you." The gruff voice floated up from somewhere below.

She sucked in a breath. *The animals.* They had so few already.

Ceridwen flew through the small attic door, yanking it shut behind her in a clatter. The musty, aged scent of the house wrapped around her as she descended the stairs two at a time.

"Ceridwen?" Jaina called from the end of the hallway. Her brow creased with worry, adding to the wrinkles marring her forehead.

The kindly housekeeper and her husband, Gerard, had followed the family to Teneboure, the only staff they could afford to keep. But they were more like family than anything. Jaina had cared for Ceridwen since childhood, especially after Mother died, and Gerard's ability to find work was one of the limited things that kept them afloat.

"Get Father," Ceridwen said in a harsh whisper. Her heart pounded as she slid around Jaina, brushing against the rough stone wall.

The floorboards creaked and groaned as she raced down the stairs and through the hall to the small yard adjacent to the house. Ceridwen's dress swished around her booted ankles as she slid to a halt on the little dirt pathway, lit only by the sliver of the moon glowing above.

"Come on, you," said the voice from the street outside, accompanied by the clomp of small hooves.

Nell. Ceridwen raced through the gate, flute in hand. She couldn't lose her, especially not to some blasted thief in the night.

"Stop, thief!" she yelled.

The man in dirty and tattered clothes turned in her direction as she raced onto the rain-slicked cobblestones.

"Go back, girl." He pulled a knife from his belt. The other clutched a rope tied around the goat's neck.

Her legs froze as she caught sight of his weapon. "Dear Goddess," she gasped.

"Ya hear me? Stay away." He backed down the street, nearing an alleyway.

The flute went icy in her grip, the keys biting into her palms. They couldn't afford more loss and misfortune. Summoning her courage, Ceridwen advanced.

The man tugged the rope and stalked her way. "I'm warnin' ya."

Father. Gerard. Her heart raced as she flicked her gaze to the house, praying for anything other than the empty yard that greeted her.

"Please." *Someone. Anyone.* But if she waited for Father or Gerard, it might be too late. The thief could get away, and who knew if they'd be able to track him down? The nearby houses loomed dark and empty. Few lived in this part of town anymore with its old houses and little yards. She'd never thought it a problem until this moment.

Goddess, give me strength. Ceridwen advanced on the stranger who stood still in the street, knife toward her. She raised her hands, flute clutched in one, the other empty. "Please don't take her from us."

The man leaped forward, thrusting the knife in her direction. Ceridwen yelped and lunged backward. Nell bleated again, struggling against the stranger's hold, but he only jerked the rope tighter.

"Get gone, girl, or I'm gonna—"

A deep growl echoed from the shadowed alleyway, sending a cold sweat breaking out over Ceridwen's skin. The thief twisted toward the sound. The rope he held dropped from limp fingers. Nell ran back to the house, never slowing.

Red eyes glowed as a form stalked on all fours into the street. Skin as black as night stretched tight over bones. Hanks of dark hair clung to its knees, elbows, and the ridge along its spine. The thing was too big for a wolf. Too...wrong with its lanky limbs.

Run, run, run. A voice screamed in Ceridwen's head. But she couldn't. Her body wouldn't respond to the panicked commands racing through her.

The monster slunk toward the man as she watched in horror, unable to move, its maw bared to display wicked fangs.

"Demon!" The man shifted his stance and swiped at the beast. It reeled away with a sharp screech. Claws swiped and missed. The second knife swipe struck home, leaving a streak of red across the monster's leathery shoulder.

Time slowed as the beast reared and then leaped. An icy chill wrapped Ceridwen in a vise, constricting her chest. A scream split the air. Both figures tumbled onto the ground.

Her eyes snapped shut. *Goddess, no.* This wasn't happening. A dream. A hallucination. It had to be. She'd wanted the man gone, but this?

The screams cut off abruptly. A shuddering, dry heave racked her body. Something scraped on stone, followed by a heavy thud. The rapid thump of her heart echoed through her soul in the sudden silence.

At length, she forced her eyes open and wished to the Goddess on her high throne she hadn't.

The creature's head bobbed, growing larger as it bounded in her direction.

"No!" Ceridwen threw her arms in front of her as the creature approached, rising to the height of a man before it barreled into her. Pain flared through her back and shoulders as they slammed against the stones. Her head followed with enough force that her teeth rattled. A scream lodged in Ceridwen's throat as her arms flew wide and her flute spiraled away.

Spots swam in her vision as she opened her eyes to darkness pierced by two red orbs.

"Goddess, spare my soul." The traditional prayer rose on instinct, her last defense against the monstrous thing looming above.

The snarling ceased, though warm, dark liquid dripped from the gaping maw onto her chin, neck, and dress. A hot, coarse tongue licked at the side of her face, sending another shiver down her spine.

"Please," she begged.

The edges of its eyes lightened, turning white, almost humanlike.

Wood cracked against the monster's side. "Off her, beast!" Father yelled.

The monster roared and leaped away. Father stood above her, brandishing the splintered end of his cane at the creature.

Ceridwen scrambled back, hands slipping on the wet cobblestones as her mind struggled to take in the monster.

Gerard stepped next to Father, swinging the metal end of a shovel toward the creature. "Stay back, fiend!" he roared.

Neither man would be able to stand against such a monster. It was a miracle Father stood at all without his cane.

The beast's eyes flicked to her, looking almost human in the pale light filtering down from the moon above. Its irises alone remained red, a dark pupil visible now in the center.

Her rapid pulse hammered in her chest. Ceridwen's older sister, Bronwyn, dropped to the ground next to her and pulled her into her arms. She stared at the monster with the fiercest look Ceridwen had ever seen, as if she could slay it with a glare alone.

In a breath, the monster turned and ran off between the houses, vaulting a stone wall to disappear into the night.

Bronwyn rubbed Ceridwen's arms. Gerard knelt and touched her face, Father wobbling behind him. Their mouths opened and closed, but only distant sounds filled her ears. Very slowly, their words came back as the shock dimmed and her heart slowed.

"—wrong, Ceridwen?"

Her hand trembled as she lifted it to touch her face. "I'm all right."

Other than a bruised back and throbbing head, the words were true. She sat straighter, wincing against the ache where she'd struck the cobblestones.

Boots thumped across the ground and splashed through puddles as Jaina ran up, holding a lit torch. The color leeched from her face, her hand flying to her mouth as she took in the scene. "Sweet Goddess, what happened? Are you hurt?"

"The blood…" Bronwyn touched Ceridwen's neck. Her hand came away wet and red.

"It's not mine." Water from the puddles on the street soaked into Ceridwen's backside through the material of the dress. She felt horrid and likely looked even worse.

"Where—" Jaina started.

"The monster," Father answered. "The one the men spoke of." He swayed. Only Gerard's quick movement and arm around his shoulders kept him on his feet.

Ceridwen shuddered. She hadn't considered the risk before rushing out to stop the thief. They'd heard rumors of a monster roaming the streets some nights, but Ceridwen thought it idle gossip or delusions conjured in the wake of too much drink. At worst, perhaps it was a dog gone rabid or a wolf that had slunk down from the mountains. But the creature she'd seen was no wolf, nor man, and certainly no illusion.

"It's been weeks since the last sighting. Could it really be?" Bronwyn asked as she helped Ceridwen rise. All the aches from her fall made themselves known anew.

Father and Gerard looked between each other, neither speaking.

"Father?" Ceridwen prompted. If he'd heard more, he'd yet to tell them about it.

"We'll speak inside," he responded.

Bronwyn picked up a silver object, long, slender, and precious, and offered it to Ceridwen. "It doesn't look too bad," she said, fingering one bent key.

"Thank you." Ceridwen took it. If her flute was all that was broken, it would be a gift from the Goddess indeed.

"So much blood…" Jaina said.

The group turned to her. Jaina peered down the street toward where the monster had set upon the thief.

Ceridwen's breath hitched as she beheld the ever-growing dark puddle and the figure lying within. The last remnants of her dinner threatened to come up onto the street. After the brief encounter with the monster, she'd nearly forgotten the thief.

Bronwyn took a step forward, but Father threw out his arm, warding her back. "Stay back, girls."

Gerard guided Father over to the body. Jaina trailed after them, holding the torch. In moments, its light would illuminate the fallen man.

"Don't look." Bronwyn wrapped her arms around Ceridwen and turned away herself, but Ceridwen had to see, had to know. A thief the man might be, but no one deserved such a fate.

Bile burned the back of her throat as a bloody face and matted hair came into view. When Gerard swore and reached for a pulse, she finally glanced away. He wouldn't find one. Glassy eyes had looked right at her from a head twisted around in the wrong direction.

CHAPTER 2
DRYSTAN

RYSTAN WINTERBOURNE SAT STIFF and stoic in the mayor's office as the sweaty, red-faced man berated him for another attack by a monstrous beast—one that the mayor believed Drystan ought to have been able to take care of months ago.

That was the trouble with mayors, especially ones of such out-of-the-way cities such as Teneboure. They were often left to their own devices, given leave to run the city on behalf of the king since such a small city was beyond the king's notice. Its remote location, small size, and general unimportance were precisely the reasons the king had chosen this, of all places, to send Drystan as punishment for his failures in the king's service.

In truth, the mayor should be glad. The city hadn't warranted the presence of a noble, a Lord Protector, for years before Drystan was assigned—or rather, exiled—there during the past winter. Having a Lord Protector in residence would give the upstart mayor some credibility among his peers should he ever choose to leave for a more opportune post.

"This wasn't just another case of missing animals or an injured drunkard," the mayor said. "A man was murdered in the streets!"

"A thief," Drystan corrected. "And stealing from an already poor family, according to what you told me earlier."

He had little sympathy for those who broke the laws, whether ones established by the royals or the Goddess herself. He, of all people, knew the danger of such transgressions. The laws weren't just there to protect the innocents, but to guard the doers themselves from the consequences of their actions. And oh, those consequences could be terrible indeed.

"It's still a dead man in the streets, Lord Winterbourne." The mayor raked a hand through his brown hair, causing it to stand on end. "I've had citizens at my door all day yesterday and since dawn this morning demanding action."

Drystan reined in a sigh. So he'd heard half a dozen times now. It wasn't like he could miss the gaggle of them outside on his way in, either. Drystan's gloved fingers dug into the cushioned armrest of the chair as he tried to maintain his calm. "It has been some time since there was an incident of this nature. We all hoped that this beast had left us for good."

"But it hasn't!" The mayor paced in front of his desk with a startling lack of decorum, the complete opposite of Drystan.

Drystan rose to his feet, and the smaller man stilled, stiffening his spine in an effort to make himself taller and more imposing, not that any of it helped.

"I assure you," Drystan began, "this monster will no longer be a threat to you by the end of winter. I will see to it myself."

"W-Winter," the man stammered. "That simply won't do."

"It's the best I can promise."

The man's face began to purple in rage, but Drystan was done listening to his ravings. "Good day, sir." He gave a stiff bow, though the man deserved nothing from him.

"T-Then I must take matters into my own hands."

The comment made Drystan stop and glance back over one shoulder.

The mayor swallowed, seeming even more uncomfortable under the Lord Protector's silent scrutiny. "I will post a reward. Any information about the monster leading to its demise will garner a generous sum."

Drystan fought the urge to roll his eyes. As if anyone could procure such a thing.

"And I will give the men who petitioned leave to hunt the beast."

Drystan tightened his hand into a fist. "That will only endanger the people further."

"We will not stand by and do nothing." The mayor notched his chin higher. "If our Lord Protector will not protect us, we must do something."

A grumble slipped from between Drystan's lips, sounding almost like a low growl. The mayor blanched but held his ground.

The man pushed him too far. Didn't he know that Drystan worked each day to keep the monster at bay? Worse, the mayor seemed to know or care nothing of the bigger threats lingering in the capital, ones that could easily come to plague this city if Drystan were unsuccessful in his efforts. He couldn't fail, and this man wouldn't ruin things for him, for all of them. If he wanted more death in the streets, getting in Drystan's way was a sure path toward accomplishing it.

Without another word, Drystan stomped from the office, throwing the wooden door open wide and letting it crack against the stone wall.

He scowled at the thing where it dangled from a broken hinge, now limp against the wall. A sudden tingle of guilt rose in his chest, but he batted it away. Good. Let the mayor remember that he was one of the Goddess-blessed, as the commoners called it, one of the nobles of the kingdom with power above normal men, a possessor of magic granted ages ago by the Goddess herself. There was a reason only certain nobles were named Lord Protectors and assigned to watch over the cities of the kingdom. It had little to do with status, a title given by humans, and everything to do with the power in his blood given by the Goddess. Sometimes people forgot that, especially in Teneboure, where royalty and nobility rarely tread.

"Lord Winterbourne." Jackoby, his butler and confidant of many years, waited outside the mayor's office. He bowed before giving a meaningful look at the ruined door.

Drystan sighed. Just the sight of his friend calmed him and cleared his senses. His weathered but balanced features consistently exuded an air of peace that Drystan couldn't help but envy. More importantly, though, with one look, the man reminded him of his greater task. He wasn't here to make a scene. Far from it. Any ill reports sent to the king could be his downfall, and he couldn't allow that. More rested on Drystan's shoulders than his own reputation, and that was precarious enough.

"The carriage awaits, my lord. I had Kent move it to the back to avoid the crowds."

"Good. Thank you." At least one of them was thinking on their feet. The mayor's office lingered in the new portion of the city near the small train station—or the city's only connection to society as some called it. It was a wonder they decided to build the line so far north at all, the steam train being a new invention to the country as a whole. The nobles, too, flocked to new homes on the southern side of the city, content to let the northern end, where his manor resided, rot. A trend he was grateful for, given the peace and privacy it offered. Though their country of Castamar kept itself cut off from most of its neighbors, isolated on the northern end of the Cerulean Sea, the nobility constantly looked for ways to connect their country within. At least it had made his journey to this city easier.

They stalked silently through the halls, slipped out the back entrance, and into the shuttered carriage. No sooner were they in than Kent had the horses in motion, not needing to be told his lord's wishes.

"Well?" Drystan asked Jackoby, who occupied the seat across from him. While Drystan had entertained the mayor, Jackoby had a separate task to see to.

"It is as you feared, my lord."

Drystan waved his hand. "No need for formalities here." He'd known Jackoby much of his life as the man had been loyal to his parents before him. More than that, though, Drystan no longer felt like he deserved any kind of honor or title. His foolish choices, those of a young man who didn't quite understand the world yet, had seen to that.

Jackoby nodded once before continuing. "The young woman involved in the incident was a Miss Ceridwen Kinsley. It took questioning several people, but I was able to confirm, to the best of the individual's knowledge, that she is the young woman who plays on the rooftop."

Damn. He pursed his lips and stared at the window of the carriage, not that he could see anything beyond the tightly pulled curtains. He loved to hear her play. It was one of the few things, perhaps the only thing, that gave him true calm and settled the agony within him. The soft tunes that floated in through the open windows of the manor some nights were all that held him together and let him focus on his mission.

Now that she'd been attacked, he could scarce believe she'd venture out to play at night anymore or that her family would allow such a risk. She had not played last night. He'd waited until the late hours, yearning for her tune, but it never came. Truthfully, that was the main reason he'd bothered to meet with the mayor today. The man always had some complaint for him, most unimportant, but this one he cared about—both because it involved the monster and his musician.

He huffed air through his nose. As if he could really think of her as his when he didn't even know her name before today.

She might not be his, exactly, but he needed her music all the same.

"What else did you learn about her?"

"The family is poor and somewhat new to the city, having moved here almost three years past. It seems they suffered some tragedy and loss of fortune, but details were few. There is an older brother in the city watch. Both daughters are of marriageable age, though one gentleman I spoke with was not optimistic about their prospects."

"And why is that?" Who could hear such lovely music and not wish for more?

Jackoby shook his head. "Unfortunate looks? The lack of fortune? A blistering personality? My sources did not say."

Most interesting, given the way people loved to gossip. As the carriage rolled on, an idea formed for how Drystan might be able to turn the situation to his favor. He steepled his hands in front of him. "I think this unfortunate event may have a silver lining after all."

"Oh?" Jackoby raised a careful brow.

Drystan banged his fist on the carriage wall, calling for a stop. "I think I'd like to pay a call on the way to the manor."

CHAPTER 3
CERIDWEN

WORD OF THE MONSTROUS encounter spread like a plague through the city. It was the topic of choice on every street corner. Or so Gerard said. Ceridwen hadn't been out of the house in the two days since it occurred, not until Bronwyn talked her into attending tea at the home of Elspeth Ainsworth.

A handful of Ainsworth ancestors stared at Ceridwen from their portraits on the elaborately decorated walls, but it wasn't their studious expressions that unnerved her. Stuffy paintings always listened. The women who attended these gatherings often did not—at least not to a girl from a fallen family who preferred music and plants to parties and gossip.

"Oh, you poor dears." Elspeth fawned over the sisters the moment they were shown into her parlor.

"Lady Ainsworth." Ceridwen curtsied in response, despite the ache that still lingered in her back from the monster's attack, displaying all the grace and poise she could muster for their hostess.

"To have witnessed such a horrible sight." Elspeth's hand flew over her mouth as she shook her head. "I can hardly imagine it."

Fine furniture dotted the space four times the size of their own rooms back home. Picture windows bracketed by heavy green curtains let in the meager light from the cloud-covered sun. Tiered trays loaded with bite-size pastries and sandwiches topped small tables. Their sugary scents and the women's perfume warred for control within the room to the point their pungency gave Ceridwen the hint of a headache. Her stomach churned at the memory of two nights ago, turning the sweet scents foul and stripping her appetite.

"Come, you must tell us what happened." Elspeth looped her arm through Ceridwen's and pulled her toward the gaggle of colorfully dressed women already sipping their tea and chatting in small groups. Ceridwen sighed. As if she wanted to recount that tale. Elspeth meant well. She genuinely liked the woman and her daughter, Lydia. It was one of the few reasons she visited them. They were kind, even if the other guests were not.

"Don't leave out any details," Elspeth added with a pat on her arm.

Whatever fanciful tale she expected, the truth was so much worse. Sightings of the monster had been reported since early spring, though some were dubious at best—drunken men stumbling home in the dark of night, shady figures with poor reputations. Occasionally one would sport wicked wounds. Claw marks to the calf. A fierce bite on their arm. A number of animals had turned up dead as well. Wolves, the doubters said, or rabid dogs. And though the monster she'd seen had certain similarities, it was no natural beast.

Ceridwen looked over her shoulder at Bronwyn in a silent plea for help as her heart twisted in her chest. But Bronwyn rolled her eyes and smoothed out a lock of her chestnut hair as she followed after. Her older sister had little patience for such gatherings, not that Ceridwen had much more. But they'd promised Father to try to fit in here. If there was one thing Bronwyn respected, it was keeping Father as happy as possible.

"Make friends. Perhaps find a nice young man," he'd said. "I won't be around forever. It would do my spirit good to know you're taken care of." As if they were helpless children. Though, the rigors of proper society left little flexibility for a woman to support herself without dropping further down the ranks of class into servitude. The sisters had an older brother, Adair. He'd joined the military and received a post in Teneboure. But Adair could barely provide for himself, much less two sisters, and someday he'd have a family of his own. Ceridwen was determined not to be a burden to him—one more mouth to feed.

A sudden heaviness in her limbs threatened to pull Ceridwen down onto the carpets. She'd longed for marriage once, prayed for someone to look at her the way Father had at Mother. But those days were gone, along with so much else. She'd met the eligible men of Teneboure. They were fine...she supposed, but none of them paid her more than a passing glance. She was pretty enough to warrant those but not much else, apparently.

Lydia set down her tea and practically ran in Ceridwen's direction, her blond curls bouncing about her head. A year her junior, and with similar coloring and complexion, she resembled Ceridwen more than her own siblings, Bronwyn and Adair. Ceridwen was the only one to turn out like her mother, whereas her siblings got her father's darker hair and eyes.

"Oh, Ceridwen, it's so awful." Lydia took her other arm, capturing Ceridwen between her and Elspeth as they came to a halt near the other women. "What was it like? That monster."

Lydia and Elspeth released her arms. Bronwyn and another young woman with blazing red hair, Georgina, joined them to form a small circle.

"Red eyes that glowed in the night. Vicious fangs dripping with blood. A lean body of shadow, more animallike than man," Bronwyn replied, her voice rising and falling as if telling the story to children.

The mere description stripped the heat from Ceridwen's skin.

Georgina fanned herself. "You must be joking."

Elspeth drew a circle, the sign of the Goddess, in front of her chest.

"Only a little," Ceridwen said. She didn't have the nerve to describe the leather skin stretched too tight over wrongly proportioned limbs. No one needed to share her nightmares.

"Is it true what we heard about the man who was killed? That he was an escaped convict and a thief?" Lydia asked.

Ceridwen nodded. "It's what Father was told." Not that it made the death any easier to take in.

"Gerard went to the constable that night to report the murder. When he came to investigate, he found the Lyndstroms' family jewels in his bag," Bronwyn said, filling in the details as she often did. Where words sometimes failed Ceridwen, they never did her sister. "And he had a dagger in his hand, covered in blood."

"The monster's?" Lydia gasped.

"Maybe. There were no other crimes reported that night."

"You think he fought back?" Lydia asked.

"He did," Ceridwen said. "I saw him stab it, but then I—"

The others continued speaking, but Ceridwen barely heard them over the jumbled buzzing in her ears. She drew her hands into fists, clenching at her dress as she willed her face to remain neutral rather than give away the terror trying to break free.

Elspeth snapped open her fan, drawing Ceridwen back to the moment. "At least there's one less criminal on the streets. Though with the king's newest tax hike, we'll see more such crimes. Mark my words."

In the short years of his reign, the king had raised taxes to the highest rate in living memory. It wasn't only Ceridwen's family stretched thin. Father's poor investments in the wake of Mother's death had left them on the brink of ruin. They owed too many loans, and with the rising taxes, how could they ever afford to pay them off? Guilt over the thief's death teased her, but if he'd stolen Nell, it would've been her family with hungry bellies this winter. Things would be tight even as it was.

"You're so lucky, Ceridwen," Lydia said, touching her arm. "Maybe the monster spared you because you're so sweet."

Her cheeks heated at the uncommon compliment, though Bronwyn's next words wiped away the momentary praise. "It stopped because Father attacked it with his cane, and Gerard went after it with a shovel."

"Such brave men," Georgina said with an exaggerated sigh. Her gaze showed little sympathy. She hadn't joined the company of the girl who said too much and the one who said too little out of concern for the siblings. She wanted the same thing as the others glancing their way and edging closer to the conversation: gossip—the true currency among the ladies of Teneboure.

Ceridwen released the skirts of her dress and smoothed a hand over the simple material, so different from the other women's layers of fine fabric, delicate lace, and perfectly tailored designs meant to accent curves and shape. Their appearance was a near-constant reminder of her country upbringing and declining fortune. One more reason the other women kept their distance. Shallow gossips. If only she had the nerve to tell them so.

"They say the monster drinks the blood of its victims. Is that true, too?"

"Lydia!" Elspeth scolded.

Lydia winced but let the topic drop.

Elspeth gave a dramatic shiver. "It reminds me too much of the stories out of the capital since the late king and queen were murdered. Goddess, give them rest."

"Goddess, give them rest," everyone echoed.

Georgina's brow furrowed. "Weren't they killed by their son? Prince Tristram?"

Elspeth nodded. "They say he was under the influence of dark magic. King Rhion had the prince executed for his crimes...and the dark magic." Her gaze turned far away. "How hard it must have been to sign his death warrant. His own nephew..."

Ceridwen sighed. Their king, Rhion Ithael, might have gotten his revenge, but what about the rest of them? Tales of death and dark magic blossomed under his reign.

Murders. Monsters in the night.

Just like the one haunting their city.

Rumors of the dangers drifted out of the capital like contraband since the death of King Rhion's brother, King Jesstin, and his wife, Queen Manon—whispered behind decorative fans between friends, shared over a pint at the pub. Between that and his taxes, the king earned more silent curses than praise. But until two nights ago, the monster of Teneboure had never killed a human—that Ceridwen knew of.

Lord Winterbourne, the city's Lord Protector, had failed for months to heed the mayor's request for aid to subdue the monster. Perhaps he would now. It was the job of a Lord Protector to guard the citizens under his watch from danger. Not that theirs did much good since he'd arrived during winter. *Lazy, useless noble.* There was the military, too, of course, but they'd not had any luck tracking the monster.

Some said it was a blessing the city had a Lord Protector at all—Teneboure hadn't had one for many years until this one arrived. But what good was it if he never left his manor?

Georgina sighed. "It's such a shame. They say the prince was so handsome."

"Did you ever see him?" Lydia asked.

"Well, of course not, but Alexa's cousin said—"

"He was rich and a prince," Bronwyn interjected. "Women would call him handsome even if he had two heads and the pox."

Elspeth gasped. Ceridwen winced at her sister's frank words, though she couldn't help but agree. Even if he had been the ugliest man in the kingdom, many women would have still sought his favor for the title and money alone.

"Well, that's probably true," Lydia replied, always one to keep the peace. "But still, to commit such a horrible crime..." She shook her head.

Shocking. Disgusting. The thought of it still turned Ceridwen's stomach.

"Well, enough about that," Elspeth said. "Tell us all about the other night. Start at the beginning." She motioned us toward the seating area where the other women waited like vultures ready to feast. The fabric of Ceridwen's skirts crumpled in her fist once more. What would be the focus of their stories later? The monster who stalked the night, or the odd country girl who saw it?

"He was so handsome," Bronwyn said in a mockery of Georgina's nasally voice as the sisters walked home arm in arm through the streets. She groaned and rolled her eyes. "And we've just fueled more of their gossip."

Heavy clouds blocked out the sun, adding a slight chill to the day and threatening more rain. The parasol they carried between them would do little good to block an afternoon shower, should it choose to fall, but the frilly accessories were in fashion, and they did happen to own one, so they'd carried it along to the tea. Another attempt to try to fit in, to please Father. The Ainsworths lived in a new home in the wealthy southern portion of the city, far from the family's home in the aged and unpopular north end.

"At least they can spread the story for us," Ceridwen said. "I never wanted to talk about it again." She shuddered just thinking about it.

Bronwyn had told the tale on Ceridwen's behalf over and over again throughout the course of the afternoon, though her version contained more of the horrific details her sister avoided. The memory pressed heavily on Ceridwen's heart. Recounting it herself was impossible, and she'd been able to do no more than pick at the rich pastries during tea, despite her love for them.

Ceridwen's attention snagged on a narrow alley running between two buildings, so similar to the one the monster had emerged from. If she'd helped the thief, could she have saved him? Or would her death be one more addition to the misery of these streets? Her flute had been easily fixed, and despite her promise to her mother, made at her grave to play for her, she couldn't summon the will to do so.

"With any luck, something more exciting will happen, and they'll get over this grim fascination quickly," Bronwyn said, patting her sister's arm. "Perhaps we can talk Adair into courting one of the women so they'll have something else to gossip about."

Ceridwen grinned. "I don't think he'd need much convincing. You know how he feels about Lydia." He'd set his sights on her at the spring ball, trailing after her like a pup.

"Yeah, I know he likes her." Bronwyn frowned. "But with how little he's likely to inherit, it will never happen. The Ainsworths would never agree to let their daughter take a step down in society."

"No." Ceridwen's gaze dipped to the cobblestones. "Sadly, they probably won't." An Ainsworth heir living in a ramshackle house? Never. Adair would be more likely to inherit their father's debt than any actual wealth. Even with the money Gerard earned from working odd jobs around the city, the family could barely keep up with their loan payments, not to mention the basics needed to get by. Ceridwen let out a long breath. At Gerard's age, it wouldn't be long before the better-paying opportunities were given to stronger, younger men instead.

"Bronwyn! Ceridwen!" Jaina waved her arms as she ran in their direction, huffing for breath, cap askew.

Home lay several blocks away. Had she run all the way here? Why?

A sudden chill stole through Ceridwen. *Father. Something happened to Father.* The family fortune wasn't the only thing to decline after Mother's death. Their father had come down with some illness two years ago that never quite left him and flared up at the worst of times.

Tension and worry froze Ceridwen in place, but Bronwyn unlatched her arm and ran. With a deep gasp, Ceridwen tore herself free of the fear and ran after her.

"What happened?" Bronwyn implored, always quick with her words. "Is it Father? Did something happen?"

"No, it's... Oh, it's... You have to come right away," Jaina lamented as the sisters approached. Sweat dripped down her face as she sucked in breaths between words. Tendrils of graying brown hair escaped from her neat cap and stuck to her face.

Jaina shook her head and inhaled deeply before continuing. "Some men came down from the manor, servants of the Lord Protector, and with them...Lord Winterbourne himself."

CHAPTER 4

DRYSTAN

THE HOUSE WAS WORSE than Drystan imagined. Though it sat in the old part of town near the manor he occupied, it was a distant cry from the polished floors, ornate tapestries, and fine furnishings that he was accustomed to. One didn't even need to step inside to notice the cracked and faded paint on the façade that might have once been a lovely shade of blue. That alone spoke volumes.

He expected some measure of surprise when he arrived at the Kinsley household unannounced, but Jackoby telling him that the poor housekeeper nearly almost fainted when he'd announced who waited in the carriage still caught him off guard. As did Mr. Kinsley, nearly tripping over his cane as he showed Drystan into the front parlor and insisted on him taking the wingback chair near closest the fireplace. For that, though, Drystan was grateful. It was the one piece of furniture that he felt comfortable wouldn't splinter under him. The rest had seen better days, as had the threadbare rugs, to say nothing of the crumbling fireplace that could give way along with a side of the house at any moment.

This family was very poor indeed to not be able to maintain a proper parlor for their guests. He could scarce imagine the rest of it. But in this case, their unfortunate circumstance might aid his goal.

The housekeeper raced off to find Mr. Kinsley's daughters the moment he informed them of his purpose and desire to speak with the woman who'd been attacked by the monster. Mr. Kinsley himself tried to offer tea, but Drystan declined. He could see the man had enough burdens as it was, and he would not add to them. Instead, Drystan tucked his hooded cloak around him and angled the offered chair toward the smoldering fire. Perhaps it was rude, but he wasn't there to chat with Mr. Kinsley, not until he'd seen Ceridwen first. Mostly uncomfortable silence lingered between the group as they waited, with Mr. Kinsley occasionally asking benign questions of Jackoby and Kent. The man's health might have seen better days, but he was wise not to push Drystan for pleasant conversation as many people would have done.

At length, the housekeeper finally returned with her charges in tow.

Drystan turned just enough in the chair to take a measure of the young women as they rushed inside. With his hooded cloak, he'd wager they could see little of him. For the best.

Mr. Kinsley rose on shaking legs and gestured to each woman in turn as they curtsied. "My daughters, Bronwyn and Ceridwen."

Both were as lovely as any lady he had seen in some time, enough that it made him stir in the chair. But where the elder one, Bronwyn, failed to hide her shrewd assessment of him, Ceridwen was more demure, staring at his booted feet rather than the rest of him. He should be glad. He didn't like being an object of attention in this place, his appearance mused over in local gossip. It was one reason he often stayed inside the manor and rarely invited anyone in. But in this case, he desperately wished she'd raise her blond head, if only so he could get a better look at her face.

Silence lingered. Drystan finally broke from his musings, realizing that everyone waited on his reply. "Thank you for returning so suddenly."

The women curtsied again but said nothing more, so he continued, "I wished to apologize to the young woman who was attacked within my city."

At that, Ceridwen's nose wrinkled, her lips pursing. A look of disgust passed across her features and was gone, but that wasn't the expression he expected given the attack. Weeping or swooning would have been more appropriate, but thankfully she had a better constitution than that. She'd need it.

"Ceridwen, was it?" he asked.

At the use of her name, she finally looked up. That lovely golden hair he admired framed a balanced face with pale eyes that he could see the blueness of even from across the room. An ember of warmth burned deep in his chest. *Yes, her face is pleasing indeed.* Not that it mattered. He needed her music and only that. There was no time for anything else, and the risk of it would be too great.

"I am glad you're unharmed and were able to scare the monster away," he said.

Bronwyn frowned. "You should thank our father for that."

Jackoby sat a little straighter. Kent covered his mouth, trying to hide the grin Drystan hadn't failed to miss. Quite the spitfire, this sister. She could be trouble.

"Just so," Drystan said. "And Mr. Kinsley shall have my thanks, as well as payment for your family's trouble." He reached under his cloak and procured a small sack of coins, which he tossed to Mr. Kinsley where he sat on the sofa. The older man, caught unawares, fumbled the bag but caught it before it could spill out on the floor.

"M-My thanks, my lord," he replied.

He didn't open the small sack but left it sitting in his lap. How proper. Though he'd be in for quite a surprise when he did. He'd wager the man hadn't seen that many gold pieces in some time. Plus, the offering had the added effect of relaxing both his daughters. Bronwyn's gaze lost some of its shrewdness, her stance easing. Even Ceridwen ventured more than a half glance his way.

Drystan crossed his legs and settled back into the frame of the chair. He wasn't here just to deliver some much-needed gold. That was only the opening act.

"While I'm here," Drystan said, "do either of you have some art, some talent you could share with me?"

He must be sure, must confirm Jackoby's information before he made his offer.

The women looked at one another, and he was surprised when the elder spoke first.

"I am a painter," Bronwyn replied.

Ceridwen's attention snapped to her sister as if she'd spilled some grave family secret. How interesting.

"Plates? Teacups?" he asked.

Ceridwen's nose wrinkled again, and this time he didn't miss the offense written in her pinched brows and sparkling blue eyes. She didn't speak, but the look alone spoke volumes of the sisters' bond.

"Landscapes on canvas," Bronwyn responded, an edge of bitterness leaking into her tone. "And some portraits."

"Very nice." If the sincerity of his voice eased some of her fire, it did little to smooth the thin press of her lips. The elder sister was quite the prickly one. "And you, Ceridwen?"

"I'm a musician, my lord." She frowned over his title, piquing his interest even more. "I play the flute."

Good. Just what he hoped. "Would you play for us now?"

Ceridwen looked at her father, perhaps seeking his approval. Other than one hand twisting around the rough, wooden cane propped on the chair next to him, Mr. Kinsley sat almost completely still. Finally, he gave an encouraging bob of his head. "She will. Please allow her a few minutes, my lord."

"Of course. A good song is worth waiting for." He'd wait all day and a night if it got him what he wanted.

The young woman gave a wobbling curtsy and rushed out of the room. Only a minute later, she returned, her flute in tow. Ceridwen's hands shook a little where she held the instrument. Could she be nervous? Surely not. The tune he heard at night always had such strength and power to it.

"Whenever you're ready." He waved a hand through the air.

Slowly she raised the flute to her lips, adjusted her grip, and began to play. He recognized the melody almost immediately, "The Nocturne of the Moon." One of his favorites. A sad song, but also a love song. A curious choice to play for a male guest.

The notes filled the small room, echoing off the walls and consuming the space in a rush of sound. Whatever nervousness she had vanished as she played. She closed her eyes as her fingers flew over the keys, playing the tune by memory. Her form swayed gently to its rhythm as if the song consumed her body and soul. No one in the room moved. If he didn't know better, Drystan would wager she held them all under her trance as she played, and him most of all. The music moved something in him, eased the restlessness that liked to creep up on him at the worst of times.

As the last note of the song faded away, Drystan rose from the chair and gave a long, slow clap in appreciation. Jackoby and Kent followed suit.

"Bravo, Ceridwen."

The compliment sent a lovely blush racing to her cheeks and had her staring at Drystan's boots once more.

Now was the time to spring his request. "I have a proposition for you. Come and play for me at the manor. I could use a resident musician, and I shall compensate you for your time."

Ceridwen's head snapped up, and she stared at him wide-eyed. "You'd pay me? For my music?" Her eyes sparkled, and she blinked hastily, glancing away.

A slight twitch pulled at the corner of his lips. Was the young woman about to cry over such a simple offer? "But there will be conditions," he continued, lest her hopes get too high.

The flush faded from her cheeks in a rush. Bronwyn stared hard at Ceridwen, some unspoken words passing between the sisters.

"You will live at the manor for the duration of our arrangement—until midwinter," he finished.

A sharp gasp cut through the room. From the housekeeper or one of the sisters, he could not say.

Mr. Kinsley frowned and shook his head. "It would not be proper for an unmarried woman to live in a man's house, even yours, my lord."

"That is my condition." He couldn't have her coming and going, spreading who knew what kind of gossip to the ladies of the city. "Further, Ceridwen shall not leave the manor grounds."

Mr. Kinsley stood, swaying slightly with his weight supported by the cane. Low fury simmered from the man, his once calm and pleasant expression suddenly hard and foreboding. He was moments away from denying him.

"How much?" Ceridwen's voice cut through the tension in the room.

"Ceridwen?" Bronwyn stared at her sister askance.

"How much would you pay for my services?" Ceridwen asked again, her voice stronger this time.

The housekeeper swayed on her feet. "But your reputation—"

Ceridwen shook her head as if such a thing were meaningless, yet it was anything but in their society. That's why he planned to pay her, and generously. Drystan knew the delicate situation his offer created.

Drystan sought another sack of coins hidden by his cloak and dropped it on the table. The family's full attention snagged on that little sack as he wagered it would. "Consider this your first payment. Assuming you accept."

"Ceridwen, we should talk about this," Mr. Kinsley began.

But it wasn't him who Drystan focused the full weight of his regard on. Ceridwen was curious, eager. He could see it in the steady resolve with which she regarded him now.

Bronwyn grabbed her arm, stealing her attention and mouthing what could only be "No."

Ceridwen shook her off. "I accept."

"Very good," Drystan replied at length, trying to keep the pleasure from his voice. He expected her agreement—they needed the money after all. He hadn't expected how it would affect him, how he would relish hearing those words from her, or the eagerness that sprang up in him to take her back to the manor that very moment. "I'll send a carriage in the morning," he continued before he could change his mind. It would be proper, and it would give the young woman time to prepare and say her farewells. He turned to the woman's father. "Thank you for your hospitality, Mr. Kinsley. I shall not soon forget it."

The man opened and closed his mouth like a fish, but whatever words he failed to find mattered not. The thing was done. Agreed to.

Drystan hastened across the room, Jackoby and Kent on his heels. He stopped once in front of Ceridwen, hoping that she would look up at him, maybe hazard a glance at his face now that they were so close and his hood would not limit her view if she looked up, but she did not. Instead, she focused on his feet again and gave a delicate curtsy.

Perhaps he could coerce her to be less demure once she joined him at the manor, but that would have to wait. "Until tomorrow," he said and left without another backward glance.

CHAPTER 5
CERIDWEN

THE HOUSE ERUPTED IN sound once the guests left. Jaina nearly fainted, collapsing onto the sofa. Father waved his cane in front of the fire and berated his daughter's foolishness. Each time he spoke Lord Winterbourne's name, Father pointed to the chair as if the Lord Protector still stood there, and he could condemn him with each accusation.

"We need money," Ceridwen protested. "I can help."

"You are of help, Ceridwen. Every day you help us here around the house and—"

A heavy breath fled her lungs as she twisted away from him. Didn't he understand? This chance would never come again. Not for them. And they needed it. He knew that. Surely he did. The two small pouches of coins Lord Winterbourne had given the family today were a blessing, to be sure, but they wouldn't last. Loans and taxes would eat them up before they even thought of spending them.

"The mayor is offering a reward for anyone who slays the beast," Father said. "It came here once. Maybe it will again, and we'll be ready for it."

Ceridwen rolled her eyes before glancing at him. He wouldn't be slaying anything. None of them would.

"That's a bit...unlikely," Gerard said from the doorway.

Ceridwen gasped, turning toward him.

"Apologies," he said. "I just got back and didn't want to interrupt." He must have come in the back entrance. A good thing, too, as the fishy scent of the docks still clung to his stained work clothes. Such a thing might have put off the Lord Protector even more than their shabby home.

"It's all too much like that gossip in the capital around the time Alis..." Jaina trailed off and looked away.

Mother. Ceridwen's chest grew tight. How long had it been since someone said her name? Or even mentioned their old home? It was like they tried to pretend that part of life never existed.

"What gossip?" Bronwyn cocked her head, hands on her hips.

"It's nothing," Gerard said before settling next to his uncharacteristically downcast and silent wife.

Father wouldn't look at anyone. Ceridwen hunched in, hugging her arms around herself. *Of course not. It's my fault Mother died after all.* She couldn't fix her mistake, couldn't bring her back, but she could help now. Ceridwen shook off the painful memories and stomped, garnering the family's attention. "I'm going. We need this."

"But then you may never get the chance to marry," Jaina exclaimed, suddenly back to her old self. "Not a real gentleman anyway. If they learn you lived unmarried with a man, even a noble, for who knows how long..." She shook her head, her eyes glassy with unshed tears.

"I don't care," Ceridwen replied. It wasn't entirely true. She cared more than she'd like to admit, but she might never find the love she longed for. That was an uncertainty where their need for money was all too sure.

"You might," Jaina insisted with a sniffle. "Someday."

"I won't be around forever, you know," Father added, looking wearier than ever with his eyes downcast and shoulders hunched. His health had been in decline ever since Mother passed. At first, Ceridwen believed it simply sorrow, but now she knew it to be something worse, something no healer couldn't find a name for and that no medicine had yet to mend. As the money thinned, he'd refused to let the family spend it on him. His condition had only worsened until the random coughs and fits became a constant plague.

Ceridwen steeled herself against the remorse in his eyes. "That's why it is even more important that I do it."

"Ceridwen..."

"We could finally get you decent medicine. And that loan to Mr. Charles comes due soon. How will we pay it if not for this? Besides, If I don't go, Lord Winterbourne might take back what aid he's already given us."

Saying his name aloud sent an odd fluttering through her, as it had when he'd spoken hers. Her name had rolled off his tongue like honey. Thick, sweet, and slow. The memory of it alone almost made her shudder.

Shame clouded Father's eyes. A low blow, mentioning the debt he tried to keep his girls unaware of, but hiding from the truth wouldn't change it. Not for him. Nor for any of them. She didn't bother to mention the others waiting to be paid. Even if he borrowed what little Adair had, Ceridwen doubted it would be enough.

"We'll tell them you're ill," Bronwyn spoke up, breaking her uncharacteristic silence. "Should anyone ask, you're staying indoors and not seeing anyone while you recover your health. I'll make excuses for you."

"It could work," Gerard piped in, scratching at his gray-flecked beard. "No one visits the manor anyway."

Father sighed in resignation and collapsed farther into his chair. "Fine." He waved his cane in defeat. "But I don't like this, Ceridwen. We know nothing about him. Lord Winterbourne is a noble, yes, but that doesn't mean he's a just one. You must be careful at all times. Be wary of him and his household."

She nodded. He didn't need to tell her that. Already her stomach tied itself in knots at the thought of what she'd committed to, so much time in the house of a man she didn't know and had never truly seen. Even today, he wore a hooded cloak that obscured much of him from sight. No amount of elation could temper that uncertainty.

Ceridwen had yearned to crane her head and stare into his hooded face to see the man beyond. His voice carried power, a hint of youth, and the richness of culture and learning. His frame spoke to strength as well—broad shoulders, steady legs, and a height that reached above every other person in the room. So why hide his face? The quandary picked at her and would certainly only worsen if she lived under the same roof with him.

"There's one person your excuse will not work on," Father said, dragging her back to their little parlor.

Adair. His name hung unspoken in the room, as heavy as his explosive personality. Bronwyn groaned, expressing Ceridwen's sympathies perfectly.

"He's on patrol," Father continued. "But once he's back and learns of this arrangement, we'll be lucky if he doesn't storm the manor himself."

Ceridwen packed her meager belongings in an old chest that might sooner come apart and spill her dresses into the street rather than carry them to the manor gate. Afterward, she found Bronwyn, who wielded a paintbrush against a new canvas with all the delicacy of their goat Nell.

She would have been famous if anyone knew the works were hers. There were tales of women artists in larger cities and the capital, but in Teneboure, as in the countryside, most people still frowned on it. So when Father or Gerard sold her paintings at the market, one of the few sources of income keeping the family afloat, the name of the artist wasn't mentioned. When pressed, Father claimed the work as his own.

A thick band of blue streaked across the canvas as Bronwyn attacked it with a huff. Painting was her great pleasure in life. Her true love. It was a wonder that she'd mentioned it to Lord Winterbourne at all rather than keeping it carefully tucked away in her heart as she often did.

"Are you mad at me too?" Ceridwen asked from the door.

"No." Bronwyn's hand dropped away from the painting. "No, not you. I'm terribly proud of you, actually." She gave a weak smile. "But I wish he'd chosen me. Not because I want to go, but to save you from this."

Ceridwen twisted her hands in her skirts. If the situation were reversed, she'd feel the same way.

"I can't stop worrying or being angry with Lord Winterbourne for his uncouth offer. Nor can I sit still. And this"—she poked the brush tip at the canvas—"is a complete disaster too."

Bronwyn set aside her palette and brushes with a clatter and wiped her hands on the stained apron over her dress. "I'm sorry. Here I am complaining when you're the one walking into the demon's den."

"Maybe it won't be that bad..." Though Ceridwen didn't quite believe her own words.

"He hid his face. We know nothing about him. He could be hideous, disease-ridden, deformed."

Ceridwen swallowed her nerves and sat on the edge of her sister's bed. "He only asked for my music, something I do every day." Once, it hadn't been the flute she had turned to daily to create music. As much as she loved to play, she'd loved to sing even more. But that was years ago, before Mother died. Before her voice refused to make the lovely lilting sounds it once had. She'd buried her singing voice with her mother, and why shouldn't she? Her singing had led to her mother's death after all. It was only fitting it rest in the planes of the Goddess with her.

Bronwyn crossed the room and took Ceridwen's hands in her paint-stained ones. "I pray that's the case. But if he tries anything, stab him with a dinner knife."

Ceridwen's eyes flew wide.

Bronwyn grinned.

"This isn't the time for jokes." Ceridwen pursed her lips in mock disapproval.

Her sister's smile dimmed. "It wasn't entirely a joke. But hopefully, he'll be a gentleman, and it will never come to that." The seriousness in her eyes didn't reflect the optimism of her words.

Ceridwen trailed her fingertips along the twisting vine of red roses stitched into the quilt atop the bed. Mother had made it long ago.

The quilt had a twin once, one with pink roses instead of red. The scratches on her pregnant stomach bled onto it after Gerard carried her into the rented house in the capital. Ceridwen never knew if the injury caused the screams or if it was the early labor that ripped her apart from within. *Dragon,* Mother mumbled in her fevered haze. But dragons didn't exist. They were children's tales. *If only I hadn't sung for her.* Ceridwen lamented in silence. *I wouldn't have upset her. She wouldn't have gone outside. She wouldn't have—*

"She'd be proud of you," Bronwyn said, a sad smile on her face.

"Mother?" Ceridwen asked in a cracked voice.

Bronwyn nodded.

How could she, when Ceridwen was the reason Mother was gone?

Her mother's death, the bed of blood, reminded her so much of the thief who'd died on the street. She couldn't save either of them, but perhaps she could save others. "The monster," she whispered.

"You'll be safe inside the manor walls, surely," Bronwyn replied.

Ceridwen nodded. If anywhere in Teneboure was safe, it should be there. "Maybe I can learn about it."

The Lord Protector must know something, even if he did nothing to stop it. The payments for her music would help, but they already had an end date, and Goddess knew they needed all the money they could get.

Bronwyn raised her brows as she sat next to Ceridwen on the bed. "It's not a bad idea. If the mayor is offering a reward…" She shrugged. "Every bit of information helps."

"Don't tell Father. The last thing we need is him worrying more or trying something foolish."

"Oh, I won't," she replied.

Ceridwen pulled in a deep breath. She could do this. Perhaps help save the city or some innocent soul and become someone others thanked and applauded rather than overlooked. This would be her chance to do some good for once, and she couldn't squander it.

CHAPTER 6
CERIDWEN

A FINE CARRIAGE ARRIVED at the house before the sun had begun to warm the day. Two solid raps upon the door announced the man who stood in front of Ceridwen's home. She recognized him from yesterday, still dressed similarly to the Ainsworths' butler, but even more refined. Today's jacket was a dark gray that accented the silver frock of hair over his forehead, so different from the darker portion of his salt-and-pepper hair pulled tightly behind his head and secured with a ribbon.

His face was serene, impassive. Had he stood still, she might have mistaken him for a painted statue. "Miss Ceridwen Kinsley," he greeted her as she stepped next to Bronwyn, who'd answered the door. "I am Jackoby, Lord Winterbourne's butler and chief aide."

Bronwyn pursed her lips when he did not turn and address her as well.

Another man emerged from around the carriage—the younger man from yesterday. He, too, had his brown hair tied back, the end brushing the base of his neck. In all likelihood, he was only a year or two older than Adair. "Kent here will see to your things," Jackoby said.

This man did bob his head to Bronwyn, which earned him a half smile in return.

Without delay, the sisters showed the men into the sitting room where Father and Jaina sat with the trunk of Ceridwen's things. She'd already said her farewell to Gerard before he left at dawn to fulfill a job at the docks.

Kent lifted the chest with more ease than expected and carried it off toward the door sitting agape.

"Now, say your farewells, and come along," Jackoby continued.

Farewells? Her throat tightened, and she grabbed Bronwyn's hand without thought.

"I'd like to see where my sister will be staying and get her settled," Bronwyn insisted.

Jackoby looked her up and down as if seeing her for the first time. "Only Miss Ceridwen is permitted entry, no others."

"May we please ask Lord Winterbourne?" Ceridwen asked, hesitant to loosen her grip on her sister lest the reality of her situation finally take hold.

"My lord was very specific," he insisted. "I will not go against his orders."

"He said I must stay, but he mentioned nothing of others not being allowed."

"Do you wish to back out of your arrangement?" He raised a careful brow.

"No, but—"

"It's all right, Ceridwen," Bronwyn said. Ceridwen started to protest, but Bronwyn pulled her into a bone-crushing hug. "I'll see what I can learn," she whispered. "I'll write and visit if he'll allow it. We all will."

Tears burned the corners of Ceridwen's eyes. She bit her lip hard, willing them away, and nodded within her sister's embrace. They'd never been separated, not once in all their years.

Jaina was on the edge of tears herself as Ceridwen pulled away from her sister, and the look on her father's face... Even notes from debt collectors didn't make him seem so forlorn.

"I'll see you soon," Ceridwen promised.

With a last round of farewells, she steeled her will and followed Jackoby to the carriage. Kent already waited in the driver's seat behind the two sturdy brown horses whose manes and trails had been trimmed and groomed to perfection. The lacquered wood of the doors shone in the morning light, more evidence of the wealth and station of the man who owned it.

Jackoby climbed in after her, more graceful than a king. Before the horses snapped into motion, Ceridwen broke the silence with a question. "Have you been Lord Winterbourne's butler long?"

He frowned. "No."

She bit her lip, debating her next question. Learning more about Jackoby might help her gather some insight about Lord Winterbourne, if the man would give her more than one-word answers.

"Whom did you butler for before him?"

"No one," he replied. "Which is why I will do my very best to be suitable for the honor Lord Winterbourne has bestowed upon me."

Something. Better than nothing. And most intriguing that a noble, much less a Lord Protector, would select an unseasoned butler.

When the carriage rocked to a stop, Ceridwen shielded her eyes and looked up at the towering manor walls whose gray stone gleamed in the morning light. The tallest spire, one that soared above the other structures of the manor and where at least one light always gleamed at night, reached high above the wall, even from this perspective.

Iron gates blocked the carriage's passage. The inner yard beyond stood empty. If she didn't know better, she would think the place abandoned despite the manicured, yellowing green grasses lingering late into the season and the well-kept appearance of the space. Jackoby exited and requested Ceridwen remain seated.

Though she lived but a few blocks from the manor, she'd never come this close. There'd been no reason to, despite her curiosity of the place. The houses nearest it stood empty, their little yards barren, as if the whole area were dead and cursed. Ceridwen shivered, more from that thought than the late autumn chill that clung to the morning.

The metal clicked and groaned as Jackoby unlocked the heavy gate to allow entry.

In moments, the carriage rolled into the yard. A knot stuck in Ceridwen's throat when Jackoby locked the gates behind them, sealing her promise along with any hope of escape. How many of the city's residents had ever stood where she did now? Likely very few. None recently that she knew of.

Another man entered the yard, grabbing the reins from Kent, who promptly strode to the back and lifted the trunk with ease. Jackoby helped Ceridwen from the lavish carriage as Kent disappeared into the manor.

No sooner had Ceridwen stepped away from the carriage onto the pathway leading to the manor than the other man led the horses off toward a large side door.

Hair rose on the back of her neck, bringing her feet to a sudden halt only a few steps across the gravel pathway. She peered around the yard, but nothing new greeted her. The tingling came again on her head, her shoulders. She glanced up at the tall tower, the highest levels just visible from this angle. The windows were dark this morning, as they always were in daylight, pits of shadow in which nothing but darkness was visible.

"Miss Ceridwen?" Jackoby asked, looking back with concern as he waited for her to follow.

No matter how she stared, nothing took shape in the dark depths. She shook her head. "It's nothing." Ceridwen faked a smile despite the gooseflesh creeping up her arms before following Jackoby into the manor.

Inside, the halls shone with the same pristine beauty and care as the outer yard, yet like the outside of the manor, it lacked life. Only their footsteps echoed through the richly appointed dim halls. Heavy curtains were drawn over many of the windows, allowing meager light from outside to slip through their seams and edges. Ornate golden sconces glimmered with low flames, offering just enough light to see by.

Although Kent entered only a few minutes in front of them with Ceridwen's things, she neither saw nor heard him. His destination remained a mystery, almost as though he'd vanished with the trunk in tow. Her flute she had packed separately, a request made by Jackoby before they departed. She carried the little box by its handle in front of her, a token of comfort in this strange place.

Rich tapestries hung from walls along with fine paintings even Bronwyn would be impressed by. The rooms and alcoves they passed were filled with an array of lavish furnishings: lamps wrought of gold and silver; finely carved, polished tables; and seating made of exotic wood and fine cloth. Yet all were empty—silent as a tomb at midnight.

The beauty and grandeur chaffed. The contents of one room could change her family's fortunes for generations, yet the reclusive Lord Protector kept it all locked away. To not even invite the citizens under his protection to view and enjoy it was unthinkable.

"Here we are," Jackoby said, drawing to a halt in front of an ornate wooden door.

He led Ceridwen into what appeared to be a study containing more of the breathtaking furnishings that occupied the rest of the manor. On the far wall stood a large stone fireplace that crackled with orange flame. Soon, such a fire would be necessary, but not yet, not if they opened the windows and let in some fresh air. Wood smoke perfumed the air instead, mixing with the faint scent of old parchment and leather. A cozy scent, or it would be anywhere else.

Ceridwen thought the room empty until a voice spoke from a high-backed leather chair turned toward the fire. "You've brought her."

The deep timbre rolled over her skin and sent her back stiffening. A hand moved on the armrest, holding a glass of dark liquid that glimmered in the firelight.

"Yes, my lord. Miss Ceridwen Kinsley, as expected." Jackoby bowed slightly at the waist, though Lord Winterbourne could not see him from where he sat.

"Thank you, Jackoby," he replied, swirling the contents of his glass. He made no move to rise or turn. "Perhaps Ceridwen would indulge me with a song?"

So that's why Jackoby had me carry the flute separately. Lord Winterbourne must have informed him of his wishes early this morning.

The glass clicked on a wooden table as he set it away, still reclining in the chair, hidden from view.

"Any requests, my lord?" Ceridwen asked before setting the flute case on a little table and removing the precious instrument.

"'The Tale of the Maiden Fair.'"

Ceridwen's blood chilled in her veins. It was the same song she'd played the night the monster attacked. She yearned to tell him no, to deny knowing the song, but she pushed the urge away. Better not to offend her patron during her first assignment.

She nearly gasped as Lord Winterbourne rose in one fluid movement. He stood tall over the high-backed chair. Long, unkempt hair trailed down between his shoulder blades. Dark clothing hugged broad shoulders. Though she could see little of him, what she saw reminded her of the wild men who lived in the deep wood, far from cities and towns. Yet this man was supposed to be a noble lord? Their protector?

His face sported a beard as dark and ragged as the hair that hung about his head. Had he never used a comb? Scissors? His butler appeared more a lord than he did. The fine dark jacket hugging his arms and shoulders shone with silver stitching. A light-colored shirt poked out from between its front lapels, crisp and clean. The pants and boots, too, spoke of wealth, yet the man...

In one movement, he lifted the chair and twisted it around. The heavy object thumped into place upon the carpets before he reclined in it once again.

Icy blue eyes locked with hers, staring Ceridwen down in return. Heat rose to her cheeks as she dropped her gaze to the ground. Even if he chose to act a hermit and keep his hair and beard like one as well, he was still a noble, and she chided herself for watching him so boldly.

"Whenever you're ready," he prompted.

A sudden tightness threatened to steal her song, but she swallowed her nerves and took a deep breath.

The first notes came out warbly, airy, and a little flat. But after a few bars, the tune strengthened. The notes rose and fell in crescendo and decrescendo, escalating to a ringing forte during the climax of the song and falling to a soft pianissimo as the tune drew to a close. At some point while playing, she'd closed her eyes, letting herself drift far away with the music. She still held them closed as the last note slipped into the heavy silence. She heard nothing, not even the beat of her own heart or the crackle of the fire.

Nothing, until a slow, loud clap drew her back to the present and caused her eyes to fly wide. It was the same reception she'd received at her house the day before.

"Perfect, just as I remembered," Lord Winterbourne said as he halted his applause. "You will uphold our agreement?"

Ceridwen swallowed and gave a jerking nod.

"Do not leave the manor grounds, nor enter the high tower. You shall attend dinner in the formal dining room and play the flute for me each day. Anything else is your own discretion."

A heavy breath slipped from Ceridwen's lips. No odd commands. Nothing to dishonor her. Perhaps she truly would be treated as a guest in this empty, lifeless place.

"That will be all, Jackoby," he said. "Ceridwen, please stay."

Her heart raced as Jackoby bowed once again and headed for the door. She followed him with her gaze, silently begging him not to leave. Terror gripped her chest at the thought of being alone in a room with this strange man. Each step increased her worry until her face flushed as the door slid shut behind the butler.

When she turned to Lord Winterbourne, he no longer sat.

"Come with me. I'll show you to your room."

CHAPTER 7
DRYSTAN

DRYSTAN TOOK HIS TIME leading Ceridwen through the halls of the manor. She had a tendency to try to trail behind him, often distracted and staring at one thing or another, but that only encouraged him to slow further. He enjoyed the sight of her taking her surroundings, inspecting his temporary home. Most all the furnishings belonged to the manor itself, used by whatever Lord Protector might be in residence at the time, but her obvious wonder and admiration still had a sense of pride swelling in his chest.

It'd been long, probably too long, since he'd spent any time around someone new, particularly someone outside the nobility and their servants. He supposed the manor would look grand in comparison to the modest home in which she lived, and he wasn't quite certain about the young woman's history before her family moved to this city. A country upbringing, Jackoby had heard, but the details of it were limited at best.

"I'm to have a room of my own?" she asked, her voice barely a whisper despite the quiet of the hall, punctuated only by the click of their boots across the marble floors. She'd left her flute behind in the study at his request since she'd play for him again that evening, and without it to hold, her hands had a tendency to twist with each other in front of her.

"Of course," Drystan replied. "You are my guest."

Ceridwen paused in a stream of light flowing in from between the curtains. Many of the windows on this hall were completely covered, but this one had been left askew by a careless maid. Normally that would irk him, but the light shimmering over her aroused a different feeling.

A frown took shape on her pink lips as she glanced away. "If I were a guest, I'd be free to come and go."

His lips twitched. "You'll have to excuse my want of privacy." Drystan held out a hand to her. "Come along."

Ceridwen tentatively met his gaze, a slight blush on her cheeks. She reached out to take his hand but stopped just short, her attention glued to his skin.

Damn it all. He'd forgotten his gloves, and with the light streaming in, she easily spied the scars marring him, a few of them still recent and scabbed.

She glanced up at him, eyes wide. "You're—"

He jerked his hand away and turned on his heel. "It's nothing. Come along."

For a moment, he feared she might protest or ask more questions, but eventually, the soft click of her boots resumed behind him, where he let her linger for the duration of the walk, his previous pleasure shattered by her observation.

Questions would follow, and he had no good answers for her, at least none that he would give.

At length they reached the door Drystan sought, which he threw open before ushering Ceridwen inside. He'd left the decision of her room to his housekeeper, Gwen, who he must admit had chosen well. The bedroom was sumptuous with its green walls and golden accents, though they'd been dimmed by time. Carved wooden couches with pale cream and gold cushions dotted the space, with matching dark wooden tables composing the sitting area. Even he could find nothing amiss with the tall four-poster bed and matching armoires. Kent had already seen to depositing her trunk at the foot of the bed. Or at least he assumed it must be hers. While much of the room, and the manor, were dated, the poor trunk looked like it could fall apart at any moment, its paint peeling badly in one corner.

Thankfully, Ceridwen was so distracted examining the room that she didn't attempt a further look at his hands—or the rest of him. He might as well have vanished the moment he opened the doors.

Something about that irked him, though it was for the best.

"My housekeeper shall be along shortly to inquire after your needs."

This got her attention. Ceridwen spun around, her skirts twirling around her legs. She stared up at him, almost as if she'd forgotten he was there.

"Thank you," she said. "The room is— It's so lovely." Her eyes sparkled, showing the truth of the compliment.

That stubborn bit of pride grew behind his ribs again, and he was thankful he'd taken the time to show it to her himself rather than passing her off to one of his staff. For more of that look alone, he'd have given up a whole day.

Lingering close to her could be more dangerous than he anticipated.

"You'll join me for dinner tonight and play after. Anything you need, my staff will acquire for you."

Before he could give in to the temptation to stay, he turned from the room and closed the doors behind him.

Inviting Ceridwen to dine with him only seemed proper, but being unused to guests, he lost track of time and was late coming down from his room in the tower.

Kent stood at the base of the stairs, waiting. He opened his mouth to speak, but Drystan cut him off with a wave of his hand. "I know. I'm late."

"Just so," the young man said, stepping into pace at his side. "Miss Ceridwen is already at the table."

Good. Something about that knowledge set him at ease. As they approached the dining room, Kent hurried to open the doors for his lord, but Drystan halted him with a whispered, "Wait."

What a person did when they thought few were watching spoke volumes about them, and he was curious to see how the young woman staying under his roof handled his tardiness. The door was already cracked, light from within spilling out into the dimmer hall.

"He shall be here soon, miss," Jackoby said from within. "Apologies, he is unaccustomed to keeping a strict schedule."

Drystan huffed air through his nose. *Accurate, as always.*

Ceridwen sat in her assigned place at one end of the table, her back to the doors. She released a fork she'd been holding, and it clattered onto the porcelain plate. Hastily, she moved it into its original position, arranging it just so and then doing the same with the other pieces. Was she nervous?

His lips quirked up in one corner as he stepped away from the door. What a curiosity she presented. Drystan nodded to Kent, an order to open the doors and grant him entry as planned.

"My lady." Drystan gave a short bow at the waist before sliding the chair out from the table and landing heavily between the armrests shaped like great paws.

"You're quite late," she said by way of reply.

Deep laughter rumbled from his chest before he could stop it. She wasn't wrong—the candles had already burned down quite a ways, but he couldn't help responding to her prod with one of his own. "And here I thought I might be greeted by a fearful mouse or meek silence."

Color raced to her cheeks. "At least I don't look like a wild man living in the woods," she muttered. Her hand flew to cover her mouth, where it gaped open after the words fell free.

Not a mouse at all. Perhaps she had some of her sister's snark, after all. What a pleasant surprise. He shouldn't enjoy it the way he did, his grin stretching wide across his features in a way it hadn't in months. Things would be easier if she were meek and quiet, but he quite liked this twist to his evening. He had the sudden urge annoy her more often, just to see how she would respond.

"Perhaps, from your perspective," he replied. It had been some time since he'd shaved, but that was purposeful. His beard hid the scars on his chin and lower cheek, and he had no desire for that to become a topic of conversation. "But even wild lords need food, and so do sharp-tongued young women."

Ceridwen flushed a deeper shade and stared at her empty plate.

Wild man, she mouthed silently, probably chastising herself.

Poor girl. It wouldn't do to put her too out of sorts on her first evening.

Jackoby cleared his throat and announced, "Dinner is served."

Servants filed in from the kitchen carrying platters of food. Generally, he wasn't one for such formality, but it seemed appropriate with a guest in residence. Besides, the staff was eager to try out the set of fine platters trimmed in little roses. A bit feminine for his taste, though he always did love to grow things, roses especially. They required work to get them to grow just right, their blooms a beautiful reward for a job well done. If only that knack for patience and diligence had taken root in him during his youth, his life might not have taken the poor turn it had. So many things could have been avoided, so much death...

Dinner passed in mostly companionable silence. Where Ceridwen had been quick to speak and sharp-tongued at his entrance, she said little the rest of the meal, only giving brief answers to his questions about the weather and her opinion of the city. Perhaps she was afraid of speaking her mind too openly and offending him. A wise fear. With most, he might have flown into a rage, but such a retort from her sparked humor in him rather than his customary emotions, though he couldn't say why. So delightfully odd.

When he was certain she'd eaten her fill, and she no longer reached for her utensils or eyed the rich fare with barely disguised lust as she had at the start of the meal, Drystan pushed back his chair and rose. He circled around the table as Kent rushed to pull back Ceridwen's chair. Silence over dinner was one thing. He didn't pay her for witty conversation. However, a deep gnawing hunger ate at him from within for a different kind of sound, one that she could grant.

As she stood, he extended his gloved hand to her. "Will you join me in my study?"

Chapter 8
Ceridwen

Lord Winterbourne closed the door to the study behind Ceridwen, sealing them in the room together like corpses in a tomb. He crossed the room to a table near the cold fireplace and poured himself a glass of dark liquid. Only the dim wall sconces illuminated the space tonight, and those gave little comfort and no warmth, just like the rest of the manor.

"The flute is over there." He gestured to the shelf where Jackoby had set the instrument that morning. Books flanked it, as well as the various other objects and trinkets that sat upon the shelves, including a miniature violin and other curiosities.

Ceridwen crossed to the shelves. Her hand hovered over the instrument while she scanned the various books. Only one title tugged her memory, an old history with a tattered binding. The others were a mystery, one she ached to explore. They'd had so few books growing up, less than two shelves worth in her family's meager study, and each she treasured.

"Come sit over here and play." Lord Winterbourne pointed to a chair near the one he'd occupied earlier that day.

Ceridwen jumped at his voice, the cool metal of the instrument digging into her palm where she gripped it too tightly. "Is no one else joining us?" she asked, turning to the sound of his voice.

He took a seat in the same chair he'd occupied that morning, with the glass of dark liquid raised aloft in a hand, elbow rested on the arm of the broad chair.

"No."

Father wouldn't like this. Not at all. Nor would any of the upper-class women, such as Elspeth. Ceridwen could almost hear her disapproving voice, see the lace fan waving in her hand, as she would say, "A young woman alone with a noble? A Lord Protector no less? How untoward. Truly shameful for her family and the supposed gentleman."

She swallowed against the tightness in my throat. "Perhaps I could play outdoors—"

"No."

Ceridwen halted halfway to him. "Is that your answer to everything? No?"

A whisper of amusement resonated from his chair. "No."

He'd been kind to her, especially after her slipup at dinner. But the thought of spending so much time alone with him made her squirm.

She sucked in a steady breath and asked, "Would it be possible to have my balcony unlocked so that I can play outside after I play for you?" Every night that it did not rain or snow, Ceridwen played for her mother, even in the dead of winter when her hands went numb after only one song. At least, she had before the monster attack. The last few days, she'd been out of her routine, and she longed to return to it, to show her mother she hadn't forgotten her, even if she was staying in this manor rather than her family's home.

She'd taught Ceridwen to play outside when she was still a young child. The stone bench under the sprawling limbs of the great tree on the south lawn had been their special place. After she passed, Ceridwen still played under that tree, mostly at night, when the sound of her song could carry to her mother in the halls of the Goddess, unimpeded by the noise of day. Her biggest fear in moving to the city was that her mother would no longer hear her songs, yet every night she'd played, she could feel her mother's eyes on her, even from the beyond. Somehow the feeling was even stronger here than their country home. To not be able to play to her for however long she resided here was unthinkable.

Don't tell me no, she prayed as she took the seat across from him.

"Hmph." The glass clattered onto the table, empty. His heavy beard hid much, but Ceridwen could have sworn the hint of a smile pulled at his lips. "It's dangerous at night, especially for a young woman alone in her room."

Heat fled her body. "The monster? Surely with the walls..."

"You think they can keep it out?" His tone held mockery despite the twinkle in his eyes.

"You're a noble lord." She'd always heard many nobles had power beyond common men. "Can't you do something about it?" As heavy silence lingered, the frustration bubbled up within her, spewing out into words. "What kind of lord cannot protect his own home, much less the city he's sworn to watch over?"

A deep growl rumbled from his chest, more animalistic than human. Shivers crept down her back. Gooseflesh rose on her arms. Before she could think, she leaped from the chair and retreated several steps before his voice rang through the air.

"Enough. No more of this." He slammed a gloved fist onto the arm of the chair. "Will you be playing for me, or should I find another musician who is interested in my employ?"

Ceridwen's legs froze under her, halting her retreat. Another retort yearned to be yelled at him, but her voice wouldn't comply, even for that. This man caused her to lose her temper more than all others combined. Bronwyn would be proud.

Unfortunately, he was the one man she could not afford to offend, not if she were to have hope of providing for her family.

Reluctantly, she reclaimed the wide chair of dark wood and crimson fabric that faced his matching one. Playing for her mother was easy, but this man... He refilled his glass from a decanter on the table as she adjusted her seat and lifted the flute from the side table.

"Apologies, Lord Winterbourne. Playing outside is important to me, and I feared not being able to do so while I stay here."

He nodded absently, his features giving nothing away.

At length, he said, "Your room is warded. It should be safe from the monster, but I cannot offer the same protections on the balcony.

"Warded?"

He raised one dark brow. "Surely you know that some nobles can work spells?"

She swallowed and gave a short nod. Yes, she'd heard that. The most powerful of them could work magic even beyond their enhanced strength and senses, but she'd never seen it, never had the chance to meet a noble. In all her years, she'd heard no more than what rumor and histories could teach her, and that was often vague at best, prone to dramatics.

"You should be safe from the monster inside your room," he replied.

"Thank you, my lord." She didn't understand the method of it, but the protection was a blessing all the same.

"I shall consider your request," he said, seeming much calmer now. "For now, proceed."

She closed her eyes, blocking out the man beyond and the unfamiliar room around her. Ceridwen's thoughts drifted away, far from the worries of the day as she raised the instrument to her lips. The melody flowed out, smooth and even. The walls of the room echoed the notes, but that, too, she tuned out. Only music remained, staccato notes teasing the tale of a hunt for the great stag of the northern wood.

When that song came to its end, she played another, her fingers flying over the keys by memory. A third followed. And a fourth.

She opened her eyes as the last song drew to its close. Soft, mournful tunes hung in the air long after she lowered the flute into her lap, the last remnants of lovers parted by death.

Not a sound came from the chair where Lord Winterbourne sat. His glass stood empty on the side table with the decanter. Had he not blinked, she might have thought him asleep with his eyes open.

His steady regard reached into her soul, tickling something she never expected. Heat rose to her cheeks. Ceridwen licked her lips without thinking, staring at the noble across from her.

Did he watch me like that the whole time? With eyes that I could drown in?

She waited for him to request another song or dismiss her.

He did neither.

"Thank you," he said at last.

His deep timbre rolled across her skin, sending a shiver down her spine. The rich voice held all softness and silk compared to the sharp, biting tone he'd used earlier.

Lord Winterbourne rose in a fluid motion and crossed the room to a large cord hanging from the wall. A bell rang in the distance, barely audible through the walls of the study.

How had two words affected her so? Ceridwen's restless hands found a home in the skirts of her dress as she waited to be dismissed, escorted back to her room, anything. The thick silence that hung between them threatened to undo her. Not to mention the feeling of his gaze sliding over her skin, all honey and velvet.

A sigh of relief escaped her lips as a soft knock came at the door, and Jackoby entered. He dipped a bow to his lord before extending an arm to Ceridwen.

As she slipped her arm through the butler's, Ceridwen looked back once at Lord Winterbourne. The sight sent a shard of ice through her heart. Red eyes.

She blinked, and they were gone. So fast, the odd sight came and went. She shook her head, clearing the image, which must have been some trick of the light.

"Good night, Ceridwen," Lord Winterbourne said as Jackoby led her from the room.

The noises that woke her could have raised the dead—shaken their spirits out of the Goddess's hallowed halls. Even her Eidolons—or Saints as the southerners liked to call them, those special humans who'd so embodied one of the characteristics she favored as to earn their own form of immortality in her service—would have been moved by the sound.

Deep growls rumbled through the quiet night—an animalistic howl unlike any wolf she'd ever heard. Worse, the sounds came from nearby, possibly within the manor walls.

She yearned to pull the covers tighter and block out the chilling symphony when the sound changed to a soft keening that threatened to crack her heart in two.

Hesitantly, Ceridwen slipped from the bed, ignoring the cold touch of stone on her skin as she traced to the floor-to-ceiling windows that lined the right side of the room. Darkness reigned beyond. Earlier in the day, she'd been so adamant about letting in the light and illuminating this gloomy manor, and the kindly housekeeper, Gwen, hadn't seemed to mind.

Were the curtains drawn in order to hide from the monster?

The balcony stood empty, its stone stark white in the moonlight shining down overhead. Only the shadow of the tall tower marred its surface.

Could the monster come within the manor walls? Would it? Lord Winterbourne himself seemed skeptical that the walls could keep it out. Despite her one horrific encounter with the beast, the pitiful sound ripped her heart anew. Did it suffer? Was that why it killed and maimed? Her palm rested against the cool glass, letting the night slip under her skin with the dark thoughts.

A sharp whine, more pained than terrible, crawled in through the cracks between the window panes and balcony doors.

How had she missed these sounds all the nights she'd played on the rooftop? Unless the monster stuck close to the manor or the forest beyond.

Ceridwen prayed to the Goddess for safety, for herself, her family, and the whole of the city. She beseeched her Eidolon of Protection, asking for him to watch over them all as well. If the Lord Protector, who was meant to represent him on this plane, would not protect the city, perhaps divine favor would, should her prayers be answered. Odd though it may be, she prayed for the monster too—for whatever it was to find peace, if even in death.

Sleep did not claim Ceridwen until long after the sounds vanished from the night. When it did, dreams reached her. In them, she played her flute on the rooftop of her family's city home while Lord Winterbourne watched her with red eyes.

CHAPTER 9

DRYSTAN

SLEEP HAD COME UNEASILY to Drystan the last few nights, despite having Ceridwen in residence and playing music for him. That calmed him where little else did. Unfortunately, it didn't fully ease the worries that kept him up until the late hours.

She was the curious sort, not content to sit idle in her rooms. The young woman liked to keep herself busy and had taken to helping the servants tend the vegetable garden, of all things. Most nobles would have frowned on such unladylike behavior, he supposed, but he admired her willingness to get dirt under her nails, the drive to do something, even so small as picking cabbages. He'd watched in secret the first time she ventured into the gardens. The glass roof overhead trapped the warmth of the sun. Between that and the heat from the kitchens below, the lush courtyard garden sprouted life through the harshest of winters like the one when he'd arrived. It was a marvel, even to someone like him raised in the capital.

The servants said Ceridwen sometimes asked about him as they worked. It both pleased and annoyed him. Digging into his past wouldn't do any of them any good. In fact, it would only make seeking his revenge harder. Sheltered as she was in this northern city on the edge of nowhere, she didn't know the horrors the capital wrought, the tangible darkness seeping through the streets and taking innocents down with it, or worse, twisting them to its own ministrations. He'd been a foolish young man once, caught up in the pleasures of life and blinded to everything around him. By the time he saw the darkness worming its way into his life, it was too late, and his family paid the price. Before he was forced to return to the capital at midwinter, per the king's command, he needed a solution to his problem. It was close. So close. But if he couldn't conquer the mess of his soul, which Ceridwen's music eased, it wouldn't be possible. He'd lose perhaps his one chance at salvation.

Conversation floated through the halls, reaching him before its speakers.

"—put him off much longer," Kent lamented, his voice carrying around the corner.

"He *is* the mayor," Jackoby touted. "He's in his right to worry."

"One day, he'll bring half the regiment with him and force an audience."

"Not if the king sends them south."

"You think he would?" Kent asked. "Not that there's much risk from invaders up here."

Drystan nearly snorted. To the north lay only some rogue settlements along the icy fjords—their citizens a people unto themselves. They never ventured south, and the residents of Castamar wisely saw nothing but bitter cold and misery in the north. That kept peace in itself. Not that there was anything to capture in this backwater city anyway.

"It's what Mayor Evans claimed."

"It's distressing if what the mayor claimed about the counsel is true," Jackoby said. "The king dismissing them doesn't bode well."

"That wretch," Kent growled. "We'd all be better off if he tripped over his royal boots and broke his neck."

"What is this about the counsel?" Drystan asked, rounding the corner and coming face-to-face with Jackoby and Kent. The mayor had demanded an audience again this morning—he'd sent them instead.

Kent paled. Jackoby swallowed thickly before answering. "The mayor says they've been dismissed. The king rules without counsel."

Drystan tightened his gloved hand into a fist. *Of course he does.* He shouldn't be surprised. The king had lusted for power, for the throne, even before his brother perished and the former king's heir was executed for causing his death and becoming corrupted by darkness. Ironic, considering the king was the worst offender of embracing dark magic and the power it offered. But dismissing the counsel was a blatant grab at unchecked rule. How could the people not see the tyrant in front of them?

"And you chose to discuss this in the halls? While we have a guest in residence?" Drystan crossed his arms, staring the men down.

"Apologies, my lord." The men echoed one another.

The information itself wasn't important—this time, but such slipups were risky. Ceridwen was an outsider, a sweet young woman, but one wrong bit of information whispered to the wrong ear could be his doom. Jackoby and Kent knew that well.

"My lord!" Another servant raced down the hall.

Immediately, the fine hairs rose on the back of Drystan's neck. "What is it?"

The young man skidded to a stop, breathing hard.

The mayor? Kent mouthed to Jackoby.

Drystan clenched his teeth as he waited for the servant to speak. *It better not be that ridiculous man.*

"Trouble at the gate, my lord," the younger man replied. "A young man demanding to see Miss Ceridwen."

Drystan's brows stretched upward. That, he did not expect. *A lover?* His mood soured at the thought.

"Gwen has already gone to retrieve her, but he's quite upset and causing a scene."

A low grumble rumbled in his chest. Yet another problem he didn't need. "I'll deal with this."

Fury simmered under his veins as he stalked down the hall.

Jackoby rushed to follow, falling into a hurried pace at Drystan's side. "Let me handle this, my lord." The older man was always quick to sense Drystan's temper and try to intervene. It was one of the reasons he trusted him so. He knew too well what could happen if Drystan gave in to his baser urges.

The thought of having to dismiss Ceridwen, to lose her music and her presence he'd come to enjoy, angered him beyond reason. But if she had some lover that was going to be a constant pain and storm the gates, he might have little choice.

Drystan and Jackoby reached the side entrance to the yard in time to see Ceridwen rush from the main doors and head with haste toward the man slamming his hands against the bars of the gate. He was young, with dark hair and wearing the military regalia of the city watch.

"Her brother?" Drystan mused aloud. The thought brought him up short.

"Perhaps," Jackoby replied. "Let me handle this, my lord."

For once, Drystan agreed. He nodded, sliding back into the shadows and watching from the doorway. Somehow, the thought of the man being her brother, not some desperate lover, changed things. He tuned his senses to the conversation and listened.

"Did Father not tell you?" Ceridwen implored.

"He told me everything," the man replied. "But you can't stay here. It's improper, even if he's our Lord Protector. Having you stay within his manor like this is wrong." He dipped his hand to the pommel of the narrow sword sheathed at his side.

The act had Drystan's lips pulling back in a snarl.

"Please don't cause a scene, young sir," Jackoby commanded, advancing on the gate.

"Let my sister go."

Drystan rolled his shoulders, releasing some of the tension stringing him tight. Definitely her brother, then. He tried to recall his name. Adair, was it?

"I chose to be here. I'm staying." Ceridwen crossed her arms and stared her brother down.

Unexpected warmth spread through Drystan's chest, a protectiveness of this woman who would choose to stay despite his rules.

"Don't mess this up for me," she implored. "Not now."

But she might as well have not spoken at all. Adair drew his sword and pointed the tip between the bars at Jackoby.

The barely leashed fury of minutes ago flared back to life within him.

How dare he? Brother or not.

"Please go," Ceridwen begged.

"You cannot be serious," Adair replied, not lowering his blade. "What have they done to you?"

"Nothing. I'm fine here." Ceridwen stepped closer to her brother, the blade barely inches from her face. Too close. Far too close.

Something in Drystan snapped, and he found himself racing across the yard with inhuman speed.

"I can't just leave—" Adair's words cut off, his gaze flying wide as it settled on him where he stopped behind Ceridwen.

"You can." Drystan wrapped an arm around Ceridwen, pulling her back from the gate and against his chest. She gasped, going absolutely still at his touch.

"You will," he continued.

"You just... From where..." Adair stuttered as his shaky sword clanked against the bars. He shook his head, recovering quickly. Instead of retreating, as any wise man would do, the arrogant idiot slid his sword farther between the bars. "Let my sister go."

Drystan flexed his arm around Ceridwen, cradling her tight against him until he could feel the racing of her heartbeat and hear her sharp little intakes of breath. She stared at her brother, unspeaking and still, possibly in shock.

"You should listen to your wise sister and leave us," Drystan said. "She chose to come here. If she wants to leave—"

"I don't," she snapped.

The strength in her resolve shivered through him, igniting a desire low within his abdomen that he did not expect. Something about her made him almost feral, possessive.

Adair adjusted his grip as his lips pulled back from his teeth in a snarl. Metal inched forward.

No more of this.

Drystan backhanded the tip of the sword with all his strength, bending the metal such that it did not return to its proper form.

"You dare raise your blade at me and those under my keeping?" Drystan demanded.

Ceridwen shivered against him, leaning farther into his embrace. "Please, Adair..." she begged, a breathy wobble to her voice.

He hadn't meant to scare her, this delicate woman unaccustomed to the strength his kind could possess, but he needed to send a message to her brother.

Adair jerked the sword from the metal bars. "If anything happens to her"—he tilted the sword up again—"I'll come back with a new sword, and not alone."

Laughter filled the air and vibrated through his chest. "Please do." *Let him try.*

Wisely, Adair held his tongue, though his lips pulled thin before his gaze sought his sister's. "I'm sorry, Ceridwen... That you had to come here, to degrade yourself like this... I..."

"Thank you," she whispered, her voice so weak he feared she might faint.

When Adair was some distance away, Drystan slowly released Ceridwen from his embrace. There was a reluctance to let her go, but he'd already held her far longer than he really should, the closeness stirring up all sorts of inappropriate ideas.

"Back inside," Drystan ordered. "Everyone."

Kent and Gwen waited just inside the main entrance.

Gwen stopped pacing when Jackoby closed the main doors, her eyes glassy. "I'm so sorry, my lord. Her brother was putting up such a fuss. We didn't want to attract unwanted attention. I thought that if Ceridwen could calm him down and send him on his way without—" She sniffled.

Drystan sighed. Once he might have flown into a rage, but something about holding Ceridwen close had calmed the dark desires within him.

"If perhaps you'd let me out to visit—" Ceridwen began.

"That would only garner attention." Drystan whirled on her, suddenly annoyed. The young woman stepped back, clearly on edge, and that sight instantly killed his fury. "Do you want people asking why you, and only you, are allowed in?" he asked more calmly. "Inquiring about me and my staff at length? Demanding knowledge?"

She stepped back again, her brows pinching together. "What are you afraid of?"

So much, Ceridwen. More than I hope you ever have to know. But he couldn't tell her that. Not only because it could compromise him and his purpose, but it might alter the easy companionship they'd settled into over the past few days while she played music for him.

"Should we expect anyone else storming our gates? Family members? Suitors?" he asked, voice gravelly and quiet.

She shook her head. "No, I don't believe so. You've met all my family now, and I have no suitors."

The comment stirred up a mess of both sorrow and joy that he couldn't quite sort out. "Take Miss Ceridwen back to her room," he said. "She's had a trying morning."

As had they all. With any luck, they'd avoid more visitors for a while.

Chapter 10
Ceridwen

Life in the manor settled back into a steady rhythm for a few days after Adair's sudden appearance at the gates. Gwen would share stories about the manor, the capital, and all number of things, though never anything about Lord Winterbourne, no matter how Ceridwen asked. It wasn't proper to share information about the Lord Protector without his approval. A fact Ceridwen knew, though it didn't stop disappointment from settling within her all the same. Kent taught her a game of cards, and others kept her company as well, especially when she worked in the gardens of the greenhouse. It wasn't a ladylike activity, though that had never stopped her, nor did anyone in the manor. Rather, she thought they seemed to appreciate her presence and company.

The manor's library, too, provided a wonderful distraction. Shelves of books lined the left and back walls. A freestanding shelf on the right separated the large desk from the three three-paned windows around a reading nook. The books numbered more than she'd ever seen. Those along the back wall out-aged the rest. One nearly crumbled when she'd touched it, so she stuck to the newer sections instead. Destroying Lord Winterbourne's library wouldn't earn her any favors.

And though she tried to keep herself busy, the steady ache of homesickness grew within her more each day.

She missed Bronwyn and the rest of the household. They'd sent a few letters. Well wishes. Encouragements. None of them were sealed. Lord Winterbourne or his staff likely read them all, as well as the ones she sent back. Ceridwen kept her messages brief and carefully complimentary of her host and her stay. But the folded pieces of paper were poor substitutes for her family's company. Letters didn't give companionship, reassuring hugs, or share winks of amusement. She couldn't linger in Father's scent of peppermint, Gerard's evening stories, or the comforting aroma of whatever meal Jaina had cooked up. Even Bronwyn's sass or Adair's temper would have been welcome company.

Her brother was always prone to bouts of dramatics, like that day at the gate, and had no trouble speaking his mind. How he maintained himself in the military, Ceridwen had no idea, for he'd never been the type to follow orders. Much like Bronwyn, he was outspoken and could easily steal the attention of a room. Ceridwen, however, had often been the opposite—the calm presence to her siblings' testy natures. But their spark of life added color to her otherwise boring one. Without them, things weren't quite the same.

But most of all, she missed playing for her mother under the stars. She played her flute by the window most nights in the hopes that her song carried to her, but it wasn't the same. And her voice... She'd tried to sing, as she once loved to, but it still wouldn't work. It hadn't since her mother died. As a child and through her youth, Ceridwen dreamed of being a great singer on the stage despite her tendency to hide at the edges of the crowd. But that dream died the day her mother did. Every time she tried to sing now, her throat closed up, choking off any sounds. Perhaps it was for the best. Her song only seemed to bring death and sadness anyway.

The only blessing over the past few nights had been the lack of the monster. Or if it had come, she hadn't heard it.

"Are you ill?" Lord Winterbourne asked as Ceridwen settled in across from him for their nightly concert. "Did something happen?"

"It's nothing," she said. Any time she brought up leaving the manor, or staying at her family's house and just traveling the short distance to the manor each day, his mood soured. Besides, her homesickness was worth whatever coin it earned. Father would need each one.

With a sigh, she closed her eyes and lifted the flute to her lips. The notes of the song slipped into the air—sad and mournful, a reflection of her spirit.

After a handful of bars, a weight pressed against the instrument in her hand. The song halted as her eyes flew wide. Lord Winterbourne stood before her. Dark brows wrinkled over deep-blue eyes as he gently pushed the flute away from her mouth with a gloved hand. Always gloves since that first day.

"You're unhappy."

She blinked at him, neither confirming nor denying his words.

"You have the best food in the city, a room fit for a noble, new dresses, and not a chore nor occupation to demand your efforts."

Color raced to her cheeks. That was certainly true. The dresses had been the greatest surprise, one brought in by Gwen one morning only days ago. Ceridwen had been terrified at first that the money had come from what Lord Winterbourne promised and been spent on such frivolous things that she could do without, but Gwen, and later Lord Winterbourne himself, had promised that was not the case. They were a gift. An unexpected one. Perhaps some attempt to make the woman staying with them look more like a guest instead of a servant, but she was beyond grateful all the same.

Everything he said was true, and though it should be enough, more than, none of it filled the needs of her soul.

She looked at him, really looked. Clear blue eyes stared into her as she reached for the depths of his spirit, trying to see beneath the unkempt noble in front of her. Yet all she found were walls, high ones covered in thorns and impossible to breach.

"I miss my family," she admitted. "I miss playing under the stars. No amount of luxury can compensate for those things."

Deft fingers tilted her chin in his direction. Ceridwen shivered at the limited contact, the smooth leather of his gloves against her skin. "You find me hideous."

She pursed her lips. *Your occasional sour attitude more than your unkempt appearance.*

His eyes widened as if he could read her thoughts or perhaps at her lack of denial of his claim.

Ceridwen stiffened, waiting for a harsh reaction, though she'd managed to keep her thoughts from slipping free in the form of words. Instead, he laughed, dropping his hand from her face.

"That spit of fire stills burns yet." He smirked before crossing the distance back to his customary chair.

Three songs later, he called an end to the performance. Ceridwen waited for Lord Winterbourne to cross the room to the braided crimson rope that would summon Jackoby to return her to her room. But instead, he crossed to the other wall and threw wide the heavy curtains, allowing pale moonlight to filter into the room.

Ceridwen's lips parted at the sight, in awe of the beauty of the night but also his odd behavior this evening. The moonlight paled his hair where it fell upon his locks, his shadow a dark form in the pool of light that stretched to her feet.

"Join me?" He reached his arm through that light in her direction, his open hand holding an invitation she dared not refuse. Yet accepting it felt just as impossible.

Ceridwen took her time returning the flute to its case before joining him.

"Who taught you to play?"

"My mother." A genuine smile bloomed on her lips.

"She lives here in the city?"

And it died just as quickly. His question sent a dagger through her heart. No matter the time that passed, it still hurt to think of her.

"She died in childbirth. Three years ago."

Ceridwen had been her last successful birth. Dierdre and Emrys were born already belonging to the Goddess, taken by her Eidolon of Rest before they ever breathed life. Fionn lived for two days after Mother birthed him, two days longer than her after the hard labor took all her spirit and caused her to bleed out. Or Ceridwen's song killed her. She never knew which. Maybe both. *If only I hadn't sung for her. If she'd never taken that walk and—*

Movement out of the corner of her eye made Ceridwen glance up under her lashes to find Lord Winterbourne sliding closer. His hand drifted a breath from her shoulder before fisting and returning to his side. "I am sorry to have brought it up."

She shook her head, blinking away the tears that threatened to form. "You did not know." An inquisitive Lord Protector who knew his people well might have heard the tale, but this man knew nothing of his people, at least nothing that he let on. "I miss her. Even now."

"She must have been quite the woman," Lord Winterbourne said.

"She was. She was so talented."

"Did she teach you other things?"

A tentative smile rose to her lips. "Most everything I know. She was an incredible singer, a storyteller, but mostly, a very kind and loving woman."

Lord Winterbourne blinked rapidly and looked away. If Ceridwen didn't know better, she might think him moved to tears by her memories of her mother.

He coughed quietly into his hand before looking at her. "Did she teach you to sing as well?"

Ceridwen's throat tightened up in response, even the mention of the talent stealing her voice. Instead, Ceridwen just nodded.

"Would you sing for me sometime?" he asked.

"No." The reply came out more sharply than she intended, and he startled. "I'm sorry, my lord. I do not sing anymore. I cannot."

"Drystan."

"Pardon?"

"My name. You may call me Drystan."

Ceridwen blinked at him. A commoner should not address a noble so informally, yet little about their arrangement was normal.

"Drystan." She tasted his name on her tongue, the richness of it surprising.

The sound of his name brought a smile to his lips, one that started a fluttering low in her stomach.

"I hope... I hope you can find some happiness here," he added.

This time he did cross the room, ringing the bell for Jackoby.

Rather than stand by the braided crimson rope that rang the bell, or return to his chair as he often did, Lord Winterbourne joined Ceridwen at the window. She flinched as he took her hand in his.

"Good night, Ceridwen."

He raised her hand to his lips. A velvet soft kiss graced her knuckles as his beard tickled her skin, but it was his eyes locked on her face that sent a pleasant shiver up her spine.

CHAPTER 11

DRYSTAN

CERIDWEN HAD OPENED UP about herself the night before, and he found he wanted to know more, so much more. The thought distracted him from his work much of the night, making his task impossible. He should be angry about that. After all, his time before returning to the capital was running short. But somehow, he couldn't be cross with her.

She intrigued him, sparked something in him other than the burning desire for revenge that fueled his purpose. It was that little flame that urged him to seek her out during the day rather than leaving her to her own ministrations or watching her from a distance as he sometimes found himself doing.

When she wasn't in the gardens, nor her rooms, he finally asked about her whereabouts and discovered her in the library. He opened the old wooden door slowly, holding his breath that it wouldn't squeak. When it was wide enough, he slipped inside and walked slowly beside the wall, looking for sight of his quarry.

He found Ceridwen sitting in the cushioned window seat, her back propped on one wall, sunlight spilling in through the window. The light added a shimmer to her golden hair and cast itself across the exposed skin of her arms, where they sat in her lap with an open book. Whatever she read held her full attention. She flipped the page. Ceridwen pulled her bottom lip between her teeth, and he almost groaned aloud.

Watching her was tempting. Joining her? More so.

"What are you reading?"

Ceridwen jumped in her seat, nearly dropping the book. "You startled me."

"Apologies," he replied, though he wasn't the least bit sorry.

Drystan walked to the window seat where she reclined. Ceridwen scooted closer to the window—giving him space to sit or moving away from him? He hoped the first and sat on the edge of the cushion, the little bit of space between their legs full of tension and warmth.

She turned the book his way, showing him the cover. The lack of wear alone marked it as a new item in the mostly aged collection. "It's the tale of the late King Jesstin and Queen Manon, Goddess give them peace."

"Ah, I see." Of all the things for her to pick.

He knew of the book, though he had not read it himself. It chronicled the late king's struggle against his father's dark magic and his efforts to restore peace and prosperity to the kingdom. A recent history, as things went, though it happened before his birth. He'd wager the printed version of the tale held must less detail than some of the rumors he'd heard.

"Quite the tale," he replied at length.

"It's...oddly vague in parts," Ceridwen said, her lips pursed. It only confirmed his suspicions. The secrecy of the royalty and nobility extended to books. No one would dare print the details of their magic and power, even if they knew what they were.

"There was little about the dark king and how he turned from such a loving father to a horrible madman," Ceridwen said. "You lived in the capital, right? Are the stories about the atrocities the dark king committed really true?"

The reminder of those dark days, and their likelihood of coming again, settled on him like a heavy weight. Ceridwen had no idea the significance of what she read and how the darkness rose once more in the capital. At length, he sighed. "The atrocities are true, as far as I know. I was not born yet, so everything I know is something I've heard from others."

Ceridwen inched closer in the seat until her leg brushed against his arm. The simple touch had desire building between his legs. "Can you tell me about the dark magic? What makes it different from yours?"

He grinned in return. "Dark magic is forbidden."

Ceridwen half rolled her eyes as if that were obvious. "Well, perhaps I'll find something about it in this library. It does seem there are books from the capital here, after all." She lifted the small book for emphasis.

Unlikely. Those secrets would never be put in books available to the public, not even ones left openly in a noble's home. "Hah," he replied, attempting to maintain some lightness in the conversation. "It may take you many years to read them all."

Her shoulders slumped as the book found a home in her lap once again.

"What is it?" he asked. But he had a sneaking suspicion. She wouldn't be here that long. Soon, he'd have to return to the capital, and she'd go back to her normal life. He thought about that looming deadline plenty, but not in relation to her, not the fact that he'd probably never see her again once she left. That fate was suddenly worse than whatever awaited him in the capital on his return.

"It's nothing," she said.

He knew well enough that wasn't true but let it go.

"It's horrible what happened to them," Ceridwen said, looking back up at him as if she needed the change of conversation as much as he did. "The king and queen, after all their sacrifice and hardship, to be killed by their own son."

The comment hit him like a punch to the ribs. *Horrible indeed.*

Ceridwen stared at the painting of the couple on the front of the book, one meant to resemble the now late monarchs in their youth. "Was it really as awful as the stories?"

"Yes." The word was thick with unspoken emotion. "Likely worse than the stories."

"Then it's a good thing King Rhion found the prince before he could escape and brought him to justice."

She spoke with such fervency, having no idea that the king she praised was as terrible, or even worse, than his nephew.

"Were you there when they executed him?" Ceridwen leaned closer, but he still couldn't quite bring himself to meet her gaze. "My friend Lydia claimed the whole of the capital attended, or at least all the nobility, though her sources are sometimes dubious."

"The execution?" Drystan asked.

She nodded, her hand settling on the cushion just an inch from his.

"That's a dark subject... But yes, I was there. Crying and begging for mercy were not what anyone expected from the prince in his last moments." A huff of air left through his nose as he pressed his lips in a thin line. "Do they include that bit in the stories?"

Ceridwen paled and leaned back toward the window. "No. They certainly do not."

"I thought not." Drystan stared at the dour expression that had risen to her face. "The execution was...uncomfortable at best for all in attendance. I'm sure no one wanted to repeat that in the tales they told their friends and relations."

She hugged her arms around herself, and he instantly regretted the frankness of his words. Even the sun retreated behind a cloud, stealing its warmth away from them.

Words to comfort her eluded him, and before he could chase them down, she spoke again, her voice a soft whisper toward the window pane. "The rumors out of the capital these days are not much brighter."

He stiffened. "You heard that here?"

Ceridwen shook her head. "The women gossiped about it before I ever came here." She glanced at him. "Monsters like our own. Whispers of terrible magic like the Dark King used to use."

So the rumors had spread to Teneboure. Things might be worse than he feared. Drystan remained silent. He could offer little in the way of comfort other than lies.

"I wish the king would do something about it. Or..."

Or me? He wanted to ask. *I'm trying.*

"The king, he—" He clenched his fist at his side. "Never mind. We shouldn't speak of it." He had more discretion in his words than his servants when speaking about their not-so-beloved monarch. He had to.

Ceridwen gave a soft gasp and turned more fully in the seat.

"What—"

But before he could ask, she reached back for him, tugging on his sleeve. "Look!"

His focus glued on her hand, that touch, and for a moment, all thought of what she'd seen vanished.

Ceridwen gave him another gentle tug and pointed out the window, a smile spreading across her face. "Snow."

The first flakes of winter. The joy of it lit the woman before him from the inside out. All talk of darkness vanished amid the spark of wonder radiating from her. A soft giggle escaped Ceridwen as she watched the flakes fall, and Drystan smiled too. Not at the snow that reminded him all too well of his time running short, but at the woman who found reasons to smile amid the coming darkness.

Chapter 12

Drystan

Drystan spent hours in the library with Ceridwen over the next few days, each taking turns reading aloud from books of myths and fanciful stories. He couldn't quite recall the last time he'd felt so at ease, so...joyful. It'd been years. Before the loss of his family, that was certain. And while he should be focused on working his spells, preparing for his return to the capital only weeks away, he couldn't find it in himself to begrudge the time he spent with her. She was a light in his dark world, one he hadn't realized he needed. He should have been working today to make up for the lost time in the library, but the thought of seeking out Ceridwen claimed the full front of his desires.

He found her just outside the greenhouse, standing atop a stone bench and reaching toward the nearby wall as if she might climb it. How delightfully odd. And curious. Why would a lady need to scale a wall? Then he noticed which wall exactly it was, one that formed the base of his tower, a place strictly off limits to everyone, including his staff, but especially her.

Jackoby had mentioned seeing the young woman at the base of the stairs to his tower, though she never ventured more. He assumed it mere curiosity, but this? Surely she couldn't know what he did up there. Drystan's chest drew tight, his jaw stiff. He liked to believe their companionship genuine, maybe even the start of something more. She couldn't be a clever spy, could she?

Her boot slipped on the edge of the bench. A scream cut through the yard as she fell, crashing hard to the ground.

All his worries from moments before vanished at the sight of her fall, worry surging forward as he raced for her. "Ceridwen!"

"Oh Goddess," she groaned, pushing into a sitting position on the yellowed grass. The few snowflakes that fell the day before had long since melted.

"Ceridwen." Drystan knelt at her side. "What's happened?" he asked, pretending he hadn't seen her failed attempt and subsequent spill from the bench. Perhaps in her panic, she hadn't heard him cry her name. His heart still raced as he looked her over for injuries. No blood, but with the thick layers of her skirts and long sleeves, he could see little of her. Some of her hair had slipped free from where she had pulled it back, the strands draping along one cheek.

"I was taking a walk and fell."

A lie, maybe to cover her embarrassment, but his desire to press her further vanished as she held her wrist and lifted it to him. "I fell on it."

"Let me see that." Gently he ran his gloved fingers along her skin, but even so, she winced. "You can't play like this."

It wasn't a question. Still, she bit her lip and nodded.

Damn. What a predicament.

Ceridwen's eyes turned glassy. Her nose wrinkled before she sniffed, almost like she was on the verge of tears. Did she worry he'd send her away if she couldn't play for him anymore? His lips thinned. Most likely. He didn't have the best of reputations, and that was the base of their arrangement. Though as much as he valued her music, he'd come to appreciate his time with her just as much.

The music, though... He *needed* that. His success depended on whatever strange magic held within her song calmed the darkness within him. At least he had a solution, even if it was one he hoped not to use.

"I can help you," he said.

Ceridwen gasped as he withdrew a thin blade from a hidden sheath within his coat. The fine silver weapon was no bigger than a sewing needle, but all he needed for this purpose. He pulled free one glove and then the other, fighting the burn of embarrassment rising to his face as she looked at his scarred hands.

There would be questions after this. So many more than he wanted to answer, but he couldn't leave her in pain, much less unable to play.

"Hold still."

Ceridwen stiffened, drawing back from him as he ran the tiny dagger across his palm, leaving a red trail in its wake. Drystan set the blade aside on his gloves before dipping a finger in the blood rising to the surface of his cut. "Magic requires blood and shape," he told her, trying to give the basest of explanations about what was to come.

"Blood and shape?" she echoed, her voice warbling.

"Don't move," he ordered. "Give me your wrist."

Hesitantly, she held out her wrist to him, though he didn't miss the slight shake in her limbs that likely wasn't all from the morning chill. Drystan wasted no time before he set to work on her wrist, drawing shapes in blood upon her arm and mumbling under his breath.

Once, twice, three times, he made the pattern. Tingling warmth spread through his hand, seeping down from his finger onto her skin. The sharp intake of breath said she felt it, too, though she managed to hold still for him.

At the completion of the spell, the blood soaked into her skin, vanishing as if it had never been.

The working complete, Drystan pulled a cloth from his pocket and wrapped it around his wound to stop the bleeding. "How does it feel?"

She blinked, opening and closing her lips in silence before finally she said, "That's where your scars come from."

"Some of them," he admitted. The ones on his hands anyway. He supposed now he might not need to hide them from her, assuming she didn't decide to stare at them.

"And your wrist?" he asked.

A small smile pulled at her lips. "So much better. It's a miracle. Like I never fell at all. But you…" Her gaze dipped to his marred skin, and he fought the urge to hide. "You cut yourself for me."

The wonder in her voice did something funny to his heart. Even so, he commanded, "You can't tell anyone."

Her brows wrinkled. "But why—"

"Not how it works anyway. Those of us skilled in the arts can use blood and shape, combined with our will and sometimes words, to cast magical spells. But you knew that, or at least the magic part. The means of it… Well, the nobility, the royals especially, don't like for it to be shared."

She pursed her lips. "Why guard it so? It's not like we commoners can use magic anyway."

"Even so, the punishment for sharing such knowledge can be quite severe." He had enough troubles on his shoulders as it was. Any more and the king might kill him rather than allow him back at court. Funny, though, that she would be curious rather than disgusted. "The blood didn't bother you?"

She dropped her gaze, a small shiver racing through her features, but she said, "Not really."

Perhaps it had, and she tried to put on a brave front.

Drystan rose to his feet and helped Ceridwen up, inquiring after any other injuries. Satisfied that she was well, he returned to his original purpose in seeking her out that morning.

"Perhaps I could offer you a tour of the greenhouse?" he asked.

"You like flowers?" A half smile twitched on her lips.

"All plants, actually. But I am particularly fond of the difficult ones." He pulled a glove over his injured hand, the soft leather tight over the makeshift bandage underneath. It would do for now. "Does that surprise you?"

"A noble interested in gardening." She looped her arm through his offered one, drawing close enough for him to catch the light floral scent clinging to her hair. "A most fascinating discovery."

They entered the greenhouse together, traversing the rows and sections of plants.

"These roses are my favorite here," he said. "I've grown them wherever I've lived for as long as I can remember. An odd hobby for a noble, I suppose. Most would leave the task to their gardeners. This place was a mess when I first moved in. The old caretaker kept some of the plants alive since the last Lord Protector left, mostly edible ones, but many we had to replant."

Ceridwen's smiles and compliments of his roses as they wandered the rows started a fluttering low in his stomach.

"I often got made fun of as a child for loving beautiful things," he admitted, gazing at the roses again. "Even so, I don't regret it. They brought me comfort when little else did."

Old memories, and some more recent, tried to claw their way to the surface. A frown pulled at his features. Ceridwen placed her hand on his arm, the gentle touch dispersing the darkness like a gust of fresh air.

"They're lovely. There's a beauty in watching things flourish and grow. I've always enjoyed it myself, even the dirt under my fingernails." She freed her arm from his and leaned down to better inspect some of the blooms. "It's much better than spending your time in that tower."

Drystan stiffened. "The tower?" He hadn't imagined things when he had entered the courtyard. She was curious about his tower, trying to learn more. He both loved and loathed that about her.

"What do you do up there?" she asked with a glance over her shoulder, trailing her fingers across silken petals.

"What do I do?" What to possibly tell her to ease her curiosity? He decided to stick as close to the truth as he could. "I keep the monster at bay."

She twisted around in a rush, her mouth forming a silent O. "You? Keep the monster away?" she asked incredulously.

A wry smile lit his face. "Do you doubt my ability?"

Her back straightened, and that fierce spark of conviction lit her eyes a moment before she spoke. "Of course I do. I saw the monster murder a man with my own eyes. I've heard the stories of it killing animals. Even here... I hear it at night sometimes."

"That was quite the accusation."

Her cheeks flushed.

"It could be so much worse, Ceridwen."

Her gaze darted away, the color of her cheeks increasing. "Can you make it go away?"

Something about her look and the desperation in her request drew him closer. He stepped near, and her gaze snapped to him. She seemed to hold her breath, her form perfectly still as he reached up and brushed a few wayward strands of hair behind her ear.

"I try to contain it every night."

"With magic?" she asked.

He longed to linger, to touch her again, but he stepped back, giving her space. "That's a part of it."

"If your magic is not enough, perhaps the city could help you. The mayor. The militia. Maybe organize a hunting party? The mayor is offering a reward. I'm sure people would help you."

"No. They would not be able to help." It would only put more innocents in harm's way, and he had no desire for more blood on his hands. He'd seen enough of death and tragedy.

"How can that be? If it bleeds, it can be killed. I saw it bleed the night I was attacked."

"Why so curious?" He fought the urge to reach for her again, to calm the edge of hysteria rising in her voice. "Shouldn't you be afraid?"

"I am." She twisted her hands in front of her, looking away for a brief moment before settling her gaze on him once more. "But one night when I heard it, it also sounded, well, sad."

"Sad?"

"Yes."

So perceptive, this young woman. She had no idea about the truth of the monster, and from what she'd seen and heard, she concluded much. Perhaps it was her talent as a musician, the ability to hear and understand without words.

"There is much you do not know." Drystan glanced toward the tower.

From the corner of his eye, he saw her open her mouth and close it again. She reached for him and then lowered her hand, twisting it with her other in front of her dress.

"Come," he said in an attempt to guide them back to safer, happier topics. "Let me show you the rest of the garden."

CHAPTER 13

CERIDWEN

THAT EVENING, GWEN STOPPED by Ceridwen's room before dinner. Heavy, shimmering fabric in shades of blue hung from her arms. Her eyes sparkled more than the cloth, matching the wide grin on her face.

"I know you have dresses of your own and some recent new ones," she began. "But I made this one just for you. With a little help from the maids."

Ceridwen gaped as she laid the dress out across the bed, displaying the layers of luxurious material, more costly than anything she could ever afford. A tight bodice embroidered with birds reminiscent of the ones on Lord Winterbourne's favored jacket topped a flowing layered skirt. Tight sleeves fanned out at the elbows, accented with the same navy and silver threads that matched the bird's design.

"It's so beautiful. But for me?" She shook her head. She was just a guest, a paid musician, and they'd given her so much already. She didn't deserve anything like that.

Gwen chuckled. "It's a gift, dear. You've livened up this tomb and brought the young lord as close to his old self as I've seen in years."

Years... How long had he been this way? But a better question. "How long have you served him?"

Her laughter softened into a motherly smile. "Since he was a small child."

"Has he always been so..." She couldn't find the right word. Secretive? Unkept? Odd? No matter how much she poked around the manor or casually asked of the servants, she could learn little about the Lord Protector. In fact, much of what she had learned, about his magic, his love of plants, came from the time she spent with him the past few days.

"No," Gwen replied over one shoulder before turning back to the dress and fluffing out the sleeves. "Not always. Would you like to try it on? We measured it off one of your other dresses, so it should fit, but we have a little time if I need to make any quick adjustments." She reached into the pockets of her apron and pulled forth a pin cushion bearing sharp bone needles and spools of thread.

Ceridwen carried the dress behind the screen to change. "Lord Winterbourne has been in Teneboure for less than a year. Where did you live before coming here? The capital?"

Most nobles did, preferring to remain among each other's company and near the royal family—or so she'd been told. She'd only visited the capital once, when Mother died, and that trip was best not remembered. Nothing good had come of it, just like nothing good so far had come from her poking about the manor. The more she tried to learn about Lord Winterbourne or about the monster haunting the city, the more the secrets seemed to close in on themselves, even if she had gotten a few tidbits more from Lord Winterbourne in the gardens today.

Her attempt to scour the tower base for some hidden entrance or other storybook-fueled nonsense? What a disaster. She'd promised Bronwyn she'd try to learn about the monster, see if there was anything that she could garner to earn the mayor's reward, but on that front, her time in the manor had been completely fruitless. Even the library was oddly devoid of anything useful—at least, in the books she'd looked through so far. Her tendency to get distracted with fanciful stories didn't help.

No response came as Ceridwen pulled on the new dress over her shift and corset, reveling in the feel of the cloth under her fingertips, along her arms, and around her legs.

She assumed Gwen ignored or missed the question until finally, she said, her voice somber, "Yes, the capital."

A tickle of unease raised gooseflesh along her arms. The rumors of death and dark magic... "I heard rumors of monsters in the capital. Is it true?"

Gwen clucked her tongue. "It's bad luck to speak of such things, especially tonight as we honor the Goddess in preparation for the winter snows. What you sow today, you reap the whole way through."

A sigh stuck in her throat. Just like that, she dodged the question.

Again.

A frown still painted Gwen's features when Ceridwen emerged from the screen, but it changed into a blinding smile as soon as Gwen beheld the dress.

"Oh, it is marvelous!" she exclaimed.

Ceridwen motioned toward the back of the dress and pulled her blond braid in front of her. The style of dress and complex laces were impossible for her own hands. This wasn't a commoner's outfit, not like the others she could fasten on her own.

"Of course, of course." Her deft hands secured the dress around her middle, ensuring it would not slip or gape. "It fits well, don't you think?" Gwen asked.

The low-cut bodice exposed more than Ceridwen would have preferred, and she fought the urge to tug it up. While stylish, it did not suit her usual preference, but even so, the rest of the dress fit like a dream. "It's lovely. Thank you."

"I was so worried," Gwen said. "It's been years since I've made such a dress." She opened her mouth to continue but slammed it closed again and abruptly looked away.

The extra bit of knowledge added more questions to the ever-growing list than it answered. How could one household conceal so much? And why?

"Anyhow," Gwen continued. "I thought the dress might be perfect to celebrate tonight. You all honor the first snow here in Teneboure, correct?"

Ceridwen bobbed her head. "Yes, we do."

The whole city would celebrate tonight—her family included. It was a tradition the day after the first snow of the season. Candles would be lit in windows all night, a prayer to the Goddess and her Eidolons for warmth and protection amid the upcoming heavy snows. The crispness in the air already teased their approach. It'd been the same in the countryside too, where a harsh winter storm could be even more punishing.

"Will we light the candles?" Ceridwen asked, attempting to push away thoughts of her family.

Gwen's smile dimmed. "Not in every window. I doubt Lord Winterbourne would approve of that, but if you want to light some here"—she gestured to the wall of windows along one side of her room—"I will have some extras brought up."

"Please. Wide ones." No point in risking one falling over and setting the drapes ablaze.

The hem of the dress swished against the stone floor as Gwen escorted Ceridwen to the dining room. Jackoby stood outside the doors, an uncharacteristic smile on his face. The expression stripped away the years and gave a hint to times of joy and laughter that had faded or been hidden behind a thick mask of formality. He dipped a bow to them as they approached.

Ceridwen curtsied in return, careful not to let the flower Lord Winterbourne gifted her during their tour of the gardens slip from behind her ear where she'd placed it before dinner. It felt right to wear it, as if the outfit were incomplete without it. Besides, she couldn't waste such a gift.

Roasted ham tickled her nose and sent a rush of saliva to her mouth, though the door to the dining room remained closed.

"Dinner is served." Jackoby pushed open the door behind him, giving Ceridwen a view of the room beyond.

A tall candelabra stood in the table center with deep-blue candles, the traditional color to honor the Goddess after the first snow. A rich array of foods already steamed in their dishes, more than two people could ever consume, but none of those things were what caused her mouth to gape open and her eyes to fly wide.

At first, she didn't recognize the young man who rose to his feet from his chair and walked the short distance of the table to hers. His unruly shocks of dark-brown hair had been trimmed and styled, falling around his ears. The beard, too, had been tamed, revealing smooth skin marred by a few scars along his chin and right cheek. Without the mass of hair, she could make out his lips as they pulled up in one corner.

Air filled her lungs as she remembered to breathe. Lord Winterbourne looked like the noble he claimed to be and, though she was loath to admit it, was quite handsome. The strong jaw and cheekbones, lips that—

Behind her, Gwen chuckled, breaking Ceridwen out of her reverie. Even so, her feet refused to cross the distance to where he waited with the chair pulled out like a gentleman. "There's so much for just the two of us," she said instead.

"Don't worry," Gwen replied. "We won't let it go to waste."

Jackoby nodded along. A smile still pulled at the corners of his mouth.

With forced steps, Ceridwen entered the room, her heart racing much faster than the slow pace of her body.

"Ceridwen," Lord Winterbourne said. "May the Goddess keep you warm in winter."

The traditional blessing brought a surge of fire to her cheeks and nearly caused her to stumble.

"May the Goddess keep you warm in winter, Lord Winterbourne," she said, stopping just before him.

"Drystan."

"Drystan," she echoed, daring to meet his mirthful gaze. His name rolled over her tongue, more delightful than the scents that had her mouth watering before she entered.

His answering smile stole her breath. For a moment, she almost forgot who he was, seeing something past the wild man she'd once thought him, the noble she knew him to be, or the reclusive lord who'd appeared to disregard the people he'd been assigned to watch over.

For the first time, she saw only Drystan.

He coughed gently, clearing his throat. "Would you like to be seated?"

Ceridwen accepted the offered chair and let him settle her at the table before he returned to his own.

Often they ate in companionable silence. But tonight, Ceridwen's gaze kept wandering up from her plate to the man across from her. And though they sat on opposite sides of the table with a mountain of food between them, his nearness unnerved her. Especially each time she found his gaze lingering on her as well, stirring up a mess of butterflies in her chest that fluttered faster than her racing heart.

"You wore the flower," he said.

A blush touched her cheeks as she squirmed under his attention. "It didn't match the dress at all, but I... Well, I wanted to."

"I'm glad." His smile mirrored his words. "It's one of my favorites."

He'd carefully trimmed the violet rosebud of its thorns before handing it to her earlier that day, a treasured piece of his most prized rosebush.

She tried to focus on the rich delicacies, but the feast didn't prove a sufficient distraction. Unable to focus on her food with the feel of his regard pushing against her ribs from the inside, she broke the silence the only way she could think of. "Do you have a favorite song?"

Safe. Music was safe. Though he'd requested a few songs, she'd never asked if he preferred one above all others.

Drystan's jaw worked as he finished a bite of food. "I have enjoyed all the ones you've played. Do you have a favorite? One you love to play?"

That was easy. "The Nocturne of the Moon."

His brows rose as he replaced his silverware with care. Chair legs scraped on stone as he stood and moved his chair. Her body tensed as he moved it around the table, closer to her, until his elaborate armrest nearly nudged hers.

"Tell me about it," he said as he sat.

Too close. Too...much. Her chest grew tight. Her neck flushed. All thought of food vanished as she focused on the servants quickly rearranging the place setting to accommodate their lord's sudden move. And he sat directly next to her, like they were a couple or something far different than they actually were.

"It's a rather dark tune," she admitted once the shuffling of plates and silverware concluded, if only to distract her racing thoughts and the almost palpable tension leaping the short distant between their bodies. "It's full of emotion. But I love the words that accompany it, the story of how the moon spirit wanders through the night, always searching for his love, the sun. Every night he almost finds her but retreats just before she appears. I suppose it's quite sad since the lovers are always kept apart, but the lengths they go to find each other are so moving, and the words that go with the tune are so fitting."

He rubbed his chin. "I had no idea it had words to it."

Ceridwen braced for mockery, for him to tease her about her girlish infatuation with the piece. Instead, he said, "I wish you could sing it for me."

A soft gasp caught in her throat. But she couldn't. Not anymore. Her voice was her first instrument, her most treasured—even beyond the flute. But her mother's last day on this plane had been the last she sang. When she left, she took Ceridwen's voice.

Old memories turned the food within her stomach. Sometimes she thought it was only fair after what she'd done, but that didn't make the loss—either of them—easier to suffer. Oh, what it would be like to sing again, especially for him!

"You're sad again."

She blinked up at him and did her best to smooth out her features and not let the sorrow leak through. "I'm all right."

He gave a slight shake of his head, seeing her words for the lie they were.

"Is there something you would like?" Drystan set his hand on the table, so close she could reach out and take it if inclined.

A flicker of hope lit within her. "Could I visit my family?" It'd been weeks since she'd seen them, and the steady ache for their company grew each day. She might have lost her mother and her songs, but there were others she loved, and being cut off from them for the first time in her life was harder than she envisioned.

He withdrew his hand abruptly. "No."

"But why?" she pressed. "It's not far, and I'll come right back." He'd given her expensive and exquisite dresses seemingly without thought or concern, but this simple request, this one that cost him nothing, he always declined.

"It's better this way." He straightened the napkin in his lap, not quite looking at her. "Safer for everyone."

Her brows scrunched together. "Safer?"

"You think I haven't noticed you sneaking around the manor?" he said, an eerie calm to his voice as his gaze slowly panned back to her. All trace of the warmth and joy of moments ago had vanished.

Breath caught in her throat. She'd tried to be discreet, never venturing into his forbidden tower, but it wasn't in her to be idle and pass up the opportunity to potentially learn something about the monster and earn the mayor's reward to help her family.

"Even today in the garden. You were trying to climb that wall before you fell, weren't you?"

She gaped at him, heat rushing to her neck and face. He'd seen her. Oh, how foolish she'd been. Worse, he'd deduced what she was about.

"And then I showed you things today, told you things, that should not be shared. At least not while I am still in residence."

"I'm not a gossip," Ceridwen snapped in return. Of all the things to accuse her of. "I only wish to see my family. Surely that cannot be harmful. I will not say anything. Not about you, the manor. None of it."

"There's so much you don't know," he grumbled, almost to himself. Though he still sat next to her, he shifted in the chair, pulling away. The casual grin and friendly facade he'd worn all night was long gone.

Without thinking, she touched his sleeve. "What are you so worried about? Tell me. Please."

A gloved hand ran through his dark hair, mussing it up. Emotions she couldn't quite place flickered across his face. His mouth worked in his jaw. "I can't."

She snatched her hand away. "Can't or won't?"

When he refused to respond, to even look at her again, Ceridwen slid the chair back from the table. "Excuse me."

He reached for her, but she ignored him, hurrying toward the door.

"Ceridwen." More panic than demand colored his voice. "I'm sorry, I didn't mean it."

Tears stung her eyes, but she refused to let him see her cry. She only wanted to see her family. Why was that so wrong? How could it possibly hurt him?

"Ceridwen, please."

That word. It struck hard in her gut. The tone threatened to crack her stubborn heart despite his callous comments. She paused and looked over one shoulder. He'd risen from the table. Something flickered in his eyes, or was it the candles?

Suddenly, he lurched forward with a groan of pain. Drystan's hands slammed onto the table as his body knocked into it, rattling the dishes and sending the candles swaying precariously on their stand. One hand grabbed at his chest. The other latched on to the tablecloth.

"Drystan!" She rushed for him.

The doors burst open. Kent advanced from his place at the side of the room. Another set of quick footfalls sounded at her back.

Someone grabbed Ceridwen around her middle just as she reached his side, pulling her away from Drystan where he practically collapsed onto the table. "Wait, don't touch him," Jackoby said.

She wiggled in his grip, but he held firm. Kent whispered to Drystan words she could not hear.

Her heart beat rapidly against her chest. "What's happening? Is he hurt?"

"Take her. Room," Drystan bit out, ignoring her plea.

"Of course," Jackoby replied. "I'll return shortly. Hold on."

Jackoby tugged on her hand, his other arm coming around her shoulders to steer her away.

"Is he? What can I—" Her words tripped over themselves as she twisted toward the table. His denial of her request had hurt, but the sight of him hunched over, gasping in pain, broke something within her.

"No time to explain. Come. Quickly."

With one last backward glance at the man still grimacing, she fled with Jackoby. When they turned a corner, he released her. "Go back to your room. Straight there. Do not leave."

"But he—"

"Now." His command rang with authority in the empty hall, a flash of emotion running across his face with the words.

Ceridwen's spine stiffened as the order sank home, but worry still twisted within, urging her to return and offer whatever aid she could. She stepped toward the dining room. However, the look of true concern in Jackoby's eyes firmed her decision. He needed to get back, to help, likely in ways that she could not.

Instead of trying to interfere, she swallowed her concern and nodded in consent.

Jackoby rushed toward the dining room, while Ceridwen hurried in the opposite direction.

CHAPTER 14

CERIDWEN

CERIDWEN PACED ALONE WITHIN her room. The winter candles lit in front of the windows illuminated the space in bright light and cast flickers and shadows against the glass and ceiling. Their wax cooled in puddles on the floor. Some of the wicks already burned low.

Was it illness? Could that be why he saw no one and did not want her to leave? A surge of anxiety spiked within her. None of the manor staff appeared ill, but neither had Drystan until today, at least other than the unkempt appearance he'd maintained until now. Would it be a contagious ailment? Something she might have unknowingly caught?

A shudder racked her body. It made sense. He wouldn't want her to leave if she could infect the rest of the city. But he should have told her. Ceridwen's nails dug little crescents into her palms. To keep something like that a secret... Her dinner threatened to come back up, and she had to sit down.

Goddess, protect us all.

A soft knock on the door pulled Ceridwen from her spiraling thoughts. At this late hour, she should have been asleep already, yet the horrible thoughts had not let her heart slow its rhythm enough to relax.

"It's Drystan."

Breath caught in her throat. Part of her yearned to run to the door and see to his health, but the other half wanted to shove the dresser in front of it. He kept something from her, some secret, and possibly worse, he might have given her whatever horrible illness plagued him. She bit her lip. Either way, she couldn't answer the door in her thin nightdress.

"One moment," she stuttered. *Too late to pretend to be asleep.*

"I'm sorry about earlier."

His words seeped through the door and followed her through the room as she lurched to the dressing screen and grabbed the heavy robe lain across its top.

"I'm not used to having visitors. Having others close to my affairs makes me...uncomfortable," he continued.

Obviously. It was ridiculous for him not to let her come and go when she lived so close, yet if it were illness, that made a certain sad sense. Deceiving her about it, though, was another matter. Yet the sincerity ringing in his apology drew her back to the door.

She closed her hand over the metal handle and froze. "Your illness... Can I catch it?"

One heartbeat was too long to wait for his reply.

"No."

"Do you promise?"

"Yes. It's not something that... It cannot be transferred to someone else."

Despite the constant thud of fear within her, Ceridwen believed his words. She twisted the key in the lock on her side of the door and pulled it open.

Drystan squinted as light spilled from the room into the dark hallway. Not even the sconces were lit. *Someone forgot to light the candles on the night they were most important.* His stiff jacket was absent. Only a thin white shirt clung to his frame, tucked into dark breeches the color of his boots.

"May I come in?" he asked.

Her cheeks heated at the question. Father would never approve of a man alone in her room. Not to mention his attire, or lack of, inspired thoughts she hastily shoved away. But the pitiful way he'd looked hunched over the dinner table had a way of pushing out common reason.

"You may." She nodded and stepped back.

He entered and closed the door behind him as she retreated into the center of the room.

What are you doing, Ceridwen? she chided herself. *Letting a man into your room at night of all times.*

"Are you better now?" she asked, forcing a smile and trying to push away her embarrassment at the situation.

"I am." He loomed like an imposing figure in the center of the room. "I'm sorry to have frightened you."

Ceridwen shook her head. "It was worry more than fright." She paced near the candles, unable to sit still as he finally moved to take a seat by the crackling fireplace.

"Will you sit with me?" He gestured to the chair opposite his.

She sighed. He was her employer after all. She needed the money he offered, even if his refusal to let her visit family suddenly made no sense at all if his disease could not be spread. It wouldn't do to ignore him. "Does it happen often? The pain, or whatever it was?"

Bracing his forearms on his knees, he leaned forward on the seat as if the weight of the world pressed upon his back. "Much more than I'd like, but you help me."

She froze at his words and rocked back on her heels within her slippers. "How do I help you?"

"Your music. It calms me, lessens the episodes that overtake me, though tonight it almost broke through anyway."

Almost? Her brows scrunched together. That was just a near miss? How much worse could it get?

"You haven't played tonight." He straightened in the chair. "I hoped you might."

The revelation had her standing a little straighter near the seat he offered. "How do you know that?"

His gaze darted to the fire. A burning log collapsed in the middle, sending a tumble of smoldering coals rolling toward the edge as the two end pieces fell in either direction. His attention drifted to Ceridwen as he said, "No one heard your music in the halls."

She pursed her lips. No one had been around when she returned to her room, and if they aided him with his illness, as Jackoby had gone to do, they would not have heard her music anyway. Something was missing again, but she let it drop—for now.

"If I'm to play, I'd like to do it under the stars, on the balcony." Far too many days had passed since she'd played under the sky for her mother, and while she hoped she heard, and she occasionally felt the tickle of someone watching, even when she played alone in her room, she longed to resume her nightly ritual.

Drystan sat up straighter, his brows rising with him. "It's cold out tonight."

"I know." It had snowed more that evening, and much of it likely clung to the balcony. But her desire to play outside outweighed her need for comfort. "It's important to me. Please."

"I do owe you quite a bit. But would you tell me why?"

The mere thought of sharing more about her mother brought the prick of tears to the corner of her eyes, but she hastily blinked them away. "I play for my mother, so that her spirit can still hear my songs from the halls of the Goddess. It sounds silly," she continued, rambling away in nervousness. "But sometimes I can almost feel her watching, and it gives me peace to know she listens, even if she's no longer on this plane with us."

When silence hung again, her gaze trailed up from the ground, climbing Drystan's body until it landed on his somber face.

"You miss her."

"Very much."

He nodded and looked toward the balcony. "Then I'll leave the balcony door unlocked and you can play for me here when the weather allows," he said. "But please, stay inside at night unless I'm with you."

Because of the monster. He didn't need to say it for her to understand the concern. Even the manor wasn't safe at night. She'd heard the beast's cries shortly after coming to the manor, so close that she'd expected to see it on the other side of the windows. A shiver, one not born of cold, racked her body.

"Thank you, I will be careful."

He rose and stretched his arms above his head. "First, we'll have to move some of these candles."

Joy bubbled up within her. "Oh, I'll—" She made to kneel, but he grabbed her wrist. "Let me."

His gloved thumb rubbed over her skin, sending a shiver down her spine. He held her gaze, far closer than she realized. A gentle smile spread across his face. "You cannot play with burned hands."

CHAPTER 15
DRYSTAN

S HE HONORED HER MOTHER with her song. No wonder Ceridwen was so eager and insistent on playing outside. Drystan wasn't entirely convinced that the spirits of those who passed could hear a thing from the Goddess's hallowed halls, but if it gave Ceridwen comfort and kept her at his side longer, it might be worth the risk—as long as she didn't go out at night without him.

That, he must insist on. It was a risk, given her penchant for snooping, and though he somewhat admired her tenacity, it put her at greater risk than she knew. Him too. Though, if she did learn anything of importance, hopefully he'd be well on his way to the capital before she left the manor and had time to spread such gossip.

At the moment, he was far less worried about that than her trying to flee or locking herself in her room in the wake of his fit. He'd tried too hard the last few nights, a vain attempt to make up time spent with her during the day. He pushed himself, and such a simple thing nearly caused a break in front of her. If it had happened, he'd have lost her for sure, and that he couldn't bear.

One by one, he moved the candles away from the balcony entrance until only a splattering of cooled wax guarded the threshold to one of the double doors. Ceridwen had traded her slippers for boots, grabbed an extra shawl, and retrieved her flute while he worked.

He slipped his hand into a pocket and pulled forth a brass key.

Ceridwen raised her brows at him. "You just happened to have a key to my room in your pocket?"

He grinned, and for a moment, he forgot what she'd asked, lost in the sight of the slight disapproving scowl on her features. Why such a look should give him such pleasure, he couldn't decide. Finally, he said, "It opens all the locks in the manor."

"Oh." She appraised the key with renewed interest, probably considering all the trouble she could get herself into with such a thing. She'd use it if she could, of that he had no doubt.

Drystan returned the key to its resting place within the pocket of his pants. "You know where to find it if you're brave enough to get it."

A soft gasp slipped from her lips as she looked away. He barely restrained the chuckle trying to break free.

Flurries blew into the room on a crisp burst of air as he pulled the glass door inward. Their boots crunched on the thin layer of soft powder as they strode onto the balcony. The cold didn't bother him much. In some ways, it was almost as comforting as Ceridwen's music. The sharp sting of a cold wind against his skin had often kept his inner turmoil in check.

Stars twinkled like little candles in the clear sky overhead, accompanied by the blue globe of the moon that lit the balcony and the manor. Puffs of smoke drifted away from Ceridwen's mouth with each breath, but she seemed undeterred. Instead, her face shone with unguarded pleasure in a way that made his lower abdomen clench. Even so, he'd have to insist she stop after a song or two. It wouldn't do for her to catch a cold.

Ceridwen's song rang out into the night, strong and sure despite the cold air. The tune was beautifully tragic, full of depth and layers that moved even his dark spirit. How anyone could listen to such music and not be affected was beyond reasoning. Even without words, the rise and fall of the melody wove a tale that could pierce the heart, stitch it back together, and then rend it asunder once more.

At the end of the second song, a livelier tune that chased away the sorrow of the first, Ceridwen lowered her flute. Her cheeks were pink. A few flakes clung to her hair, and she had to be freezing.

"Your songs are lovely, even when your hands are numb," he remarked. "Perhaps some gloves would help?"

She smiled at him. "It's hard to play in gloves." She traced her fingers over the holes in the keys. "If we cut off the fingertips, that may work, but it'd be such a waste of a good pair of gloves."

Always worried about the cost. He admired that, even when a pair of gloves was nothing to him. "I'll see to it."

"But—" she started.

"Don't worry about the price. Consider it a gift."

She dipped her chin, the flush along her cheeks rising. "That's very kind."

"It's nothing," he said, though it was clear to her it meant a great deal. He should have thought of it sooner.

"I love to watch you play," he admitted. There was something magical about it, even more than the enchanting tunes she wove into the night. "To see the way you lose yourself so completely in the melody. The softness of your face. The flutter of your eyelids as the song lures you somewhere far away from me." He closed the distance between them and swept a gloved hand down her cheek. "The gentle pucker of your lips."

Her gaze snapped up to his, wide-eyed and mesmerizing. "Drystan."

He cupped her cheek, savoring the soft inhale of her breath.

"Perhaps we should go inside." She stepped away, aiming for the balcony doors, but he caught her about the waist.

She whirled around at his bold touch, her flute a last barricade between them as he drew her close. "W-What are you doing?" she stuttered.

When she didn't try to flee again, he tugged her even closer, his forehead leaning in to nearly brush hers, the fog of their breaths mingling together. "What I've wanted to do for days."

He thought she might pull back then, turn away from him again, but when she blinked up at him, leaning ever so gently against his chest, it was all the invitation he needed. The warmth of her breath swept across his lips moments before he claimed them with his own.

So soft. So warm.

He felt her stiffen under his palm, but it was quick, gone in an instant before she relaxed again, her body pliant and willing in his embrace. Her lips brushed his in the gentlest touch, nearly breaking something within him.

The ice encasing his spirit melted in a rush of fire, flowing outward from his chest. Drystan groaned as her lips moved against his own, a tentative answer to the initial question of his kiss.

Her flute pressed awkwardly between their bodies, but he guided her closer until she was encased in his warmth, the floral notes of her scent stirring up the desire buried deep within him and setting him aflame. She dug her hand into the material of his shirt, so warm and insistent in contrast to the chill night air against his back.

It was the greatest gift and the most agonizingly delightful torment, one he thought perhaps lost to him forever. He didn't deserve to kiss someone so lovely, so innocent.

Drystan forced himself to relinquish her kiss, to let her go before he lost himself in her completely. Her eyes fluttered open, her heavy breathing and dilated pupils making his cock strain painfully against his breeches.

"I thought you might whack me upon the head with your flute," he teased. It would have been worth it. So worth it.

She glanced away, pulling her bottom lip between her teeth. The act nearly had him groaning in pleasure.

"Is that what you wanted?" Ceridwen glanced at him from under her lashes, as if she couldn't bear to fully look at him. In truth, if she did, he might lose the last of his resolve and kiss her again.

"No." He flexed his hand against her side, unable to relinquish that last bit of connection. "You've already given me so much more than I'd dared to hope."

"Why me?" She glanced away again.

A fair question. He was noble, she a commoner, and the two rarely mixed, but their status had little to do with desire. In fact, he'd gladly give whatever shred of status he had left to linger with her. "You enchant me." He slid a hand up her side, eventually cupping her cheek and angling her face toward his. "Your songs, your spirit, they show me a glimmer of the person I used to be."

She met his gaze, her eyes filled with a mix of emotions he couldn't quite decipher.

"I'd almost forgotten him, lost here inside my lonely tower," he added.

Ceridwen ran her fingertips along his shirt, the brief and fleeting touch stirring up more emotion than she could know. "Who were you?" she asked.

"It doesn't matter."

Her mouth parted, questions sure to follow, and Drystan pulled away, heading into her room. Ceridwen followed, quick on his heels.

"Who were you?" she asked again.

He glanced at her sidelong. "A failure of a man who made poor decisions."

Too many of them to name. More than he could bear to share with her. He'd been a fool, trusted the wrong people, and done things that still made him wake in a cold sweat at night.

"But what—"

"Ceridwen." At the use of her name, she stopped, staring at him from just within her bedroom, the darkness of night spilling in behind her. "Let it lie. Please."

"I'm sorry." Her shoulders drooped. "If I can help..."

You do. So much. "Someday...maybe..." He shrugged as if it mattered little, but it was anything but.

"Good night, Ceridwen. It's late, and I shall leave you to your rest. Be sure to keep the balcony closed." Drystan gave a short, stiff bow before striding across the room to the open hallway door. Gripping the handle, he halted, looking back once over his shoulder. Ceridwen still watched him, so many unspoken questions lingering on her parted lips.

If only he could tell her everything. But that would ruin whatever they had, this tentative bloom of something, and he wouldn't risk it. Instead, his gaze swept over her form, savoring one last look before he turned and forced himself out into the dark hallway.

CHAPTER 16

CERIDWEN

CERIDWEN SPENT THE DAY scouring the manor for Drystan, yet he was nowhere to be found. His words and actions from the night before played over and over in her head. Who had he been? How much had his life changed? The man had more secrets than anyone she'd ever met. Considering them nearly drove her mad. And that didn't even include whatever he knew about the monster that stalked the night.

Eager to distract herself, Ceridwen tried to read, but after a line or two, the words became a blur, and whatever scene she read twisted itself in her head until it became the balcony from the night before with Drystan standing just in front of her.

Your songs, your spirit. You enchant me.

She slammed the book closed and set it aside with a heavy thump. "What were you thinking, kissing him back?" she mumbled to herself.

Nothing good could come of it. Not from kissing a lord. But even so, she couldn't entirely make herself regret it.

Ceridwen readied for dinner and strode to the dining room. She'd be early, but distracting herself proved ineffective, and Drystan was nowhere to be found. Probably stuck up in his tower, the one place she was forbidden to go. Tempting as it was to search for him there, she couldn't risk angering him and being dismissed.

"Miss Ceridwen." Jackoby gave a stiff bow as she approached. "I'm afraid the dining room is still being set."

"Can I be seated anyway?" she asked.

Jackoby's lips tugged downward, ever the one to enforce the proper way of things.

She'd tried to occupy her mind as long as she could. Even her songs did not come easily today. Drystan would come to dinner. He always did. Perhaps she'd play outside again for him that night. Maybe he'd... She bit her lip. *Don't go there, Ceridwen.*

"Please?" Ceridwen asked, blinking innocently at the butler.

Jackoby's lips thinned. She waited for the rejection sure to come, twisting her hands together behind her back.

The quick, heavy thump of boots on stone captured both of their attention as Kent turned a corner and rushed toward them. The maroon curtains and oil lamp flames ruffled in his wake.

"Kent, what—"

The younger man's eyes flicked to Ceridwen as he came to a halt, back stiff, though his chest rose and fell with each deep breath. A tangle of hair had fallen free from his normally perfect slicked-back ponytail. "You're needed immediately. There's..." His attention jumped to her again as he swallowed before returning his attention to Jackoby. "Lord Winterbourne would want you to handle this situation."

Ceridwen nearly groaned. *Please don't be Adair.* If her brother stirred up more trouble, she'd never forgive him.

Jackoby sucked in a breath. "The decorum of this manor falls apart in a moment," he mumbled to himself. "Be seated," he ordered to her. "I'll be back shortly. Kent." He waved his hand in the other man's direction.

If it was her brother, they might need her help. "Should I come—"

"No," both men replied at once.

Ceridwen startled, standing a little straighter.

"Apologies, miss." Kent gave a short nod as Jackoby hustled in his direction as fast as his manners permitted.

Odd. So odd. She watched them go, her brows wrinkling until they rounded a corner out of sight. A trickle of apprehension crawled under her skin. If not her brother, could this have to do with the beast? It never came during the day, not that anyone knew, but it had to go somewhere during that time.

The dining table had already been set for two. The serving dishes stood empty, the candles unlit. Heavenly smells—roasted meat, a whiff of potato, the barest hint of sweet pastry—wafted in through the closed door leading toward the servant's entrance, which connected to the kitchens down a flight of stairs. The cook's food never failed to please. In fact, whenever her services came to an end, Ceridwen would miss the food. Once, it might have been the thing she missed most, besides the money, but no longer.

She trailed one finger over her bottom lip, recalling the unexpected softness of Drystan's lips, his soft groan when she'd melted for him, and the odd spiciness that invaded her nose.

A door creaked, giving her a heartbeat to pull her hand back into her lap before two maids entered carrying steaming dishes. The first raised her eyebrows when she caught sight of Ceridwen but said nothing about her early arrival. Nor did the second. They made a second trip a few minutes later, finishing off the arrangement of food in the center of the table.

Her stomach rumbled at the savory scents filling the room from the covered dishes. Where was Drystan? Or Jackoby and Kent, for that matter.

The double doors behind her groaned open. *Finally.* With them came a flood of conversation.

"—just wait," Jackoby ordered, sounding more ruffled than she'd ever heard him.

"Does my dear cousin expect me to starve?"

The unfamiliar, rich male voice practically pulled her shoulders back, straightening her in the seat. She dug her fingers into the wood of the armrests as she grasped for purchase among the wave of surprise flowing over her. *Cousin?* Drystan never mentioned...

"Honestly, I'd expect more hospitality than—" His haughty words cut off abruptly along with the heavy tread of boots across the floor.

She ached to turn and look at the guest at her back, but wariness held her in place. The candlesticks on the table flickered and wavered more than she did.

"Now, what do we have here?"

The amusement in his voice twisted a knot within her stomach, one that tightened as the footsteps turned light and moved in her direction. At that, she did turn, catching sight of the man.

At first glance, he reminded her of Drystan, with the same dark hair and strong cheekbones. But this was not the lord of the manor. Green eyes twinkled in a smirking face, and his skin was a shade darker than Drystan's. His piercing look pinned her to the chair like an insect in a collection.

He pulled a brooch off his coat before she got the full look of it. Iron? An animal, perhaps? He tucked it away into a tailored, fine-stitched coat that radiated wealth. Whatever it was, it paled in comparison to the rings on his hand that glittered with gemstones only someone of great importance could possibly own.

A noble. He had to be.

"A pretty bird, hidden away in this dingy manor. Such an unexpected surprise."

Leather with a hint of spice tickled her nose as he stopped next to her chair and bent slightly in her direction, tilting his head this way and that as his gaze raked her body.

Ceridwen studied her plate; heat flooded her cheeks as she fought the urge to squirm under his inspection. *Oh, to be able to disappear through the floor.*

"Have my charming looks stolen the words from your delicious lips?"

Ceridwen snapped her head in his direction. "Not even a bit." His looks were charming, but his attitude, and the leer in his eyes that made her want to run, overrode his physical beauty.

He threw his head back and laughed, a deep rumble that rolled across her and filled the room. "Oh, that fiery look in your eyes," he said, reining in his laughter and pinning her with his stare once again. "You are interesting. What are you to him, hmm?"

"Perhaps you'd take a seat and wait for—"

The visitor cut Jackoby off midsentence with a quick scowl and wave of his hand. Jackoby stepped out of view as the annoyance slipped from the visitor's face to be replaced by mirth once again.

Her lips thinned as she held back the retorts rising to the tip of her tongue. Anyone who could silence Lord Winterbourne's butler with one motion was not someone she cared to anger. The newcomer tapped his index finger on his smirking lips while she dug her hands into the chair to keep from smacking the lecherous look off his face.

"A hired courtesan, perhaps?" he mused.

Fury simmered under her skin, and she could no longer sit still. Ceridwen rose to her feet, sending the chair back with a clatter as she moved away from the male at her side. "Do not dare call me such a thing."

His hand dropped as his grin widened. "I thought not."

"What's going on here?"

Drystan. Thank the Goddess. He hustled into the room, Kent quick on his heels and looking even more disheveled than before. Jackoby, too, appeared unnerved where he stood a few paces from the door, his shoulders even stiffer and more squared than normal, as if a cord from the ceiling pulled him upward.

"Ah, dear cousin," the man said with a flourish of his hand. But Drystan's scowl only deepened despite the familiarity of the man's words. "I was just meeting this lovely lady that you failed to ever mention to me. Who is she?"

Drystan's gaze flicked to her, cold and impassive, before returning to his cousin. "Just a local girl who plays music. Nothing to get excited over."

The words hit like a blow to the stomach. It took everything she had not to hunch in phantom pain as they worked their way into her heart like small daggers. *Nothing to get excited over.* Memories of the night before flashed through her mind. His kind words. His kiss. All felt foul and dirty to her now.

Her gaze fell to the place setting in front of her chair, the only safe place to look as tears threatened to fill her eyes. *What a fool I've been to think we could be anything more.*

CHAPTER 17

DRYSTAN

SAYING THE WORDS, CALLING Ceridwen nothing special, was painful. Seeing the immediate effect they had on her was so much worse. He'd rather cut his hands and bleed himself a hundred times than hurt her that way, but nothing good could come of Malik realizing his true feelings for her. In fact, nothing good could come of Malik's visit at all, but it was too late to avoid that.

The arrogant bastard hadn't even sent word that he would come. Perhaps he should have expected it. It wasn't Malik's first visit, after all, but this close to midwinter, to his return, he thought himself safe from interference from the capital.

Should have known better. Letting his guard down was a fool's error. Drystan had little doubt who sent his cousin up for a visit, and he knew exactly to whom Malik would be whispering whatever he learned during his visit upon his return—the king.

"She's quite attractive for a commoner," Malik said, his smirk fixed firmly in place as he admired Ceridwen with far too much interest.

He couldn't have Malik speaking to the king about her. If he had any idea that she meant more to him than just some hired help, the king would find a way to use her against him, another tool to keep him in check. Worse—it would put her in more danger.

Drystan shrugged, trying to appear unfazed by Malik's appraisal of Ceridwen as he crossed to the table with casual grace. "Are you planning to join us for dinner?" Drystan asked, ignoring the plaintive look Ceridwen aimed his way. "There should be plenty of food."

If only he could tell her exactly what transpired, but there was no method of it. Malik had caught him unprepared, and he'd had no time to warn Ceridwen of possible visitors and what such a visit might mean for him, or for her.

"Perhaps." Malik straightened a serving utensil set near a platter of food. "Though I've developed a craving for something else." His gaze drifted to Ceridwen, his smirk broadening in a way that had Drystan seething within.

At the side of the room, Kent took two steps forward, but Jackoby grabbed his sleeve, holding him back. He admired the young man and his eagerness to rise to Ceridwen's defense, but he should know better than to interfere where Malik was considered. His cousin was a pest that only he could deal with.

Drystan rolled his eyes and cut his cousin a hard look. "She's my guest, not your entertainment for the night."

"Ah, but that's the thing. You never have guests." Malik rounded Ceridwen's chair until he stood just behind her. She stiffened, going absolutely still as Malik placed his hands on the edges of the back of the seat.

"Have a seat, pet," Malik crooned, leaning in so close to Ceridwen that his lips might have brushed her hair.

Drystan bristled, his teeth grinding together.

Silently, she raised her chin and stared across the table at him—begged him for help. Drystan inclined his head ever so slightly. If she followed Malik's command, maybe he'd leave her alone.

Ceridwen tightened her hands into fists at her side, but she sat.

"An obedient little thing," Malik remarked. "Curious that she's here with you. No family present. No others either. It's quite..." His palm slipped from the chair to land on Ceridwen's shoulder, causing her to jolt in her seat. "Intimate," he punctuated each syllable of the word.

Fury coursed through his veins, but Drystan fought it down. "I told you—she's just my musician. Leave her be."

Malik released his grip, and the act let Drystan suck in a much-needed breath. But Malik didn't fully retreat and stepped to the side of the chair as he rubbed his chin and continued to appraise Ceridwen. "She is a lovely little bird. Too lovely to be trapped in such a dreary place with such limited company. Does he make you sing for him all day, little pet?"

The careful expression on Ceridwen's face broke into something almost like a snarl as she snapped her head to the side to stare at Malik. "No. And I am not your pet, nor anyone's."

Good girl. Pride sparked in him at her fight, her fury.

Then, her features smoothed out all at once, and she lowered her eyes. "Lord..."

She pulled for the rest of his name, a careful brow ached in question like a proper lady, as if her momentary fury had never existed. Impressive.

"Just Malik will do." He smirked.

"Is that not too intimate for an acquaintance?" she countered.

Far too intimate, though not a surprise where his cousin was concerned. In fact, Drystan wouldn't be surprised if that, too, was a ploy to get under his skin.

"Then let's be more than acquaintances." Malik closed the distance to Ceridwen's chair once more, trailing his fingers along the back.

Drystan found himself rocking forward on his toes, ready to spring. "Malik…" He ground out.

But his cousin's grin only widened. "If you're nothing special to him"—Malik caught a bit of Ceridwen's hair and pulled it to his lips, even as she leaned away as far as she could—"you could be to me. What do you think?"

A small thread of doubt tugged at something in his chest. What if she said yes? Surely she wouldn't, but if she did…

"No. Thank you." Ceridwen managed to lace the polite rejection with venom sharp and piercing.

A sigh of relief crept up his throat, but it was too soon for that.

Malik dropped her hair, and Ceridwen bolted from the chair, accidentally knocking into the table and rattling the dishes in the process. A few glasses tipped, one rolling to shatter on the floor.

Run. Go. Drystan silently pleaded to Ceridwen as he edged around the table to get closer to her. But if she thought to flee, Malik was faster.

His cousin moved with a swiftness only nobles possessed and grabbed Ceridwen's wrist. "Ah, don't fly away yet. The fun's just getting started."

Ceridwen tried to jerk away from him. "Let me go."

"Oh, I will, but not yet," Malik promised.

Ceridwen twisted her head toward him, eyes pleading as she pulled against Malik's grip. "Drystan," she whispered. The sight nearly gutted him.

"Let her go, Malik," Drystan warned.

"Now, now," Malik crooned as he brushed the back of his other hand along her cheek. "She may come to enjoy my attentions. You never really know until you try, do you?"

Malik leaned in to steal a kiss, and something in Drystan snapped.

Before he could think, Drystan sped across the space between them, jerked Malik back, and hurled him at the wall with such fury that he sent the other man flying.

His cousin smacked against the wall before sliding down its surface, a crack marring the spot where he'd slammed into it. The force of such a hit might have killed a normal man, but only a trickle of blood seeped from Malik's lips to drip down his chin.

Drystan's fingers curled and uncurled at his side. His breaths came sharp and quick as he stepped in front of Ceridwen, attempting to block her view of what he'd done—the damage he'd almost brought upon her as well. Malik could have easily grabbed her and pulled her with him. The pain it would have caused her was unthinkable. He shuddered before letting out a cry of anguish that was almost a roar.

The fact that Malik hadn't grabbed her, had almost seemed to anticipate what he'd do, was the only reason Drystan didn't stalk across the marble floor and do even worse.

Malik touched his lips, his fingers coming away red. Laughter with a maniacal edge slipped from him as he beheld the blood and then looked at Drystan.

"Well," Malik began, pushing off the wall and sending a small shower of rubble tumbling to the floor. "I think we've established that the girl is not nothing after all."

CHAPTER 18

CERIDWEN

THE STEAMING WATER SHOULD have soothed her, but no matter how Ceridwen scrubbed, the feeling of Malik's gaze or his hands on her could not be washed away. Her blood ran cold despite the wet warmth cocooning her in the tub.

Drystan had thrown Malik against the wall with more force than a man should be able to muster. Another reminder that even though they'd shared a kiss, he was a noble, different, and she was just her, a poor commoner living in a city at the edge of the kingdom. There could be nothing between them.

Lord Winterbourne ordered Jackoby and Kent to bring her back to her room while his cousin laughed at the mess of their dinner. The entire time, Drystan's voice had been cold and callous. The previous night felt more like a dream or a tricky snow phantom than an event that had actually occurred.

When they'd come upon Gwen in the hallway, her eyes had widened, and a lightly wrinkled hand had moved to cover her gaping mouth. She hadn't left Ceridwen alone since. Gwen said nothing of their guest but did her best to distract her charge with talk of clothes, plants, and tales of the capital.

"All of this was during the late king and queen's reign?" Ceridwen asked in response to Gwen's story—a happy one about the former monarchs and the prosperity they brought to the people.

"Oh, yes," she replied. "Before that...well, those were dark times indeed. I still remember the constant worry and fear. Those times cannot return, no matter the cost." An uncharacteristic sharpness clung to her words with a passionate fervor.

The dark king was dead. His grandson, the prince who'd fallen to his grandfather's dark magic, was dead. But if two monarchs could fall to its embrace, what prevented the others?

"You worry about King Rhion. Could the darkness pervert him the way it did the prince?"

Silence reigned. The nonanswer was answer enough. She thought it could, and it worried her, where even the monster haunting this city did not. Ceridwen shivered, sending ripples through the water.

"My sister still lives in the capital with her family," Gwen said at last. "She sends me letters from time to time. The stories out of the capital are not ones that anyone wants to hear."

Elspeth had said the same, and Ceridwen had heard the rumors. Death. Whispers of dark magic. Not to mention the king's erratic behavior of late. "Do they have a monster like ours?"

"Possibly several— Well, it's hard to be certain. Rumors and all. And I should not have told you. Lord Winterbourne would not approve. But things are certainly dark indeed."

More monsters like ours...worse ones? And what did the king do about it? The former monarchs would never have let this happen.

Taxes. Death. Dismissing his counsel. King Rhion was a plague on them all. Ceridwen took out her frustrations on the water, sloshing it dangerously close to the edges of the tub.

"Ceridwen."

She snapped her head up at the sound of Gwen's voice.

"This knowledge does not leave the manor. Some nobles do all they can to keep word from leaving the capital, and it cannot spread here. They'd find out where it came from."

And that would be bad for all of them. Whatever the nobles had done, it had not been enough. The gossip had begun to spread before she'd come there. Ceridwen thought to mention it but nodded instead.

"Are you doing okay in there?"

"I'm fine." Not at all. But the bath wouldn't be what killed her. Drystan's curt words, the monster, or Malik's games would do that easily enough if they continued.

"Why don't I go bring in a comfortable nightdress for you to change into? Oh, and I could fetch some rose water. That might do nicely to ease your worries. Or perhaps some hot tea? Yes, I think I'll have some brought up with the tray."

Gwen's kindness eased the stiffness from Ceridwen's shoulders where she hunched in the water, but her care would not be enough to heal her inner wounds. "Tea would be lovely," Ceridwen said.

"Perfect." Gwen rose from her perch and ventured toward the exit. Before she closed the door behind her, she turned back. "I'll— Oh. One moment." She called the last part out louder than usual. Someone must be at the door. Probably a maid with a dinner tray since this evening's meal had been thoroughly ruined. "I'll be back with your clothes," she finished.

With effort, Ceridwen rose from the tub, gooseflesh breaking out over her skin from the cool air. A thick towel, so much finer than the worn, holey ones she had at home, embraced her body while she used a smaller one to rub the water out of her clean hair.

The oddity of having someone wait on her still sat uncomfortably, but Gwen had been determined, at least tonight, to make sure Ceridwen was well cared for. It reminded her so much of Bronwyn or Jaina tending to her when she'd been ill last spring that she did her best to enjoy it. At least this time, she wasn't waiting for the Goddess to claim her, though there was a moment during dinner when she'd briefly considered asking her to.

Ceridwen expected a nightdress, but the outfit Gwen helped her into moments later was just as fine as the one she'd worn to dinner. The dress was lined cotton in pale blue and white, with dark-blue ribbons accenting the trim. A wearable cloud meant to comfort on this dark night. Another blue ribbon tied back her hair, which Gwen braided behind her head. It'd be wavy instead of its usual straight by the time it dried, but Ceridwen didn't mind that a bit.

Her bare feet halted on the cool stone floor as soon as she entered the bedroom proper from the little bathing room. Drystan stood near the fire, his hands behind his back.

"Ceridwen," he said, turning to her.

A thousand emotions flowed with one word, yet his face still remained stiff.

She flicked her gaze to Gwen, who'd come to her side, not bothering to hide the hurt and betrayal in her wide eyes and parted lips.

Gwen winced. "He asked me not to tell you." Her gaze drifted to Drystan. "I'll be going now."

"Wait." *Please.*

Gwen took one of Ceridwen's hands in hers and gave it a little pat. "You'll be fine. He'll explain everything. Won't you?" She cocked an eyebrow at Drystan on the question. From her tone, one would think she scolded a young schoolboy, not the lord of the manor.

He nodded, and Gwen gave one in return. "Good night, dear."

Ceridwen's toes curled against the stone as Gwen left, ruined dress in tow, and closed the heavy wooden door behind her. Tension filled the room, thick as porridge, but even that paled to the knot stuck in her throat.

"Please come have a seat," Drystan said. He motioned to the chairs near the fire where two trays had been laid out on the low table between them, fully occupying the small table space.

When she didn't move, he continued, "I'm sorry for what happened. For what had to be said and done." He ran a hand through his hair, the icy calm of his face melting away to be replaced by something real and almost frantic. "I tried, yet in the end, I still failed."

Her brows drew together. His words made no sense. He'd stopped his cousin...eventually. Though it stung that he hadn't intervened earlier, that any of it had happened at all. Perhaps it was her curiosity or the genuine pain in his voice, but something drew Ceridwen across the room.

"Explain everything. Who is he? Why would he—" She balled her hands into fists. Goodness, the impropriety of it all. Maybe his cousin only meant to kiss her—a scandalous enough thing after she'd rejected him—but something about the way he had looked at her made his advances seem much more sinister. "Why did you..." She couldn't put words into it. His indifference left her too raw, and another cut might just let her tears slip free, and she couldn't allow that in front of him.

Drystan nodded and took a seat. He scrubbed his hands down his face before he finally began. "Malik is my cousin, as he said, though we are not close as some cousins may be." His mouth worked in his jaw. "He's come here before, but he did not write of his intent to visit this time."

"You never planned to tell me about him?" she accused, keeping the high-backed chair between them and leaning on its back. The least he could have done was give her some warning about the monster of a man.

He ran his hand through his hair again, a few dark strands sticking out haphazardly in his wake. "I did not expect him to visit again, certainly not unannounced."

As if that was some excuse. She dug her fingers into the fabric along the top of the chair. Too bad it wasn't him they strangled instead.

Drystan's gaze flicked from her face to her hands and back again before he slumped in the chair. With a sigh, he said, "I thought he'd dismiss your presence if he thought you were unimportant to me. I was wrong."

Her brows arched skyward. "Is that supposed to be an apology?"

"Yes. I messed up. Miscalculated. And you paid the price for that." His elbows rested on his thighs as he leaned forward once again, constantly wiggling in the chair. "We don't have many guests here. I wasn't prepared. Somewhere along the way, I became complacent, and that cannot happen. I never wanted to hurt you. And when he advanced on you...I couldn't hold back, no matter what ruse I played."

A ruse? Truly? So why did it still hurt so badly?

"Has he left?" Ceridwen asked.

"No."

Her spine stiffened. The idea of locking herself in the bedroom became infinitely more appealing. "Will he be quite so...rude going forward?"

Drystan's eyes locked with hers, solemn and resigned. "I have no idea what he will do now. But I believe he learned what he wanted to know, and he'll find a way to use that against me."

The girl is not nothing after all.

The words chased themselves through Ceridwen's mind. A thread of heat wormed its way into the icy chill surrounding her heart. "He wanted to know what I meant to you."

Drystan nodded slowly, his eyes never leaving her face. The intensity of his cool blue gaze nearly stole her breath.

On silent feet, she rounded the chair and sat in its cushioned embrace, staring at Drystan across the still steaming plates of food. The rich scents had yet to stir her hunger around the knots of anxiety twisting there.

"And what am I to you?"

Her heart clenched as she waited for his response, braced for more pain and indifference.

"More than I expected, and more than I ever wanted him to know."

The tourniquet around her heart loosened, sending heat flooding through her body. Though not the words she secretly wished for, they were so much more than the terrible callousness she'd feared. Truthfully, it was much more than she should dare hope for, given their difference in status, to say nothing of her family's poverty.

Drystan rose with a slight groan to stand in front of the fire. The flames highlighted the dark material of his overcoat. "Malik may be here for some time," he said into the fire before turning to her.

"You cannot send him away?"

"Unfortunately not. No." His back stiffened. "He outranks me, my cousin, and doing so would only draw his suspicions further." One hand clenched into a fist at his side.

"He outranks you, yet he wished me to call him simply Malik?" It wasn't done. Nobles loved their titles more than the gold in their pockets, and that they all but worshiped, or so some said.

Drystan scrubbed a hand down his face. "He's not one for manners or propriety, as you observed. Quite the opposite, really."

It was a wonder such a reputation hadn't preceded him there, though perhaps not since Teneboure was so out of favor with the nobility. She wiggled in the chair. "And you said you are not on good terms, so why is he here?"

"To keep an eye on me and make sure I do not step out of line."

Another answer that fueled more questions. "What does he think you may do?"

"Ceridwen..."

Her lips thinned as she stared him down. She'd been pulled into this mess, intentionally or not. The least he could do was explain it a bit.

Weary eyes bored into hers as he sat heavily and stared at her across the open space. "The king does not trust me."

Her mouth gaped in silent exclamation. That, she had not expected.

"Sending me here was a test, a show of goodwill, but one mistake, and I will lose what little favor I have curried. So Malik comes, and he watches, and he reports back to the capital."

No wonder Drystan never wanted guests in the manor or ventured out into local society. Ceridwen hugged her arms around herself despite the rising warmth of the new fire. In a heartbeat, he could lose it all. One wrong step. One bad report. And it all depended on Malik. She never wanted to see that man again, yet it seemed she had little choice in the matter.

"Are all your relatives so repulsive? Will more of them visit?"

Drystan's countenance darkened. "Possibly worse, though they will not visit here."

Worse? How could they possibly be worse? Especially someone of noble blood. She picked at the sleeves of her dress.

"In any case, you should rest if you can," he continued. "Tomorrow may be a long day."

"I haven't played." Though, deep in her heart, she didn't want to. The day had rattled the song from her fingers and stripped it from her heart.

"Play for me tomorrow." His shoulders slumped as if the weight of the world pressed down upon him and only her songs gave him strength. How could someone so young have so many burdens? A noble alone at the edge of the kingdom was a lonely one indeed.

"You're exhausted." The thought slipped from her like water between her fingers.

"Sleep does not come easily for me, especially when I keep the monster at bay."

With a real monster of a man in the house, she'd almost forgotten. "Is it safe tonight? Will it come too?" She couldn't handle another demon in the same night.

"Not tonight, I don't think. We should be fine."

She should have asked more, but the certainty in his voice brokered no questions. Drystan rose to his feet, and Ceridwen feared he prepared to leave her alone.

"Wait." She held up a hand. "Malik won't come in here, will he?"

The hint of a smile pulled at his lips. "I'd thought to sleep in here."

She gaped.

"Or I could put up a magical ward."

Magic. The word hung between them. He pursed his lips, gaze darting, as if he were a young child waiting for a reprimand. "I could sleep in the hall if you'd rather me not stay here or use magic to protect your room. Though," he drawled, "that doesn't protect the balcony or the windows. And truthfully, I'd prefer not to sleep on the floor."

"Not the hall, then." She shook her head. A noble on the floor—impossible.

"So what shall it be? Magic or the sofa?" he asked.

Blood or impropriety. Such choices. Heat flooded her cheeks as she debated the answer. "Whichever you prefer," she said at last.

Drystan crossed the narrow space between them and lifted her hand to his lips, placing a chaste kiss upon the back that sent a shiver down her spine. "A little of both, then. Magic to see if he tries himself against it, and myself in case he does."

"What about the monster?" she asked. It'd sounded so close before, almost within the manor walls.

"I warded your room against that before you arrived." He looked away. "I try to keep it at bay, but it's quite challenging."

"That's one of the things they are watching you for? Part of your test?" One he didn't seem to be passing if it involved ending the monster for good.

He nodded.

"So it's not a twisted pet?" She'd wondered, especially hearing it so close to the manor.

His brows rose. "A pet? Never. I'd love nothing more than for it to be gone forever. But until then, stay in your room at night where it's safest."

"You can't kill it?"

He held her gaze for a long time before he answered. "I want to." Sorrow tinged his words as his hand opened and closed. "A stronger man might be able to, but I can't. Not yet. Soon." He glanced away. "One way or another, I'll make sure this monster is gone for good."

Ceridwen watched as Drystan worked his magic on the room. He took the little blade he'd used in the garden and cut his hand—another scar for her. The blood he painted on the doors and windows soaked into the wood and glass as surely as if it had never existed to begin with. Yet Drystan promised the wards held true—ones specifically designed to keep out any male she did not invite inside, though as the caster of such a spell, he was immune.

An extra spell he wove as well, almost without effort it seemed, to let him know if anyone tried his wards. Though the blood had sickened and terrified her when he'd first demonstrated his skill, the more she watched him work, the more she became entranced by the magical designs.

The slide of his bloody fingers across a surface reminded her of Bronwyn painting a new canvas. Each stoke precise and measured, shapes taking form from whatever vision enraptured her mind and gave her inspiration for a new work—often a landscape or snippet of winding city streets. Though occasionally, Bronwyn chose to paint a subject, either animal or human. Each took her breath away, but they were never a mirror of their subjects. Yet, at the same time, Ceridwen could not say what her sister added or took away to give them their own unique air.

Drystan's patterns were like Bronwyn's paintings. Intricate. Beautiful in a way. Yet elusive to the mind all the same. She could not have copied one from memory had she tried, despite watching him hastily draw the same symbol on each potential entry into the room.

At length, he lay upon the long divan near the fireplace and said not a word as she climbed into bed and hid her face with the blankets. When worry refused to let her sleep, she peeked out from the coverings toward the smoldering embers of the hearth.

A breath lodged in her throat as light gave shape and life to the room. Drystan lay wide awake, his hands propped behind his head, where he sprawled upon the divan, watching her.

Their eyes locked.

Seconds turned into minutes. Silence grew heavy and thick in the air.

What could she possibly say? *I'm frightened? I miss my family?* But their health and happiness relied on her staying, no matter how uncomfortable she might be at times. A recent letter from Bronwyn only solidified that when she shared that the money Ceridwen earned was enough to buy new medicine for Father, some that actually seemed to help him regain his strength.

It wasn't just them who relied on her either. Somehow, impossibly, Drystan might need her too. The secrets he kept frustrated her, but some deeper pull drew her in, like it did as she stared at him across the room.

He'd join me in bed if I asked him. She could feel the truth of that in his gaze as certainly as the blankets wrapped around her. Part of her yearned for it, her fingertips aching to wave him over. But a last bit of self-preservation held her back. What could she hope to gain from sharing a bed with him? A night of pleasure, perhaps, but she knew he planned to return to the capital at midwinter. Would he return after that? Would he bother with her? He had no reason to, despite his proclaimed love of her music. She was a commoner, and there was no future between them that didn't end with her in pain and possibly ruin.

Even so, the pull of desire toward him was strong enough to hold her still, to hold his gaze across the room in the dim light.

What are you thinking about right now? She yearned to know, to ask. What could possibly fill his mind as he stared at her in the dark?

If she went to him now, would he reveal his secrets? Open his heart?

A log in the fire split, sending up a spray of sparks and tumble of glowing embers. The movement drew Ceridwen's attention, breaking the invisible connection between her and Drystan. She hid back under the covers, not trusting her head or heart. Tomorrow. Tomorrow she'd figure something out.

Eventually, she did find a few minutes of rest.

When Gwen woke her the next day, Drystan had already left. In fact, if she hadn't known better, nothing in the room would have indicated he'd been there at all.

"Did Malik die during the night?" she asked the housekeeper. It would be generous of the monster to take himself off their hands.

Gwen huffed a laugh before ushering her to the dressing screen, where she changed into a gown of evergreen with creamy lace and ribbons. Yet another dress Drystan had commissioned on her behalf. Despite her initial reluctance, she had to admit that the dresses were a dream. The soft material caressed her skin. The layers kept away the winter chill. Each dress was more fashionable than anything her family had been able to afford since childhood, when she'd been far too young to appreciate them.

"Unfortunately not," Gwen replied. "And Lord Winterbourne has insisted that you meet them both for a casual breakfast in his study."

Ceridwen's hands paused in their efforts to smooth the heavy skirts. Never once since she arrived had Drystan attended a meal with her other than dinner. Yet now, he wanted her to eat breakfast with him and a man he knew she loathed? This must be another front. Another attempt to convince Malik that nothing was amiss. But why involve her? Ceridwen shuddered. She pinched her eyes shut as she wrestled control of her worries and pushed them down and out of sight. With a deep and steadying breath, she turned toward Gwen. "I'm ready."

CHAPTER 19
DRYSTAN

Having Malik in residence was far more of a nuisance than in the past. No sooner had Drystan left Ceridwen's rooms at dawn than he encountered Malik strolling through the hallways of the manor, probably poking his business into everything. At least the man hadn't tried to enter his tower. The magical wards he placed upon it would have let him know, nor had he attempted to enter Ceridwen's bedroom the night before.

Drystan's fitful sleep had little to do with the too-short sofa he had used as a bed. And while he expected his mind to be full thinking of strategies to both satisfy and evade his cousin's curiosity, it was Ceridwen who garnered most of his churning thoughts. Staying in the bedroom with her, longing to touch her, to talk to her, when they both really needed to rest, was a twisted form of self-torture.

Just when he was almost certain she slept, she'd peeked out from under the coverings where she hid like a frightened lamb. He stayed silent, fearful of spooking or disturbing her, but oh, how he'd longed for her to say something or, better yet, invite him to her bed. To say he fantasized about the numerous things she could have said or done was an understatement. It had been one scenario after the other, playing itself in his head, and he tried and failed to rest.

And then he just had to run right into Malik in the hall—caught like the foolish young man he thought he no longer was. His cousin had deduced much in moments without even a question—entirely too much. The mischievous sparkle in his eyes said he knew exactly where Drystan had been and with whom. To ignore him or deny it would have only made it worse, more incriminating, so Drystan did the only thing he could—he invited Malik to his study.

Sometimes it was best to get the poison out of the wound quickly rather than let it fester. His cousin came here to garner news, to appraise his actions—it was easiest just to give him the show he desired.

It was at Malik's insistence that Ceridwen come and play for them that morning. He so badly wanted to know why Drystan was enraptured with the young woman, and he failed to believe it simply because of her music. That had been the case, the truth, at first, though it was no longer. But maybe that origin would show through if she played, though Drystan was in no rush to wake or hurry her out of bed, especially if she'd slept as little as him.

Instead, Drystan spent the morning talking about everything and nothing with Malik. Their conversation was as strategic and important as a battle waged during a war. Tell him what he wanted to hear, but don't make it sound that way. Show just enough deference to the king and his reign. Appease him with easy truths so that he was less likely to spot the lies. Malik's questions and Drystan's answers were a carefully choreographed dance, with neither wanting to step on each other's feet or, worse, falter in their planned steps.

When Jackoby arrived to show Ceridwen—flute case in tow—into the study, Drystan both heaved a sigh of relief and tensed all at once. On one hand, she was a balm to his weary soul and a break from his cousin's casual inquisition. On the other, she entered the viper's pit with him, and he had no idea how Malik would react.

"Just as lovely as I remembered," Malik commented with a grin, rising to his feet.

Sarcasm or sincerity, Drystan wasn't sure, but he rose to his feet as well. Ceridwen's gaze passed right over Malik, as if he didn't exist, to land on Drystan. Warmth swelled in his chest as he took her in. She'd taken time with her appearance this morning, and her eyes appeared free of dark circles under them or any other tell that she had not slept. Hopefully his presence had not disturbed her rest as thoughts of her had his.

"Good morning." Ceridwen dropped into a perfect curtsy.

"Please have a seat." Drystan gestured to the chair to his left, farther from Malik. The seat would leave a low table set with a tiered display of pastries and fruit between his cousin and his musician. A thin barrier at best, but better than nothing. Malik had sampled some of the delights on the table, but he'd managed little himself. Gwen rushed in as Ceridwen took her seat, replacing the cooled pot of tea with a steaming one.

"I apologize for our introduction," Malik said once Gwen and Jackoby had left.

Ceridwen raised her brows at him as she smoothed out her skirts. "Really? Do you introduce yourself to everyone that way?" When he didn't immediately reply, she folded her hands in her lap and continued. "It's a wonder no one's stabbed you."

Drystan barely contained the laughter eager to burst free. Jackoby's inquiries about the young woman had given the description of her as quiet and demure. Perhaps she was in society and around her family, but here, outside her sibling's fiery personalities, it seemed Ceridwen was able to find that spark of defiance within herself, or maybe she finally wasn't overshadowed. He hoped for the latter. If her time here gave her the freedom to find herself, to be herself, he would be grateful, no matter the pain of leaving her in the end when he returned to the capital.

To Drystan's surprise, Malik laughed as well and leaned back into the cushioned chair. "Who says they haven't?"

"You look quite alive to me."

He leaned forward with his elbows on his knees. "Only thanks to my cunning charm."

Ceridwen huffed in annoyance.

Drystan coughed, breaking up their duel. "Would you like some tea?" He'd already lifted the teapot to pour.

"I would." Ceridwen's pleasant smile returned instantly as she looked at him. "Thank you."

Drystan poured the steaming amber liquid with practiced ease, not spilling a drop, and passed the cup to Ceridwen.

"When did a gentleman learn to serve so well?" she teased.

The hint of a smile passed across his face and was gone. "A recent talent. I haven't always had staff to attend me." The truth, unfortunately.

Malik watched them both with eager interest, not saying a word.

Ceridwen's brows pinched as she blew on the steaming liquid before taking a dainty sip, but thankfully she did not ask more. She set the little teacup aside with all the grace of a fine lady and refolded her hands over the flute case in her lap. "Why did you ask for me this morning?"

"It was Malik who requested your presence," Drystan replied.

Ceridwen glanced at his cousin. "Still just Malik? Not Lord Something-or-other?"

"Malik will do." He leaned forward in his chair, sliding back into the conversation as easily as he'd stepped out of it. "Drystan mentioned that you play music, and I happen to be a great patron of the arts."

"*You* are a patron of the arts?"

He grinned. "I'm quite serious. Perhaps you'd indulge us this morning?" For all his cousin's scheming and pandering, that much was true. He'd always been enamored of the arts, the theater and opera especially, much to his father's dismay.

Ceridwen considered the request in silence, rubbing her fingertips across her instrument case in small motions.

"If you'd rather not—" Drystan began.

"It's fine," Ceridwen replied quickly. "I do love to play."

She set about righting her instrument, and after a minute, she began to play. Drystan was unfamiliar with the tune—something deep and moving. As always, Ceridwen's eyes fluttered closed as she played, seeming lost in a trance of her own making. Malik, too, relaxed in his seat, consumed by her music and taken somewhere far away.

Though too on edge to relax completely, Drystan appreciated the soothing atmosphere that Ceridwen's music brought to an otherwise tense moment. If he let his guard down, he had no doubt her song would sweep him away as well.

After the second song, one that must be related to the first for their similarity, Ceridwen lowered her flute, ending the spell she'd woven over them.

Malik leaned forward in his chair, a blinding grin upon his face, a rare and true one if Drystan had to guess. "Lovely. No wonder he procured your services."

Ceridwen looked down at her lap, the hint of a blush on her cheeks. Instantly, jealousy reared its ugly head within him, and Drystan frowned at his cousin. But Malik didn't pay him any mind, his focus solely on the young woman across from him.

"A concerto?" he asked.

"*The Blessings of the Goddess*," Ceridwen replied.

"Don't those typically have three movements?" Malik tapped a finger on his chin. "Would you play us the third as well?"

"Apologies, I cannot." Ceridwen shook her head. "The third movement is missing. I have never seen it. I'm not sure anyone has."

"Unfortunate." Malik sat back in the chair, crossing one ankle over his knee.

"You should eat something," Drystan offered to Ceridwen, nodding toward the breakfast display.

"Food does taste so much better after such a show." Malik plucked a pastry from the tray and stuffed the entire thing in his mouth.

Seemingly reluctantly, Ceridwen selected a pastry and nibbled at it in the ensuing silence. Drystan wasn't sure quite what to say, and Malik only asked benign questions about the recent snow, which Drystan answered, leaving Ceridwen to pick at her food.

Halfway through her selection, Ceridwen set the plate aside. "I should leave you to your meeting," she said, her gaze locked on Drystan. The silent request in her eyes was easy enough to pick out. She wanted a reprieve from Malik's company. He couldn't blame her.

"Indeed," Drystan replied. "Thank you for the music, Ceridwen."

"I look forward to another concert tonight," Malik said, rising from his chair.

He and Ceridwen rose as well. She didn't even bother to return her flute to its case, just held each at her side.

"I'll miss this while I'm gone." Malik sighed.

Ceridwen stood a little straighter. Drystan's attention snapped to his cousin. *Gone? Could he be so lucky?*

Drystan asked the natural question, trying to hide his eagerness. "Leaving again so soon, cousin?"

"Only for a few days, starting tomorrow morning." Malik appraised him, a slow grin forming on his lips. "But then I'd hoped to stay until midwinter. Why, we could even venture back to the capital together. Wouldn't that be grand?"

The blood in Drystan's veins ran cold. So that was how it was to be. Malik would likely take the early train back tomorrow, report his findings, and then return to keep a close eye on him until midwinter, at which point he'd drag him to the capital and the king himself. He might as well have pronounced a death sentence right then and there. Even Ceridwen looked at them with wide eyes, her tone paling, and she didn't know half of Drystan's fears or the disaster that Malik could bring upon him, should he choose.

Drystan crossed to the thick rope on the side of the room and pulled it, ringing for Jackoby to show Ceridwen back to her room. It was the only thing he could think of to keep his fury in check and his anger from spewing out. He sucked in a deep breath and turned to his cousin. "Well, won't that be something to look forward to?"

CHAPTER 20
CERIDWEN

THE DAY MALIK LEFT for his venture, Drystan did not make an appearance. Not at dinner. Nor after to request her songs.

She played anyway in the confines of her room. After two wistful melodies, she stepped out into the knee-high snow on the balcony, hoping Drystan might somehow appear. The night she'd played for him out there was forever burned into her memory, along with the feel of his lips on hers.

He had not tried to kiss her again, not with Malik's disturbance. But with him gone, she had hoped things might change. Instead, he was curiously absent.

The lights in his tower flickered, but Ceridwen spied no movement beyond their reaches. As she raised the flute to her lips to begin a new song, a sound cut through her, one more chilling than the biting cold soaking into her stockings and slipping through the material of her gloves.

A moan-like howl pierced the night. Close. Possibly just outside the manor walls.

"Drystan."

His name was a prayer, a plea.

Ceridwen stumbled through the snow back toward the glass balcony door. Her heart thundered louder in her chest with every slow step.

Another ghastly wail sounded, even closer than before. Her heart leaped into her throat. Her hands shook, and not just from the cold. *Faster, Ceridwen.*

The balcony door had never felt so far away. She tore toward it like a dead man racing for the Goddess's loving embrace. When she finally grasped the handle and pushed it open, she practically fell into the room, savoring the warmth emanating from the crackling fire and assumed protection of the walls. In another heartbeat, she flung the door shut behind her, sending the glass rattling in its frame.

She clutched the flute like a shield in front of her, where she huddled in a puddle of damp skirts on the stone floor, breathing heavily. Outside the windows, she could see nothing past the blanket of snow barely illuminated in the cloudy night. When at last her shaking legs allowed her to stand, she pulled all the curtains shut—a final barrier against the monster. They wouldn't save her. Not from that. But they gave comfort all the same.

When the eerie wails echoed only in her thoughts and no longer in the still night beyond, Ceridwen finally crawled under the layer of blankets upon the bed and willed herself to sleep.

Drystan never came.

But neither did the monster.

Before dinner the next day, Ceridwen came upon Jackoby, Kent, and Gwen arguing in hushed tones in a tight cluster at the base of the winding staircase leading up to Drystan's tower. The one place that she had been forbidden from entering.

Their conversation halted as her booted steps echoed in the hallway, muffling whatever words had been spoken between them before she appeared.

"Good afternoon, Miss Ceridwen," Jackoby announced with a short bow as if nothing were amiss and this day was as common as any other. Yet she had a suspicion of what they discussed and why they discussed it in this location. That same concern had driven her to this very spot, unable to sit still and not worry over the missing lord of the manor. Particularly given the monstrous sounds echoing through the night.

"Has he not come down today?" she asked.

Gwen fidgeted with her apron. Kent looked away. Only Jackoby got straight to the point. "No. He has not."

An invisible hand clenched her heart. "Has anyone been up to check on him?"

Jackoby's lips thinned. Kent and Gwen both refused to meet her steady gaze.

"Something might be wrong. What if he's had another attack?" She'd seen that only once, but if it could happen one time, it could happen again.

"We're not allowed in the tower," Gwen admitted, finally releasing the apron she'd wrinkled with her hands. Jackoby slid her a side-eyed look, but she ignored him.

"None of you?" She'd thought his rule only applied to her. Why would he prevent his trusted household staff from entering his rooms as well?

"She spoke truly," Jackoby added. "No one is allowed in the lord's tower."

Incredulous, she shook her head.

"No one," Jackoby echoed.

Ceridwen pursed her lips and closed the distance between them until she stood amid their cluster of bodies. "Are you not worried?" She stared them each down in turn. Was she the only one who heard that monster in the night? Permitted or not, someone needed to check on him.

"It's only been two days..." Kent began, but his words were unconvincing.

"Of course we are worried," Gwen stepped in. "But going against his orders..." She shook her head. "The steps are warded. He will know if we go up them, even to simply peek into the rooms. Going against his wishes would break his trust and endanger our place here."

"Or worse," Kent mumbled.

A stern look from Jackoby caused Kent to flinch. Yet his words sparked more curiosity in Ceridwen than anything else.

Drystan did not seem the type to unjustly punish those around him, not over such a small trespass, especially if done with his best interest in mind. And if he had tried to keep the monster at bay last night and had been injured, he might need help—desperately.

While a silent conversation passed among her companions, Ceridwen eyed the stairs. Her family needed the money that Drystan provided. She needed it. And in a way, she needed him. He'd reignited her dream of sharing her music and freed her heart from its lonely isolation. To risk his ire and lose out on this miracle of an opportunity would be stupid. Yet she couldn't shake the feeling that something was wrong or the mental image of him lying bloody and injured on the floor.

"You all heard the monster last night?"

Reluctant nods from Gwen and Kent confirmed her worries. Jackoby stood stone-faced. For once, he refused to meet her gaze.

"He could be hurt! Worse!" She stomped at their complacency. If he'd fended off the monster and something had gone wrong, he could be in terrible pain. Her whole body vibrated with barely contained anxiety.

They might not be willing to risk their position for the health and safety of their lord, but sitting still was out of the question for her, even if it risked the money her family needed. Surely he would not send her away over this, not something done out of care and concern.

"I'm going up." She trudged toward the staircase without waiting to see their response, yet a sharp intake of breath teased her ears.

A step away from the first stair, a hand wrapped around her wrist, pulling her to a stop. Her head snapped to Jackoby. His eyes shone with an emotion she couldn't place. For the first time, his role of butler fell away to reveal the man underneath.

"Don't." A soft tug on her arm accompanied his words.

But she shrugged off his grip and stepped onto the wide first step. "I have to."

Behind him, Kent wrapped his arms around Gwen, a show of comfort, much like a mourner at a funeral. Ceridwen swallowed her nerves and continued on.

As soon as she crossed fully onto the stairs, sound stopped, all but the echo of her boots on the polished stone. Over her shoulder, she could see Jackoby's mouth moving and Kent saying something to a distraught Gwen, but the words were lost to silence.

Drystan had warded the staircase in more ways than one, but for what purpose, she could not say. Ceridwen followed the twisting steps as they took her up and up into the darkness of the unlit staircase until only a faint glow ahead of her and the residual light from below lit her way in the darkness.

Her pace slowed as the top of the landing came into view. She'd likely traveled at least two floors up into the darkness of the stairwell without passing so much as a door or window. An oil lamp flickered at the top of the stairs, one that burned low. She could barely make out a trace of oil in the well at the bottom. Another few hours would see it burn itself through if left untended.

"Drystan," she called softly, hoping not to walk in on him unaware.

The door at the top of the stairs had been left wide open, yet no response greeted her.

She gasped, her feet rooting themselves to the stone at the threshold. Beyond the open door, the room lay in shambles.

Papers were strewn across the floor, along with an assortment of accessories she did not take the time to examine. Black ink pooled in a spilled puddle on the floor next to a shattered lamp, its oil swirling with the edge of the ink puddle. Sheets had been partially pulled from a bed on the right wall and lay heaped upon the floor. Little feathers floated near their edges and graced the bedcoverings. A table was upended, a chair's navy-blue cloth ripped on one armrest. Petals covered the floor around the base of a pot near the window.

The monster came inside.

The thought stripped the heat from her body. Somehow, impossibly, it had crept into Drystan's tower. Yet no blood marred the floors or any surface she could see. Nor did she find what she most feared—a body.

But the stairs continued upward. Another floor loomed above.

Ceridwen ran up the stairs, desperate to find Drystan.

Please be all right. Please be—

She stifled a scream as the steps ended, dumping her into a room even more destroyed than the one below. But it wasn't the overturned bookshelf, the scattered dried herbs, broken plants, or even the arrangement of weapons knocked from their displays that caused her heart to clench in fear.

A stone altar stood in the center of the room, covered in bloody designs. A blade as long as her forearm and coated in blood lay poised in the center of the pattern. Unlike the workings Drystan performed in her room, this blood had not disappeared upon casting.

The working drew her like a beckoning call. Without thinking, she crossed the space and stared at the gruesome mess in a chilled daze. *Incomplete or interrupted?*

She reached her hand toward the altar.

Deep rumbling from behind froze her body to the core. A scream lodged in her throat as she whirled toward the noise.

A dark beast.

A monster.

The monster.

It hovered in the shadows near the far wall, not far from where she'd entered. Its red eyes glimmered in the rays of sunset filtering in through the windows. A clawed hand scraped against the gray stone floor with a shrill screech, leaving behind white grooves.

"Goddess, no." Her head spun. Her body shook.

Drystan had tried to keep the monster at bay...and lost.

The monster lounged on all fours like a wolf. Yet it was too large, its limbs oddly formed in a way she hadn't noticed the first time she'd glimpsed it. Dark fur marred the skin of its back, face, and what little she could see of its chest. But the arms and legs were mostly hairless, dark flesh strung tight over bone.

Her hand slipped on the altar where she gripped it for support, coating her palm in sticky wetness as she held herself upright. The beast stretched and slunk toward the stair.

Never taking her eyes off it, Ceridwen moved behind the altar on shaking legs, a last defense against the beast. The weapons she'd spotted stood too close to the monster itself.

Reaching them would be a gamble, one she likely would not win. The bloody dagger on the stone slab was the only reasonable item within range. Yet as she stretched her fingers toward it, something halted her—an invisible tug on her sleeve, a whisper she could not quite hear—as if the Goddess herself warned her against that course of action.

She left the dagger where it lay.

"What did you do to Drystan?" she demanded of the monster subtly pacing near the stairs, fear giving force to her words. From this angle, she could see that no one else occupied the top floor, living or dead.

The beast's head bobbed. A soft growl floated through the space between them—more a wail of the dead than any animalistic sound. The chill of it nearly stopped her heart. If it could speak in human tones, it chose not to. Instead, the monster slunk forward, gliding along the floor with catlike grace despite its awkward limbs.

Another scream threatened to tear its way from her throat. A window stood behind her, but if she could get there in time, the leap to the ground many floors below would certainly kill her.

Ceridwen had no illusions regarding how quickly this monster could kill. Likely it could leap upon a grown man and tear out his throat in two heartbeats. She'd seen the result. That horrific sight would never leave her mind—not for long.

The best chance lay in making it back down the twisting stairs to the main hall, where hopefully, the others would still be waiting. Together, they might have a chance.

Maybe.

The monster gave another wail that made her skin crawl and set her teeth on edge. She grabbed the sides of a heavy wooden chair nearby. With effort, she lifted it between herself and the monster, a last defense and distraction as it slunk around the edge of the room, rounding the final edge of the stone altar that had lain between them.

She flung the chair with all her might. It clattered to the stone and slid across the ground to tap into the monster's foreleg and side. As soon as it raised its clawed limb to swat at the offensive object, she sprinted for the stairs.

Goddess, please. She prayed, lunging for the pathway down.

A firm tug jerked one leg backward and sent her body crashing forward. Ceridwen screamed, but the impact knocked the air from her lungs and sent her teeth rattling. Sharp pain echoed through her bones, accompanied by the piercing stab of claws that poked through the leather of her boots at one ankle.

"No, please! Let me go!" She twisted around to face the looming monster. She prayed to the Goddess as she thrashed her legs and held her arms in front of her. The movement increased the stab of its claws where it still dug into her boot.

Finally, the claws released. The curved tips dripped blood as the monster raised them to its fanged maw and sniffed. A long, almost black tongue flicked out to lick her blood from its talons.

Ceridwen attempted to push herself away from the monster in its moment of distraction but halted as a deep growl ripped from its throat.

"Goddess, spare my soul," she prayed. "Don't let it end this way. Not now."

Death stared her in the face, its gaping maw exposing jagged teeth ready to shred her to ribbons. Tears blurred its form.

"Drystan." Like a prayer all its own, his name slipped from her lips.

The red of the monster's eerie eyes dimmed. Its head reared. Its mouth closed.

"Drystan," she whispered again, praying that somehow the name that cracked from her throat all rough and heavy had caused the change.

After what might have been a deep sniff, the red receded from the creature's eyes until she gazed into familiar pools of dark cerulean. Claws clinked upon the ground near her boots as it scooted back like a dog shamed by its owner. Garbled noises filled the space between them.

Cold swallowed her, freezing more completely than if she'd lain naked in the snow. At first, she didn't recognize the sound the monster made, but on the third try, the certainty of it settled like a weight upon her bones.

"Ceridwen."

It said her name. The monster knew her.

"Drystan?" she whispered.

Her lunch threatened to come up onto the stones.

He leaned away, traces of humanity coming back into the monstrous face that peered at her with human emotions—sorrow, grief, fear.

"You're the..." But she could not say the word. Her whole body shook, barely able to form the truth that spilled between them. She scrambled across the ground, aiming for the stairs.

"Please." His voice cracked in a pained rasp from chapped, almost human lips. His eyes begged and pleaded.

But he was the monster who haunted their city. A killer. A demon in the night.

He kept the monster at bay, he'd said. A humorless huff of laughter bubbled to her lips as tears blurred her eyes. The Lord Protector who had been assigned to protect this city terrorized it instead.

The man she cared for. Whom she kissed.

"Ceridwen." A hand, more human now than monstrous, reached for her. "Please."

The word pierced her heart, but with it came the sharp stab of reality that cleared away the fog of terror shrouding her mind.

She couldn't stay here.

Not with him. Not now.

Ceridwen rose unsteadily to her feet, ignoring the pain in her ankle, and backed toward the stairs.

"Stay..." The end of the word trailed into an inhuman hiss as he wrestled with the monster within. A flash of red filled his eyes, sealing her decision.

With one final glance, she turned and hurtled down the stairs.

Each step sent the same thought echoing through her mind.

Drystan is the monster.

CHAPTER 21

CERIDWEN

CERIDWEN FLEW OUT OF the bottom of the staircase into the waiting embrace of Gwen and exclamations of concern from Jackoby and Kent. Tears streaked down her face. A sob shook her shoulders as she slumped against the older woman, the weight of moments ago crashing down upon her.

"Are you hurt?"

"What happened?"

"Miss Ceridwen—"

Their voices swam through her head, but she barely heard them. *Drystan is the monster.* The monster looming just upstairs.

"He—" She hiccupped. "The monster."

Gwen sucked in a breath. Kent swore and stomped away.

"Upstairs. He—" But as she looked around, not a glimmer of surprise or concern wove through their expressions. If anything, they looked defeated with downcast eyes and slumped shoulders.

"You knew." The dark certainty dried her tears. She wiped the tracks on her face.

More somber looks. More resigned defeat. "There is a reason we are not allowed upstairs," Jackoby replied, adjusting the edge of his stiff collar.

She swayed on her feet. "You know what he is..."

Jackoby nodded, answering for the group.

"His attack that time in the dining room..."

"It came on him suddenly," Kent said, barely a whisper. "But that one we calmed down. He must have tried something two nights ago after Malik left and—"

Jackoby cut him off with a quick motion of his hand. He'd said too much.

"I can't stay here." Panic clawed its way up her chest. Not with a monster. Not with the demon they all feared. And especially not when everyone kept that knowledge from her—a lamb in a pen of wolves.

"Oh, but you can't go," Gwen replied, reaching out. Her voice held a note of panic, worry.

Ceridwen brushed past her, aiming for the large doors at the end of the hall that opened into the yard.

"Please stay. He's been so much better," she continued.

"Better?" Ceridwen spun around. Another humorless laugh clawed at her chest. "He stalked me down like a rat who'd invaded the kitchens, and I'm supposed to think that's better?" She turned and fled.

Words and footsteps echoed after her as she pushed open the main door.

The setting sun dipped toward the horizon, painting the sky in shades of orange that faded into blue. Its colors reflected on the ungroomed snow that had fallen across the yard. Without regular visitors to the manor, no one bothered to shovel a pathway to the iron gates. She made one now, lifting her hem and trudging through the drifts as fast as her legs would carry her. The tears streaking down her face turned icy. A fitting pain given the sharp rending feeling that kept carving up her heart, as if Drystan sliced it with his monstrous claws.

She winced as the cold seeped into the holes clawed into her boot, awakening the ripped skin underneath. They'd be ruined from the blood soaking into the leather.

Gwen sobbed a plea, uncaring that they were outdoors and might be overheard. It did not stop her.

Kent caught up with her a few feet from the gate, his long legs giving him advantage traversing the snow.

"Wait, let us explain." He stepped in Ceridwen's path, barring her way to the gate. Not that it much mattered with the lock shining strong and sure. She'd need one of them to unlock it.

"What is there to explain? Is he not a monster?" she asked in a harsh whisper.

His jaw slid side to side before he finally uttered one word. "No."

Then it didn't matter. None of it did. "Let me out. Please."

Jackoby had come around her other side, snaring her attention where he held an object before him. A key. The key.

"Jackoby, you can't mean to—"

He silenced Kent with a look. "Our guest has made her decision," he said with authoritative finality. With that, he trudged the few short feet to the gate as Ceridwen trailed after, wading through his footprints to ease her path.

The key slid into the lock and turned with a click. Jackoby pushed the metal gate under the stone archway open as much as the snow spilling near it would allow. Her heart fluttered at the small gap. Too narrow for a horse or cart, but plenty of space for a person to squeeze through. Freedom beckoned beyond despite the ungroomed, snow-covered streets that awaited. No one had bothered to shovel all the way to the manor gate, not for a Lord Protector who did not visit his citizens or invite them in.

At once, thoughts of Drystan twisted her racing heart. A quick glance at the tower and the fading sun illuminating the windows near the top did nothing to ease her pain. It wrecked her heart all the more.

"He was doing so much better with you here," Jackoby said, drawing her attention back to him and the gate. "If only you could've seen past the monster. He might have had a chance. We might all have."

She recognized the look in his eyes, the one deep beyond his stoic demeanor. Disappointment. It hit like a slap to the face. His master was a monster, yet his disappointment was aimed at her, not the creature lurking in the tower. Somehow, she'd failed him—failed them all.

She could stop now. Return to the manor and forget what she'd seen.

A stiff, cold wind rushed through the gate. Except she never could. How could she reside with a monster? Have dinner with him each night? Play for him alone? A sick, hard knot tumbled within her. She'd kissed him. Kissed the same mouth that had clamped down on the thief's throat.

With that unsettling thought, she squared her shoulders and faced Jackoby through the tears burning the corners of her eyes. "I'm sorry."

Without another backward glance, she fled out the gate and into the streets. She hurried home, her feet taking her along the streets she hadn't walked in weeks. Intuition led the way as her mind reeled with flickers of memory and the knowledge she'd gained that afternoon.

A sob tore from her as she turned the corner onto the street with her family's home. In her haste, she'd left her flute, her most valuable possession. How could she play for Mother now?

CHAPTER 22

DRYSTAN

DRYSTAN FLUNG THE RUINED chair across the room, savoring the shattering of the wood as it smashed into stone. His beast had finally receded. His humanity returned, and with it, the horror of what he'd half witnessed while trapped within the monster's thrall.

Ceridwen had come.

The foolish, brave, bewitching woman had ventured into the one place he'd ordered her not to go and stumbled right into the worst thing imaginable: him fully lost to the darkness in his blood.

When the monster broke free, his mortal mind slipped far into the recesses of his consciousness. Usually, he only could recall glimpses of what happened when the beast had control of him—bits of memory, like pieces of a dark dream. Somehow, her voice cut through the monster's hold and reached him deep within the shadowy place where it locked him away. It responded to her as it rarely did to anyone else. The first night they'd met in the streets, it was her voice that stopped the monster from making her another victim of its rage. Again, she'd stopped it here in the tower, though not before he'd done the unforgiveable.

Drystan slunk to the floor, staring at his hand, at the blood—her blood—coating his fingers from where his monster had grabbed her with its claws.

He'd hurt her. She'd fled.

An anguished cry tore from his chest.

She wouldn't play for him now, not since she'd seen what lurked beneath his skin. No sane person would. She'd probably run right down those stairs and out of the manor for good. The thought caused a shudder to rack his body. The monster was still on edge, prowling just beneath his skin.

People prayed to the Goddess and thought her merciful. To the south, they even called her the Mother, praising her gentle and nurturing side. But in Castamar, they remembered that the Mother was only one side of the divinity that watched over them. The royalty and some nobility could certainly never forget her darker side. Long ago, she'd gifted some of her children power beyond mortal men and women. Strength, increased senses, and the ability to work magic from blood and shape. The power was guarded, limited, and kept by the bloodlines that possessed it. Hoarding of it was one reason nobles rarely married outside their ranks, but there was a darker reason too.

With any power came temptation.

The Goddess's gift wasn't just a blessing but a curse as well. The magic she granted was powerful, but it only went so far. It could be stronger. It could do more, and the temptation of that was ever present in anyone who held the Goddess's touch. But giving in to that temptation was damnation. It meant giving in to the monster lurking within each of them, granting it the power to take control. Worse still were the ones who tried to harness that inner monster for themselves, a sin he refused to sink to.

To tempt darkness at all was an offense punishable by death. At least, it had been before the King Rhion had risen to power, determined to harness that darkness for himself and those loyal to him. Any who weren't? Well, they went the way of the king's nephew, no matter if their magic was light or dark. The public execution hadn't been just a punishment, but a threat.

However, Drystan needed darkness. Light alone wouldn't give him the strength to work the spells he needed for his revenge. Time dripped ever closer to its end for him in this place, and Malik's wandering of his halls would make the spell casting even more tricky. One slip in front of him, one show of his monstrous side, and he'd be done. His cousin would know what magic he used and deduce what he attempted.

He lay back on the floor, begging the coolness of the stone to soothe the pain and regret coursing through him.

Malik might not get the chance to out him. If Ceridwen fled, if she shared what she'd learned in the tower, it would be the end of him. The mayor and the city watch would be at his gates, demanding justice, a mob of citizens in tow. He could see it in his mind's eye, the glimmer of their torches against the night as they sought out the beast to slay it once and for all.

He was a plague upon them. He deserved whatever torment they could muster.

But they didn't know about the king in the capital or his followers who embraced the darkness. They didn't know the danger that could easily spread if left unchecked. It would be a terror unlike any seen in this generation. Death and bloodshed to slake the endless lust of monsters, both human and otherwise. The citizens of Teneboure didn't know that the worst of them wore a human face, sat upon a throne, and received their praise.

Not all monsters crept through the night, baring their fangs and claws for all to see.

With effort, Drystan pushed himself off the floor and slunk to the window. It was sunset now. Had a day passed since he'd lost himself to the monster's thrall? Two? Time was meaningless in that abyss. He'd tried one of the final spells he needed for his working. He'd been close, so close, but that fueled the monster inside him. For days, he'd held it in check despite his use of the darker powers, only to have it break free and consume him. He'd hoped Ceridwen's music would be enough, that her calming presence and songs that seemed to placate the monster would keep it at bay.

But it wasn't enough. Nothing was ever enough.

Drystan pushed open the window pane and peered out toward the city. His focus immediately fell to the main yard below and the stammering of footprints marring the otherwise pristine snow. And there, heading away from the manor, was a lone figure in the near dusk streets. He didn't need to see her to know who it was.

Grief bellowed from him in a roar before he sank to his knees and held his head in his hands.

CHAPTER 23
CERIDWEN

"Oh—Oh my—" Jaina exclaimed as she beheld Ceridwen standing on the front stair. "Ceridwen, what's happened?" She practically pulled her inside as the young woman hiccupped through her tears.

The moment the front door shut, she wrapped Ceridwen in her arms, encircling her in the warmth of her body and the thick shawl she'd held closed over her arms and shoulders. The scent of fresh-baked bread and spice clung to her, lulling Ceridwen into the comfort of her arms.

"Dear girl, what's wrong? And where are your things?" she asked.

"Ceridwen?"

The voice Ceridwen missed more than all the others jolted through her like lightning.

She raised her head from Jaina's shoulder, sniffling away her tears. Bronwyn stood in the doorway, gaping at her sudden appearance. A fine dress hugged her curves in layers of dark blue with lace and ribbons in cream. The heavy skirts falling from her waist spoke to warmth yet held an air of fashionable elegance as well.

Her sister had not owned such a fine dress before. Either Father finally allowed her to find a patron for her art, or even more impossibly, had her stubborn heart been swayed by a suitor who saw fit to shower her with luxurious gifts?

"Bronwyn." Ceridwen wiped at her face with a cold, bare hand.

Jaina stepped away as Bronwyn rushed to fling her arms around her sister. Ceridwen practically collapsed against her, sobs coming anew.

"Your father and Gerard are out," Jaina said with a little sniffle of her own. "But I'll bring us all some tea, and then perhaps you can tell us what's happened."

Bronwyn guided Ceridwen into the sitting room while they waited for Jaina. Here, too, she noticed changes: a new rug to replace the old one that had worn thin and bare, a soft blanket of fur folded over one arm of the sofa, and repairs to the cracked stone of the fireplace. Even the musty scent that always tainted this section of the house seemed fainter, replaced instead with sweet, fresh pine.

"The first payment showed up a few days after you left." Bronwyn shook her head with a smile. "So much gold that Father raged against that stern-looking servant with the frock of white hair on his brow and said he hadn't sold his daughter off permanently."

Her description of Jackoby almost tugged a smile from Ceridwen's lips. Almost.

Unlike Jaina, Bronwyn hadn't asked what was wrong. She knew her sister would tell her when she was ready. Instead, Bronwyn took to distracting Ceridwen's thoughts with all she'd missed and that hadn't made it into a letter. Adair had finally requested permission to court Lydia. Her father rejected the initial request, but a second more adamant plea earned a grudging allowance with a reminder that many other, more suited, gentlemen sought her hand.

Father's health had improved with new medicine, as she mentioned in her letter. So much so that he could move about on his own and go into town as he had today.

Drystan had sent money to the family as promised. More than Ceridwen could fathom for her meager service. Enough to buy medicine, pay off the most urgent loan repayments, and supply some simple upgrades for the house.

"We didn't expect any more, not after that first generous gift, so we rationed it out. But I made sure Father saw the new physician and spent the money on the treatment he recommended." Bronwyn smoothed out her fine skirts, no doubt a byproduct of Drystan's patronage. "If only we could have afforded that years ago."

Or that old physician hadn't been such a rotten thief. He'd claimed his tonics could work miracles, but they'd only made their father worse, if anything.

"But then more payments did come," she continued. "One each week. Sometimes just coin, and other times they contained gifts, like this dress." She pinched the top layer of fabric and lifted it for emphasis. "Honestly, I tried to reject it. It was bad enough that he wouldn't let you visit. I didn't want to like the things he sent, but..."

Bronwyn's shrug said more than words. She didn't want to admit to liking pretty dresses. She never did, not even when they were small. But put one in front of her, and she couldn't resist it, especially not one given for free. It warmed Ceridwen to know her sister had something pretty, something she enjoyed. If they benefitted from her time with Drystan, it was worth all the pain and heartache she suffered now.

"And it's a good thing too. It wouldn't do any good to go rejecting such generosity," Jaina jumped into the conversation as she entered the room, carrying a tray arranged with a steaming teapot, three cups, and an assortment of baked goods that smelled of apples and spice. Nicer fare than they would have had in the past.

After she'd poured tea and Ceridwen started to nibble on the flaky edge of a pastry, Jaina finally asked her questions again. "Your color looks better already. You were white as a sheet on the doorstep. I thought you might have been a spirit sent by the Goddess. Now, will you tell us what had you showing up in such a state? Was he... Did he do something to you?"

She almost choked on the pastry. He had done something to her, but not what Jaina implied. The Drystan she knew would never consider assaulting a woman that way. Yet she never would have believed him to be a monster either. Now she wondered how much she really knew him at all. The thought turned the pastry to ash in her mouth.

"I'll kill him," Bronwyn said. "Lord or no, I'll—"

"It's not like that." Ceridwen waved her arms, calming her sister's burst of anger.

The least she could do was defend his reputation after he'd upheld his end of their arrangement. And he'd done it to a degree she never anticipated. Malik was another matter—one she intended to avoid altogether.

Bronwyn's lips thinned, but Ceridwen continued, "The monster...the one we saw that night. It lives in the manor."

"Goddess protect our souls," Jaina uttered, aghast, before making a circle in front of her chest with her hands—the sign of the Goddess's protection.

The color drained from Bronwyn's cheeks. Jaina fanned herself with her hand, blinking rapidly. Ceridwen had only seen her like that one other time, and then she'd fainted upon on the sofa with great dramatics. Jaina had shown less worry when she faced down the bloody monster itself, but the mention of it now, living so close, nearly sent her spilling onto the floor.

The plan had been to tell them everything, but Jaina's reaction to that one detail almost sent her over the edge. What would she do if Ceridwen confessed that Drystan was the monster she feared? She simply couldn't mention it, not now.

"Does he know?" Bronwyn asked.

Bronwyn stared at her sister hard, trying to figure out what she wasn't saying. They knew each other too well. Ceridwen would have to tell her. Later.

"Yes. He knows. He tries to..." What could she possibly tell them? "Contain it."

Deep in her heart, she knew he didn't want to be monstrous or to cause pain and suffering.

"That's why you left." Bronwyn pinned her with her steady brown-eyed gaze.

"I couldn't stay. Not after…" The tightness in her throat swallowed up her words. Instead, she pulled up the edge of her damp and dirty hem, showing the ruined boots below. A dark stain spread out on one side where her blood had soaked through the puncture holes.

The sight had Jaina wobbling in her chair before she sucked in a deep breath and gripped the cushioned arm for support. With a shake, she came back to the present. "Dear girl, why didn't you tell us straight away?"

It wasn't the worst injury she'd ever had. When they'd lived in the countryside and been able to afford horses, a new mare had bucked her off onto packed dirt interwoven with tree roots. Every part of her had screamed in pain. It'd taken weeks to heal then, and only the village doctor's careful work ensured she had no permanent disability.

The fear of Drystan's monster had been much worse than the wound it inflicted, and in her flight of terror, she'd nearly forgotten the injury all together.

"It looks worse than it is," she said, covering the offensive sight. "But I couldn't stay there. Not with something like that in the manor."

"I'd say not," Jaina replied, making the sign of the Goddess again. "We need to tell someone. The mayor. The watch. Perhaps—"

"No," Ceridwen snapped, shocking both Jaina and her sister.

"Whyever not?"

Because they would find out Drystan's secret, too, or bring some other disaster down on his head. They might kill him. The monster would certainly kill innocents if unleashed. She couldn't have his death on her conscious, but could she let the monster run free? "I can't explain. But you cannot repeat this. Please. If you love me, don't speak a word of what I've told you."

Jaina still fussed, but Bronwyn nodded slowly. "There haven't been any more attacks in the city since you left."

A surprise given how often she'd heard the monster in the manor, but also good news. Ceridwen sat a little straighter. Perhaps Drystan truly was close to containing it somehow.

"We won't tell," Bronwyn promised, staring hard at Jaina, who finally nodded.

"I'm so sorry about the money," Ceridwen said, changing the topic. "There won't be any more now." Hopefully he wouldn't request they return his payments since she left so abruptly.

Bronwyn laughed.

Both Jaina and Ceridwen swiveled to stare at her as she reeled in her humor. "*That's what you're worried about?*" She shook her head with a smile. "We're fine, Ceridwen. We have more than enough now. We'll get by. I'm just glad you're home. We'll put this behind us like a bad dream—a profitable one."

Ceridwen wished she could believe her, but somehow, she knew they hadn't seen the end of the Lord Protector—or his monster.

CHAPTER 24
DRYSTAN

DRYSTAN DIDN'T BOTHER LEAVING his tower until the morning after Ceridwen's departure. When he finally gathered the will to descend the stairs, his stomach rumbling from the lack of food, he found Jackoby waiting at the bottom.

The man said nothing of Drystan's disheveled appearance, simply bowed at the waist with a polite, "My lord."

He'd never felt less deserving of the title. From anyone else, he might have seen it as a mockery, but Jackoby's loyalty and sincerity never faltered. How he managed to deserve such a man in his life, he couldn't quite say. Jackoby had been loyal to his parents before him, raised in their service since his boyhood. Perhaps it was easier to stay in his employ after their deaths than seek out someone else, but that didn't stop most from doing so. Even in his darkest days, Jackoby had been there to make sure he ate, saw to his needs, and kept going, even during the times when Drystan hadn't wanted to.

His butler, his friend, knew exactly what lurked under his skin and the horror it could conjure, but he never once turned his back on him.

"She's gone," Drystan said. Even if not for the sight of someone fleeing from the manor the day before, he could sense a difference in the very air, a void of emptiness no one else could fill.

"She is," Jackoby said. "I'm sorry. Truly. I tried to stop her."

"Perhaps it's for the best." No one could blame her for fleeing after what she had learned.

Jackoby huffed. "She helped you. We all saw it."

"Yes." He swallowed, his throat suddenly thick. For a time there, he'd been as close to happiness as he had been in years. But her music, her calming presence, also made him complacent. He risked things perhaps he shouldn't in his eagerness to finish his task before Malik returned.

The few staff he had knew of his monstrous form but remained loyal. Even so, only Jackoby knew the truth of what he worked on in his tower at night, what caused him to seek out and use the magic that occasionally forced him to become a monster.

"Were you able to finish your work?" Jackoby asked, keeping his words carefully vague.

"No." Drystan groaned, nearly stumbling. Jackoby rushed to aid him, but Drystan waved him off. He was just weak. Food would help. "I'll have to try again."

Creating the Gray Blade, the legendary weapon against darkness, was a tricky affair, even for someone skilled in the arts such as he. If Malik found out what he worked on, or worse, the king, he'd be doomed. He'd never get the chance to wield it and have his vengeance. There would be no redemption for all those who suffered because of the king's dark inclinations.

"Your cousin may return any day," Jackoby said.

A fact Drystan was too well aware of. He wouldn't put it past him to stroll in that very moment.

"Let Kent and I venture into the city. We can try to convince Miss Ceridwen to return."

"She's gone, Jackoby." The pain of saying it aloud was almost too much. "Just see me to the dining room."

"As you will, but if I can be of assistance…"

"You are," Drystan assured him. "Every day."

The older man's lips thinned. "Not yesterday. The young woman was so determined to leave, and I didn't want to cause a scene. I unlocked the gate for her. I let her go." His voice rose uncharacteristically, shaking with emotion as if he'd just committed the worst treason. "It was a mistake."

"It wasn't," Drystan said. "I'm…I'm glad you let her go."

The look on her face when she realized what he was would haunt him forever after. The horror etched there, the revelation… It was almost too much to bear. Seeing that look on her face again, especially if he locked her within the manor and forced her to linger after that revelation, would be too much. He had enough sins to pay for. He wouldn't break the lovely young woman who made him feel like a man again.

They walked in silence the rest of the way to the dining room. Jackoby seated Drystan in his traditional chair and called for an urgent meal for his lord. "Something simple. Cold is fine," Drystan said, though Jackoby ignored him.

He didn't deserve fine foods. He didn't deserve any of these people's loyalty.

A serving maid filled his glass and rushed into the kitchens. When she'd gone, Jackoby turned to Drystan. "Miss Ceridwen left her things in her haste." He tucked his hands behind his back, standing a little straighter. "Should I have them delivered to her?"

"Yes, but not this moment." He had no desire to hold her things hostage, and the dresses he'd commissioned were a gift. She was meant to have them when she left, as he always knew she must—he just thought it would be when he departed for the capital, not sooner. Once her things were gone, the last vestiges of her in this manor would be as well, though he had no doubt memories of her would taunt him. He'd picture her everywhere, from the greenhouse and the roses he loved, to the halls, the dining room, and the library. His study would be quiet without her music, as empty as the hole in his heart.

No, he couldn't quite give up the last bit of her, not yet.

It took two days for Drystan to work up the courage to enter Ceridwen's former room. Someone had been in, straightening the bed and removing the pitcher of water and cups that had stood on the side table. Even so, the room still held a trace of her scent, one that wrapped around him as he entered, beckoning him to stay.

He warred with the desire to linger there versus the pang of longing it caused. Spending time in her former room, holding her things hostage, wouldn't bring her back.

Drystan knelt by the trunk at the end of the bed with its worn sides and peeling face. The clasp groaned as he opened it, but the dresses stacked inside rewarded him with another blast of her scent. He ran his fingers over the fabric, memorizing the design so he could remember her in it.

A minute later, he rose, shutting the trunk. With another glance around the room, he noticed another object and stilled. Her flute case sat on the table, her precious instrument no doubt still within. Guilt coiled around him, stringing him up tight. How selfish he'd been keeping her things in the manor. What a coward he was not to face this last bit of her before now. She would miss her flute. She needed it to play for her mother.

Without another thought, he exited the room, determined to find Jackoby or Kent and have them return Ceridwen's things immediately.

Unfortunately, someone else found him first.

"Ah, there you are." Malik strode down the hall, his traveling cloak still around his shoulders. An iron brooch pinned it closed, one bearing the symbol of a dragon—a sign of those loyal to the king and within his inner circle.

Drystan's jaw stiffened. *Of all the damnable times for him to show up.* "My servants let you in?" He'd gotten through the gate somehow.

"Yes, Jackoby, and what was his name?" Malik tapped a finger on his chin. "Kent?" He shrugged. "They were most accommodating. Should be delivering my trunks to my room right now, in fact."

"And you just thought to take a stroll of the halls this morning?" Drystan asked, a droll boredom in his tone. It'd be so much easier if he could dismiss him or send him away without arousing suspicion.

"Hmm." Malik smirked, crossing his arms and leaning against the wall. "Actually, I'd hoped to find that lovely young woman staying with you and request a song or two. I have been so looking forward to hearing her play again."

The words hit him square in the chest. Malik would bring her up the moment Drystan was about to let her go forever. "She's not here," he ground out.

"Oh?" Malik shoved off the wall. "I thought she was staying in residence."

"No longer."

Drystan continued on his way, but as he passed by, Malik said, "Lovers' spat?"

The question still rang in the air when Drystan twisted toward his cousin, grabbed him by the neck, and shoved him roughly against the wall. An inhuman growl rumbled in his chest before he took in his cousin's grimace of pain and released him. Malik slid down the wall a few inches before getting his feet back under him and rubbing at his neck.

"Seems I was right."

Drystan snarled. The gall of Malik to provoke him this way.

"She just left?" Malik asked, refusing to let the topic drop. "And you let her go? That doesn't sound like you."

The growl that slipped from Drystan echoed down the halls, but Malik stared back, unfazed.

"You certainly cared for her," Malik continued.

"Don't speak of her. Never again," Drystan warned. He turned away from his cousin, determined to leave this conversation before he could do something even more stupid, more...permanent.

"Why not?"

"This has nothing to do with you."

"Doesn't it, cousin?" He drew out the title, almost like an endearment.

Drystan halted and looked over one shoulder at Malik. His cousin said nothing, just stared at him with his arms crossed.

The man provoked him to no end. Drystan ignored him, stalking down the hall. He was about to turn the corner out of sight when Malik spoke again.

"Too bad. You almost seemed like your old self with her."

Drystan's nails dug into his palms as he skidded to a stop. That should be the last thing Malik wanted. His old self was no good to anyone. Not anymore.

Drystan turned on his heel, his fury spiking back to a boiling point. "What is this to you, Malik? Some game? Why do you care?"

"Perhaps I'm not as terrible as you like to think me," Malik said, striding down the hall toward him.

As if he could believe that. Anyone loyal to the king was a plague upon the country and certainly not to be trusted. But once upon a time, years ago, things had been different. He and Malik had never been the best of friends, but they were easy companions dueling with fake swords and learning the basics of magic together. Malik had never tended toward darkness. In fact, his mother was one of the staunchest supports of the former monarchs who favored the light.

But she was long dead, the former king and queen too.

The boy he'd known in youth was one to seek pleasure, not pain, but then, no one had expected Drystan to touch the darkness either. The things he'd done were unforgiveable, yet still, there were those loyal to him, those who didn't hold the past against him as they should.

"We were friends once," Malik said, as if reading the thought straight from his mind.

"Years ago," Drystan said.

Malik shrugged. "Even so." He stopped just in front of Drystan, in easy reach of his fury. "For what it's worth, I believe she cared for you too." Malik made to move past him but halted and clapped Drystan on the shoulder.

Drystan stared his cousin down across the length of his arm.

"An apology can go a long way," Malik said, then released him to saunter on down the hall. Over his shoulder, he called, "You should try it sometime."

CHAPTER 25

CERIDWEN

O N THE THIRD DAY since her return home, Bronwyn dragged Ceridwen from the kitchen where she gathered scraps to take out to the animals.

"You're not going to believe this," she insisted while pulling her through the hallway decorated with faded and peeling wallpaper.

"What? What is it?" Ceridwen asked for the third time.

She didn't answer. Bronwyn's silence held more terror than any words she could speak.

As they came into the front room, Ceridwen realized the reason for her silence. It stripped the words from her thoughts as well.

Jackoby stood just inside the front door near a heap of chests and smaller items that someone had brought in. Father was with him and had opened the largest chest. Within lay layers and piles of luxurious fabrics in colors and patterns she wouldn't soon forget. Her dresses. The ones Drystan had commissioned.

Tears pricked her eyes at the sight of the small, long box in Jackoby's arms. Her flute. They'd yet to order a new one—not that she'd even considered playing since her return. Leaving Drystan had crushed her will to play, even for her mother.

"Lord Winterbourne asked that these be brought for you since you accidentally left them behind in your departure."

Ceridwen barely heard his careful words as she searched for any hint of a deeper meaning in his face. As usual, Jackoby gave little away.

"He also sent this for you as well." Jackoby lifted the sealed envelope in his hand for emphasis. With the other treasures he'd brought, she hadn't noticed the thick paper with a rose stamped upon its closure in crimson wax.

Ceridwen took the letter and her flute case with shaking hands. "Thank you." It meant more than he could ever know.

He nodded. "I will pass along your appreciation to Lord Winterbourne." Then his face softened, showing something resembling friendly concern. "Please read the letter and consider it. Not just for him, for all of us."

The words struck deep in her chest. She hadn't just left Drystan. She'd left them all.

"I will." She could promise that much.

Jackoby left a final sack of gold coins with her father—payment for services rendered, plus extra. So much more than she deserved. After his departure, Bronwyn and Ceridwen relocated the chests of clothing to her room.

"This will be perfect for the winter ball," Bronwyn said, airing out the blue dress she'd worn to honor the first snow—the same night she'd witnessed Drystan's attack. She hadn't known then about the monster lurking beneath the surface. Looking back, she should have, but she never considered it possible that a man could become such a beast. Especially not Drystan.

"You're going to go, aren't you?" Bronwyn asked.

Honestly, she hadn't realized the ball would be held so soon. Within the manor, one day seemed much like the next, and the ball wasn't even a consideration while she'd lived there.

From the corner of her eye, Ceridwen saw her sister lay the dress over a cushioned chair before coming to sit next to her on the bed. She took Ceridwen's hands in hers. "You haven't heard a word of what I've said, have you?"

"I'm sorry. I have a lot on my mind." Ceridwen flashed a weak smile.

"Are you going to open it?" Bronwyn nodded toward the envelope on the side table, the object that had held Ceridwen's almost full attention since Jackoby had placed it into her hands.

A deep sigh slipped from her lips. "There's something I haven't told you. Several things, actually, but one important one. The real reason I ran."

"It wasn't because of the monster in the manor?" she asked.

"It was, but there's more than that." She licked her lips, hesitating before sharing the next bit. "If I tell you, it can never leave this room. Promise me."

She raised her free hand in front of her. "By the Goddess and the sanctity of the old oak we played under as girls, I solemnly promise not to tell." Their greatest promise and vow of sisterhood.

Satisfied, Ceridwen began. "He wasn't the lazy vagabond of a lord we suspected him to be when he came here. He seemed that way at first, even within his home, but then something changed. He softened somehow. Even cleaned himself up. Underneath it all, he was kind. Charming. A handsome young lord."

"You liked him," she said.

Her heart twisted. "I did, and I believe he cared for me too. And how wonderful it was to play for him. He made music come alive in my heart again."

"Oh, Ceridwen..."

That was the easy admission. The harder one came now. "I accused him of being a lazy lord and not caring about his people being terrorized by the monster in their midst. That's when he told me that he worked every night to keep the monster at bay." She shook her head, recalling their time together. "I heard it sometimes while I stayed there. Always at night. But not once did I see it. Not until that last day."

"Bronwyn..." Her hands tightened on her sister's. "Lord Winterbourne *is* the monster."

Bronwyn's eyes flew wide. Her lips parted.

"It must be magic," Ceridwen hurried on, looking away from her sister's wild expression. "He's one of the nobles that can wield it. Though I don't know why it causes him to change like that."

"Magic..." her sister murmured in apparent shock.

"He'd not left his tower for two days, and I'd grown concerned. All the residents of the manor had. Yet no one would enter the tower to discover what had happened. I didn't know why. I do now. At first, I thought it was empty, ransacked. I feared that Drystan may have been killed by the monster he claimed to protect us from. But then I found it on the top floor."

Her chest grew tight, burning with emotion. "The monster attacked me as I tried to flee. But then it began to change, to become more human. It spoke with Drystan's voice. He called out my name and begged me to stay, but I—" The memories finally choked off her words.

"You ran," Bronwyn finished. Her earlier surprise faded into sadness.

Ceridwen nodded as Bronwyn pulled her into a bone-crushing hug. Tears streamed down her face.

"It's all right. I would have too. I think anyone would when confronted by a shock like that. But—" She pulled Ceridwen back until she could look her in the eye again. "If you care about him, as I believe you do, you need to read his letter. See what he has to say. It won't change what happened, or that he kept such a thing from you, but you should do it for yourself, if nothing else."

Ceridwen nodded and breathed deeply. "I know. I will. I just…"

Bronwyn patted her leg. "Take your time. I'll be here if you want to talk about it afterward. You've become so much braver since you left us. I know you can handle this." With that, she left her alone with Drystan's words, still sealed with the crimson rose of wax.

It took time for her sister's praise to sink in. Braver? She didn't feel like it, though she'd done a number of things she never could have imagined only a few weeks ago. Ceridwen was the quiet younger sibling. Always polite. Never outspoken like Adair and Bronwyn. Yet she'd been the one to criticize a noble and face down a monster. Perhaps, outside their shadows, she'd finally started to find her own spark.

After a few more minutes of indecision, she finally pried open the seal and pulled out the letter—one thick sheet of paper folded twice.

Dearest Ceridwen,

An apology would be insufficient for the event that occurred between us. But know that if I could have kept you from that, I would have.

I thought I was keeping you safe, protecting you from the things I wish I could change. I see now that I was wrong. I'd give anything to fix what happened, and it destroys me that I can't.

Your music helps me more than you know, and your bright spirit is the light that brought me back from deep darkness. I miss it. I miss you.

If you would deign to return, I would be willing to increase the terms of our arrangement.

I pray the Goddess grants me your presence again before my time is up.

Drystan

She expected anger or hurt. Yet all that filled her after reading his letter was empty, numbing sadness. He'd been carefully vague, but of course he would be. Putting his monstrous side into words, and signed in his hand, would be damning if Ceridwen chose to wield that against him.

Of all his words, the last line bothered her the most. Drystan mentioned returning to the capital at midwinter, but why not say that? Such travel would not be unexpected for a noble.

A cord of unease slithered its way into the emptiness within her. Drystan held more secrets than she ever imagined, and worse ones than anyone would reasonably believe. But perhaps, she'd yet to learn the extent of them. Whatever plagued the Lord Protector of Teneboure and led to his monstrous form, she had a suspicion that he did not expect to survive it.

That night, Ceridwen chose to play again. The song she picked had been her mother's favorite and the first she had memorized. The words of the song sang themselves in her heart as she played the tune with practiced ease from her customary perch on the usable portion of the roof of the house, letting the notes float out into the cold night.

A second song followed the first. Despite the cold that stiffened her limbs through layers of fabric, she raised her flute and began a third. As the warmed metal came to rest against her lip, an imaginary spider skittered down her back.

Always she felt eyes on her when she played outside. Her mother watching from the Goddess's hallowed halls, she assumed. Though often, the tingles came from the direction of the manor. Perhaps Drystan had listened and watched long before they'd been introduced. Actually, she was almost certain of it.

But this new feeling was more intense. Stronger. As if whomever watched stood just behind her. She lowered her flute with shaking hands but could not will herself to turn.

"Drystan?" she whispered.

The world grew still, holding its breath with her.

When the reply came, the familiar voice nearly chilled her to the bone. "Ceridwen."

She spun around, desperately seeking the source of her name. The rooftop was empty, but near the edge, the snow had been marred and scraped away as if someone had climbed onto the roof from the street below. Yet she'd never heard a sound.

She hustled through the packed snow to the edge of the low railing. Her hand found purchase in the marred snow, the imprint almost warm under her glove, as she gazed down into the street below. Empty. No Drystan, no monster, nor anyone else. With the snow shoveled in haphazard mounds and the tracks of many footprints and animal hooves in what remained, finding fresh tracks proved impossible. Yet she knew what she'd heard, what she'd felt.

"Drystan…"

Sleep did not come easily after the strange, almost encounter the night before. When the rooster finally crowed with the dawn, Ceridwen had already been awake and staring at the dark ceiling of her room. She slipped back inside after feeding the animals to hear a deep pounding echoing down the stairs from the main hall. Someone knocked at the front door. Aggressively.

They weren't expecting anyone. The whole town would be busy preparing for the winter ball that evening, yet this visitor had no intention of waiting. Or being polite.

Only one face came to mind, and that image had her rushing through the halls toward the door. When she finally made it there, lightly huffing for air, Bronwyn had arrived from somewhere, only a few paces behind her.

Ceridwen's pulse raced with excitement as she closed her palm around the heavy metal handle and pulled. The sight that greeted her, however, sent her heart plummeting into her stomach.

Malik stood on the doorstep, dark hair slightly tousled. His green eyes sparked with mirth, and his characteristic smirk pulled at one corner of his mouth.

Of all the people Ceridwen imagined showing up at the door, he'd never come to mind at all.

"Hello again, dear Ceridwen."

"Is that…" Bronwyn began.

Malik's brows rose as a grin stretched wide across his face. "Oh, so you've heard stories about me, have you?" He brushed by her and strode toward Bronwyn. To her sister's credit, she held her ground and stared him down.

"No. I haven't spoken of you at all." Ceridwen stepped in front of Malik. "You're not welcome here."

Malik cocked his head to the side.

"She said you're not welcome here," Bronwyn echoed in a show of solidarity.

His grin dropped into a dramatic frown. "Really, that's such a pity." He leaned on the wall, showing no intention of leaving. "Though before I go, tell me one thing. Why did you leave him?"

Her heart skipped a beat. "That's not your business."

"Oh, it might be," he said.

His gaze settled on Ceridwen like a slimy eel as his lips quirked up in one corner. That's right. He'd been sent to watch Drystan, to report on his actions. Turning into a monster would certainly be a mark against him.

"We had a disagreement."

"Is that all?"

Ceridwen pursed her lips and held her ground.

"Well, just a *disagreement* doesn't sound too bad. Perhaps you'd consider returning?" He cocked his head in question.

Her brows furrowed. "Why do you want me to return?"

He smirked. "Who doesn't want a pretty view around such a dreary manor?"

Ridiculous. She crossed her arms over her chest and frowned at him. Bronwyn rolled her eyes.

"But honestly, you help him," he added, his smirk smoothing out into something resembling a decent gentlemanly demeanor. "The last time I was here, I saw a glimmer of the man he used to be, and perhaps could be again—with your help, that is."

"You want to help him?" Ceridwen asked, incredulous.

"Maybe, depending on his intentions."

So vague. Just like Drystan's letter. Some puzzle piece eluded her, but Ceridwen couldn't begin to find it or determine where it fit.

"Besides," he added, finally crossing the room and stepping out the door onto the threshold of the house. "We are cousins. What's family for?"

"I'll consider it." Anything to get him to leave and stay gone.

"Good." He nodded before looking past Ceridwen. His gaze fixed on something, likely Bronwyn, and glittered with mirth before he turned to walk away.

Ceridwen didn't waste a breath before she slammed the door closed behind him with more force than necessary.

"Who was that?" Bronwyn asked. When Ceridwen turned to her, she slid a metal hairpin into her pocket. *That's* what Malik found amusing? Her sister's desire to skewer him?

"Drystan's cousin," Ceridwen replied, letting all her bitterness fill her words.

A soft whisper slipped through her sister's lips. "Is he a monster too?"

"Of a different sort." Though if he turned beastly in the flesh as well, it wouldn't surprise her.

CHAPTER 26
CERIDWEN

BRONWYN TALKED CERIDWEN INTO wearing the blue dress embroidered with birds she'd worn to celebrate the first snow. Her sister wore one of her new ones as well—a confection of forest green that accented her eyes and dark hair, reminiscent of their father's coloring in his younger days.

"Is someone finally trying to attract a husband?" Jaina teased as she came in to help with their hair.

Bronwyn pursed her lips and balled her fists on her hips. She'd never once trailed after a man and had little interest in marriage. Unless, of course, she could find some magical gentleman that adored her painting and didn't mind the occasional sharpness of her tongue. She'd decided years ago such a man didn't exist, though. Two weeks in this city had ruled out just about all the men of marriageable age and confirmed her conclusion.

"I can look pretty just for myself, thank you," Bronwyn replied.

"You'll be the most stunning woman at the ball," Ceridwen said.

She rolled her eyes. "A better topic," her sister began, "is how shall we do your hair?"

"Something that will work with the mask." Ceridwen lifted a bird mask from the dressing table. It was mostly blue with accents of black, gold, and silver paint, a perfect complement to her dress. Everyone wore masks for the winter ball. Hers was small as masks went, just wide enough to halo her eyes from one edge of the face to the other while leaving her nose, mouth, and hair uncovered, but she preferred that to being weighed down by some monstrosity.

The tradition sprang from many years ago when the locals wore them to ward off the winter sprites said to freeze animals and humans alike within their beds at night. How a fanciful bird could ward off a sprite, Ceridwen had no idea, but the legend brought a playful air to the event that she appreciated all the same.

Bronwyn's mask resembled a cat, painted in gold and white with hints of orange and brown. No one knew what Adair had chosen, but they'd find out soon enough.

Jaina and Bronwyn wove Ceridwen's long blond hair into braids and pinned them upon her head like a crown—or a bird's nest. Fitting, given her outfit.

Once they were dressed and primped, Jaina shooed the young women out of the room. "I'm sure your brother is already waiting."

She wouldn't be going with them. Neither would Gerard nor Father. None of them enjoyed such raucous events, despite Father's penchant for gossip, and with an older brother to escort his sisters there and back, it would not be misperceived for them to attend without their father's presence.

Adair waited in the front room downstairs. With his crisp shirt, fitted tailcoat embroidered with crimson, and tailored pants, he looked a man above his station. The fox mask pushed up high on his forehead mussed his dark hair at the front where it fell free from the tie binding the longer ends at the back of his head.

Undoubtedly, their father had given him some of the coin Ceridwen earned playing for Drystan. Adair couldn't afford to waste his money on such frivolous things, not when saving for a wife and a home of his own. He wasn't that much of a fool, even if he often acted before he thought. Though, with Lydia the object of his affection, perhaps he had sprung for the new clothes himself, if for no other reason than to impress his would-be future in-laws.

He gave a shallow bow. "My lovely little sisters."

"You make us sound like children," Bronwyn retorted.

"No one could mistake either of you for a child, especially not with those dresses." Adair shifted his attention to Ceridwen. "Are we expecting any *special* guests at tonight's event?"

The bitterness he managed to inflect into his tone shocked her. Adair had no reason to dislike Drystan other than their one ill-fated encounter and Ceridwen's temporary residence with him. A fact the family had kept secret lest ugly rumors spread concerning her reputation, and by proxy, the family's. To the rest of the city, she'd simply been unwell and staying indoors for her health. Ceridwen had told her brother nothing of Drystan's monster. With his penchant for saying too much, especially after a drink or two, he'd never be able to keep it a secret.

"No, I should think not," Ceridwen replied with confidence. A society party was the very last type of place she'd expect to see the reclusive Lord Winterbourne.

A steady stream of finely dressed and masked citizens wound their way through the main doors of the public hall. Oil lamp sconces bracketed the doors and had been set on poles leading up to the entrance from where coaches deposited their occupants. Full night had fallen on the world, leaving the lamps, the glow emanating from the windows of the hall, and the dim shine of the moon overhead the only sources of light.

Adair craned his neck out the window of their carriage, one he'd hired specifically to improve his image for this evening. Ceridwen had little doubt whom he searched for. Lydia would likely arrive slightly late, always one to make an entrance and to be sure people saw her do it.

A young woman with brilliant red hair stepped from the carriage two in front of theirs. Georgina took the arm of a well-dressed young man Ceridwen couldn't name and let herself be led toward the hall. When their turn came, Adair exited the coach first and helped each of his sisters out in turn. They left the furs covering their legs in the coach for their return.

"Well, dear sisters, are you ready for the ball?" He pasted on a blinding smile and held out an arm to each of them.

"Not as excited as you," Bronwyn teased.

Ceridwen pulled in a deep breath that iced her lungs, but somehow steadied her all the same, before taking his offered arm.

Why, oh why, did I agree to come? Ceridwen asked herself. *For Bronwyn. For Adair.* In a twisted way, it was for her too. If she put all her focus into appearing happy and enjoying the evening, she couldn't think about Drystan.

"Gentlemen." Adair nodded to the two young men attending the doors, dressed in military attire. No doubt friends of his, or at least acquaintances. Adair made it a point to know as many people as possible and make friends wherever he could—the opposite of his sisters.

A wave of sound crashed over them as the doors were pulled open and they stepped inside. Ceridwen bit her lip, her gaze darting around. Though they were not late, the main room already housed a jumble of people laughing, drinking, and beginning a circular dance within the center of the open floor.

"I'll find you later," Adair assured them, his brotherly duties fulfilled.

"Good luck with a certain lady," Ceridwen said with a wink despite the burning sensation building behind her ribs.

He only smirked and headed off in pursuit of said lady, or drink, though likely both.

Bronwyn and Ceridwen each snagged a glass of punch, the only thing likely to loosen their nerves, or at least Ceridwen's. The press of bodies, mingling pungent scents of perfume, and rancorous conversation begging to be heard over the music already being played by the small band made her stomach churn.

"Drink that and find someone to dance with," Bronwyn remarked, pointing to her sister's saucer of punch.

The warm apple and spice mixture had been spiked with something, though Ceridwen couldn't begin to deduce what. At least it tasted better than the ale many of the men gulped from larger tankards.

"You first." She raised her brows at her sister.

Bronwyn smirked and took a long sip.

"Oh, Ceridwen!" Lydia exclaimed, pushing through two nearby men in matching hound masks to join their spot near the back wall. Georgina was two steps behind her, having lost her escort somewhere in the crowd.

Lydia clasped Ceridwen's free hand in hers and tugged her close, almost spilling the punch. The frilly white lace of Lydia's gloves matched the pure white and delicate lace of her gown, along with the white swan mask adorning her face, accented by her blond hair done up in curls. She looked like a fanciful bride in a fairy tale, dwarfing the rest of the crowd with her pure radiance. In contrast, Georgina had played up the red of her hair in the russet of her gown with a brown ermine mask.

"We were so worried when Bronwyn mentioned you were ill," Lydia continued, still clutching her hand.

"It was most troubling," Georgina agreed, though Ceridwen sensed her sympathies were mostly for show. She didn't look the least bit troubled or excited to see her. If anything, she already looked bored.

Typical.

"But look at you!" Lydia beamed, ignoring her companion. "Healthy as ever by the look of it."

"I am much better now." The lie came easily. She'd prepared for this, after all. "Thank you."

"I tried to come and visit once, but your father suggested it best to leave you in peace." Lydia pouted and finally released her hand.

Bronwyn faintly nodded, confirming her words. "For which we are very grateful," she added. "It cheered Ceridwen's spirit to know she had a friend who worried for her."

"Oh, I'm so glad. And your dress!" She touched her lips with one hand, eyes sparkling as she took in one sister then the other. "Both of you. My, they're absolutely stunning."

"And new?" Georgina raised a careful brow. "Someone's fortune's have improved, I'll say."

The slight insult behind the comment was impossible to miss, or Georgina's circumspect look. Ceridwen's smile settled into something forced and sharp around the edges. Bronwyn frowned, and only Ceridwen's quick move to grasp her sister's hand and squeeze kept her from responding with something unfortunate. "We've been lucky of late on multiple fronts, that's true," Ceridwen replied.

"And I'm so glad for it." Unlike Georgina, Lydia's reply rang with sincerity and smoothed out some of the tension among their little group.

Lydia continued to ramble on about the recent gossip as Ceridwen drained her saucer and handed it off to a passing boy picking up empty glasses. A pleasant warmth settled in her chest as she nodded along and made appreciative comments. Bronwyn had already told her the more interesting pieces of news, but Ceridwen suspected that Lydia liked to share gossip just as much as hear it, so she let her continue. Besides, her company gave Ceridwen an excuse not to seek out others with whom she'd be less comfortable.

Commotion picked up behind them. Conversations halted abruptly to start up again with gasps and questions. Every muscle in her body went rigid.

"Who are they?" Georgina blurted right in the middle of Lydia's story.

Bronwyn twisted to the side and stilled. Lydia pouted at the interruption but did the same. Her expression slid into one of shock as her mouth parted in surprise.

It can't be. The thought lodged in Ceridwen's mind, repeating over and over.

"I truly don't know," Lydia said, recovering quickly.

A familiar tickling grazed her head and shoulders before moving on. But a moment later, it settled on her anew, crawling down her back with spiderlike fingers. And she knew. She knew without looking who had entered the hall.

Chapter 27

Drystan

Attending the winter ball was a terrible idea. Drystan still couldn't quite figure out how Malik had talked him into it, though deep within, he knew it had something to do with the lovely young woman he'd spied across the ballroom.

She hadn't written to him. Had not responded to his letter nor shown up at the manor's gate as he'd secretly hoped. And where his cousin was often not to be trusted, in Drystan's recent experiences, he'd been right on this account. Ceridwen attended the ball.

By some twisted blessing of the Goddess, it was a masquerade, an excuse to hide his face, and Malik's, lest anyone recognize them and it cause a stir. Drystan had chosen an elaborate mask shaped like a bird of prey. Fanciful grays wings stretched out to either side of his face, the beak covering his own nose. Malik wore a cat mask, complete with golden whiskers that glinted in the light. Entirely too fitting given his playful amusement at the whole affair, especially since it was his idea to attend.

But even if these people weren't sure exactly who strode into their midst, they'd garnered more attention within a minute than he'd hoped to receive all night.

They were strangers to these people who seemed to know one another well—finely dressed outsiders who caused a wave of whispers to spread out from them with each step into the room.

No matter. It was done. The damage of it he would deal with later. In that moment, there was only one person he wanted to see.

Ceridwen turned his way from where she stood with a gaggle of other young women. Despite the mass of bodies and yards between them, their eyes locked across the space. All at once, he was too warm in his tailored tailcoat. Such an effect she had without a word or touch.

Someone—her sister perhaps, by the look of her—whispered something to Ceridwen, who nodded, her focus never leaving him.

Whispers swarmed around Drystan and Malik.

"Someone's relative?"

"Those clothes." One woman gasped. "Could they be nobles? Nobles at a ball in Teneboure?"

No one knew. They didn't recognize their Lord Protector. But of course, they shouldn't with the way he kept to himself. Drystan relaxed his stance and pasted on an easy smile, attempting to look comfortable, at ease, as if this were a daily occurrence for him.

The crowd parted as Drystan and Malik strode into their midst. Despite the mass of people and the noise, the woman across the room consumed him. Every moment between them flashed like lightning through his mind.

And then she was there before him, frozen solid like a statue of ice, resplendent in layers of blue. He recognized the dress immediately as one he'd commissioned for her, and his chest swelled with delight at the way it accented her coloring and natural beauty. And of all the things for her to wear, she'd chosen the dress embroidered with shimmering silver birds, so like the one her dainty mask was meant to portray.

Ceridwen's sister grabbed her hand, trying to pull her away. To save her from him? *How quaint.*

"May I have the next dance?" Drystan gave a courtly bow and extended his hand to Ceridwen.

Some of the other young women nearby gasped, whispering among one another, but he only had eyes for one. It wasn't lost on him that they matched, her pale blue and little birds the feminine compliment to his hawkish mask and brocade vest under his coat of navy. Dark and light. Predator and song bird.

He held his breath, waiting to see what she would do, fearful she might flee out into the cold night.

Finally, she slid her hand from her sister's and extended it to Drystan. "You may."

Thank the Goddess. Drystan closed the meager distance and took her hand in his. Despite the gloves he wore, his heart gave an involuntary leap when they touched. He relished in the feel of her dainty hand in his.

Someone nearby gave a dramatic, swooning sigh. Another woman giggled. This night, this moment, would be the topic of gossip for days to come, but right then he couldn't make himself care.

Malik slid into the space next to him, his attention focused on Ceridwen's sister. "May I have the honor?" he asked, extending a hand.

Bronwyn looked him up and down slowly, her frown deepening all the while. "No, thank you." She turned in a flash of skirts and pushed through nearby spectators, moving away from them.

Drystan didn't fight the grin managing to break free. Malik rejected. What a rare thing.

Malik stood dumbstruck, his hand still outstretched toward Bronwyn's retreating back. He recovered in a flash, reeling in his hand as he threw his head back and laughed, but Drystan knew it was likely an act to cover his embarrassment. Malik always had easy luck with the ladies. It wasn't like one to reject him so bluntly.

Other women jumped into the space to offer their hand in the dance, but Malik ignored them all as he turned and walked away, his smile blinding. Perhaps he was amused by the rejection rather than offended. Who could really tell where he was concerned?

But that wasn't the important thing now. Drystan slid an arm around Ceridwen's waist, earning a small gasp. The intimate gesture wouldn't go unnoticed, but the risk was worth it to hold her close and savor the feel of her in his arms.

The band struck up a new tune, slower and less festive than the ones they'd played before. It was perfect—a tune that wouldn't require him to pass off his companion to others or bounce around like some fool.

"Why did you come here?" Ceridwen whispered, her eyes wide.

"Isn't that obvious?" He let the pleasure of her presence drift to his face, his eyes, hoping she could see it despite the mask.

She glanced away. "Among so many people..." How sweet that she worried for him.

"You look lovely tonight." His comment drew her attention back to him. "Besides, would you have met me otherwise?"

She stumbled in the dance, but Drystan covered her error and kept them moving. It pained him that she might have kept him waiting, possibly forever—all the more reason he was glad he came.

"People will talk. They'll know," she said.

"Worth the risk." He rubbed her side through the fabric of her dress. "Besides, I don't have long left. Not here."

Ceridwen's hand flinched on his arm and she winced, almost like she took a painful step.

"Your leg?" he asked, suddenly concerned he'd done far more damage as his beast than he knew. Any was too much, but to cause her daily pain would be an unbearable torment.

"It's fine. You came here just to see me?" she asked before he could press her on it.

"Yes. And to ask you something."

Her breath hitched, and she nearly stumbled again.

"You read my letter?" he asked before twirling her around in a grand swirl of skirts. Upon her return to his arms, she nodded.

"Then give me the chance to explain in person. Come back to me, Ceridwen."

The agony of his monstrous form was easier to suffer than the wait for her answer. He spun her again, as the song required, before drawing her back to him.

Ceridwen's expression broke as she rested her palm on his upper arm. "Drystan..." Her chest heaved. Her brows pinched as she halted mid-dance. The oncoming rejection tried to break him, and he couldn't let it, not here.

Drystan gently tugged her toward the side of the dance floor. People closed in around them, likely hoping to take one or the other's place, but he didn't give them time to offer.

"Let's talk outside," he said as he laced his fingers through hers and headed for the main door. If she were going to carve his heart out, it wouldn't be in this room of strangers.

"The back." Ceridwen led him the other way.

A wise suggestion. It would be quieter there with fewer people to witness his failure. The crowd parted for them as they went, conversations halting and then restarting with fervor in their wake.

A flurry of snowflakes swirled around them as they exited the back door. The crisp, wet smell of the falling snow rushed into his lungs, calming him. A gentle breeze tugged at a few tendrils of hair that had escaped Ceridwen's hairdo and sent them caressing her exposed neck.

She'd be cold out here. He wouldn't have long.

Only a few others gathered around the back entrance, mostly men smoking pipes and rolled cigars while muttering to each other without paying them any mind. Two oil lamp sconces near the door provided the only light other than what slipped out the window panes or filtered through the clouds from the moon above.

"Are you all right? Truly?" he asked. She'd claimed to be fine, but her voice had lacked conviction.

She stepped away from his embrace and wrapped her arms around herself. "I've endured worse. As you can see, I walk just fine."

Indeed, she did, but still, he couldn't forgive himself for the pain he caused her—physical and non.

"You should never have suffered at my hand," he whispered. "For that, I am forever shamed. But your music helps me more than you know." He closed the distance between them, wishing to pull her into his arms and barely holding himself back. "It keeps...*me* in check. Even your voice. I pushed it too far, tried too much. I thought with you there that I had enough control, but I was wrong. Please, give me another chance, just until midwinter."

She turned away again, hugging her arms more closely around herself. Snowflakes fell on her exposed skin, melting immediately, though a few clung to her hair. Drystan hastily unbuttoned his coat and shrugged out of it. If she wouldn't let him hold her close, at least he could warm her in this way. He draped the coat around her shoulders, causing her to gasp softly and turn within the cage of his arms.

"You'll freeze," she protested, reaching for the edge of one lapel.

He settled his palms on her shoulders, holding the coat in place. "It doesn't matter."

"But it does." Her throat bobbed as she looked up at him from under her lashes. "To me."

And just like that, she shattered him in an entirely different way than he expected.

"Ceridwen." He cupped her cheeks, framing her face within his grasp.

Hesitantly, she drew closer, the space between them vanishing until the front of his coat pressed against his shirt. He should be cold in just that, but with her so close, he'd never been more content.

"Drystan." Her eyes fluttered closed, and his heart nearly stopped.

He leaned in, intent to savor the gift of her kiss until a loud voice boomed behind him, "Step away from my sister!"

CHAPTER 28

DRYSTAN

T HE FINE HAIRS ON the back of his neck rose. Ceridwen gasped, her eyes flying open. She made to step away from him, but he cocooned her in his arms, holding her close from the threat at his back.

His monster roared within him, echoing his own fury at the untimely interruption. Drystan turned his head just enough to take in the sight of Ceridwen's brother. His mask had been cast off at some point, leaving his dark hair slightly mussed, a match for the anger flashing in his dark eyes. Other men flooded out of the back exit behind him, and one woman—her sister, Bronwyn.

Worse than the crowd forming outside the hall was the object in Adair's hand. A sword. Drystan's lips nearly pulled back from his teeth in a snarl. The boy had no idea what fury he tempted.

"Stay out of this, Adair," Ceridwen demanded with as much fire in her voice as he'd heard the night she met Malik.

In this, they were aligned. *Good*.

Her brother ignored her, but Bronwyn didn't. Something that might have been regret flashed across the young woman's features before she retreated a few steps.

So she had informed their brother about Ceridwen's whereabouts. His jaw stiffened. What else had she told him?

"This wannabe Lord Protector only appears to flirt with the ladies," Adair said. Some of his words were slurred, and now Drystan could make out the hint of a flush on his cheeks.

A hothead and a drunk. A terrible combination, especially in someone who knew his title.

"I'll handle this," Drystan whispered to Ceridwen before releasing her from his embrace and positioning himself between her and her brother. To Adair, he said, "Go back inside before you embarrass yourself further. You forget your place."

If he had any sense left, he'd take the warning.

"Oh? And where is that? At least I protect this city. We all do." He gestured to the men around him. Friends in the city watch? One could barely stand. Drystan huffed air through his nose. What a pitiful group they made. "What have you done for this city that's not to please yourself?" Adair continued.

Drystan wrestled for control of his fury, using the last shred of his calm to don the casual attitude he'd worn when he entered the damnable ball. He raised his chin and forced a smirk to his lips. "I keep the monster at bay."

"Hah." Adair slapped his leg in mock amusement. Grins spread across the faces of some of the other men. "Yes, the monster, the one few have ever seen. I'm sure one rabid wolf gives you much trouble. I think I could take it easily. One swing of my blade." He swung the sheathed sword in a slow arc.

They truly had no idea that the monster could take them all down with ease. Drystan clenched his hand into a fist at his side, even as he kept his casual facade in place.

Ceridwen had stepped away from him, forming an odd triangle between the three of them. Her sister had found her, coming to her side instead of the men. But whose side would Ceridwen take? He appraised her from the corner of his eye. She hadn't spilled his secret yet, that he knew of, though she'd had days to do so.

Would she now? Something dark within him demanded she try it. Let her join him or condemn him. Either way, the agony of her indecision had to end.

Drystan turned his head to stare at Ceridwen, pinning her with his gaze and twisted smile. "A wolf, you say?" he said with an even calm. "Ask your sister. She saw it last."

Bronwyn clutched her arm, pressing in against his coat that her sister still wore. The men waited for her response as he expected they would.

But Ceridwen paid them no mind. She looked only at Drystan as she said, "It's true. He protects us all."

A shudder racked his form, desire surging between his legs. In that moment, he wanted nothing more than to lift her into his arms, carry her away, and show her exactly how much her words meant to him, propriety be damned.

"Ah yes, he protects us all," Adair slurred, ruining his daydream. "And that's why he made a certain deal with you."

The slander implied in those words made him snarl. "How dare—"

"Adair, go back inside before you embarrass us!" Bronwyn shouted over him.

Normally, such an interruption would be unwelcome, but this one gave him the moment he needed to think. He had one chance, this chance, to save Ceridwen's reputation, and he'd be damned before he failed her again. "Your sister had a close encounter due to my failure," Drystan replied, raising his voice so no one would dare miss it. "I sought to ease her burdens, and that of your entire family, in compensation for my error. Surely you cannot take issue with that."

"And what about the rest of us? You're supposed to protect us all, yet that *thing* still haunts the night," one of the men shouted.

"I've been ill. Ceridwen"—he looked at her for emphasis—"has been able to heal my ailment better than any medic I have come across. She is invaluable to me," he added, letting emotion flood his eyes and hoping she saw it, that she understood. He glanced at the men. "Unfortunately, I require further treatment while I am here, which is why I have requested her continued service. Such an honor it is for a commoner to aid a noble." His gaze shifted to land squarely on Adair. "Your house is brought higher by her service and care."

"Now, this is a sight." Malik whistled as he joined the growing group of onlookers standing to one side, Bronwyn and Ceridwen at their front.

Goddess, help me. Drystan groaned. The night could scarcely get worse.

"Who are you?" Adair practically spit, having lost any regard for class or station.

Malik raised his hands in the air. "An interested party? Ladies," he said to the sisters, inclining his head in a courtly nod. The scathing look Bronwyn shot him could have stripped paint. How he offended her, Drystan had no idea, but it was the least of his worries at the moment.

"Enough of your excuses." Adair pulled the sword from its sheath and tossed it away. "Let's see who's more of a man. Duel me!"

"Stop it!" Ceridwen rushed between them, turning this way and that to look at them both. "This is nonsense!"

"I won't hurt him," Drystan promised. *Much*, he added silently. The man was deep into his cups. Besting him would be easy. And for Ceridwen's sake, if nothing else, he'd make sure her brother suffered no lasting ill effects.

Malik smirked, enjoying the scene way more than he should. Another man hustled forward from behind Adair, offering Drystan a sword, which he accepted.

Ceridwen grabbed at his sleeve. "Drystan, please."

The pleading look on her face made him want to give her anything, but he needed to teach her brother a lesson. "Trust me." He pulled away from her touch. "Stay with your sister."

Drystan loosened his cravat and rolled up his sleeves, but kept his mask in place as he faced Adair in the falling snow. The young man had shirked his coat, tossed it to a nearby friend, shed his cravat completely, and rolled up his sleeves as well.

"Last chance to reconsider," Drystan offered.

"Preparing to lose already?" Adair ran his hand through his snow-dampened hair, mussing it up worse than before.

Adair raised his blade and charged with a reckless lack of caution, roaring like a warrior on the battlefield.

Drystan chuckled as he sidestepped, easily dodging the onslaught without the need to parry. Adair skidded to a halt on the snow-slicked ground before whirling around like an angry bull, reading for a charge once more.

Even sober, Adair would stand little chance against him. Drystan had years of lessons in sword fighting, and though it had been some time since he'd had to use such skills, the sword felt as natural and easy in his grip as it ever had, old honed instincts returning to him like a hound called home.

With a grunt, Adair pushed a stray strand of hair from his face. He regripped the blade, took a few quick steps forward, and swung. This time, Drystan blocked the blow with his sword. Metal sang in the air before Drystan flicked the opposing blade away.

Another swing yielded a similar result. And another. The young man's swordplay was sloppy at best, wide swings projected far in advance with little skill and less grace. He'd stab himself before ever landing a solid blow.

Another young woman dressed in white ran to Ceridwen's side—a friend, possibly—letting out something caught between a gasp and shriek as she spied the duel.

Adair charged again, aiming to skewer Drystan on the point of his sword. Instead, Drystan deflected the blade and twisted around, sending his opponent lunging several steps toward the growing crowd.

Adair stilled as he spied the new onlooker. A young woman he desired? Drystan blew a huff of air through his nose. If so, this sordid display surely wouldn't help his chances.

Drystan adjusted his stance. The young man hesitated, distracted from his opponent. It would be an easy opportunity to end this nonsense, but that would likely enrage Adair more and earn Drystan no favors with Ceridwen. Instead, he waited.

With a grunt, Adair whirled. Eyes wild, he stalked to his opponent and swung with both hands clenched around the hilt. His poor form, not to mention his attitude, would have offended his commanding officer, especially if they knew who he fought.

If this continued, it would ruin Adair and possibly cost him his position.

This time, Drystan pulled his blade back before he swung it into Adair's oncoming attack. A hush spread across the crowd as Drystan's blade sent Adair's flying from his hands and skidding across the snow-covered ground.

"Enough," Drystan said, his breath fogging in the cool air.

But the fool wasn't done. He moved in a flash, attempting to land a kick to Drystan's stomach. A mistake. Instead, the move unsettled his stance. His arms flailed in the air. A short curse left Adair's lips, and with a slip and crash, the young man landed unceremoniously on his back upon the icy ground.

A deep groan filled the air as Adair attempted to rise before submitting to the ground.

"Idiot," the young woman in white shouted, tears glistening in her eyes before she fled into the hall. Ceridwen watched her go, frowning all the while.

Too bad she hadn't chosen a wiser beau or one who could handle his drink.

Adair's friends helped him to his feet as Drystan crossed the space to Ceridwen. Congratulations and shouts of praise rang out from other citizens who'd been drawn by the scuffle, but he only had eyes for one, and she stood silent, that pinched and sorrowful expression stuck to her features.

"Pity. Things were just getting fun." Malik shrugged as he approached. The movement showed off his silken shirt to great effect. At some point, his coat had disappeared too. It didn't take long for Drystan to spy it wrapped around Ceridwen's sister, Bronwyn. She'd rejected his offer to dance but not his coat. How very odd. Drystan's brow arched as he looked from her to Malik. His cousin's smirk broadened, and he fought the urge to roll his eyes. Whatever happened, he'd clearly missed something.

"I'll give you a ride home," Drystan offered, turning to the sisters. "Both of you."

"Thank you," Ceridwen replied. Her focus wasn't on him, but rather something or someone behind him.

Drystan looked over his shoulder in time to see Adair regain his footing. He stared at them, his gaze briefly catching Drystan's before flitting away. In that brief moment, though, he caught the regret in his eyes...and the shame.

Good. Hopefully he learned a lesson this night. Most would not have been so lenient.

The carriage ride back to the sisters' home passed in mostly terse, uncomfortable silence. No one seemed apt to speak, and the conversation he desperately needed to have with Ceridwen wasn't one he wished to have in front of her sister or Malik.

The only bit of amusement during the chilly ride was Malik's obvious looks of interest toward Bronwyn and her equally scathing appraisals in return. Ceridwen, meanwhile, seemed not to notice any of them as she stared at nothing out the window.

Once the carriage rolled to a stop, the men hopped out first and offered assistance to the women.

"Here." Bronwyn unwrapped herself from Malik's coat and held it as far away from her as her arm would allow. Her nose wrinkled when he didn't immediately accept it, as if the thing repulsed her. It hadn't when she'd huddled in its warmth the whole ride home, sitting as far from him as possible in the tight carriage.

"Happy to be of service, my lady." He accepted it with a flourish and a smile. If Drystan didn't know better, he might think his cousin genuinely interested in the young woman. But the cousin he knew flirted with just about everyone who crossed his path, and he couldn't recall him ever settling on one long enough to truly care, especially not one who rebuked him—not that such a thing often happened.

With a harrumph, Bronwyn turned and stormed off into the house without a backward glance. Not for the men or her sister who still stood in the snowy street. Malik laughed and returned to the carriage, leaving Drystan alone with Ceridwen at the bottom of the short stairs to her house.

"You'll think about my question?" he asked.

He held his breath as Ceridwen slowly slipped his coat from her shoulders, taking care not to let any of it touch the ground.

"I already have." His tailcoat hung from her arms, untouched, as Drystan took in her impassive face.

He braced for the worst, for the doom certain to spill from her lips in the next second. His jaw worked as he took the garment without a word. The mask still adorned his face, and he was grateful for the meager shield to hide the impact of her impending rejection.

With the coat secured around him once more, Drystan took her hand in his. "I'm glad I got to see you one last time." The chaste kiss he placed on the back of her hand was a mockery of all the longing he still possessed.

"Last time?" she whispered.

The question hung frozen in the air between him. Drystan stiffened as his eyes flew wide, his heart lurching against his ribs.

"I'll come to the manor in the morning." Her gaze flitted away before landing back on him. "We'll talk. If that's okay with you," she hurried on.

"Ceridwen." Warmth tingled through him, as if she'd lit a candle in his chest on that dark night.

"That's all I can promise for now." She pulled her hand from his. "You'll see me again," she said with a weak smile before she turned, rushed up the short steps, and entered the house.

It wasn't the easy agreement he'd prayed for, but it was a chance, a hope—so much more than he truly deserved.

CHAPTER 29

CERIDWEN

CERIDWEN AND BRONWYN STOOD at the imposing manor gates in the morning sunlight. The day had dawned crisp and clean. A fresh layer of white powder covered the ground, which they'd disturbed on their short trek. A few gray birds scratched at the snow on the other side of the gate, trying to get at the ground below.

"Are you sure you want to do this?" Bronwyn asked, looking over at her sister.

Telling Drystan goodbye would have been easier. It would hurt. It might cut out a part of her heart that would never grow back. But facing down his monster, his darkness? That could crush her even more. Her family could still use the money, though, especially since Adair's foolishness could cost his job. And she needed...something. A sense of life and passion she'd lost somewhere along the way. Gwen said she made Drystan more like the young man he used to be, and perhaps he did the same for her, too, in a way.

Was she sure? *No.* But she'd regret it forever if she didn't come. That much she knew. "He's coming now." Ceridwen tilted her head to the approaching butler, avoiding her sister's question.

Jackoby, dressed in a jacket of navy blue and silver, strode through the yard in more haste than usual, walking down a path from the manor doors to the gate where the snow had been scraped away in preparation for visitors.

"Miss Ceridwen," Jackoby announced as he reached for the key always secured inside his jacket. The barest hint of a smile pulled at his lips. "We are quite pleased by your return."

"We'll both be coming in." Ceridwen motioned between Bronwyn and herself. If she returned to Drystan's employ, it would be on her terms.

She expected an argument or a stern reminder that Lord Winterbourne did not allow guests. Instead, Jackoby nodded and swung the gate wide to permit them entry. "Very well. I'll see you both to Lord Winterbourne's study."

Ceridwen blinked, dumbfounded. Since before dawn, she'd practiced her argument to permit Bronwyn entry as well, yet she didn't need it. One hurdle crossed without a fight.

Without another word, they entered the gate and waited for Jackoby to lock it behind them before following him inside. The manor reminded Ceridwen of how it had been on her first visit. Clean. Ornate. Dark. But most of all, quiet. Lifeless.

Somehow, she expected it to be as she'd left it, but the spark of life she'd found and nurtured within these walls had vanished in her short absence. Ceridwen searched every hall and doorway they passed for signs of the people she knew, yet they came across no one. Not until they reached the study.

Jackoby rapped three times on the door before a muffled confirmation sounded within. A knot twisted in her stomach. Her throat grew tight. Ceridwen hadn't been nervous...until now. Suddenly, she wanted to run, but she'd come this far.

Her choice slipped away when the door opened.

The curtains were drawn, as they nearly always were, leaving the room shrouded in darkness pocketed by flickering oil lamps spaced around to provide light. This room remained much how she remembered it, with its smattering of fine furnishings, shelves with assorted books and items, a mammoth writing desk, and more space than anyone truly needed in a study.

"Missed me already?" Malik reclined in a cushioned armchair like a reckless boy, his legs thrown over one armrest and his back propped against the other.

Bronwyn froze, her lips drawing into a thin line. Ceridwen winced, feeling the tension in the room press tight around her.

"Malik..." Drystan sat near him, two glasses of dark liquid on the low table between them.

"Ah, right. I promised you some privacy." He rose in one fluid movement, stretching his arms over his head as he crossed the distance to the sisters. "You're welcome to visit any time," he said to Bronwyn. "Even if this one says no." He hiked a thumb at Drystan before departing with Jackoby.

Everything Ceridwen planned to say fled her mind as soon as the door clicked shut. The room grew smaller, despite its impressive size, and for all the world, she couldn't make her legs cross the room to the seating area that he occupied. Drystan's gaze had not left her from the moment she entered the room. Nor now, as he rose and relocated the glasses near a silver pitcher on a far table.

Bronwyn coughed lightly into her hand. The sound brought Ceridwen back to the moment. Bronwyn stared at her, brows raised.

We're here for a reason, right? She could almost hear her sister's silent words.

When Ceridwen still didn't make a sound, Bronwyn spoke up. "Our apologies for our brother's actions last night, Lord Winterbourne. He can be quite troublesome."

Understatement.

"I've dealt with much worse," Drystan replied. "Would you both like to have a seat?" He gestured to the collection of chairs surrounding the table where he and Malik had been sitting.

A seat. Yes, I can do that. Her legs complied before her mind fully processed the request, gliding her along the fine carpets to the chair nearest Drystan's. The leather hugged Ceridwen into its embrace as she reclined in the deep brown chair, trying to keep her hands still while they yearned to twist in the fabric of her dress.

Bronwyn raised her brows again. She'd come for moral support, not to lead this discussion.

The knot in her throat tried to block her speech, and Ceridwen had to swallow it down. "I've come to discuss your request."

The quiet intensity of Drystan's steady gaze urged her to continue.

"If I return," Ceridwen began, "I want to be able to leave to visit my family. I want them to visit too."

Drystan's lips thinned. "Your brother?"

She winced. "Perhaps not him. But what about my sister?"

Bronwyn shifted her gaze to him as well, reminding him of her presence.

Drystan steepled his fingers and reclined in the chair. Ceridwen could practically see his mind working behind the blue eyes that skewered her to the leather. "You know how I feel about..." He pursed his lips, but she knew what word he omitted. *Outsiders.*

Stepping gently around certain topics wouldn't help with this discussion. Ceridwen took a deep and steadying breath, smoothed out her dress, and stated simply, "She knows about the monster."

A sharp gasp filled the silence. His eyes flew wide. Drystan stood and began pacing back and forth, his hands moving in motions that made no sense but spoke volumes. "Ceridwen. You—" He rubbed his hands down his face.

She hugged her arms around herself. "We've kept your secrets. We won't share them."

"No one can know." Drystan's voice had all the softness of steel as he looked between the sisters. "Whatever you witness in this manor, whatever you learn, it cannot leave."

"And should anyone ask?" Bronwyn said, completely unruffled.

The hard stare Drystan gave Ceridwen's sister might have sent some people running, but Bronwyn merely cocked her head to the side and waited.

"You'll tell them you saw me little, if at all," he said. "Tell them that I don't like company and prefer to keep to myself," he said. "Tell them it's for my health and exertion from keeping the monster at bay, but never tell them what you know."

She leaned forward now, showing the courage Ceridwen often wished she had. "And is it hard? Keeping the monster at bay?"

Bronwyn... Ceridwen groaned inwardly. Perhaps bringing her had been a mistake after all.

But Drystan did not bat away her question or demand she leave. "More than you can imagine."

The confession stripped the heat from Ceridwen's body. She needed to learn more about his transformation. Soon. Today. She pressed her lips together as she stared between them. "I think that—"

"One more question." Bronwyn cut her off, one finger raised as she glared at Drystan. "Will my sister be safe amid such difficulties?"

With a glare of his own and arms crossed in front of his chest, Drystan replied, "I wish I could promise that, but I can assure you, I'll do everything I can to keep her safe." The last part, he directed at Ceridwen.

The nerve, talking about her as if she were some child in need of coddling.

"I believe you, and that's what matters." Ceridwen jumped in before they carry on with their exchange. Her sister wanted the best for her, yes, but she could take care of herself too.

Bronwyn gave a brief nod and settled back into the chair, silent for now.

One discussion resolved, Ceridwen shifted her focus to Drystan. "If I'm to return to your employment, I need to know more about the monster." She pinned him with her steady gaze as he often did her. "What causes it to appear. How to prevent it. How you change back. Everything."

A muscle jumped in Drystan's clenched jaw. Eventually, he nodded, a move that disheveled some of the dark hair curling around his ear. "That's fair, but you and you alone shall know. Tell no one. Not your family, not Malik, nor any in the household.

Don't write any of it down. And no one, save you, shall enter my tower." His steely gaze slid to Bronwyn. "Not for any reason."

She crossed her arms but nodded.

"And my family will still receive payment for my services?" She couldn't forget that, no matter whatever else he'd provided or agreed to. Her father would need more medicine, which only money could supply. Despite her own worries and hesitations, his very life depended upon her actions. That certainty helped Ceridwen's lingering apprehension to slide into the background.

"Of course," Drystan replied.

A smile crept to her lips without thought. "Then I accept."

Ceridwen made to rise, but Drystan's quick reply held her down. "Wait."

The air rushed from her lungs as she slipped back into the leather.

"Take a walk with me first." He held out a hand to help her up. "I want to tell you more about my monster. You deserve to know that before you finalize your decision."

CHAPTER 30
CERIDWEN

W HEN THEY EXITED THE study, the halls were no longer empty. Gwen rushed up immediately, wrapping Ceridwen in a tight hug. Kent stood nearby, a broad smile on his face. Even Jackoby looked pleased.

"Oh, we're so glad you've returned," Gwen said, nearly squeezing the breath from her lungs. She drew back to look her up and down. "I'm so terribly sorry about what happened before. I worried you'd never forgive us."

In truth, she hadn't, not fully. They'd lied to her. She understood now that they'd done it to protect their lord, the one they'd served for years in some cases. However, their defense of him did not fully erase the slight against her. Not that they owed her anything.

"It hasn't been fully decided yet," Drystan said, saving her from a response. "Though if Ceridwen agrees, Miss Bronwyn will be visiting us more often. Perhaps you could give her a quick tour of the manor while I talk with Ceridwen?"

Gwen switched to fussing over Bronwyn, much to her sister's discomfort, and led her off with the rest of the group. Drystan didn't say the destination he had in mind, but once they stepped into the spiral staircase, Ceridwen's suspicions were confirmed. Her chest rose and fell, one deep breath after another, as she willed herself onto the stairs. Thick silence hung between them, full of so many unsaid words and emotions. They continued up the steep stairs, past his living quarters, to the top floor of the tower.

The mess and destruction his monster had wrought were gone. Likely cleaned by Drystan's own hand unless he'd decided to finally let others in the tower. The stone altar sat empty. Orderly shelves lined the walls. The grand desk had been organized, and the shattered chair had been replaced with a new, slightly finer one carved to illustrate vines and plant life. A winter breeze stirred through the windows, though that wasn't what made her shudder and hug her arms about herself.

Ceridwen waited for the monster to reappear from the shadows, to leap at her, and try to tear out her throat. Logic did nothing to calm her fear as she hesitantly stared at Drystan. His eyes did not change, nor did his body shift and bend. He was simply Drystan.

For now.

"Ceridwen..." He reached for her, but she stepped away.

"What did you want to tell me?"

He sighed and walked to the opposite side of the altar. "I promised to explain, to tell you about the monster and what happens to me." He paused, placing his palms on the stone. "It's a side effect of my magic. When the Goddess gifted some of us with it generations ago, she did it in two forms. Light and dark."

Ceridwen nodded. Everyone knew the lore, at least anyone who bothered to read and learn it. Though even if they hadn't, everyone had heard stories of the former dark king who wielded darkness and how his son, King Jesstin Ithael, and Jesstin's queen, Manon, used the light to overthrow him. *Goddess grant them peace.* The Ithael line knew such extremes. Powerful darkness, but also powerful light.

"The magic that most everyone knows is the power of light. It heals, protects, strengthens, and many other things. But darkness..." Drystan continued. "It offers strength and power far beyond the light. But it's hard to control—the Goddess's punishment for giving into temptation, I suppose. When someone uses dark magic, it can become wild and control them—take on a life of its own." His eyes held a solemn truth he refused to speak.

Ceridwen's legs shook beneath her. *Oh Goddess...* Her hand flew to her mouth, holding in the horror threatening to crawl up her throat.

Somber resignation flashed across his features before he clenched shut his eyes. "And that's why I wanted to tell you before you agreed to stay."

She stumbled forward, gripping the edge of the altar for support. "Why?"

"I didn't want to deceive you into staying again when—"

"No." She shook her head. "Why use the darkness?"

He looked away and sighed. "I need the power it offers. Light magic alone isn't enough. But using dark magic stirs the monster within me. I could wake it on my own, give myself over to it to satisfy the dark urges under my skin. I do sometimes. But if I don't, and I dip too much into the dark ways, the monster wakes whether I want it to or not."

"But why do you need it?" He was a noble already. Powerful. Wealthy.

"Revenge." His gaze turned steely, hard as the frozen ground. "My family was murdered. My reputation destroyed."

Her heart skipped a beat. She hadn't known, had no idea. But it made sense—the terrible kind that stirred a desperate ache deep within. Why else would such a young lord hold the title himself rather than his father or another more senior relative? Why would he be here with only servants for company if any close family were still living?

Drystan looked away, out at the wintery landscape beyond the window. "I intend for the one responsible to pay dearly, but the power of light alone will not be enough. They wield the darkness, and only with the power of darkness and light can I hope to craft the blade that can kill the demon lurking in the capital."

Darkness in the capital, like the rumors said. A shiver racked her. "Surely the king..."

He turned to her, his features grave. "He knows."

Her legs would no longer hold her. Ceridwen slid to the ground, her back against the stone as his words threatened to drown her, to unseat everything she thought she knew.

The king knew...and did nothing. Bad enough that he taxed the people to death, but to bless the use of darkness and the death of innocents at its hands? Unthinkable.

"Ceridwen!" Drystan crouched before her, his hands on her face. "I'll take you home. We can discuss the rest another day."

She placed a palm over his hand, holding it to her cheek and sending a little shudder through him that she couldn't miss.

"No." There was no turning back. No running from this. "Tell me now. All of it."

"Are you sure?" He stroked her cheek again, and despite all that she had learned, her greatest wish at that moment was to continue to feel his skin against her own. His nearness sparked a fire deep within her more terrifying than the truth he shared. It threatened to burn away everything else until only they were left.

"Yes." Whatever else there was to hear, she needed to know it.

Drystan nodded and withdrew his hand. "If I don't destroy the one leading the darkness, it will spread. It has too much already. Disappearances. Murders. Victims missing blood. I can't let that happen. I won't."

The cloud of darkness spreading from the capital was a real one, and no one tried to stop it, not even the king. No one, except possibly the city's very own monster.

"That's why you're going to the capital at midwinter?"

"I'm required back anyway. But yes, once I'm there, I'll end this or die trying."

Tears burned the corners of her eyes, blurring her vision. "I don't want you to die." Her truth. "Stay."

He wiped away a tear that slipped free to trickle down her cheek. "Every time I look at you, I want to." He gave the smallest hint of a smile that didn't quite reach his eyes. "But the things I've done... They're unforgiveable already. Even more so if I were to run. I couldn't live with myself."

What had he— But she didn't need to ask. She knew. His monster had killed. She'd seen it with her own eyes.

Grief surrounded her, a familiar, if unwanted, companion. Her actions had led to a death, her mother's, and the guilt of it plagued her every day. How much more did the death he'd caused with fang and claw haunt his steps?

Guilt was a wicked burden on both of their hearts.

"Blood fuels magic. My own"—he lifted his hand, reminding her of the scars that marred it—"and others. And dark magic..." He pulled back from her, sitting on the ground a foot away. "It's not enough just to wield shape and blood. True dark magic requires something more. The consumption of it."

His words did not immediately register, the thought so foreign and strange. When they did, bile burned the base of her throat.

This time, he didn't reach for her, but the feeling of his eyes on her never faltered, despite the panic threatening to rip her apart.

Blood.

He drank blood.

Like some beast or wild animal. No one knew. She'd never heard of such a thing. Or had she? Somewhere in the back of her mind, a song called to her. Familiar, but just out of reach. In her panic, she couldn't think, couldn't sort through the memories to find that lyric.

"It's not wine that you drink in your study, is it? Even this morning, you and Malik..."

He nodded.

"Does he become a monster too?" One monster unnerved her enough. If there were a second... She shivered.

"Not that I have seen. But that doesn't mean much. I haven't seen Malik paint or cast a spell in years, but his father... He favors the darkness. It seems likely that influence may have spread to him."

Ceridwen squeezed her eyes shut. Another wielder of darkness. One who'd set his eyes upon her sister. Just when she thought she couldn't dislike him more.

The cool stone behind her back gave odd comfort. Of all the men in the kingdom, she'd fallen for one who became a monster, one determined to die for his revenge.

Running would have been easier. Or shunning him and never looking back.

But somewhere along the way, she'd unwillingly given him a part of herself. Never seeing him again would mean losing that part forever.

A tear leaked down her face. "Can you win?" she whispered.

"There's always hope." His voice reflected little of it.

"What can I do?"

"Your music helps me. I can't explain it, but it soothes the monster. If you play for me, I might be able to control it long enough to finish the blade." He rose, movement stiff as if his very body ached, and crossed to one of the shelves.

The object he selected did not stand out among the rest. Others held more sparkle and grandeur or more sense of mystery and macabre. The blade he carried to the altar lacked any adornment, all gray metal without shine or frill. The blade itself was shorter than Ceridwen's forearm, with a simple hilt crossing perpendicular to the blade just above the grip wrapped in plain strips of brown leather.

"The Gray Blade." He laid it with reverence upon the altar as she rose to stand near his side. "Or it will be, if I can complete it."

In this position, she recognized the blade from the last time she'd stood there. Then it had been encircled in patterns of blood.

"You need magic to complete it? I think you were working on it when I came here last."

"Yes. If I can finish it, the blade should nullify the magic of anyone it pierces, though no one has seen a completed one for an age. It's my best hope."

She nodded numbly, examining the blade. "What if I played for you while you work?"

"No." The refusal was quick and definite, shaking in the air between them. "It's too dangerous. If the beast were to emerge anyway—" He shook his head.

But he was almost out of time. Her family had always looked forward to midwinter. The darkest and coldest of days. Once it passed, they would begin the countdown to spring, half the winter gone by. Despite the long night, the day gave hope to people far and wide that warmth and sunlight would bless them once again. But what was a joyous day for most wouldn't be to him. It was a deadline. An ending. Possibly a deadly one.

Lightning zipped up her arm when he closed his hand over hers. "I won't have your blood on my conscience too."

She placed her free hand over his, where it still rested on her other. "And I won't have yours on mine."

It was her choice, her life and fate. She'd stay. She'd help...as best she could.

CHAPTER 31

DRYSTAN

I N THE FEW DAYS since her return, Ceridwen settled back into life at the manor, livening the place up instantly. Though Drystan thanked the Goddess on his knees for her return to his life, he also guarded his optimism. It was impossible to miss the way she jumped at unexpected sounds or seemed to stay in her room more than she had before. When they were together, her gaze often drifted to any shadowy places in the room. He knew what she saw there—ghastly visions of his alternate self.

It would be easy to lie and tell her she would be safe, that his monster would never harm her. But though her voice had stopped him twice, he couldn't offer that false hope, no matter how much he wished it. It was best she stayed far away from him and from danger.

For that reason, he kept a careful distance between them and didn't invite her back into his tower. That, and he could never let Malik deduce what he worked on up there. His cousin believed Ceridwen a romantic intrigue, and that was far safer than him knowing the effect her music had on his monster.

Ceridwen still played for him each night, usually alone, though sometimes during the day, she would play for him too, usually with Malik and some of the staff in attendance. He hadn't known how many of his servants had lingered in the halls to hear her songs, but the confessions had slipped out slowly during her absence, the loss felt by many. It cheered Drystan to see those he cared for enjoy her music, and Ceridwen was more than happy to play for them as well. One evening, she even disclosed to him a secret dream from her youth of being a musician beloved by the masses. If he could make her dream happen, in even this little way, he wanted to. Whatever comfort and joy he could give her before he left for the capital, he owed her.

That was one reason he allowed her sister to visit and Ceridwen to leave the manor and visit her family as well. Drystan had been tense during the duration of Bronwyn's visit for tea the day before, but the young woman had come and gone without issue. Even Malik gave the sisters peace to enjoy one another's company. Recent news from the mayor's office said that her brother's unit had been deployed to the capital for the remainder of the season and through spring. Something about a training rotation. Drystan thanked the Goddess not to have the young man around to stir up more trouble, but he couldn't hold back the pesky bit of worry that clung to the shadows of his mind. If anything happened to him, Ceridwen would be devastated.

That morning, Drystan had retreated to his one oasis within the manor outside Ceridwen and her music. The rose garden within the greenhouse.

There was something refreshing about spending his time among the plant life, pruning the bushes into perfection, and getting a little bit of dirt under his nails in the process. As a child, his mother had often scolded him, declaring the hobby below his station and something that should be left to the servants. No matter her ire and his love for her, he couldn't quite abandon his passion for plants and making them grow. After her death, it was one of the few places that gave him peace. It was the same at this manor, and thankfully, no one tried to talk him out of it.

Drystan's acute hearing alerted him to someone's approach as he knelt among the roses, pruning away a cluster of browning leaves off a bush. A servant would have given him a clue of their approach, and Malik was never so quiet. His pulse picked up as he glanced over one shoulder and confirmed his suspicions.

Ceridwen looked resplendent in the morning light filtering in from the glass roof overhead. She wound her way through the rows of vegetables that supplied fresh food for the manor even in the depth of winter.

"Ceridwen." A grin stretched his features before he set his clippers aside and rose to his feet.

She smiled in return, an act that sent his heart kicking against his ribs. That she could still look at him that way, even knowing what lurked beneath his skin, was a miracle in itself.

"The roses look lovely," she said, coming to stand near him.

The hint of a frown tugged at his expression. "Mostly, but something has been bothering them lately. Look here."

A few brown leaves and stems marred the bush of violet roses and several others nearby.

"They're still quite beautiful to me." She beamed. "You might be a perfectionist."

"Perhaps, though I usually don't have much trouble with these. It's warm inside. I fertilize them the same way." He shrugged. "I'm not sure what's making them look peaked." Drystan favored their unique color above the others and had brought them with him from the capital. He might have thought the transplant to blame, except they'd flourished under his care until recently. Perhaps they didn't favor the northern winter, despite the protection the greenhouse afforded them.

"What brings you to the gardens today?" he asked, shifting his attention from the blooms.

Her gaze skirted down the stone pathway before she looked at him again. "I hoped to see you."

Desperate longing filled him, its surge so sudden it took a moment to bring it under control. He cleared his throat, a poor attempt to rein in the flood of emotions. "Is there something I can do for you?"

"Bronwyn came for tea yesterday."

"Yes, I know. Did you enjoy her company?"

"I did it. It was lovely, but..." All at once, her look darkened. "She said that the monster was seen two nights ago."

He winced, his shoulders dropping. It was too much to hope she simply wanted to spend time with him. "I slipped while working on the—my project," he corrected himself. Even here, he was careful not to reveal his secrets. "I remember bits and pieces. Scaring a group outside a pub. Spooking a horse or two. Did I..."

Goddess above. If he'd killed again, how could he face the shame and horror of it?

"No." She laid her hand upon his arm, stirring up a mess of feelings, but drew it back almost as quickly. "No one was hurt. But..." She pulled her bottom lip between her teeth. "I thought my music helped."

He took her hand in his, savoring the tingling that zipped between them. "It does help. More than I can express." He lowered his voice to barely a whisper. "But the spells I have left are difficult. Even with your help, I struggle to retain control. Without you, I wouldn't have a chance at all."

She closed the distance between them, wrapping her hand around his. "Then I'll play more. Longer. Whatever it takes."

"I don't deserve you." He cupped her cheek, savoring her soft intake of breath.

"But you do." She tilted her head into his touch. "You gave me a dream I thought impossible. To play music and aid my family. No one else has ever offered a gift so precious." A fragile smile broke across her face. "It took encountering a monster to give me something I love and turn my world upside down."

A monster. That he was, but for once, it didn't seem so terrible, not coming from her.

He leaned in until his forehead nearly touched hers. "Your presence helps too. Just spending time with you like this."

A hint of color rose to her cheeks. "Then perhaps you shouldn't spend so much time in your tower," she teased.

"A necessary sacrifice. Though one day..." His voice trailed off as he stared down into her eyes. If only he could promise her more, days where they could linger without the threat of his monster or the darkness spreading from the capital. That was the dream. One so fragile and unlikely he couldn't bring it into words.

But there was something he could do. Something he yearned for. Her eyelashes fluttered as he tugged her closer, his face leaning in, intent to take her mouth with his.

A piece of his heart splintered as she pulled away, popping the moment like a bubble.

"I could play now," she said, only half looking at him. "A few extra songs couldn't hurt."

"Couldn't hurt at all," Drystan replied with a mildly sarcastic grunt.

And just like that, the moment was gone. Ceridwen trailed away from him through the gardens, eager to get her flute and play her songs.

He'd wished for more, pushed the slightest bit, and she'd shrunk from him.

Drystan swallowed thickly, his footsteps leaden as he walked after her. Perhaps his monster had stomped out the fragile bloom that grew between them forever.

CHAPTER 32

CERIDWEN

Not kissing Drystan was a mistake. A terrible one. She wanted to kiss him again, yearned for it, but as he'd leaned in, the looming specter of his monster wrenched her away. She should have explained, should have leaped into his arms and kissed him herself, but like a coward, she'd walked away and used her music as a shield for her insecurity.

Guilt drove her into the greenhouse again the next day. She couldn't change the past, but if she was lucky, she might be able to redo the moment. Drystan loved his plants. If she had a chance of finding him anywhere outside his tower, it was there.

Today she wouldn't step away. Today she'd kiss him—if she had the opportunity.

But Drystan wasn't in the greenhouse when she arrived. No one occupied its glassy walls outside its permanent residents, the plants.

If I wait, maybe he'll come.

Ceridwen fingered the leafy fringe on a head of cabbage ripe for harvest. Perhaps tomorrow she could take it to her family. The green vegetable would surely brighten their day and provide a change from the thick stews and baked spuds Bronwyn had droned on about when she'd stopped by for tea. Though they had the coin now, such things were hard to find in the market this time of year.

A strangled sound snapped her reverie among the vegetables. She'd been alone in the greenhouse minutes ago, she was sure of it, but someone or something lurked beneath the canopy with her now. Someone she'd never heard enter despite her vigilance.

Muffled noises came again from her right, sending a shiver down her spine despite the heat of the blazing afternoon sun through the glass. A wide trellis covered in vines separated her from the sound and obscured the view beyond. The rose garden lay on the other side, the one Drystan had worked on so carefully the day before.

She recognized the sound as she drew around the edge of the rows of trellises.

Retching.

A dark form hunched among the roses. Masculine. Strong shoulders. Dark hair.

Not Drystan.

Recognition chilled her skin. Malik had seemed fine earlier in the day when she passed him briefly on the way out of the library, yet now he crouched bent over among the thorny bushes. Only one reason made sense. He held a monster as well, and now that monster rose to the surface, even in the light of day.

Fear urged her back, away from the monster about to spring to life. One step, two. Her back crashed into the trellis, rustling the leafy vines coating its surface. The racket carried through the otherwise quiet space like her flute on a cold winter's night.

Malik's head flew up, pinning her to the trellis with just a look. Something red, too much like blood to be anything else, coated his lips and dribbled down his chin. He stared her down in shock with wide eyes, unblinking, until another lurch rolled up his back and had him heaving a splash of watery crimson to the rich soil below.

Ceridwen bolted, running as fast as she could through the paths toward the door.

"Wait!" The strangled call sounded behind her.

But she didn't stop, couldn't stop.

A hand latched on to her arm, drawing her to a sudden, jarring halt between rows of vegetables. Ceridwen jerked against him.

"Please," Malik begged, voice gruff.

A scream crawled up her throat, but his hand clamped over her mouth as he drew her against his hard, still human body.

"Stop, just listen to me," he implored when she strained against him without avail. "I won't hurt you."

He hadn't, not yet, not truly. But she trusted a snake in the grass more than this man.

"Ceridwen, please, I need you to listen."

Something in his voice, the desperate plea, slowed her struggle. Malik always exuded calm arrogance—perfect control beneath a surface of cocky amusement. Even when Drystan had thrown him bodily across the room, he'd laughed it off as nothing. Yet now he begged, a touch of fear in his words as they rolled across her ears.

He loosed a deep breath that tickled her cheek as she finally stilled against his unmoving form. "If I let you go, don't scream, and don't run." His chest rose and fell against her back, far too intimate a position to be in with anyone, much less him. "Please."

She nodded, if for no other reason than to escape his scent, so like Drystan's, and the warmth that reminded her of other arms she wished to be held in.

Malik released his hold. Ceridwen stepped away and whirled on him fast enough to catch the smear of blood still clinging to his lips before he wiped it away with the back of his hand.

"What did you see?" he asked. His green eyes searched her like a puzzle, as if he stared hard enough he could pull the truth from her mind with his will alone. Perhaps his magic allowed that.

Despite her wariness, she replied, "You, retching blood into the roses."

Her back stiffened as silence hung in the air between them. Suddenly she knew the source of his fear, his panic. The greenhouse crashing down around her would have been less surprising.

She thought she knew this man. She was wrong.

"I see... Drystan's told you even more than I expected." He rubbed the back of his neck. "You know what drinking blood means for our magic?"

"Yes." She swallowed thickly. "It's necessary for dark magic."

Malik nodded, somber.

"And I've seen you drink it with him, but just now, you threw it up." The roses, just out of sight, pulled her gaze like a bonfire. Now she knew what bothered Drystan's favorite plants, what hampered their growth. But even more remarkably, an unexpected certainty settled into her—this man didn't practice dark magic. He couldn't without consuming the blood he tried to rid himself of.

"You can't tell him."

Her attention snapped to Malik.

"Everything depends on it. He can't know I vomit up the blood."

"Why not?" He wielded the light. Drystan sought to stop the darkness. In a way, they were on the same side.

"That look." He cocked his head to the side. "You know something."

Too much. More than he knew. She willed her features into neutrality despite the thoughts churning through her mind. Drystan didn't trust him with his secrets. But Drystan didn't know Malik's secret either. Somehow, she'd learned both. Not that it made it any easier to know what to do with them.

"Of course you do. He cares for you, perhaps more than anyone," he said.

This admission sent a flush of heat to her cheeks that muted the racing thoughts.

"But why do you care for him?" Malik asked.

"I—" she started, stepping back.

"You do, don't deny it. I see it, even if you refuse to admit it. You've seen the blood he drinks, and you know what that means. Even at that ball, I heard rumors of the monster who haunts this city. I know what he is. I know the darkness he wields, and so do you. However, I don't know why you still care for him despite that."

He'd begun to pace as he talked, looking her up and down with a piercing gaze that saw too much.

"He's more than a monster," she replied.

Malik halted and raised his brows. "Is he?" When she didn't respond, he started to pace once again. "What does he do in that tower all day?"

"I don't go in the tower." As close to the truth as possible.

He paused again, a small smile pulling at his lips. "You don't know, or you won't tell me? Fine, keep his secrets. Though I'll need you to keep mine as well."

"Why should I?" She had a certain loyalty to Drystan, but not to this man.

"I can make it worth your while. He pays you, right? What if I sent money for your family after he leaves, enough to ensure that you and your fiery sister want for nothing?"

The offer stole her breath away. Money had been her goal, her purpose in coming here. She couldn't begin to picture the amount of gold he offered. For her family to want for nothing... She'd never hoped for near so much.

"How do I know you'll keep your word?" she asked. As a noble, he could afford it. Maybe. But why give so much away for a secret she only needed to keep for a short time?

"Who am I?" he asked in return.

Her brows scrunched. A trick question. It had to be. But she couldn't work out the twist in it, so she said the first thing that came to mind. "Malik. Drystan's cousin."

He smirked, slinking closer until their boots almost touched. Ceridwen stiffened and fought down the urge to back away. *Too close. Too familiar.*

"That's the name you know, but everyone has more than one name. I think it will explain a great deal."

She sucked in a breath as he leaned in, his cheek nearly grazing hers.

His breath tickled her skin as he whispered, "Alistair Malikant Ithael."

He didn't give his title. He didn't need to.

Everyone knew the name of the prince of Castamar.

CHAPTER 33

DRYSTAN

CERIDWEN SAID LITTLE AT dinner, uncharacteristically distracted by something he couldn't place. Jackoby had informed Drystan that she'd left abruptly that afternoon to visit her family for tea, something she generally apprised him of in advance but hadn't mentioned during their time together the day before.

Perhaps he'd been too eager in his affections, too hopeful to reignite that spark of something that had blossomed between them before she'd discovered his secret. He wouldn't put it past the Goddess to taunt him by putting the only woman he desired so close, an unscalable wall wedged between them at the same time. He deserved no less, in truth.

Drystan had ventured questions about her family and if anything was amiss, but Ceridwen perked up at that, saying that they were quite well and that her father actually seemed to be as strong as he'd been in years. She'd even poured out her gratitude for the money he provided, which allowed for her father's medicine. Yet even in the line of that good news, her edginess remained. Perhaps it had something to do with her brother and his deployment, though they'd talked of that too, and it hadn't appeared to affect her mood one way or the other.

Malik did not join them for dinner either, as he had most nights since Ceridwen's return to the manor. In fact, he'd been curiously absent all afternoon, though Jackoby couldn't account for him leaving and venturing into the city.

Drystan mused over that quandary as Ceridwen played for him in his study after dinner. Could their behavior be connected? Had Malik dared to try something with her? But Ceridwen's behavior was much different than after Malik's unfortunate arrival and the incident that occurred between them. Then, she'd been scared and flustered. Now, she had a determined set to her shoulders, a fervor to her music.

Every night she poured her heart and soul into her music, bringing the sounds alive in a way that moved him deep within and even calmed his monstrous side. Tonight, however, she added a little something extra. When she finished her song and lowered the flute, her chest rose and fell. A hint of perspiration clung to her brow. Drystan fought the urge to rise to his feet and respond with thunderous applause. Instead, as she pried open her eyes once more, breathing hard, he gave a slow, appreciative clap.

"Lovely," he said, meeting her gaze. A smile pulled at her lips, matching his own. How anyone could not marvel at her music, he would never understand. "I wish I could listen longer, but I need to work a complicated spell tonight."

He was so close, more than he dare say, to completing the Gray Blade, and the power of her music tonight might be enough to keep his beast in submission. It lay down within him like a tame dog for her, content to be stroked into a restful state by each line of her song.

"For your project?" she asked, giving him a meaningful look as she placed her flute back in its case.

"Just so." He rose and crossed to the large windows. He'd left the curtains open this evening, letting in the dim rays of moonlight filtering between clouds. "You should stay in your room once you leave here tonight. And tomorrow…" He turned to Ceridwen as she rose to join him near the window. "Don't come looking for me if I don't leave the tower."

If the worst happened, if the music wasn't enough, he wouldn't have her in harm's way again.

Her eyes filled with concern as she stared up at him. "What if you don't change back? Or if someone in the city gets hurt?"

"Then it'll be one more horrible mark on my conscience." Without thinking, he caressed her face with the back of his hand. He'd swear she shivered as he jerked his hand away with a silent reprimand to himself, but she did not flee.

"Perhaps Malik can help you?" she asked.

Drystan huffed air through his nose. "He wouldn't help me. Especially not if he knew what I work on."

"Then let me play for you while you work the spell."

"No," he snapped, every muscle in his body going rigid. "It's too risky. You saw what I can become firsthand. If you were there and something happened—"

She cut off his words with a finger over his lips, and he nearly forgot how to breathe. "I know the risks." Her other hand grazed over the stubble on his cheek, sending a tremor under his skin. "Let me help you. Please."

The simple touch threatened to wreck him. Drystan held absolutely still, terrified of ruining the moment. "You do. More than you know. More than I could have hoped after all that happened between us."

Impossibly, she stepped closer, leaving barely any space between them. She grazed his chin with her fingertips, tracing the lines of an old scar down his jawline. The subtle scent clinging to her was more intoxicating than any wine, muddling his senses until his thoughts slipped free.

"Will you ever be able to see me as a man and not a monster?"

She leaned in, her bosom brushing his shirt, and he dared place a hand on her hip, cradling her close, savoring the closeness he believed long gone. The wait for her reply was agonizing, even more than the gentle glide of her pink tongue over her lip as she stared at him.

"I see only you."

Drystan's knees nearly buckled. Even in his best dreams, her reply had not been so generous. He tugged her forward until their bodies pressed together, only layers of cloth separating them. The intimacy of the position, the way she molded to him, sent a bolt of desire straight to his groin.

"I've dreamed of this," he confessed, voice thick. "Longed for it. To hold you in my arms, to kiss you again."

"Then do it." She caressed his face, brushing the ends of his hair with her fingertips.

The smallest hesitation held him back. He couldn't bear to push it, to lose her again. "Yesterday, you—"

"I was wrong. Scared. Uncertain. But I know now. I knew the moment I stepped away then, but it was too late. I want you."

I want you.

And oh, how he wanted her. As much as life itself. His body tingled as he closed his eyes and leaned his head down toward hers.

But just before their lips touched, she whispered, "Kiss me, Tristram."

He froze. His eyes flew wide. Drystan's heart leaped into his throat as he ripped away from the beauty before him and stared at her in horror.

CHAPTER 34

DRYSTAN

S HE STARED AT HIM wide-eyed, her mouth gaping open before she covered it with a delicate hand. "Oh, blessed Goddess, it's true."

He balled his hands into fists as he turned away from her and stared at the fireplace. "Tristram is dead."

Publicly executed for his crimes. Buried without ceremony. A fitting end for the monster he became.

Blood roared in his ears. His chest rose and fell. He never even heard Ceridwen approach until she laid a hand upon his back that caused every muscle in his body to stiffen.

"He's not," she whispered. "But I don't care about that. To me, you're Drystan, no matter what you were once called."

He slammed his eyes shut, fighting against the pain of that name and the monster rumbling once more under his skin. Drystan jerked away and crossed the room to fall into his customary chair, head in his hands.

She didn't even know his greatest sin and shame, but she knew enough, more than he'd ever wanted her to know. How? How could she have learned such a thing when he'd been so careful? Tristram was dead, Drystan Winterbourne reborn in his place. A noble sprung from the shadows to serve the king or receive the punishment he truly deserved, one that had been bestowed on some unfortunate man who bore a passing resemblance to him that the king had dug up to execute in his stead.

He was nothing more than a ghost, a shadow in an already dark world.

Where the king planned to wield him like a cruel blade for his own uses, and had, to his shame, only one thing gave him the courage not to lie down and die or accept the torment he so readily deserved: the chance at revenge.

Ceridwen was a beautiful light in the dark despair of his recent years. A bright spot amid all the grief, loss, and guilt that plagued him. She was so much more than a monster like him deserved, yet he'd been unable to stop yearning for that light, for the beauty of her spirit that shone through in her songs and smiles.

He gasped when Ceridwen stepped before him and placed her palms on his shoulders. She shoved him, forcing him to recline in the chair.

"Ceridwen—"

Before he could protest further, she hiked up her skirts and climbed atop his lap.

"Goddess above," he groaned.

"You can't run from me now unless you plan to tip me off onto the floor." Her words were near breathless, her chest rising and falling with breaths as heavy and uneven as his own.

He planted his palms on her waist, holding her in place. "We can't have that." Of all the things he'd damaged, he wouldn't let her be one of them.

If this was her reprisal for his secrets, her way of tormenting him, he'd gladly take it.

Once again, her tongue peeked out, moistening her lips as she stared him down. That act, along with her nearness, had his cock stiffening again despite her revelation moments ago.

"It's true?" she asked. Her gaze dipped to his chest where her fingertips scrunched the soft material of his shirt. "Are you really Prince Tristram?"

He swallowed the tightness in his throat. The moment she'd said that name, his eyes had flown open, and he'd seen the conviction in hers. The name, his old name, hadn't been a random question. It was a test, and his reaction already gave away the answer.

"How did you figure it out? I was so careful..." He'd had to be—for years. Outside his staff, the king, and a few of those in the king's central sphere, no one knew that he still lived. Despite the nagging worry that lingered at the back of his mind, he was almost certain the staff hadn't given him away. They'd been loyal long before his fall—handpicked from only those he knew he could trust to keep his secrets. People loyal to him, to his parents, not to the wicked king now reigning from his stolen throne.

Ceridwen shifted her position, nearly making him groan in pleasure as she slid in his lap, before she responded. "Malik told me his true identity."

Drystan bucked in surprise. "That bastard. I'll—"

She silenced him with a finger over his mouth again. "Don't. I don't think he was trying to get you in trouble or even reveal your secret. It was just one puzzle piece, but it helped all the others to fit together."

Drystan's lips thinned. As if that bastard wouldn't want to ruin him one way or another.

Ceridwen continued, "You keep everyone away from the manor and don't show your face in town. Even at the ball, you never removed your mask. No one knows anything about Drystan Winterbourne. It makes sense if that's because you're trying to hide who you really are. Even Malik's visits make a certain sense."

He rubbed a path up and down her side with his thumb, the soothing motion helping him remain calm amid her revelations.

"It would cause problems in the capital if anyone found out the dark prince was still alive after his execution," she said. "That's why he comes to visit and to watch you, isn't it?"

So easily she figured him out. Drystan's gaze hooded as he stared at her in admiration. If he didn't already love her for her kindness, music, and beauty, he would have fallen headlong in that moment over her mind. "Have I ever told you how clever you are?"

"No," she huffed. "I don't believe you have."

"An oversight on my part. One I won't make again." He slid her closer to him, causing the fabric of her dress to further bunch between them. Ceridwen squirmed atop him, unknowingly, or even perhaps knowingly rubbing against his stiff cock through his breeches. Drystan didn't bother to muffle his groan of desire.

He released one hand from her hip to twirl a strand of golden hair near her face. *So lovely.* If he could focus on her, it might give him the strength to confess all, but there was one thing he needed to make sure she knew straight away.

"It's true, what you've said. But I didn't kill my parents." His throat tightened up again as his shoulders hunched. Years had gone by, but speaking of them still threatened to crush him. "You have to believe me. I loved them. I would never have wished them harm."

"I do. The man I know wouldn't do such a thing," she said. "But who did?"

He sighed and slumped forward until his forehead pressed against hers. "The king."

Ceridwen stiffened, as he expected she might, so he snuggled her closer, clung to her like an anchor in turbulent seas.

"The man said to have helped purge the darkness destroyed the light instead," she whispered, a slight tremor running through her.

"I wasn't entirely innocent in the matter, though," Drystan confessed, drawing back ever so slightly until their faces were only inches apart.

Ceridwen fisted her hands in his shirt, as if perhaps he was her anchor as well.

"My uncle introduced me to dark magic."

She gasped. "But why do it?"

"I didn't know what it was, not really. I was an ignorant boy back then." Such a foolish young man, consumed with the pleasures of life and missing every warning sign. "He presented it as a way to obtain power and help my family. So, like the fool I was, I believed him." He shook his head. "He left out the side effects, of course, not telling me the cravings that dark magic bred, that I'd become a monster. There was always a temptation toward the dark, even for those of us who practice light magic. Almost like a faint itch just waiting to be scratched. But it was so dull I never noticed it, not until my uncle pointed it out. And that craving only grew. The more I touched darkness, the more I wanted it."

"He trained me himself, in secret. I relished in the power at first. It hit me like a high, so much stronger than booze or parties. Soon, it consumed me until I started to black out, to lose time. I didn't know then that I became a monster." Sadness settled on him like a heavy weight, and he drew quiet.

"What happened with your parents?" Ceridwen asked.

A sad smile crept to his face as he leaned back into the chair.

Ceridwen followed him, closing the distance he created.

This time, he smiled genuinely. "It's hard to talk with you like this."

"I'm not moving until you finish," she replied.

He ran a hand through a fall of her blond hair, which had slipped over one shoulder, swirling it around his fingers again. "Then I may talk all night. I just wish it were a happier topic."

The answering blush that tinted her cheeks was reward enough as he dropped her hair and let his head recline against the back of the chair. "Anyway, rumors of a monster spread around the capital and especially within the palace. My father knew immediately what that meant—he'd fought his own father and his followers, after all, some who transformed into monsters, like I do. By the time Father told me of the rumors, I'd started to be somewhat lucid during the change, just enough to understand why I woke up naked and sometimes covered in blood that wasn't my own. The darkness craves it, and if you don't feed the craving once you start, the monster takes its due."

"I confessed to him what had happened. The dark magic, the change, all of it. He and Mother tried to purge the darkness using some complicated spell, but it caused me to change as they worked. As the monster, I attacked them before they could complete their working. The rest is hazy, though I've begun to remember more and more of it as time goes by. I didn't kill them, but the injuries..." He shuddered, trying to shut down the horrible memories racing behind his eyes. "I can never forgive myself. My uncle appeared in the wake of the disaster and finished what I started."

"Drystan..." She caressed his cheek, the touch a balm to his sorrow.

"He could have finished me off too, but he didn't," he continued. "He convinced me I'd killed my parents, and in the haze of magic and grief, I believed him. He promised to guide me, to help me, but he used me as a weapon instead, doing his dirty work around the capital while he faked my death and put himself on the throne. He made me one of his pawns."

"You told me you watched the prince's execution." She tilted her head, brows scrunching.

His lips twitched. "I did, or at least the poor man who looked enough like me that no one questioned it after they'd beaten him bloody and dragged him in front of the crowd. He begged and sobbed, proclaiming his innocence. And to my shame, I watched it all from my uncle's box while disguised. That part I didn't lie about."

One of his greatest sins. He'd been too consumed with grief over his parents to think straight. Too angry to form a plan or do anything to stop his uncle's actions. And still too much of a coward to take the punishment that was his due.

"As my memories came back, I realized the lies and how my guilt had been twisted and used. It's like I was trapped in a haze for months, unable to do anything except what I was bid. But finally, it cleared. That's when I started to plan my revenge."

"But how did you get here?" she asked. "Wouldn't he have wanted to keep you close?"

"I told you he used me to do his dirty work? Well, I always wore a disguise when I did—a mask like the rest of his followers—something to hide our identities." The king favored masks resembling dragons, his nickname for his followers, and the symbol he forged in iron for each of them to carry and wear so that they would know one another as loyal to the king and his dark ways. The beast of myth no longer existed, if it ever had, but the thought of them made his teeth grind together.

"However, I started to let myself be seen instead. Sure enough, a rumor spread around the capital that Tristram might not be dead after all. He could have killed me then, but it was worth the risk." Every bit of his plan was risky. Any number of times, someone could have betrayed him, or the king could have chosen to slaughter him then and there. But without risk, without trying, he would never have his revenge.

"I couldn't work the magic I needed to with him so near, and I had to risk that he'd banish me instead of kill me for my error. To my luck, he sent me away for one year to the most out-of-the-way place he could think of with strict orders not to share my identity. I brought only those I trusted, servants of my parents and myself who knew my truth and kept it safe. Though I'm still surprised Malik hasn't reported something to his father that would give him cause to sign my death warrant. The king would certainly kill me if he knew even a bit of what I plan. He likely will when he's done using me anyway."

Being a pawn, a shadow in the form of one of the king's loyal dragons, was never a long-term prospect for him. Drystan was powerful, more so than even his parents, and the king liked power so long as he could control it. But the king was no fool either. He knew the risk of keeping Drystan alive. If that outweighed whatever use he had planned, he'd end him—quickly and quietly.

CHAPTER 35

DRYSTAN

DESPITE THE SERIOUSNESS OF the topic, a small smile formed on Ceridwen's lips, and humor twinkled in her eyes.

Drystan's brows pinched together. "What is it?" It surely couldn't be his tale. He'd seen the sorrow in her face as he spoke, watched her skin pale, and felt little tremors run through her body where she still sat atop him.

"I'm sorry." She shook her head, the look fading. "It's just that even the king thought this city so unworthy of notice and out of the way that he could hide his greatest secret here and send his own son to watch over it and make sure it never came to light."

A puff of laughter caught in his chest. That it was. Teneboure might be sneered at by nobles in the capital, but they had no idea the beautiful treasure it held, one he currently had in a most advantageous, if improper, position.

"You have to let me help you now." She gripped his shirt tighter in her fists, pressing the heels of her palms into him. "If the king really wields the darkness, then this is bigger than your revenge, me supporting my family, or any of this." She gestured to the room around them. "Please."

"It would put you in danger." The very last thing he wanted.

"But I could make a difference," she insisted. "For once in my life, I could help not only my family but also so many others. I wouldn't be just the youngest child or the woman broken by her mother's death. I'd be...more."

The passion in her voice, the pain laced behind the names she had for herself, pulled at something in him. He knew what it was to be broken by grief, how deeply the loss of a parent could cut someone, bleeding them out until they were a shell of themselves.

"I want to help." She pushed on his immoveable chest for emphasis.

He caressed her face, savoring the way she leaned into his touch. "A fire flower that bloomed in winter. Who knew such a woman lived in this tired city? Especially one whose music would please even the Goddess herself." He slid his thumb across her lips, which she parted for him.

The hooded, glassy look in her eyes snapped his restraint. He'd be damned before he had the woman of his dreams in his lap, not running from him despite all the horrors she knew, and didn't do something about it.

"The magic can wait."

In a heartbeat, his lips replaced his thumb, crashing into hers with enough force to tip her backward in his lap. Her shock faded, and she melted into him. Drystan groaned against her mouth as Ceridwen slid her arms up his chest to wrap them around his neck and hold him close.

The world around them faded. All the dark memories he'd shared slipped into nothingness as he kissed her with all his heart. In that moment, it was just the two of them, locked together in grief and affection that bound stronger than iron.

Their first kiss had been chaste, sweet. Drystan had kept a tight leash on himself, lest he scare her away. But now she knew everything—the worst of his secrets—and she hadn't fled. She listened patiently as he shared the horrors of his past, never balking or condemning him, though he deserved it. She was a wonder, a gift, and he planned to savor every moment with her.

This time, he poured all his desire into their kiss. He demanded everything, and she gave it willingly, almost like she tried to soothe his pain and suffering with the touch of her lips. And oh, how it did. She had no idea. His light. His beauty.

Drystan slid his hands down until they cupped her backside. With a gentle nip on her bottom lip, he pulled her tight against him, grinding up against the softness between her thighs.

When his tongue teased her lips, she parted them with a soft sigh. He tasted, he conquered, claiming all of her that she would give.

Finally, he released her, sucking in one deep breath after another, his head spinning. Anymore, and he'd give into the temptation to tumble her onto the floor, push up her skirts, and delight her with an entirely different kind of kiss.

Ceridwen's cheeks were flushed, her lips kiss-bruised, and hair tousled. She'd never looked quite so lovely, and right then, he wanted to give her everything she could ever ask for.

"I'll let you play for me while I try the spell tonight," he said between heavy breaths.

She nodded eagerly, wiggling a bit in his lap and rubbing against his cock in the most delicious torment. He gripped her hips again, holding her still. If she kept moving like that, he'd lose his control, not to mention his train of thought.

"If I feel the change coming on, I'll stop immediately. And if I don't feel it in time, you have to run." He leaned his forehead against hers, sharing her breaths. "If the monster breaks free, get to your room and don't leave it."

"I promise," she whispered.

With careful movements, he slid Ceridwen from his lap. Drystan groaned as he stood, adjusting his pants as she averted her gaze from the incriminating view. Her sheepishness was precious, another rare treasure. Perhaps it was best he hadn't taken it further with her.

He took her hand in his. When she glanced up at him, he rewarded her with the most genuine smile he'd shared in years. With one hand in his and her flute case in the other, Drystan led Ceridwen through the manor and up the stairs to his tower.

Ceridwen gagged as he sipped from a cup of blood. He hadn't considered this element of his magic and how it might affect her to see it in action. He'd told her, but knowing something and seeing it weren't the same.

"Are you all right?" He set the cup away, hiding it from her sight.

"Fine." She gave him a tight smile, one that all but said she was anything but fine, but was willing to continue. This strong woman—she only added to the many ways he didn't deserve her.

"Where do you get—" She broke off quickly with a shake of her head. "No. Never mind."

The blood? Best she didn't ask. She wouldn't like the answer. He could use his own, and did for the spells he painted, hence many of the scars on his hands and arms. The one on his face was one of the few he hadn't given himself. That one came from his uncle after his fall. His blood had limited effect when it came to consumption, though, as did animal blood. Most of what he used came from his staff, which they gave freely in small doses to aid his cause. It'd be a lie to say he didn't ponder what Ceridwen's would taste like or how it might affect him, given the power she had over his monster from her music and presence alone. That, however, was one thing he could never ask of her and might decline, even if she offered.

Instead of answering the half-spoken question, he said, "I tried a similar spell that night you found me." It was the last spell he needed to complete and the most difficult.

Ceridwen nodded, shifting her gaze to one of the shadowy areas of the room. "If the monster rises, I'll run," she promised and looked at him. "Should I play now?"

Drystan traced to the bookshelves, hands ungloved and bloody, and selected the Gray Blade from its innocuous place upon the shelf. "Yes," he said, almost to the blade rather than to her. "Go ahead and start now. Stay near the stairs."

He allowed her here at her insistence, but he wouldn't let her anywhere near him while he worked.

Before he'd returned to the altar, Ceridwen lifted the flute and began to play. She chose a lighthearted tune, one that brought to mind lush wisteria, sunshine, and spring days. Yet none of those happy thoughts settled the unease building with him as his monster prowled under his skin, wide awake since tasting the blood. So strange that a weapon meant to defeat darkness required dark magic to craft it.

Drystan placed the blade in the center of the altar and willed his body to relax and the monster to rest. He spent long minutes with his eyes closed, listening to the song, letting it feed happy thoughts into his mind, and blocking out the world. Only when he felt his beast settle did he begin to trace patterns in blood upon the stone. A hint of sound flowed from his lips to join the music as he murmured words of magic in addition to the blood and shape, willing it to take.

Ceridwen's music picked up in tempo, faster, he'd wager, than intended for the song. From the corner of his eye, he noticed she'd turned her head away from his working and kept her eyes tightly closed, as she often did while playing.

At one point, she peeked her eyes open. Her breath hitched, sending an awkward note into the air. The tune faltered for the briefest moment, but she slammed her eyes shut once more and continued on as he worked the pattern over and over.

The first tune ended, and she started another, her playing calm and controlled once more. Her confidence and strength bolstered his spirit and encouraged him on. He was close, he could feel it, but each swipe of his finger through the blood roused his beast despite the music. It prowled inside him, waiting for weakness and the opportunity to pounce.

So close. A few more.

The beast sprang, rising up within him and warring for control. Drystan's body lurched forward, slamming into the stone altar. He curled his fingers against the bloody surface. An agonized moan tore from his throat as the beast stretched against him, throwing itself into his form.

Ceridwen's music faltered. The flute dipped from her lips as she stared at him wide-eyed.

He moved to grip the edge of the altar. His back bowed. "Go," Drystan bit out through gritted teeth. The beast was insistent, hurtling itself at him again and again.

She shook her head, her lips settling in a suborn line. "No." She raised her flute to continue.

"Go!"

Their eyes locked across the room. The monster made its final push. Drystan groaned as his limbs began to shift and warp. "Please!" he cried.

This time, she listened. His vision blurred as the monster took over, and the last thing he saw was the pale color of her dress as she fled down the stairs.

CHAPTER 36
CERIDWEN

CERIDWEN NEARLY SLIPPED TWICE on the steep stone steps. Her music failed. It couldn't help Drystan when he needed it, just as it hadn't helped her mother. At least her song hadn't killed him—yet. The altar he'd worked at reminded her far too much of another bed of blood. The one where her mother died. She'd sung to her through her hard labor and right into the Goddess's hallowed halls. As if that hadn't been enough, it was her song that drove Mother out of the house to begin with, her singing that she insisted on despite Mother's claim of a headache.

Back then, Ceridwen still clung to her foolish, girlhood dream of being a great singer on the stage. If she sang during their family's visit to the capital, even inside, surely someone would notice and offer her that dream. It led to a nightmare instead. If she'd listened, Mother might not have gone out that day. She might not have gotten hurt and ended up in labor weeks too early. And then, Ceridwen just had to go and sing to her again when her mother asked between her cries of pain. One final song that took her life.

"Miss Ceridwen." Jackoby halted as she flew out of the stairwell and nearly barreled into him. "Is he—"

She sucked in a deep breath and bit her lip. "Maybe." She hadn't waited to be sure.

He straightened despite his already stiff posture. "I'll sound the servant bells." He took off at a near run, as fast as decorum would allow. "Get to your room," he called over one shoulder.

But she didn't need to be told. Already Ceridwen hurried in that direction, lifting her skirts to speed her progress.

Alone in her room, failure overwhelmed her. She'd been so certain her music would help, that it would contain the beast if she'd played. Yet it had risen anyway. Ceridwen wiped at the tears leaking down her face. They wouldn't help anyone. Tears hadn't saved her mother. They wouldn't help Drystan now.

She waited by the windows for long minutes, listening for sounds of the beast roaming the manor grounds. All night she remained there. They never came, but that didn't mean it hadn't risen.

When at last she calmed down, she played her flute until her fingers tingled from overuse, and sleep blurred the edge of her vision.

Only as she finally gave in to the urge to rest did a sharp howl pierce the wintery night.

Ceridwen paced near the stairs to the tower half the morning, but Drystan did not emerge. Nor had anyone seen him.

An ominous sign.

The temptation to lose herself in the paths of the greenhouse beckoned. She yearned to dig her hands into the dirt, to prune the hedges, to plant late seedlings—anything to keep her mind off the man she longed to see. However, thoughts of another man kept her from those glass walls. She couldn't handle Malik right now. Not in her current state.

The temptation to climb the stairs was almost too much. A few times, she'd ventured the first step, but the thought of what she'd find at the top, and Drystan's stern warnings, urged her back down.

Visiting Bronwyn might help. But her sister would know something bothered her. And worse, Ceridwen might just tell her everything. Something she simply couldn't do. She hadn't mentioned a word of her suspicions during her visit the day before—hard as it had been. However, seeing her family had given her the courage to confront Drystan about his past and give voice to the suspicion Malik's reveal had fueled.

Instead of venturing home or outdoors, Ceridwen fled to her other sanctuary with the manor: the library.

The sweet, musky scent of old books washed over her like a balm as soon as she opened the ornate wooden door. But the reverie didn't last.

"Ah, our lady of music. I thought you might appear."

Her nails dug into the edge of the door. Too bad it wasn't his neck.

"Before you run off, do come inside for a minute." Malik beckoned her toward the table he stood next to, where books of various shapes and sizes were strewn open in front of him.

Anything sounded better, even facing down Drystan's monster. But his cocky, know-it-all smile drew her in. It begged her to agree with his request despite the way her legs locked up. Besides, he was a prince. *The* prince for all the world knew. Even if he didn't parade around here as such, who was she to insult a royal?

Ceridwen released the door and stepped inside.

"Close it." He motioned with a wave of his hand.

Reluctantly, she complied, but not before looking both ways out the door with a quick prayer to the Goddess that someone would notice and join them.

No one did.

With the door securely closed, she dipped into a low curtsy. "Your highness."

Malik's face held a deep frown when she raised her head at the end of the gesture. "Don't," he snapped. "You can't treat me that way. Not here. And don't you dare call me Alistair either."

"Why not?" Her brows reached skyward.

"It's how I'm regarded in the capital. In front of my father. But it's not what I prefer. And yes, the people here know who I am, but that's not the point. Secrets only work when people keep them. We had a deal, remember?" He drummed his fingers on the table. "Besides, what if your lovely sister chose today to come for a visit?"

Then she'd likely have one more reason to despise him. Not that it should bother him what a commoner thought. "I agreed to keep your secret about the blood," Ceridwen said. "But you gave me your name on your own."

"I don't—" He opened his mouth, closed it, and shook his head. "It doesn't matter. How about a peace offering? Something for keeping both secrets?" He raised a thin book in one hand. No, not a book. She knew the size of those pages, the narrow thickness of the binding. Malik held a bound composition. An old one by the weathered and yellowed look of the thing.

Curiosity beckoned like the Goddess herself.

"The first composition I heard you play was *The Blessings of the Goddess*, but you didn't know the third movement."

"No one does," she insisted. "It's lost."

His lips twitched. "Perhaps to most people, but there are a few copies left. And one..." He laid the bound composition on the reading table before him.

The impossible sight sent the world tilting beneath her. "Oh Goddess, it can't be." *Right here, under my nose.*

Tears threatened to fall, but she blinked them back and reached for it, tracing a finger along the letters of the title on the cover page. "It was here?"

He gestured to the back wall, to the stacks and sections of books so old they'd nearly come apart when she'd touched them. Such a treasure waited there, and she'd missed it completely.

"Why show this to me?" She could hardly believe it existed, much less that it lay in front of her.

He shrugged. "I thought it might be helpful, especially if you're going to play for Drystan while he works dark magic."

Breath caught in her throat. Her mouth gaped before she could stop herself. "He doesn't..." She shook her head, letting her brows pinch in faked confusion.

"I saw you leave the tower." He leaned on the table, closing the distance between them. "And I heard the monster in the night. It wasn't hard to put the two together."

Well, that was unfortunate. And something she couldn't refute. Even so, she wouldn't admit it. "That doesn't mean—"

He cut her off. "It does. You think I don't know? There's no need to lie for him. What I'm still working out, though, is why you would aid him with dark magic? You don't seem like the type. In fact, you're about as far from it as they come. So why? What is he doing up there?"

"You've never been up there yourself?" she asked, if only to give herself time to think.

"No, I—" He pursed his lips.

"You're here to watch him, yet you only guess at what he does?"

"Watch him?" He cocked his head to the side. "Yes, of course he told you that." He sighed. "But he's been more careful than I expected. Guarded...with everyone but you."

She could no longer hold his gaze, the one that dug into her soul as if he could pry loose the secrets he so desperately craved. She looked away, down to the table where the various tomes lay open before him. And her heart nearly stopped.

The page his fingers drummed upon contained a large illustration of a simple dagger, and below it, words she could easily read even upside down. The Gray Blade.

Color leeched from her vision as she stared at the impossible sight. Unmoving. Unblinking.

Of all the things that he could read about, he'd chosen that one. It was no mistake. He'd left the book open for her to see. He suspected, if he didn't already know.

Motion and color rushed back as she pulled in a deep breath.

Malik tipped her chin up until she was forced to look him in the eye. "You might just be the key that saves us all."

Chills raced down her spine. When had he gotten so close?

The main door creaked open in a rush of wood, sending Malik and Ceridwen leaning away from each other, the table safely between them.

"There you are," Kent said, brushing away a lock of dark-brown hair that liked to fall free from the binding at his neck. He straightened as he took in the other man in the room, one he clearly did not expect. His gaze flitted nervously between them before he continued, directing his words to Ceridwen. "Lord Winterbourne has come downstairs and is asking for you."

Thank the Goddess! "One moment. I'll be right there."

Kent looked between them again but said nothing before giving a short bow and leaving as quickly as he'd come.

"You don't want to run into Drystan's arms?" Malik asked with a smirk as the door shut.

Ceridwen ignored the jab and steeled her will. "What do you want?"

"We're to be confidants now?"

She pinned him with her gaze, refusing to give in. "Well?"

Finally, he sighed. "Freedom."

The word sat heavily between them.

"You're not free?" If a prince wasn't, then who was?

"No one is more watched than me, and no one has more to lose."

It was her turn to be surprised. "You're the one watching Drystan."

"And he watches me. If he reports what I am, or what I'm not, I'm done."

Because his father led the darkness, a path Malik refused to follow. Ceridwen jerked back, seeing him in a new light. The king must not know. His own son turned his back on him, and he had no idea. Most ironically, Drystan felt the same way about him. Both watched each other, neither trusting the other.

But that fact solidified her decision. "Come to my room just before luncheon."

His smile grew blinding. "Now that's an invitation I did not expect."

Ceridwen groaned and rolled her eyes.

Malik laughed in return.

"Just do it. Please." She snatched the composition off the table, whirled around, and left the room with the precious pages clutched to her chest.

CHAPTER 37

DRYSTAN

DRYSTAN COULD NOT HAVE been more apologetic if he repented before the Goddess herself. His monster hadn't hurt anyone. There was no blood on him when he finally returned to himself around dawn in the snow-ridden courtyard. But he hadn't been able to contain his beast either. Ceridwen had been there. She'd seen the change and been in harm's way, even if she dodged it this time.

"We won't try that again. It's too risky," he insisted.

"But we're running out of time," Ceridwen replied.

How could she not understand the danger he put her in? If she hadn't left when she did, he could have fully transformed in front of her. He could have harmed her. He'd wrestled with the beast long after she left, trying everything to contain it despite the agony it caused, but it won. It always won.

Yes, it was less than two weeks until midwinter. The sand in his hourglass was nearing its end, but he'd rather fail than harm her.

Drystan paced in front of the crackling fire in Ceridwen's room. She'd led him there, a safe place where they could talk. He usually preferred his study, but he was grateful for the change today. With light flowing through the windows and her scent teasing him, it soothed some of the aftershocks of his transformation.

Still, exhaustion pulled at him, begging him to sink into a chair, or even better, a bed, but not before he spoke to her and told her what he realized as he crawled through the snow and back inside the manor in the dim, predawn light.

Drystan pulled Ceridwen into his arms, savoring the way she came to him despite all he was and all he'd done. Warmth built in his chest, burning away the pain still clinging to his limbs. He ran his fingers through her hair, relishing the way it tickled his chin as he held her close. "I'll go it alone. I'll find a way."

She clutched at his chest and looked up at him. She traced a path with her fingertips through the prickly hairs on his chin. "You don't have to do it alone."

He captured her hand and placed a kiss upon her knuckles. "We tried. I almost turned on you." His brave woman.

"I know." She stepped from his embrace and walked to a nearby table. With care, she opened a wide, thin book. He joined her and stared over her shoulder. It wasn't a book at all, but a musical score—an old one by the looks of it, and not one he recalled seeing her with.

"Where did you find that?" he asked.

"The library." She turned the page slowly, almost like she thought it might crumble apart.

"I didn't know we had any sheet music here."

She flipped the page again to what looked like the beginning of a new song and read the words inked under the lines. "To test the hearts of man, she gifted darkness too. A temptation one can only resist if they stay true."

"The Goddess?" he mused aloud.

Before Ceridwen could read on, a knock sounded at the door.

"Who is it?" Drystan asked, more a demand than a question.

But Ceridwen didn't wait for a response. She hurried to the door and threw it open, sweeping her hand in an invitation that released the magical binding he placed on the threshold weeks ago.

Drystan stiffened as Malik strode in. "Why are you in here?" he accused. *And why, oh why, would Ceridwen let such a man in her room?*

"Ceridwen invited me," Malik replied with his ever-casual air.

Jealousy flared hot and angry through his center. Drystan's attention snapped to Ceridwen, not bothering to shield the look of betrayal he knew must be evident upon his face.

Ceridwen winced but offered no response.

Malik crossed his arms and stared at him. "You're not the partner I would have chosen for a ménage either."

An inhuman growl slipped from Drystan's throat and rolled through the air with menace.

"Stop." Ceridwen stepped between them. "Both of you."

Drystan's rumbling growl ceased, even when his frown deepened.

"Neither of you trust one another, but you should," she continued.

Perhaps he was wrong. Maybe his monster had hurt her somehow, or she'd slipped and hit her head upon the stairs in her flight down. "You don't know him," Drystan grumbled, trying to edge between them.

Ceridwen planted her hands on his chest, willing him to a halt. "You're on the same side."

"The same side?" Drystan echoed in confusion.

"And what side would that be?" Malik asked, sliding up behind Ceridwen, entirely too close for Drystan's comfort.

Ceridwen looked over one shoulder at his cousin and then back at him. "The side of the light."

She might as well have punched him in the chest and knocked the air from his lungs. Stabbing him would have been less painful. The woman he loved, he trusted, had spilled his secrets to the one man in this manor he tried to keep them from. Worse, she knew exactly what she did.

Drystan bared his teeth, his body shuddering. But when he looked at Malik, expecting him to be beaming with triumph, he found only an echoed look of shock and betrayal.

What in the name of the Goddess...

"Ceridwen—" Drystan began.

"We had an agreement," Malik cut in, staring at her with fury.

"We did. We do." She held her hands aloft, staring back and forth between both men. "But you two have to talk. No more secrets. No more games."

Drystan's chest rose and fell as he searched her face, trying to ponder out her meaning. To his surprise, Malik turned to him and stared him down in somber silence until Drystan met his steady gaze.

Finally, Malik spoke. "I don't practice dark magic," he admitted. His voice lacked all humor and playfulness.

Drystan stared at him, unmoving. "I've seen you drink blood. We drank it together."

"I throw it up. Ceridwen caught me in the act." Malik's shoulders slumped.

Impossible. It couldn't be true. "But your father..."

"Would kill me if he knew. Or worse, force me to use the dark magic," Malik finished, leveling Drystan with a hard look.

The world spun around him. Drystan placed a palm on the tabletop for support.

"He already thinks me weak. Worthless," Malik continued, letting all his bitterness leak into his tone. "That's why he chose you, after all. The nephew who did what his own son couldn't, or rather, wouldn't do."

Malik stood still as a statue, only his throat bobbing as he swallowed. His admission hung heavy in the air.

It couldn't be true. It went against everything Drystan believed, all that he'd been so sure of. But there was an honesty in his cousin's expression, a vulnerability he hadn't seen since they were young. The man before him suddenly reminded him of that boy, the innocent kid so like his mother in his kindness and humility. But her death years ago had changed him, or so Drystan believed. It turned him more like his father with his mercurial ways, tricks, and false smiles.

Unless...it hadn't.

Drystan looked at Ceridwen out of the corner of his eye, catching her slow nod where she stood silently by. This was his decision, his call, but she believed Malik. Perhaps she hadn't meant to betray him but to give him another weapon in his fight. Could it possibly be true?

With a silent prayer to the Goddess, Drystan heaved a heavy sigh. "I won't tell him. I plan to kill him instead."

Malik blinked, his only movement as he took in Drystan's words. Finally, Malik whistled and shoved his hands in his pockets. "Well, I sure hope you have a good plan."

Tension slipped from his shoulders, all that pent-up worry shifting in an instant to a heady rush of adrenaline that sent his body humming.

"I suppose you've been working on something up in that tower of yours," Malik continued. "So how can I help?"

"You'd go against your own father?" Drystan asked.

"With pleasure. He's made my life a misery, and my mother..." He shook his head. "It's only a matter of time before he stages my own disappearance. A permanent one. I'd guess he's done plenty to you as well."

"More than you can imagine." So much more.

Malik raised his brows. "I can imagine quite a lot. I know why and how my mother died, and I can hazard a guess why you want him dead as well."

Malik's mother? She'd been the sweetest woman he knew, taken by an illness far too young. But that was what he'd been told, like the whole kingdom believing him dead for the murder of his parents. How many lies had the king spun in his quest for power?

"I didn't kill my parents," Drystan said. Those old memories tried to creep in again, to hunch his shoulders and squeeze his throat until he could barely breathe.

"I see that now, because of how you are with her." Malik nodded toward Ceridwen.

She crossed the short space to Drystan and wove her arm through his, leaning in close, offering support without even a word. Her touch alone sent his nightmares fleeing back to the recesses of his mind.

"So you'll help me kill the king," Drystan said. "You're that eager for the title yourself?"

"No," Malik snapped. "I never want to be king."

The sincerity in his words made Drystan rock on his feet.

"To have my life scrutinized at all time... The responsibility..." Malik ran a hand through his hair, mussing it up. "I just want my old life back. A spare royal with no expectations."

"You swear it?"

"In the name of the Goddess." Malik stuck his hand out toward Drystan. "Do you?"

Drystan took Malik's hand. "In the name of the Goddess."

Hope blossomed between their clasped hands. If his cousin held true, they might just have a chance.

"So." Malik grinned like a cat. "About that plan..."

CHAPTER 38

CERIDWEN

For the three nights, they worked on the Gray Blade.

Drystan had already completed the light spells required. Only the dark remained. Unfortunately, that meant Malik couldn't work the spells himself given his avoidance of dark magic. However, he still found a way to assist. Malik wove a ring of light magic protection spells around the altar, ones to help contain the darkness should Drystan lose control again.

Ceridwen played the flute to calm the monster within while Drystan worked the remaining spell.

The night before, he'd almost transformed into the monster again. His eyes flashed red. His limbs warped and stretched. Only her music held the magic in check, and barely at that.

He'd halted his spell, unwilling to let the monster break free.

But they were running out of days. He couldn't put it off forever. So tonight, he resolved to try the last spell one more time.

Ceridwen hugged her arms about herself as she stared out the window of Drystan's tower. Courage failed her when she tried to ask what came next. How did Drystan plan to kill his uncle? Who would keep him safe? Would he take her with him?

Part of her knew she wouldn't like the answers.

Malik's muttered words tickled her senses as he worked. The falling snow and cold air couldn't distract her grim thoughts or knowledge of the patterns of blood he traced.

So much blood...

Some of it theirs. Some animal. Other donated by the residents of the castle. She'd offered hers, but the men refused. Both of them would bear new scars on their bodies, preferring to use their own as much as possible.

The faintest hint of moonlight crept through the cloudy sky, highlighting the heavy flakes as they drifted down to join their brethren upon the manor and the city beyond. Ceridwen could almost see her family house just a few blocks away.

Drystan slid next to her, wrapping a fresh bandage around his hand.

"Why work the spells at night?" she asked.

"Dark magic is stronger at night," Drystan said. "Light magic works better in the day. I need the spells to be at their strongest for this working."

She nodded along. It made a certain sense since the monster always reared its head after sunset—nights when Drystan must have worked the strongest of his spells, or the most reckless ones.

Ceridwen jumped when his arms wrapped around her. A cocoon of warmth settled over her as she relaxed against him. A hint of leather and a light floral note, likely belonging to one of the many plants Drystan tended, lulled her into a momentary peace. He kissed her with passion each night and each day, but never tried for more. A part of her resented that. Another part chided herself for not being more forward with him herself. But deep down, she knew it probably had something to do with his plans to return to the capital, the uncertainty of his—their—future.

She let herself float away until Malik's voice interrupted the bubble of warmth. "It's done."

Cold rushed back in as Drystan released her. He had work to do. As did she. Malik would stay nearby in case he needed to reinforce his spells, or to protect her if the worst should happen.

Ceridwen took a seat in a cushioned chair set up near the stairs. Drystan had even managed to pull together a makeshift music stand so that she could play the third movement of *The Blessings of the Goddess* as he worked. It wouldn't be her best performance—she'd yet to memorize or perfect the melody. However, it would likely be only the first of many songs if everything went according to plan.

Three songs in, she thought they were finally safe.

The third movement turned out more beautifully than she imagined. So much so it nearly brought tears to her eyes. Finally, she'd gotten it right on her first playthrough. Ceridwen played the second and first movements after it, playing the whole concerto in reverse order.

Then, Drystan's posture shifted abruptly. A groan marred the words of his spell. Ceridwen nearly dropped her flute when his eyes flickered to red instead of their traditional deep blue.

"Keep playing," Malik whispered beside her, calm amid the change threatening to take place before them.

Fear dried her throat, but she continued as best she could. The song she began told of traveling through winter snows to visit a lover. A happy tune, or it should have been.

Drystan's back hunched. Fabric ripped at the seam of an arm. A shimmer of darkness hovered about his form, one so close to changing.

Not again. Please not this.

Malik leaped from his seat and paced around Drystan, holding his attention. "Calm, cousin," he said over the song. "You can control this."

Drystan gritted his teeth. With a shake, the blue returned to fill his eyes. He dipped his fingers in the goblet of blood on the altar and moved them through the pattern of the magical working. Sweat beaded on his brow and dripped down his skin as Ceridwen continued to play despite her worry.

Ever so slowly, the blood began to disappear.

It's working. Oh Goddess, please let him be successful this time.

"Almost there, Drystan. Breathe." Malik coached him from outside the circle of protection he'd crafted.

A shimmer passed over the blade as the blood disappeared completely into the altar.

"He's done it."

Drystan closed his eyes and breathed deeply. The flute slipped from Ceridwen's lips as she stared at the blade still lit with an eerie glow. She gazed in rapture at the object that had taken so much effort to craft. As the light faded, it looked no different from a simple blade any commoner could own.

Drystan's body shook. A half grunt, half growl split the air.

"Drystan!" Ceridwen lurched from her chair.

Malik waved her back. "Play! He's losing it."

Her legs gave way as she thumped onto the seat, flute flying to her lips. She played in earnest, pouring everything she had into the song. Her fear. Her love. Her own deep sorrow.

It didn't help.

Fabric ripped. His eyes flashed bright red. Claws elongated from his hands to scrape against stone.

They were losing him.

Ceridwen looked away as more fabric ripped, revealing skin turned inky black and stretched tight across bone. Tears blurred her vision. The music didn't help. It wasn't enough. Just as it hadn't been enough to keep her mother alive after she sent her into danger.

A sharp howl pierced the room. The flute slipped from her lips as Malik cried out in pain. Ceridwen's head snapped to the altar where Drystan's monster stood upright, fully dark and horrifying. Only a few frayed bits of cloth clung to what once had been a human body. Malik gripped his arm and fell back against a wall, his teeth gritted at the monster.

Drystan swiped again, feet shuffling at the edge of Malik's working, stirring up red sparks that rose from the stone floor as the magic frayed.

"Drystan, stop!" Ceridwen waved her arms. Blood rushed to her ears, drowning out the monster's loud breaths.

It swiveled slowly in her direction, head bobbing ever so slightly. Pointed fangs filled its gaping mouth.

"This isn't you." Tears slid down her face.

"Try again," Malik said. He'd managed to shuffle along the wall, keeping well out of range of the circle he'd drawn. A dark stain marred his navy coat where he held his other hand tightly against the wound.

Drystan's attention slipped back to his cousin. Red irises flickered as drops of blood fell and splattered onto the stone tiles.

Ceridwen swallowed and raised her flute again, continuing the tune where she'd left off. To her side, Malik traced a pattern on his arm with his own blood.

The monster lunged for the barrier. The movement knocked the chalice of blood off the altar, sending it splashing across the floor in a gruesome display. A horrid squeak slipped out of the flute in the wake of her shock as more crimson sparks fluttered up from the ground. The monster's tantrum grew worse as it pawed and roared in the narrow space.

"It may not hold much longer," Malik said, edging ever so slightly in front of her.

His action only spurred the monster on. Ceridwen's heart cracked with every swipe the monster took.

"We need to go. Now."

But her body wouldn't move. Couldn't. To leave him here again? Like this? How could she? He could hurt himself or someone in the manor. He could flee and hurt someone in the city. She had to do something.

"Go!" Malik shoved her toward the stairs. Ceridwen tripped over her feet. Her knees slammed into the ground, jarring the flute from her hands.

Pain radiated up her body as an unholy roar practically shook the room.

"Don't!" Malik yelled.

A haze of red sparks hung in the air as she twisted around and saw the monster lunge at Malik. He grabbed the music stand and smashed into the monster's side, sending it skidding across the ground.

Music fluttered through the air. Ceridwen screamed. *Drystan! The concerto!*

Black claws scraped grooves in the stone as the monster slid across the floor, scrambling for purchase.

Ceridwen lurched back, suddenly numb. The beast gained its footing and shook its body like a dog shedding water.

Malik crouched beside her, the broken stand still in hand. "We have to go!"

Drystan's monster roared again. The sound alone threatened to crush her.

Ceridwen shook herself. Malik was right. They had to go. Run.

Drystan.

The monster lunged, breaking through the barrier, crashing into Malik, and knocking her aside.

"Stop!" Malik screamed, the stand a flimsy defense between the claws and his skin.

"No!" *No, no, no.*

"Run!" Malik yelled.

Her body shook, but she couldn't let someone else die for her, for her failures. She wouldn't. And Drystan...killing Malik might kill him too.

Ceridwen lunged at the monster, wrapping her arms around its neck.

It flung her away. Pain flared in her back and head. Spots swam in her vision.

Wood clattered. Malik groaned.

As her sight cleared, the monster took shape before her. Ceridwen's heart skipped a beat. Terror gripped her. He loomed above her, saliva dripping from his fangs.

A clawed paw thumped next to her head.

Would he kill her this time? Another death on his conscience? Tears leaked down her face. A memory flashed before her, cloaking the room with its vision. Mother lay in her bed. Fresh blood marred the sheets around her lower half. Fionn whimpered nearby, the thin cry of a child not fully in the world and already looking toward the embrace of the Goddess.

"Sing for me, Ceridwen," she asked, her voice a soft rasp.

The tight rope that bound her throat snapped. Fear flowed away like water. Her song had caused death, but death would follow her silence this night. The certainty of it echoed in her soul. She couldn't allow that.

"Drystan."

A sharp whine broke from its maw.

"Keep talking to him," Malik groaned.

A deep growl cut him off. Ceridwen stared at the monster, trying her best to see the man beneath the surface. She touched his leathery cheek, pulling his focus to her.

"Sing for me, Ceridwen." Mother's phantom voice slipped through her mind.

"Your music helps me," the memory of Drystan echoed.

Could she sing? If she loved him, truly loved him, she had to try.

Red eyes stared into hers as she swallowed her fear, sucked in a breath, and began to sing.

"Each night...the moon rises...from his bed."

The monster continued to stare, red eyes blinking where it loomed like a ghastly statue above her.

"Searching for his one love that hath fled."

It tilted its head to the side like a dog assessing its master.

Ceridwen stroked his cheek, the hot, hard skin, the bits of matted hair. "With brightest light, she tempts him onward. The object of his nightly quest for love." Her voice grew steadier, more confident, coming alive with song as it hadn't in years.

The monster retreated and crouched at her feet.

Ceridwen pulled herself up, ignoring the pain in her body, her racing heart, everything but the monster of a man before her.

"Each morning, the sun raises her head. Longing for her love, she dreams to wed."

It sniffed in her direction, dipping its head as she raised her hand toward its muzzle.

"His soft white glow beckons her to him."

"Ceridwen!" Malik yelled, but she ignored him.

"The answer to her longing for love."

Coarse fur tickled her fingertips. Another wayward tear rolled down the crease of her nose and over her lips.

"Drystan," she whispered between lines. She stroked his face over the hard ridges of bone and ears like a bat's wing, as she continued to sing.

The monster did not rip out her neck. Not as she caressed his face, nor when she wrapped her arms around him as if he were a gentle creature that would lick her face or purr like a cat. He was none of those things, not now, but he allowed the touch.

His fangs did not bite. Claws did not scratch. His whole form seemed to relax under her touch at the sound of her voice as she held him and sang through the tears that continued to fall.

Tears for Drystan. For Mother. For her.

For all that she'd lost and all she'd found. And all that would still endure should they live through this night.

Her heart pounded as the monster wiggled in her grip. She shut her eyes against her death and sang through the fear threatening to cut off her song once more.

She no longer heard Malik. Perhaps he fled. A small screech slipped out among words as the monster thrashed and jerked under her arms.

Something changed. The hair she grasped with one hand vanished. Soft skin replaced the cracked leather surface under the other. A groan more human than monstrous echoed in her ears and trickled over her skin like water.

Through it all, she kept singing, willing sounds out of her throat no matter how they tried to stay inside.

Ceridwen's eyes flew wide as a human hand gripped her side, pulling her close. The sight that greeted her choked off the song. His dark hair was matted and sticking out in odd directions. The grimace on his features spoke of pain. But his eyes were clear of their red haze.

"Drystan." His name cracked from her lips.

He winced, flexing his hand on her side as he tried to move. She scooted back to give him space. A soft gasp fell from her lips as her gaze traveled down his chest. His naked chest. His arms, too, laid bare, covered in a dusting of hair and marred by scars. And below that—

She looked away before she could give into temptation, heat rushing to her cheeks.

"You brought me back." His voice was gritty, rough like the sandy soil near the sea's edge.

Hesitantly, she met his gaze. Ceridwen's lips quivered with the emotions coursing through her body. Without thinking, she lunged for him and flung her arms around his neck. He gave a slight oomph as she landed against him, their bodies tilting backward until he righted them and clutched her in return.

"It wasn't a dream. You saved me. You...you sang." Awed wonder rang in his tone.

"I did," she mumbled against his chest, still trying to rein in the tears wetting his warm skin.

Drystan drew back, quickly taking stock of her with his gaze and holding her face in between his palms. "Are you—? What I did—" His breath hitched as he beheld the blood on her dress.

"I'm fine," she promised. A little sore, achey, and with a few new bruises, no doubt, but so much better off than she could have been.

"But the blood—"

"It's not mine," she said in a hurry.

"Goddess, Ceridwen." His voice cracked over her name. "I could have killed you."

"You didn't," she promised, placing her hand atop his where it still lingered on her cheek.

"But I knocked you away. I hurt you." Drystan slid his palm down her neck, her shoulder, and to her arm, as if he needed to touch her everywhere to assure himself she was whole.

"It wasn't you. Not really," she said.

His pupils flared, and then his arms were around her again, pulling her back against his chest and cradling her close. "I'm sorry. So sorry," he whispered against her hair, a kiss following in the wake of his words.

Malik cleared his throat behind them. Ceridwen twisted around just enough to catch a glimpse of him from the corner of her eye. A hint of amusement lit his face. "Should I leave you two alone?"

"Malik. Damn it all, I...I almost...." Drystan's voice cracked once more as he beheld his cousin.

Malik shrugged with a grimace. "I've had worse. A few more spells will fix this up." He held up his arm. Angry scratches were visible through the shredded fabric of his sleeve. His earlier spells had healed some, but not all, of his wounds.

Drystan drew in a shaking breath and released Ceridwen from his embrace.

To Malik, he asked, "Can you help me downstairs? We'll clean up this mess later."

Malik nodded in return and offered a hand to Drystan.

Ceridwen scooted away, averting her gaze once again as Malik heaved Drystan to his feet with more groans and grunts. The change took a toll, a physical one as well as mental it seemed. Her flute had been discarded on the floor. She picked it up with care, placed it on the chair, and hurried down the stairs without a backward glance.

CHAPTER 39

CERIDWEN

I N DRYSTAN'S ROOM, CERIDWEN caught sight of herself in a long mirror. Blood-stains marred the skirt of her eggplant dress, likely from the cup that had been knocked upon the floor. More tainted her hands and arms. Some of her hair had gone askew and fallen from the simple ribbons she'd tied it back with that morning. It hung like thin, pale vines that curled down her chest.

A chair creaked as Malik settled Drystan on it.

"No wonder you wear so many different outfits," Malik mused. "And I thought perhaps you had a taste for fashion."

A bitter chuckle filled the air. "I did. Once."

Wood slid against wood. Fabric ruffled as she busied herself staring at nothing on the wall. Water splashed as Drystan hastily cleaned away the blood on his skin.

"Those will do," Drystan commented to Malik.

From the corner of her eye, Ceridwen caught him bringing clothes to Drystan, whose naked form was hidden from her view.

"I'll leave you," Malik said. "I need to see to my wounds."

"I'm so sorry. I didn't think—"

"Yeah, yeah," Malik said. "Sorry for your...ribs? What did I hit?"

"I deserved it." Something splashed into the water.

"True," Malik replied.

The slip and slide of fabric reached her ears, but still, Ceridwen refused to look, giving Drystan the privacy he needed.

A gasp caught in Ceridwen's throat as Malik took her hand and raised it to his lips. "Good night, brave Ceridwen."

With a wink, he turned to leave. Boots clicked down the stairs as he excused himself from the tower.

"I-I should go too." Ceridwen turned to the stairs, prepared to slink away.

"Please stay." The softness in Drystan's words nearly broke her heart.

Her feet wouldn't move. They'd rooted themselves to the ground near the rounded section of wall concealing the staircase.

She swallowed the lump in her throat and turned to the beckoning voice. He sat shirtless on his bed. A dusting of dark hair coated the hard planes of his chest, a fine trail disappearing down into the waistband of the dark trousers he'd donned. He'd hastily washed much of the blood away, leaving a sheen of dampness on his skin. Scars marred his chest as well as his arms. Self-inflicted? She didn't know, but their shape and thickness were reminiscent of the ones she knew he'd created himself.

His scars told a story with as much heart and emotion as any song. Some marked his fall, others his suffering, yet the newer ones paved his path to vengeance.

"All right."

He rose and crossed the room to her.

She resisted the urge to step away, not for fear of his monster. No, not that. The tightness in her chest came from something within herself, an all-consuming desire.

He knelt before her, taking her hand in his.

"I'm so sorry. Tonight I...I could have killed you. Again. And I promised myself, I promised I wouldn't—" His words cut off as she placed her other hand upon his head. He gazed up at her, eyes glassy and pained. "Ceridwen."

"Drystan."

He held her gaze. Vulnerable. Open. "I want your forgiveness, but I don't deserve it."

"It was my choice." Staying. Helping him. And this. She knelt, taking his face in her hands.

"Ceri—"

Her kiss captured his words. Soft. Tender. Acceptance of his apology. A whispered promise.

Their breaths mingled as he pulled back. Drystan stared her down, an unfamiliar glimmer in his eyes. "We...um..."

A sheepish smile broke out over her features before she bit her lip, holding it in.

"We should get you cleaned up." He lifted her off the floor and carried her to his bed.

Butterflies fluttered in her stomach, a whole swarm of them that continued even when he set her on the edge and stepped away to retrieve a pitcher and fresh cloth.

She tugged the bloody sections of the dress until they bunched in front of her, away from the fine coverings on the bed. Her backside clung to the edge of the mattress. One inch farther, and she'd fall onto the floor.

Ceridwen willed away the heat rising to her cheeks and pooling deep within her, but it refused to obey, especially as Drystan returned with the water and cloth. He frowned at the stains as he gently washed away the blood on her skin. "I'll have the dress replaced."

"It's not a problem. I have many others, thanks to you." More than she'd ever had. Having one ruined was no great loss, though it did make her heart ache to see something so fine tarnished. She hadn't considered its welfare when she'd gone to Drystan's monster. She'd barely considered her own.

"You told me you couldn't sing. Or didn't sing?" His brows scrunched as he worked. "But your voice is lovely."

She fisted her hands in the fabric bunched together in her lap. "I don't... I haven't. Not for a long time anyway." How could he think it lovely? Her voice had warbled, cracked, broken, and sounded worse than anything she'd ever played him on her flute. Talking and singing were different. She could speak without thinking about it. It used to be the same for singing—not anymore.

He closed his hand over her arm. "It reached me where nothing else ever has." His eyes held such sincerity they stole her breath. "Usually, I have to wait for the magic to run its course. If I'm lucky, I retain some control over the beast, but not always. Sometimes it blocks me out so completely that I don't even recall everything it does." He set the washbowl aside.

"But your music holds a magic I can't explain. Something more powerful than anything I've known." He slid his hand down her arm to take her hand, leaving gooseflesh in its wake. "I wish I could admonish you for being so reckless and coming near my beast as you did." He shook his head.

"I'm glad I did," she admitted, leaning into him. "But I'm so surprised my song helped. It's never helped anyone before. The opposite usually." Her attention faltered, falling to the floor as old memories rose to torment her.

"Something happened." He rubbed a pattern on her newly cleaned skin with thumb, the act almost enough to distract her spiraling thoughts. "I've told you about my scars. What happened to cause you to doubt such a beautiful gift?"

A gift. She blinked up at him.

"You said once you used to sing? Until?"

She shuffled closer on the edge of the bed, savoring the warmth of his body and the comfort it provided. "I told you my mother died?"

"In childbirth."

She nodded. "Father had rented a house in the capital for the weeks before the spring fair. He had numerous profitable business dealings then and had brought the family along as a treat. It was my first time in the capital, and it brought to mind all my foolish, girlish dreams of being a great singer upon a stage. I sang for Mother that morning, but we had a fight, an argument. She had a headache and asked me to stop, but I wanted her to hear the tune I'd memorized. I'd been so proud of it then, certain someone in the capital would recognize my talents and bestow me with my greatest dream." She shook her head. What a foolish young woman she'd been, stuck on the dreams of youth. No one had given her the dreams of her heart. Instead, those dreams created a very real nightmare that destroyed everything.

"I pushed her too far," Ceridwen continued. "She...she got upset with me and went to walk through the city. Alone. She forbid me to come." Her throat tightened, threatening to steal her words. Even so, she pressed onward. "If I hadn't sung, if I hadn't been so insistent that she listen to me, she might not have left, and then..." Someone should have gone with her, heavy with child as she was, especially at her age. Sometime later, Father was the first of their household to hear her scream, but not the last.

"Father and Gerard found her stumbling up the front stairs, blood trailing down her legs from a labor already underway. Scratches marred her arms and stomach. She mumbled nonsense. Something about a dragon." Drystan stiffened, but she continued, the memories spilling out in a torrent she could no longer hold back. "But those creatures of myth do not exist. She must have fallen and hit her head. Encountered some robber in her walk? I don't know. She had a hard labor. I still remember the screams, the blood..." She'd been out of the room at the time, waiting just outside the door with Bronwyn and Adair. The thick wood had done nothing to halt the horrific sounds from within.

"We sent for the doctor immediately, but he wasn't fast enough." Jaina and another maid delivered the baby. A small thing with little life of its own. Despite its size, it managed to inflict such pain on Mother during its delivery.

"The baby came quickly. She didn't linger in pain too long, but it... Something happened, and they couldn't stop the bleeding. I still remember the blood on the bed when they finally let us in the room. The sharp metallic scent. The way Mother's blond hair was matted to her face and the sweat that still ran down it as she reclined on the pillow. It was springtime. There were roses next to her bed, pink ones I'd brought her the day before when we'd gone to the market."

Drystan laced his fingers through hers and gave a tight squeeze.

"Mother taught me to sing and play the flute. She was a great singer herself. Her songs lit up our home even in deep winter. I wanted to be like her, or better, if I could. She beckoned me over as she lay on the bed, just a small movement of her arm. I suppose it's all she could manage. 'Sing for me, Ceridwen,' she said. 'Sing something happy to help me feel better.' It was the first lucid thing she'd said since we found her."

"And so, I sang. I picked her favorite song, the first one she ever taught me. I sang it over and over until my voice was hoarse and my throat ached. I still remember the peaceful look upon her face, despite the sweat that still beaded and fell. Others tried to talk to her, but she waved them away. She looked so calm, so pleasant. I thought surely my music helped."

An unbidden tear streaked down her cheek. "I didn't stop until our housekeeper Jaina led me away, telling me that she was gone and couldn't hear my songs anymore. My music...it didn't help her. It killed her instead. I couldn't sing after that. Anytime I tried, my throat closed up, my eyes watered, and the sound wouldn't come out."

Drystan wiped away her falling tears with his free hand. The other still clutched her as a lifeline amid her sadness. "You didn't kill her, Ceridwen. You gave her peace and joy in her last minutes. She chose to go out into the city. She chose where to walk. And whatever happened, you didn't cause that."

She sniffled, trying to hold back the emotions threatening to overwhelm her. Logically, she knew his words were right. But logic had no authority when it came to guilt and grief. Perhaps she hadn't landed the killing blow, but Mother had left the house because of her. No amount of logic or reason could dull the pain of that or the scars her death left. Mother's death marked the end of Ceridwen's happy childhood, one that likely lingered too far into her womanhood anyway, but it was the first time she knew true sadness. Everything went downhill afterward. Adair grew distant and hotheaded. Father made poor investments and lost his health. Bronwyn grew a sharp tongue and stubborn demeanor. And Ceridwen...she lost even more of herself trying to please them all and make things as they once were. Not that it did any good.

"But I couldn't save her either," she admitted. Ceridwen pulled away and scooped up the bowl and soiled cloth. "You need rest," she began as she returned the bowl to the table.

An object on the desk caught her eye where it sparkled in the dim light. A dark iron pin in the shape of a dragon. Her hands shook. Some of the tainted water spilled onto the floor.

"Ceridwen?"

Memories rushed back, choking her as pieces clicked into place.

Nearby, a mask, even more elaborate than the ones worn to the winter ball, sat on the table. But this wasn't the proud bird Drystan had worn that day. It was something much more sinister.

Dragon. One of the few words her mother moaned after they found her bloodied on the stairs. Nonsense words.

Unless they weren't.

The deep scratches. The blood. Fear to start a labor so suddenly. Danger in the capital. And a dragon.

The bowl fell from her limp fingers.

CHAPTER 40

DRYSTAN

"Ceridwen!" Drystan lunged from the bed, racing across the room as the bowl fell from her grip to clatter upon the floor. Fear seized him over some injury he'd missed, throbbing worse than his aching ribs.

Ceridwen whirled, eyes wide. Color had leeched from her face. Her hands shook.

He reached for her. "What—"

"You!" she sputtered. "Three years ago. Where were you?"

"The capital," he replied, bewildered.

"Where *exactly*." She drew the second word out, her voice as hard as he'd ever heard it. Fury flashed in her blue eyes.

Drystan glanced past her to the items spread on the table, ones gathering dust from how long they'd sat untouched. There, he spied the ornaments of his fall, the symbols of the king's dragons, which he'd left out just in case Malik should venture into his tower when he still believed him an enemy.

Oh, holy Goddess... The blood drained from his face. "You can't think—"

"I certainly can!" Ceridwen grabbed the iron brooch and shoved it toward him. "A dragon, Drystan! And the mask." She gestured to it. "Why else would Mother mutter such nonsense before she died, unless—" Her words cut off in a sob, tears leaking from her face.

Before another tear could fall, Drystan wrapped her in his arms and pulled her close, uncaring of the way his body protested its aches. Ceridwen fought and squirmed, all but stabbing him with the pin on the brooch and likely adding to his bruises. And easy price to pay.

"Let go!"

"I didn't kill your mother," he replied, keeping his voice calm and even as he suffered the wrath of the thrashing beauty in his arms.

"Why should I believe that?" She slammed a fist into his chest, knocking some of the breath from his lungs and sending a wave of fresh pain down his form. "You said you blacked out. She had scratches, like from the beast!"

"It wasn't me." He cradled her head as gently as he could despite her efforts to pull away. "It couldn't have been me." Of this, he was certain.

"How!" she demanded, jerking her head back to skewer him with her stare. "How can you be sure?"

"It was spring," he reminded her. "The prince—I—had been executed that winter."

"So? That hasn't stopped the monster."

The verbal jab slipped between his ribs as vicious as a dagger. No, it hadn't. But he wasn't the only monster roaming the capital, and he hadn't been in the streets then at all. "I was all but imprisoned then," he confessed. "Kept near the king and out of sight, sometimes even...chained."

The king had kept him like a sick and twisted pet. Alive, ready to serve, but never free. Many nights he would order him chained by the wrist in his assigned room—the dark place no larger than a closet, just in case his beast should rise and he should think to leave. It was almost a year before he'd been given any measure of freedom, before he saw anything outside the castle walls.

"Chained," she echoed, suddenly still.

He nodded, the ghostly weight of the shackle on his wrist weighing on him even now. "I could not have been in the streets that spring. It was not me, Ceridwen."

"But the deep cuts on Mother, the dragon mask..."

He wiped at the tear streaks on her cheek. "I'm not the only monster in the capital. There are many loyal to the king. His dragons, he called us. I told you we wore masks when we carried out his handiwork. Well..." He gestured to the mask still gathering dust on the table.

"Then my mother..."

"Must have run afoul of one of them." Probably in the process of carrying out some other heinous act. But to attack a woman, especially one heavy with child, was a terrible new low, one that turned his stomach and made his blood boil in equal measure. Another senseless death to lay at the king's feet.

Ceridwen swayed before nearly collapsing against his bare chest. He held her close, petting her hair as she sniffed away her tears. "All this time...I thought it was some weird accident, that I was the only one to blame."

"It wasn't your fault, Ceridwen."

She nodded slightly, her tears leaking onto his skin. "And the king knows about all this and condones these villains?"

He wasn't entirely sure it was a question, but all the same, he replied, "He does." Which was why he had to stop it. Too many innocent lives were already lost to the darkness, and it would only grow if allowed to spread, like a deep rot that would eventually consume the kingdom. For generations, Castamar kept tight borders and rarely let in outsiders other than for trade. Wariness that others should learn of their magic and lust for it themselves, his father once said, not that it was something a person could claim unless born to it. But maybe there was another reason, too. The havoc a wielder of darkness could cause against the innocents of the world was formidable, something those who valued the light saw in themselves to prevent and contain as best they could.

Eventually, Ceridwen shuddered against him, sucked in a breath, and stared up at him with her tear-stained face still leaning against the top of his chest. "I want to help you kill the king."

"You..." He blinked at her, awed and surprised in equal measure. "You already have."

"I can do more," she insisted.

"It's dangerous. If something happened to you—" He shook his head.

"My music can help you. Whatever it takes to stop this, it's worth the risk."

"Ceridwen—"

"Please. For Mother."

He sighed, his shoulders slumping. She would not be dissuaded, no matter what he said. Drystan ran his fingers along the soft skin of her cheek, savoring the blush that rose in its wake. "How could I tell you no?"

He led her back to the edge of the bed. Silence sat heavily between them, worse than the grief and guilt that had spilled through their words.

"So what led you to play on the rooftops?" he asked. Anything to distract her, and himself if he were being honest.

Ceridwen gave a tentative smile and wiped away the last of her tears. "Music had been Mother's great gift to us all. I couldn't replace her if I tried. If I played near Father, he'd get a faraway look or even leave the room, so I stopped playing for my family too. Only for Mother. I played for her each evening, and I have most days since. I thought it would make her happy to hear me play, though eventually it became more of a comfort to me than it probably ever was to her spirit."

"I always wondered," he said. "When I heard your music for the first time in the spring, it was a light in the darkness of my soul. I often waited by the windows here in the tower, hoping I would hear your songs, especially if I planned to perform a spell that night. It gave me peace. Calm."

"It was you. All this time..." She stared at him in awe.

"What?"

"Watching me." She pulled her bottom lip between her teeth. "Many nights I could feel a strange presence, like someone nearby listening to my song. I thought it might be Mother, but it was you."

He cupped her face, drawing it toward him. "I wanted your music. Craved it. That's why I asked you to come here. I never expected to want the woman who played it even more."

Ceridwen met him halfway with a kiss so delicate and trusting it threatened to carve out a piece of his heart. Only moments ago, she'd feared the worst, but that was gone now. He could taste the acceptance of his truth in her touch, the way she gently sighed against his lips before leaning in farther. Goddess, how she slew him with her tenderness.

Warmth suffused his body when they parted, a balm to some of his physical aches. His stiff cock strained against his breeches, but he wouldn't take more than she offered, no matter how much he wanted her.

"When we first met, I thought you a recluse with the pox who cared nothing for anyone but himself," she admitted.

Drystan laughed, a deep rumbling roar that brought a smile to her lips. "Hopefully I disappointed on that score."

"You did." She traced a finger down the hard lines of his chest, causing his muscles to grow taut. "Eventually."

The comment earned another laugh, one shorter lived. Something swelled in his chest, pressing against his ribs almost painfully, but it wasn't his monster or the lingering pain from Malik striking it. This was something else, a desperation he hadn't felt in years.

"Drystan?"

"Stay here with me tonight." *Please.* More than anything, possibly even his revenge, he wanted her.

Ceridwen gaped at his suggestion. "The dress..." She held up a stained section of the skirt.

His gaze raked her from head to toe. "Take it off."

"Oh!" She covered her mouth with one dainty hand, the flush on her cheeks deepening.

"If you want to, I mean," he replied, suddenly sheepish, a boy caught taking an extra piece of cake. "I know I don't have much to offer anymore. I'm supposed to be dead after all. I might be soon. Of course, there's the dark magic, and you know what I become when—"

She silenced him with a soft palm against his chest. "You're right, but none of that has stopped me from falling in love with you."

"Love," he echoed, dumbstruck. "You love me? Even with the monster?"

When she smiled up at him, the sight was blinding. "Monster and all."

The tightness in his chest transformed, turning into liquid warmth that spread in a slow wave through his body. She really was the most beautiful treasure. One he could never deserve but would savor every day for the rest of whatever remained of his life.

"I love you too, Ceridwen."

CHAPTER 41

CERIDWEN

H E LOVED HER. THE mere thought made her dizzy with joy.

She'd known it already—had felt it in the gentle way he touched her, seen it in his eyes when he looked at her, tasted it in his kiss—but hearing the words from his lips trumped all the others.

He took her hand and brought it to his lips. The chaste, gentlemanly kiss only undid her further. "I don't deserve you, but I started to fall in love with you that day I gave you the tour of the greenhouse."

The admission sparked an entirely different kind of tear in the corner of her eyes.

"It struck me like a blow from nowhere. I tried to ignore it, to remind myself that you deserve better than me." Drystan's head drooped as he released her hand. "I can't give you the life you deserve. Peace, security, happiness..."

She touched his cheek, and he lifted his face to her.

"You already have. My family has the money they need to live a much better life than before. I sang again. And for the first time in many years, I've done what I wanted—for me. You gave me the freedom to be myself, not always the dutiful youngest child trying to keep her family together while breaking apart herself. You brought me back to life and helped me find a beautiful melody in my dreary world."

Drystan tipped her onto the bed, his body coming to cover hers.

"The blood—" she began.

"I don't care."

His lips caught hers, soft but demanding all at once. Ceridwen wrapped her arms around his neck and shoulders, embracing the man she loved as his weight pressed her into the pillow-like softness below.

Her head swam. Her breath drew short until she no longer cared about the mussed dress. She didn't feel the softness of the sheets, or Drystan's heavy weight. Only his lips and hers, locked together in an embrace she wished would last forever.

"Can I take this off?" He fingered the edge of her dress, voice thick and rich.

She licked her lips and nodded, unable to form words.

He helped her rise. With infinite care and slowness, he unlaced the back of the dress until it gaped about her form and slipped to the ground.

Gooseflesh broke out over her skin as Drystan ran his fingertips across her face, around her ear, and down her neck, while he worked behind her, unlacing the corset. Every nerve ending tingled. Heavy breaths and the slip of material accompanied the pounding of her heart, the only sounds in the room.

She yearned to see him, to trace the muscles of his bare chest and the dusting of dark hair that graced its surface. Yet she dared not move. Instead, she savored, letting herself feel rather than think or pursue.

Piece by piece, he undressed her. Nerves in her gut twisted tight as the last of the clothing fell away. The cool air teasing her skin did nothing to ease the blazing warmth within. She bit her lip, strategically positioning her hands in a final show of modesty.

Drystan circled, his gaze raking her from head to toe before he stepped in close. The warmth of his skin jumped the narrow distance between them as he brushed her hair back from her shoulders.

"You're shaking."

She hadn't even noticed. Her eyes were glued to his, the brilliant blue that threatened to undo her even more than his touch. He encircled her with his arms, pulling her close until her hands slipped away and their chests pressed together in the most delicious way.

"Are you having second thoughts? If you are, it's fine, I'll—"

"No." She smiled up at him. "None. I want you. I've never wanted anyone half so much." *And I don't know what comes next. What our future holds.* She'd never forgive herself if she walked away from him now. She wanted all of him, even if only for a short while.

"You're my treasure. The light that keeps me going. I love you, Ceridwen."

She stood on her toes, reaching up to kiss him with her whole heart. His embrace spoke more than words. Each press of his lips was a promise, one she accepted and gave back in return.

She couldn't recall how they ended up on the bed or when he shed his pants, but none of it mattered. All she could think of was Drystan.

Ceridwen gasped as he reached between her spread thighs, gliding his fingers through her slickness. He rubbed his thumb over her taut nub, and she bucked her hips toward him, eager for his touch. Books were her only experience of such things, but she knew what came next. She yearned for it. Feared it. Needed it with every speck of her soul.

"Drystan?" She tangled her fingers in his hair as he worked kisses down her body—her collarbone, one tender nipple, her belly—only stopping and glancing up at her after placing a kiss below her belly button.

"I want to taste you here, Ceridwen." He palmed her between her legs.

"I—" She didn't know what to say exactly, but she'd deny him nothing. She nodded, biting her bottom lip in anticipation.

Drystan's devastating grin alone made her whimper, and then he settled in between her legs. He had kissed her mouth like a master, but the way he kissed her there put even that to shame. Each stroke of his tongue brought more pleasure than touching herself ever had. The short stubble on his cheek grazed lightly against her thighs, only heightening the sensation of his wet tongue against her opening. Ceridwen wiggled, unable to hold still amid the torrent of pleasure. Drystan flatted his palm against her stomach. The other gripped her thigh. She clenched the sheets, holding on for dear life as he brought her closer to the pinnacle of pleasure.

An entirely unladylike gasping moan tore from her lips as he slid one callused finger deep into her wetness. He thrust into her, firmly but gently, rubbing something within her. And then she tipped over the edge in a blinding spiral. She called his name, begged, as he drew out her release.

Sweat dewed her skin as she came back to herself, panting, pleasure tingling through her body, which settled in languid contentment atop the bed.

"You're a beauty, Ceridwen," Drystan said, wiping her wetness from his face. He crawled atop her, careful to keep his weight from pressing on her too heavily. "A wonder."

"So are you," she replied, breathless, before caressing his cheek.

Only a rare man could manage to remain such a tender lover and protector while containing a monster within.

Raised on his forearms, Drystan looked down in pure rapture. "I'll love you all the days I have left and even beyond."

She traced a scar on his arm, the evidence of years of magic and struggle. "Yet I'll love you even longer."

The hair on his legs tickled her thighs as he slid against the wetness between her legs, earning a whimper.

He adjusted his weight, sliding one hand between them to graze over one stiff nipple, around her naval, and lower still until he positioned himself. Their gazes caught and held in the meager light.

She gasped as he pressed into her. The fullness of him stretched her in new ways.

"Ceridwen?" He froze, breathing heavily.

"I'm all right." She brushed away the hair falling around his ears as he eased his weight on top of her. The pain subsided as quickly as it came, a sharp stab that faded as she relaxed against Drystan and savored the feeling of him seated within her.

Another prickle of pain flashed through her when he began to move again, but she bit her lip and held on to the man above her. By the second thrust, it'd already begun to fade. The friction of his gentle thrusts stirred up pleasure even greater than what he'd given moments ago.

"Perfect. Glorious," he praised with every motion of his hips.

Fire licked through her body as she moaned against him, unable to contain the sweet feelings he elicited as they moved together. Slow. Steady. Claiming. Infinitely more exquisite than a perfectly played sonata.

With each near withdrawal, she gripped him tighter, savoring the feel of his hot skin under her hands as they grazed his back, his shoulders, and tangled in his hair. Her body moved on instinct alone, her hips arching for his.

"Ceridwen," he groaned the first time she moved, meeting his thrust with eagerness of her own.

A knot built in her core, constricting with each coming together. She was beyond words, beyond thought, giving in to the will of their bodies moving together as one in perfect harmony.

She slipped her hand from his hair to dig into the sheets when he adjusted his weight and grasped her backside to pull her tight against him. Impossibly, he slid deeper, testing the limits of her giving body in the most delicious way.

With two more deep thrusts, something within her snapped. Ceridwen screamed as pleasure like she'd never known barreled through her. Her toes curled into the sheets. Her back arched. Her head swam until she saw spots before her eyes.

Drystan still moved within her, drawing out her pleasure as she came back to the world, clinging to him with everything she had. "Drystan," she breathed against his fevered skin.

His body shook as a groan slipped from his lips. She cupped his cheek as his eyes closed. With a few more quick thrusts, he stilled. His weight pushed her into the sheets as he nearly collapsed atop her, but she didn't mind. Instead, she savored the feel of his skin against hers everywhere they touched.

Being with him was perfection, bliss. Everything she'd never known she needed.

He found the nook between her neck and shoulder as he kissed a path from her ear and down her upper arm, heavy breaths floating over her skin between each love mark.

"My beauty. My love." The trail of his hand over her thigh, still locked around him, sent a new tingle through her. "You're all right? I didn't hurt you?"

A sweet ache filled the space between her legs, one he still occupied, but she'd never call it pain. "Better than," Ceridwen promised. "I didn't know. Had no idea..." A small laugh slipped from her lips. "We should have done this sooner."

His chest rumbled, reigniting the fire within her. "This is already more than I ever hoped for. When you figured out what I was, I thought all hope of you loving me to be lost."

At first, she'd thought so too, but she'd never admit that to him. Not now. Certainly not like this. "It's a good thing I'd already fallen in love with you," she replied instead. "Light. Dark. I accept it all."

He groaned as he slid from between her legs to lie at her side. Instantly, she missed him. The closeness. The connection. Ceridwen snuggled against him, lacing a leg over his as she trailed her fingers down his chest.

Sadness seeped into his features as he turned to her, their faces only a breath apart. "Whatever happens to me, I'll make sure you're safe. Provided for. Protected."

"Don't talk like that," she chided. "Not tonight." They'd figure out a plan, a way forward. But that darkness could wait until tomorrow. She didn't want anything to cloud the beauty of this night.

"If you command it."

"I do." She sealed her words with a kiss, deep and full of the lingering desire building anew under her skin. His hand sliding along her side and over her hip only fueled that ache.

"Can we do it again?" she asked, near breathless.

He raised his brows. "Again?"

Heat blazed to her cheeks. She bit her lip, slightly embarrassed at her eagerness.

Deep laughter rumbled from his lips, vibrating against her body where it lay against his own. "Who knew I found such a lusty savior?" His wolfish grin melted her further. "Give me a little bit, but I think I can accommodate my lady's desires."

CHAPTER 42
DRYSTAN

D RYSTAN WOKE BEFORE DAWN. Ceridwen lay curled on her side in his bed, chest rising and falling with easy breaths. The oil lamp on the table burned low. It gave just enough light to see Ceridwen's blond hair strewn across the pillow like a golden cloud.

Watching her was a dream. What they shared the night before, even more so. His chest drew tight as he imagined a future with her, one he'd be determined to have if he were any other man with any other past. How easily she slipped into his life and his heart. How wonderful it would be to wake to the sight of her each morning and cherish her in his bed at night.

He'd give every piece of gold he had to clear the sins of his past and live a simple life together with her. But he wasn't some normal man, no matter how much he might yearn for it. He knew darkness, tasted it, lived with it. It would grow until it crept across the whole of the country, seeking him out once more. More than that, he couldn't live with the guilt of being able to do something—to kill the king and stop the darkness from spreading—and choosing not to.

Drystan quietly slipped from bed and donned fresh clothes. At his desk, he wrote two letters, and then he crept down the stairs in search of Jackoby.

The task complete, he briefly returned to the tower. For the still-sleeping Ceridwen, he left two things: fresh clothes and a rose from his favorite plant.

No, that wasn't entirely true. He left a third there with her in the tower: his heart.

It was the hardest thing he'd ever done, but there was no one more precious to him, no one he longed to keep far from the danger and darkness in the capital more than her.

He packed a few essential belongings and descended the tower stairs again. With a quiet farewell to his friend and butler, Drystan left the manor to catch the morning train.

CHAPTER 43

CERIDWEN

LIGHT SPILLED INTO THE room through the window and roused Ceridwen from sleep.

A smile pulled at her lips as memories of the night before rushed back, flooding her with happy, glowing feelings that wrapped around her, body and soul. Her muscles had never felt so languid. Even her spirit was lighter. Free.

"Drystan." She smiled at the taste of his name on her tongue. She rubbed the last bit of sleep from her eyes. His scent tickled her nose from the sheets, only deepening the fire kindling to life again within her.

Any second now, he'd wrap her in his arms, kiss her hair, and wish her a good morning. She could see it in her mind's eye. She longed for it.

But the silence stretched. A coil of dread slipped into her happiness.

"Drystan?"

She twisted toward his side of the bed to be greeted by empty, ruffled sheets. One object lay where he'd rested the night before: a single purple rose.

Drystan loved his roses. He'd clipped other flowers for her, but never those, yet now he'd left one on the pillow. Tentatively, she ran her fingertips over the silken petals and down the stem, dodging thorns. When she reached the cut end, it was still moist.

The beautiful sight should have filled her with further joy, but foreboding crept in instead. Why the rose instead of him? She'd never considered that he might be absent when she woke. Not after the night they'd shared.

Chills raced over her naked skin as she sat upright in bed. The man she loved was nowhere to be found, nor could she hear any sound from the floor above.

"Drystan?" Ceridwen called again, eyeing the doorway. Any moment now, he'd walk in, and all the tension building against her bones would rush away.

But moments passed, and only silence greeted her.

In haste, she slipped from the bed, wincing against the cold, and donned the clean underthings, nightdress, and robe that someone—likely Drystan—had left at the foot of the bed.

With still mussed and tangled hair, she rushed down the stairs. *He's just gone down for breakfast. Everything is fine.* But she didn't believe her own excuses.

Each step notched her panic a note higher until she practically jumped down the last steps and out into the main hall. Voices swarmed her, including one she did not expect.

"You haven't explained anything," Bronwyn snapped. "How many times do I have to ask?"

"At least a few more," Malik replied, though he didn't sound the least bit annoyed.

Her sister stared daggers at the prince. If only she knew. But Ceridwen had more important things on her mind. "Where's Drystan?"

Their attention snapped to her, silencing the argument between them.

Bronwyn gaped. "Ceridwen...you..." Her gaze trailed over her sister's mussed hair and robe. "Are you all right?"

"I'm fine," Ceridwen assured as her sister rushed to greet her. Past her, Malik's smile had died. He shifted from one foot to the other, not looking her in the eye. Her heart started to crumble. Something was wrong. Very wrong.

"Was Drystan here?" Ceridwen asked.

"Yes, he came down," he replied at length. "Or so I was told."

"And?"

She didn't want to know. She had to know.

"He's gone. He left for the capital on the early train."

She didn't hear him correctly. Couldn't have. The world before her shifted. Her legs shook. Bronwyn lunged for her as she slumped to the floor.

"He...he..." *He left me.*

Bronwyn pulled her tight against her chest. "You bastard!" she yelled over her shoulder. "You had to tell her something hurtful with such callousness?"

"I didn't ask to be the messenger," Malik retorted. "But I did think to fetch you to be here for her."

She snapped her mouth shut, cutting off whatever she planned to say as she focused on Ceridwen again.

Ceridwen saw her sister and felt her embrace, but everything was numb and far away. Nothing filled her but deep emptiness.

"It's okay. It will be okay," Bronwyn crooned.

But it wouldn't. If she never saw him again... She shuddered. It was unthinkable.

"Let's get you up. A bath will help. Maybe some breakfast." Bronwyn tried to pull her to her feet, but Ceridwen's body refused to move. After a minute, her sister gave up and sat on the floor next to her.

Malik neared. His feet shifted on the floor he gazed at like a scolded child. "There's a letter too. If you want it." He slipped a thin piece of folded parchment from within his jacket.

From the way he held it, Ceridwen could just make out the looping scrawl of one word that started with a grand C. Her name.

"Give it to me," she demanded, not caring that she sounded and looked like a petulant child. Hair a mess. Teary eyes. Only wearing a nightdress and robe. He probably saw her as a wild woman. Yet his eyes held no judgment as he slipped the letter into her waiting hands.

"Perhaps we should take her to her room," Jackoby intoned. Ceridwen hadn't seen him enter, but his voice displayed no surprise. Someone must have told him.

"In a minute," Malik replied on her behalf.

Ceridwen unfolded the letter with shaking hands.

Dearest Ceridwen,

You'll know by now that I've left ahead of plan. I couldn't risk you asking to come with me again. How could I have ever told you no?

Know that I love you. You've given me joy in my last days—more than a monster like me deserves.

Malik will see to your family's well-being and that of everyone who resides within the manor.

Live a good life far away from the taint of magic and blood. Forget about me, but never lose your music. It's a magic of its own, filled with the beauty of your soul, that only you can weave.

No matter what happens, I'm blessed beyond worth or measure to have heard your song and felt your love.

Yours always,

Drystan

Short and sharp like an arrow to the heart. She'd expected nothing less, but the brevity of his last words sent tears streaking down her face.

"You know what it says?" she asked Malik through her tears.

"I do. He told me in my letter. And I'll uphold every word," he promised, arms crossed across his chest.

"What's going on?" Bronwyn asked, looking between the two of them.

Ceridwen sniffed away the tears, rubbed her eyes, and stood. Bronwyn kept a hand on her the whole time, probably worried she might sink to the ground in a heap or puddle. "I'm going to the capital."

Malik's eyes widened. Bronwyn's hand tightened on hers.

Jackoby was the first to speak. "Miss Ceridwen, you should stay here for now. We'll look after you and your family if you'd like."

Forcing a smile took effort. "That is very kind," Ceridwen replied, "but Drystan has already set up provision for them and everyone here."

She looked to Malik, who nodded, the surprise gone from his face. He reached into his front jacket pocket and pulled forth an elaborate silver key. "The key to the vault. Allocations have been set aside for Ceridwen's family as well as all the manor staff. You may stay for a few days to get organized and then start anew somewhere else with the blessing of Tristram Ithael."

Bronwyn squeaked, hands flying to her mouth.

"And should anyone question it"—Malik slid a large, ornate ring from one finger—"show them my seal."

Jackoby approached and took the items Malik offered. "Highness," he said with a courtly bow.

"Holy Goddess," Bronwyn blurted. "You're the dark prince."

Not quite. Apparently, Malik and Jackoby were ready to let Bronwyn in on the secrets they held, though she might not be ready to hear them. Of course, if Drystan succeeded, then perhaps he could reclaim his old name and title. If he failed... She couldn't consider that. She wouldn't let the king and his dark magic steal another person she loved.

"Only half right," Malik replied, striding toward Bronwyn with an amused smirk on his face. He took her hand, though she tried to pull away, and bowed before her. "Prince Alistair Ithael, at your service."

Bronwyn paled considerably. A myriad of emotions raced across her face. Ceridwen could tell the moment her sister sorted out the puzzle. She looked at Ceridwen as Malik released her. "Then Drystan..."

"Is really Tristram Ithael," she supplied. A weight lifted from her shoulders. Finally, her sister knew. She'd never kept secrets from her, not before she came to the manor. Sharing them now brought a sliver of peace to the turmoil in her heart.

"But he...didn't he..." She'd never been quite so tongue-tied.

"He didn't kill his parents. He was framed by our current king, a practitioner of dark magic." Ceridwen shivered at the reference and looked over at Jackoby. "You know everything?"

One solemn nod confirmed everything before he even spoke. "That bit I knew before we came here, but only this morning did we learn his full plan. Goddess, give him strength."

Malik nodded in confirmation. Some discussion had happened that morning that she hadn't been privy to, but none of that mattered now.

"Do you trust her?" Jackoby asked, tipping his head toward Bronwyn.

"Completely." Ceridwen took Bronwyn's hands in hers, snaring her sister's full attention. "Drystan plans to kill the king, and I intend to help him."

Very rarely was Bronwyn ever stunned into silence, but she was at that moment, her eyes widening and mouth gaping open. Ceridwen looked past her sister at Malik. He knew Drystan's plans, of course, but her following after had never been part of them.

To her surprise, Malik responded, "Good." As if he was somehow glad Ceridwen planned to defy Drystan's expectations and whatever orders he might have left for Malik to keep her there and out of trouble.

A grin tipped his lips up at the corners. "But I wouldn't be much of a gentleman if I let you go alone. I'll escort you to the capital. No one should stop you if you're with me."

Bronwyn's grip on her hands tightened. "I'm going too."

"No." Ceridwen's heart leaped into her throat as she swung back toward her sister. "It's too dangerous." Risking herself was one thing. Getting her sister mixed up in this deadly plot? Unthinkable.

Bronwyn jerked her hands away, crossed her arms, and stared her sister down. "I'm not letting you run off into danger alone. Especially not with that one." She pointed an accusing finger at Malik. "I'm coming. You've carried too many burdens by yourself for too long. No longer. I want to help."

"But—" Ceridwen began, her panic rising with her voice.

"Let her come," Malik interjected. "Surely I can keep two young women safe."

Bronwyn pursed her lips but stayed silent.

Ceridwen looked between the two of them, and her shoulders slumped with a weary sigh. She couldn't win against them both. "Fine." Letting Bronwyn get herself in danger once they got to the capital was another matter, one she'd find a way around. Truthfully, it would be nice to have company, if even just for the benign part of the journey. She'd never traveled alone, especially not with a man, and having Bronwyn with her might help on that front. However... "What are we going to tell Father?" Her absence might not be noticed since she already resided at the manor with Lord Winterbourne, but their father was bound to notice if his oldest daughter didn't come home.

Bronwyn shrugged. "I'll think of something."

As if that were a viable plan. Ceridwen gave her a withering look.

"Whatever it is, do it quickly," Malik said.

"I'll keep an eye on your family personally until I receive word of your return," Jackoby promised. "And before you go, you must pack your things. You'll need clothes in the capital if nothing else. I can send Kent to assist your sister. Besides, Gwen would flay me alive if I let you leave before she could give you a proper farewell or if I let you out looking like that." He appraised her from head to toe with raised brows.

A touch of heat flamed Ceridwen's cheeks. He was right on both counts. She'd fled out the front door without thinking once before, and she couldn't do that to them again. Plus, she really needed to clean and change, but time wasn't on their side. "The train..."

"The train to the capital only runs twice a week," Malik said, pacing a narrow trail a few feet away. "We've missed today's, but perhaps we can hire a carriage to take us to the next city south and catch one from there. It would be faster than waiting around. Plus it will give you time to ready yourselves."

Twice a week. Ceridwen barely held back a squeak. How silly that she lived here and didn't know the train schedule to the capital. But then, after Mother's death, none of them wished to ever return there. How strange a turn life took, sending her back once more.

"Fine," Ceridwen agreed. "If that's the fastest way, we'll do it. Now, let's all get to it."

Chapter 44

Drystan

THE CAPITAL WAS WORSE than he remembered. Factory smoke and the stench of human waste tainted the air. Hollow, hungry faces watched him as he passed, despite his efforts to dress as nondescript as possible and shield much of himself in a heavy cloak as he'd done when in Teneboure. The looks would only worsen if they knew who he was. The station attendant in Teneboure had nearly fainted when he, as Lord Winterbourne, purchased a ticket to the capital. The conductor had been just as bad, practically tripping over himself.

The worst part of the return, so far, was the number of missing person signs tacked to building walls and lampposts. The knowledge of what led to those disappearances and the certainty that the victims would never be found turned his stomach. But it also steeled his resolve. That was why he returned, why he ventured just outside the station and hired a carriage to take him to the castle.

Guards stopped him at the main gate, as expected, inquiring over his identity and his request to be let inside. One quick show of his family sigil, one the king himself created for him after his fall, appeased that request. No one seemed to care that there hadn't been a Lord Winterbourne before. Nor did anyone seem to recognize him as the prince he used to be. Too many people believed whatever they were told, looking no further than for an easy reason to agree and be on their way.

Long minutes he waited in the king's audience chamber for the man to appear. Servants had offered to take his luggage to a room for him, but he refused to let the case out of his sight, keeping it beside his chair instead. It contained the Gray Blade, and he would not risk its theft or discovery.

Drystan tapped a slow rhythm with the toe of his boot on the elaborate rug while he waited, the only thing keeping him sane. Even his beast paced within him, impatient and uncertain.

Finally, the door groaned open, and the king entered, waving off his guard who waited outside the doors. Killing him now would be possible—risky, but possible. However, it would ensure his own demise, and he wouldn't have the chance to dismantle the damage the king wrought during his horrible, albeit short, reign. For true success, he needed more, something public, damning—an act he wasn't quite sure of yet but would search out every moment until he found it.

Drystan jumped to his feet and dropped into a bow before his uncle, as expected.

"Lord Winterbourne," the king boomed, smiling all the while, though that was no true indication of a welcome reception. "And back much earlier than I expected, with no staff and few belongings, I hear."

"Apologies, Your Grace." He lifted his head but remained standing, the iron dragon pin in proud display upon his chest. "I tired of the dreary winters up north and wished to return to your service. My servants will finish tending the manor and arrive with my things in due time."

The orders he'd given were quite the opposite: Stay for a few days so as not to draw suspicion. Pack and shut down the manor as they would have upon midwinter and their return to the capital. But then, take the gold he left in the vaults and whatever around the manor could aid them to start a new life. If he was successful, he could refurnish the manor and offer his staff a place with him in the capital, should they choose. If unsuccessful? Well, if a future lord or lady complained about the sparsity of their new residence, they could be damned for all he cared. There would be bigger things to worry about then.

Drystan had no regrets on that front. The only regret was leaving Ceridwen before dawn. But she would have surely begged to go with him if he'd told her or if he had waited until midwinter. How could he refuse her anything? Hopefully the money he left for her family would ease the sting of their parting, even if every moment without her was an agony for him.

"Hmm," the king mused, slipping into his favorite chair of crimson velvet and gold-painted wood. "I suppose the north is quite dull at the best of times. And my son, is he not with you?"

"Prince Alistair wished to remain a few days longer."

"That boy." The king tsked before pursing his lips. "Always ignoring his duties."

For all that he was a monster in truth, the king's fair looks, ones so similar to Drystan's father, still unnerved him. His dark hair, liberally streaked with gray, fell just the same way his father's had. They shared the same strong jaw and nose, as well as the bright-blue eyes that Drystan inherited also. It would be easy to believe the best of him, if one didn't know the heinous acts he committed, a fact he used to his advantage with commoners and nobles alike.

"Though I will say, the reports I've received from my son thus far have been most assuring, as well as your own. That mayor up there though, whatever his name is"—he waved a dismissive hand through the air—"loves to send his complaints."

Damn it. Drystan's jaw stiffened. He knew the mayor would find a way to cause him trouble.

"Complaints about a beast stalking citizens?" The king arched a dark brow. His ring-decked fingers steepled in front of him.

"Apologies, Your Grace," Drystan forced out. "I thought it best to keep my skills in practice so that I may be of service to you. However, I have been most discreet in that and my stay in Teneboure."

The king crossed his legs, the top one bouncing a bit. He never could sit still. "Good, I'll have use of them. More of his complaints were about your inability to kill it." He laughed. "Ironic that? He also confirmed that you were quite...absent from society."

Drystan shifted slightly in his seat, unsure how to take the king's upbeat mood. It could be a sign of acceptance or the taunt of a viper waiting to sink in its teeth. "All with your reign in mind, my king. I offended you by accidentally being seen and confused for someone I was not." To the king, Tristram was dead. He created Lord Winterbourne, but Drystan picked out his own first name to go with the title. Still, it was best not to annoy him by making any reference to his shamed nephew. "I thought it best to keep well out of sight and let my title and mere presence in their city placate the citizens. I hope I have not displeased you in this."

The pandering, the constant need to appease the king's ego, tasted foul on his tongue, but such words were necessary. With one word, the king could order a real execution this time, and his efforts at revenge would be for naught.

"No, you did well." The king stood once more, pacing slowly in front of his chair. "I don't care what one upstart mayor thinks." He paused, tapping a finger on his lip. "Perhaps I'll have him replaced with someone more...docile. In any case, settle in today and rest from your travels. I may have need of your services, so your return is timely."

"Oh? And how may I be of service?" Drystan asked, hoping to appear conspiratorial.

The king smirked. "I'm to have a midwinter party, and a few nobles have rejected my invitation. Can you imagine that?"

"No, Your Grace." He certainly could, especially if they favored the light. But a party? Now that could be an interesting opportunity. "Who would reject such an invitation?"

"Who indeed," the king echoed. "One claimed illness or such nonsense, but still, I may need your assistance aiding some of your fellow dragons in convincing them. It wouldn't look good if the party isn't crowded. You understand, of course."

"Yes, Your Grace." *A large crowd...* If only he could find a way to expose the king's true nature to them.

"Well then, we shall talk tomorrow." Without a backward glance, the king left the room.

Drystan smiled broadly. The Goddess blessed him twofold, first sparing him from the king's ire and, secondly, giving him the seed of a plan.

CHAPTER 45
CERIDWEN

T HE SIZE AND SPRAWL of the capital still boggled Ceridwen's mind. They'd started passing farms an hour before the steam-powered train pulled into the station. When houses began to fill her vision with regularity, she'd been certain the train would draw to a halt at any moment, but they'd kept going until she could hardly comprehend the number of people who must reside among the many cramped buildings and narrow streets. Somehow, it had seemed less intimidating when she'd visited with her family some three years ago. But then, it was just a fun family trip—albeit one that ended terribly. This time was much different.

Colorful awnings and painted walls gave life to otherwise gray stone buildings. Trees were sparse, gardens even rarer, within the dense sprawl of the city proper.

Sound overwhelmed Ceridwen when they stepped from the train car. Unlike Teneboure, where no one seemed in a rush for anything, people ran this way and that, shouting and carrying on as if everything must happen in a moment or the Goddess would claim their soul. At least it was a change from the near-constant scowls and verbal taunts exchanged between Bronwyn and Malik for the better part of their journey.

"I still don't see how anyone can stand this city," Bronwyn said as she avoided a dubious puddle on the way to whatever nearby destination Malik had in mind.

"It has its beauty, if you know where to look." Malik plowed ahead, navigating the maze of streets like a captain at sea.

"You're sure our things will be safe?" Ceridwen asked for possibly the third time. She'd brought the sheet music for *The Blessings of the Goddess* concerto after recovering it from Drystan's tower before their departure. The poor sheets were a little worse for wear with a few bloodstains and tears, but still readable. She should have left the concerto behind for safekeeping, especially with the state it was in, but it made its way into her trunk anyway. Her flute had been packed away as well until Malik insisted she fetch it for this little venture.

"I paid the porter more than enough. I have no doubt they'll be at my apartment once we arrive."

"You don't have a more official residence?" Bronwyn asked. A jab. Of course he did.

He smirked over one shoulder. "You know why we can't stay there. Besides, having a place of my own away from prying eyes has its advantages."

"Such as?" she prodded.

The hooded smile and wicked grin he shot her way sent her stumbling over the cobblestones. Ceridwen's own feet turned sluggish as well. It didn't take much imagination to figure out his implication. A reckless, carefree prince indeed.

"Ah, here we are," Malik announced, turning the corner onto a wide street.

A grand building rose before them, several stories in height. Marble pillars stretched up to the high roof from the landing atop a flight of wide stairs that started at the street. Paintings in golden frames hinted at shows and performances, either past or present. Doors two stories high stood at the front, just below a sign in gold letters that read Grand Opera.

"An opera house." The sight nearly stopped Ceridwen in her tracks.

"The most renowned venue. Every show draws the city's best like flies to a corpse."

She gagged. Between his vile description and the stench of the city, she was lucky not to spill her meager meal from the train into the street.

"Why are we here?" Ceridwen asked once she'd recovered.

"Trust me, you'll see."

Dread washed over her as an inkling of his plan settled in, but she followed him to the side door without question. Outside the door were small posters resembling ones they'd seen at the station. Missing people—all who'd disappeared at night.

They'd heard the rumors, even in Teneboure. Now that they were here, the signs of trouble, of darkness, were impossible to miss if one knew what to look for.

Three solid raps drew the attention of an attendant who showed them into a small parlor. Plush velvets of crimson, gold, and shades of pink highlighted the cushions of elaborately carved furniture within the gaudy room. Painted posters of former shows and acts hung from the walls. A vibrant arrangement of greenery and winter flowers occupied a table in the middle of the seating area, so large Ceridwen could barely see over it.

After a few minutes, a busty woman with ringlets of long, golden hair burst through the door. Heavy makeup painted her entire face, from bloodred lips to coal-darkened eyelids and rouged cheeks. An equally curious woman with bright-teal hair and dark skin followed.

"My favorite patron has finally returned to pay me a visit," the first announced.

The woman's masculine voice did not fit her appearance. And as Ceridwen looked closer, neither did the slight bulge on her neck.

"Wynni." Malik bowed and kissed the back of her hand, which she'd offered to him. "Your *favorite patron* has come to ask a favor. An urgent one."

Her eyes glittered. "You know I do love a good intrigue. Speaking of, I don't think you've met my new assistant, Chesa. She comes up with the most fascinating tales."

Chesa gave a quick bow before her grin stretched wide to flash bright-white teeth as she tilted her head this way and that, studying them each in turn with rapt fascination.

"We'll have an incredible opera this next season for sure. There's the one she's come up with about a secluded island ruled by two families, the sons of which are both in love with the same woman, who—"

Malik coughed loudly, cutting her off. Though Ceridwen had only heard half of what she'd said since Chesa kept staring at her like she could see every single thought in her head—a truly terrifying possibility.

"Ah, apologies. I get so excited, you know," Wynni said, stifling a laugh. "We'll talk later. Now then who are these lovely ladies with you?"

Bronwyn stepped up first. "Bronwyn Kinsley," she said with a curtsy. "And my sister, Ceridwen."

"It's a pleasure to meet you," Ceridwen added with a curtsy of her own, doing her best not to let her unease show.

Boisterous laughter, pitched too high to be natural, filled the room. "Lovely. I'm Wynnifred Prosser, though I suppose he's told you that." She pointed a manicured nail at Malik. "Welcome to my opera house."

She waved them toward the seats. "Now that the pleasantries are out of the way, what is this favor?"

Malik made himself comfortable on a pink settee before he said, "I'd like you to let Ceridwen perform on your stage."

Wynni took her in appraisingly.

"Tonight," Malik added.

Ceridwen's breath hitched and she sat a little straighter. Wynni's sculpted eyebrows reached higher as her gaze shifted between the prince and Ceridwen.

"And the next several nights if needed."

No. Me? Perform on a stage? She couldn't. Yes, it had been a dream once, but playing for so many people... The possibility of it made her dizzy and she clutched the cushion beneath her for support.

"She looks like she might faint first," Chesa whispered to Wynni, but the other woman ignored her as she pulled a paper fan from her dress pocket, unfolded it in a snap, and fanned herself.

"My, that is quite the request," Wynni replied.

"She's very talented." Malik leaned in and began gesturing with his hands, his chin lifting with the practiced confidence of someone used to getting their way. "Besides, I could make your house renowned. Famous for all time."

A small smile lit her face. "It already is, darling. Besides, I have plenty of my own singers."

Ceridwen's heart skipped a beat. He couldn't mean for her to sing. She shifted in her seat. "I can't—"

Chesa stood abruptly, and Ceridwen's protest died. The woman with teal hair stepped in front of Ceridwen's seat and bent over until their faces were nearly level. But Chesa wasn't looking at her, not exactly anyway. Her gaze seemed to be far away and so close at all once. Suddenly she straightened and looked back at Wynni. "She has a story, this one. A song, but not a spoken one."

The idea of the woman prying into her mind suddenly felt all too plausible. Ceridwen glanced at Malik, not bothering to shield the panic she knew must be visible in her eyes.

However, Malik's pinched brows smoothed out as did his stiff posture. "How astute," he replied, unruffled. Then to Wynni, "She plays the flute better than anyone you've heard. And she happens to have the third act of *The Blessings of the Goddess* in her possession."

The fan halted. "It doesn't exist," Wynni said, but her eyes gleamed with interest, her voice carrying an intensity that begged for what he claimed to be true even though she'd been quick to deny it. "It does. I've seen it myself," he said, reclining with a smug smile.

A silent conversation passed between Chesa and Wynni. Then, Wynni took Ceridwen in again, finally noticing the case she clutched for dear life. "Well then, why don't you play for me, dear?" She snapped the fan closed. "But if I'm going to rearrange my schedule at the last minute, it better be good."

Bronwyn cinched her sister into the corset, pulling the string so tightly Ceridwen gasped.

"I won't be able to play if it's too tight," she reminded her.

"The dress Wynnifred found for you won't fit if this isn't tight." Her regular cast were all tiny or curvaceous, with few in between, much to Ceridwen's misfortune. This dress, a confection of pink-and-white lace, proved the best she could find on short notice.

"Besides," Bronwyn continued. "She loved your playing so much that she agreed to completely change her evening program for the entire week. Even her strange assistant clapped like a little kid after just one song. I doubt the rare off note will hinder her regard."

"It's not her attention I'm after."

Their plan was haphazardly pieced together at best. Get Ceridwen on the stage in front of a massive audience to play a song most didn't believe existed. Her music, along with the song, should spread gossip around the city in no time, especially if Wynnifred gushed about it as well, which she promised to do. With any luck, Drystan would hear the rumors and make an appearance of some sort.

If they weren't already too late. She pushed the thought away, refusing to let it fester.

One thing was certain, though. They couldn't just wander into the castle looking for him. Malik was reluctant to return yet for fear of his father restricting his movement or immediately ordering him off on some other venture.

Malik left the sisters in Wynnifred's care while he went to retrieve the sheet music. Ceridwen hadn't memorized the third movement yet, not all of it. Improvising would not work for this show. To impress such a particular audience, used to seeing and hearing the best talent in the country, she would need to be perfect.

Bronwyn helped her into the dress and then stepped back as two women rushed in to attend to her hair and makeup.

"Nothing will do but the very best. Wynni's orders," the older one informed Ceridwen as she gaped at the baskets of supplies they toted with them.

While they worked to transform her into a new woman, Ceridwen thought of Drystan. More than once, the ladies reminded her not to mar their work when her eyes turned glassy and far away.

Even if Drystan could kill the king, one couldn't simply murder a monarch without repercussions. Not easily. Malik didn't want the title and surely wouldn't take it seriously. No one else stood in line for the throne.

Unless a certain prince were no longer dead...

For that, they'd need to clear his name. And sully the king's.

Ceridwen jumped as the doors burst open. With her makeup complete to the women's exacting standards and her hair done up in waves and curls, she looked like something she never expected to be—a high-class lady. Ceridwen couldn't imagine a way to improve the look, yet the two women still poked and prodded the curls, adding pins here and there.

"Isn't it perfect?" Wynnifred exclaimed. "She's lovely. Let the poor girl be so she can look."

The women stepped away. Freed, Ceridwen turned and gasped at the sight before her. Chesa held a large piece of parchment, and on it shown Ceridwen's likeness. Or what she assumed to be her likeness. A dainty blond woman played the flute on a grand, lighted stage. Her name stood out in bold print at the top. The painted image faded at the bottom to give way to further words. "Hear the incredible third movement of *The Blessings of the Goddess*. This week only!"

She gaped in wonder. Her dream from long away would be coming true, yet instead of the urge to jump for joy, all she felt was apprehension—worry for Drystan, for herself, for all of them.

"It's lovely," she managed.

"Better than lovely." Wynnifred laughed.

"And by tomorrow, we'll have made enough copies to paste them all over the city. Plus, I may have written a little story to accompany some of them." Chesa's eyes gleamed. "A poor lovesick woman prayed to the Goddess for aid, and in return the Goddess blessed her with a song, and now she's sharing it with the world."

Ceridwen's smile faltered a bit. Had Malik told her about Drystan? Surely not.

Wynni clapped twice, and Chesa rolled up the poster, retreating with a little bounce in her step.

"Don't let me down out there." Wynni patted Ceridwen's shoulder. "Ten minutes."

So soon?

When the time was right, Wynnifred led Ceridwen to the stage. Her music had been set up on a stand in the center. Bright light from the gas lamps lit all around the edge of the wooden platform blinded her view of the audience. They were there, though. Murmurs filled the air, along with the occasional cough, laugh, and jostle of bodies as people took their seats.

"A full crowd." Wynnifred smiled before strutting onto the stage to introduce her. In the opposite wing, Malik and Bronwyn looked on, each giving Ceridwen an encouraging smile.

Goddess, give me strength.

The crowd quieted when Wynnifred demanded their attention. "And now, for your listening pleasure, may I introduce Miss Ceridwen Kinsley."

CHAPTER 46

DRYSTAN

DRYSTAN FIXED HIS DRAGON mask over his face and pulled the hood of his cloak over his head before venturing out into the streets—his task fulfilled. The few flurries of snow that stuck to the ground that morning were long melted, as was often the case, the capital being situated near the southern end of the country, not far from the Cerulean Sea.

The meeting he left could have gone one of two ways, and he whispered thanks to the Goddess and all her Eidolons as he climbed into the waiting carriage that it had gone in his favor.

The king hadn't been joking about his fury that some of the nobles refused his invitation to the midwinter party. In light of their refusals, the king had dispatched some of his most loyal dragons—Drystan included—to help the nobles see things the king's way and promise their support and attendance.

A bloody, terrible task.

Or it could have been.

But when Drystan arrived at the home of Lord Stellan and was let inside, he didn't find the malleable elder he expected. Instead, Lord Stellan, proud man that he was, spouted praise for the former monarchs and railed about all the ways the king disappointed him and was leading the country to damnation.

Reckless, foolish talk. The kind that could have ended with him imprisoned or worse, had Drystan been any other dragon.

But during the minutes that he silently endured the tirade, Drystan spied an opportunity. He needed allies, members of the nobility who might believe his story and support him should be successful in overthrowing the king. So he took a chance on Lord Stellan, recalling memories of his youth when the lord used to play cards with his father, or how the late Lady Stellan had been fond of his mother and the two used to have regular walks through the castle gardens to chat about their little dogs.

The older man wept by the end of it, but not in the way the king had hoped. Drystan had the lord's vow of loyalty and the promise to gather others to the cause. He and those loyal to his father's memory would attend the midwinter party, where Drystan would reveal the king's ills for all. How exactly he would do that was a puzzle still taking shape in his mind, but the pieces were forming, moving into place. Lord Stellan was just the latest of the few lords and ladies he'd appealed to over the past days while on errand for the king, but each pledged to his cause.

It was a risk, one not taken lightly. Some other nobles had seemed less zealous, so Drystan did not venture his luck on them, but he knew one thing for certain: Without some risks, he could never win, and he'd come too far to stop now.

The carriage rocked to a stop. When the halt lasted more than a handful of moments, the driver informed Drystan of a spilled cart ahead, blocking the way. With other carriages crammed into the busy street behind them, there was little room to move. They would have to wait it out.

Eager to see more of the city, Drystan excused himself to continue on foot. It was short blocks back to castle—not a risk with his hood up and the spilled cart drawing everyone's attention.

He was halfway when he spied something that rooted his feet to the cobblestones. Drystan stared at the newly nailed poster, certain he must be seeing things. But there was no mistaking the name scrawled across the bottom of it. He traced the letters with his fingertips. "Ceridwen."

His blood ran hot and cold at once. The woman he loved was here, impossibly fulfilling the dream she'd once told him of. But there was only one reason she would venture to this city she loathed, the one that had taken her mother. He'd wager it had nothing to do with her brother, whose unit was likely here somewhere, and instead everything to do with him.

Did you hope to get my attention, dearest Ceridwen?

She certainly had it now, and that of many others by putting on such a show at the Grand Opera. His chest swelled with pride at the thought of her on the stage. She should be safe there, far from what he planned.

But what if she wasn't? Or worse, what if she tried something even more reckless?

He snapped his hand back from the poster and clenched it tight into a fist. He had to see her, make sure she was safe, and find some way to keep her that way.

Without another thought, Drystan turned on his heel and ventured toward the opera house.

Patrons swarmed the main entrance when he arrived, already making their way in for the early performance—Ceridwen's. A sold-out sign had been hung over the ticket window, and he'd never make it in the main entrance anyway. They'd demand he remove his hood. The mask would draw too much gossip, and without it? Well, he might be able to see the show if he could procure a ticket, but he doubted they'd let the average attendee see the star.

"Three nights in a row now. Can you believe it?" someone whined to their companion as they trudged away from the opera house.

"And tomorrow, too," the other said. "How will we ever get tickets?"

Bravo, Ceridwen.

Drystan smiled in spite of himself as he watched the strangers leave. The city loved her, as it should.

Around the back of the building, a few stagehands sat on stacks of crates and smoked pipes a short way from a narrow door. That was his way in. Easy enough—he'd done a good bit of sneaking into places on behalf of the king, but finding Ceridwen once he got in before someone spotted him and threw him out would be another matter.

Drystan pulled free a small blade and quickly slid it across his palm, just enough for blood to well and pool in his cupped hand, ready for his use. He painted one quick spell on a crate in the shadows of the alleyway across from the theater. In a few moments, it would turn into flame, enough to catch attention but hopefully not to cause any real damage. Another spell he traced onto himself, one to coerce the shadows to cling to him. It wouldn't hide him perfectly—that was beyond his skill—but it would help.

Once the flames ignited, the men took notice and rushed to put them out, just as he'd hoped. The distraction presented the perfect opportunity to slip inside. The halls were dim and cluttered, full of props and crates of supplies. He wound through the passages, ducking into shadows and holding his breath as people wandered by, praying for the Goddess to aid his magic in cloaking his presence.

The sound of a familiar voice around a corner made him go deathly still. All at once, he knew exactly how Ceridwen had gotten a show at the opera house, though whether he was grateful or furious, he couldn't say. Perhaps both in equal measure.

He waited patiently as the conversation wrapped up and footsteps headed his way. A familiar figure rounded the corner, and Drystan stepped out from his hiding place. "Malik."

His cousin jolted and stumbled back a step. "Goddess above!"

Drystan pulled back his hood, only belatedly realizing he still wore the mask when his cousin's eyes widened. He jerked that free as well. "It's me."

Malik heaved a sigh. "If you wanted to kill me, there are easier ways."

Drystan's fist tightened at his side. *Of all the times—*

"But good, you're here." Malik patted him on the shoulder. "You saw the posters?"

Some of the tension slipped from his form. "Yes. She's..." Words tripped over themselves. *Here? All right? Safe?*

"Just fine. Her sister too."

Drystan's brows rose. Bronwyn was there too?

"Come with me, quickly. She's about to go on stage."

Malik led him up a twisting staircase he was sure might break under their combined weight and into a place near the rooftop where various curtains and set pieces were secured.

"Here." Malik stopped, kneeling near a low railing. "She'll be on in moments."

From this angle, he could see both behind the vast crimson curtains blocking off the stage and the audience finding the last of their seats.

"You can watch the show from here and then venture back down," Malik whispered. "No one should bother you up here if you stick to the shadows." He glanced at Drystan's still-bloodied hand. "A spell wouldn't hurt. Just to be sure."

Drystan pulled the shadows to him once more, his previous spell still active, and Malik's brows rose.

"One step ahead of me, I see."

"I've had to be." And ahead of just about everyone else's scheming too if he wanted to keep his head.

"Ah, yes." Malik's gaze darted away before settling back on him again. "Well, once she's done, meet us in Ceridwen's dressing room. At the base of the stairs, take three lefts, then a right. There's a storage room with a mirror. It's double-sided with a short passage in between, and the other side goes into the dressing room she uses."

"How do you know about this?" Drystan asked, suddenly suspicious.

Malik stared at him side-eyed with a little smirk. "I had a thing for dancers for a while."

It figured his cousin would know the way into a woman's dressing room. He nearly rolled his eyes. Of all the reasons he could give, that one absolutely fit.

"You're not into them anymore?" Drystan prodded. If he dared say he preferred a certain musician, any good favor he'd earned would vanish right then and there.

Malik shrugged. "I may have found other interests." At Drystan's scowl, he added, "Of the brunette variety."

A certain sister, he'd wager. Drystan relaxed his stance, finding an almost comfortable perch. "Bronwyn?"

Malik didn't reply, but his grin widened.

"She hates you," Drystan replied. Or it seemed that way.

"Oh, she wants to," Malik said. "But she doesn't. Not really."

Right...

At that moment, a figure appeared behind the curtains, resplendent in a pink gown that sparkled even in the shadows. His heart leaped into his throat. Recognition surged through him before the announcer, who pranced onto the stage in front of the curtains, ever said her name.

"Ceridwen," he whispered.

A hand clamped down on his shoulder. "I'll leave you to enjoy," Malik said, edging past him. "Besides, I might be missed if I'm gone long. Three lefts, and then a right. Find the storage room and the mirror."

"I will," he replied, never taking his eyes off the woman he loved.

The curtains parted. The audience cheered as she was revealed, a glimmering beauty like the Goddess herself at the center of the stage, her silver flute clutched in her hands.

When the cheers quieted, she raised the flute and began to play. Her music washed over him, seeping deep into his heart and soul and carrying all his troubles far away. Somehow, in front of all these people, her tune was even more powerful, lulling him into a sense of peace and calm he feared might be lost forever.

No matter what future awaited, he was blessed in that moment.

To see her, to hear her music one more time, and witness her dream finally realized.

Chapter 47

Ceridwen

T HE HOUSE LIGHTS FLICKERED to life, slowly illuminating the crowd, as Ceridwen took a bow. Cheers erupted, and the crowd rose to their feet from chairs cushioned in plush red fabric. Golden paint on the walls and balconies caught the light, sparkling between the press of bodies like fancy necklaces in a jewelry box.

Three days. Three sold-out shows.

The first day she'd been all nerves. The second still hadn't felt real. Today, she finally let the joy of playing for a crowd sink in, relishing in her dream come to life.

As a little girl, she'd pretended to be a great singer on a stage. Now, she was, almost. She played her flute rather than singing, but for brief moments, the applause managed to drown out her worry for Drystan. Though, for much of the show, she could have sworn she felt eyes on her, someone watching. Not the crowd. This was a tingling from above, almost like the nights she'd believed her mother watched from the Goddess's hallowed halls.

Long-stemmed roses splashed onto the stage, thrown by audience members in the front rows. Favors for the artist. For her. Such flowers would be very expensive this time of year, having been grown indoors during the cool season.

She gave another bow, her dress bunching on the polished wood, before making her way off the side of the stage.

"Beautiful!" Bronwyn wrapped her in a tight embrace, where she waited in the wings. Malik smiled nearby, as content and peaceful as she'd ever seen him. Perhaps this was his element after all, a place that provided him with more comfort than the role of spy or even prince.

Malik slipped in close, brushing Bronwyn's shoulder. For once, she didn't stare daggers at him or move away. Ceridwen cocked her head, observing the touch, but neither seemed to notice.

"There's a fan to see you," Malik whispered.

Ceridwen barely heard him over the din of the crowd wrapping up their praise and murmuring among themselves. Another performance would follow, but blessedly it wouldn't be her giving it.

Ceridwen opened her mouth to reply when the words sank in. Her heart leaped. One hand flew to cover her mouth. *Drystan. Finally.*

Malik nodded.

"Take me there at once!" Excitement threatened to bubble out, and she couldn't hold still.

"There's my star!" Wynni swooped in, wrapping Ceridwen in a strong hug that nearly crushed the flute still in her grip. "You were brilliant tonight, just brilliant!" The heavy floral scent of her perfume flowed around them like a wave.

She nudged Malik out of the way and swooped her arm through Ceridwen's. She'd never seen a person disregard status the way Wynni did. "There's someone who wants to see you." The opera house owner practically vibrated with glee.

"Oh, I know, we just—"

Malik dug his hand into her shoulder, cutting off her words. A quick flick of his head said everything.

Wynni didn't know about Drystan. *Then who?*

"This is such a rare opportunity. We must go right away." Wynni plucked the flute from Ceridwen's hand. "Be a dear and put this away for us," she ordered, passing it off to Chesa, who replied with a grin.

She didn't wait for a reply before tugging Ceridwen along with her through the crowd backstage. Malik stuck close to her other side. In their haste, Ceridwen lost track of Bronwyn completely.

Behind the stage, people rushed this way and that, preparing for the next act, a troupe of singers who'd been a mainstay of Wynni's shows for many years. Ceridwen nearly sighed as they escaped from the mass of movement into the quieter hallways.

"Who is it, Wynni?" Malik asked as they strode through the painted halls at break-neck speed.

"You don't know?"

"Of course not, who—" Malik's words choked off as two men came into view. Both were dressed alike in red jackets with black pants and boots. Their outfits resembled Adair's military attire. These men could have been his peers in Teneboure, except for one difference. Each wore a sash across their chest, colored in purple and gold.

The men stood silently on either side of an innocuous door. Wynni practically ignored them as she rushed up, but Malik had gone pale and stiff. The thin line of his lips replaced his characteristic grin.

What's wrong? Tell me!

Malik said nothing as Wynni presented Ceridwen before the men who knocked twice upon the polished wood. A muffled acknowledgment came from within.

One guard opened the door. Before Ceridwen could clearly see beyond, Wynni pulled her into the room.

"Your Majesty."

Breath left her as shock gripped her heart. Wynni bent at the waist, pulling Ceridwen's joined arm along with hers and forcing her into a bow.

The king. Holy Goddess, it's the king.

"Ah, the musician." His voice rang with command and authority—deep, strong, and with a slight lilt like his son.

Ceridwen's body followed Wynni's movements, unable to function on its own. Thoughts raced through her mind as she attempted to focus on the man in front of them, flanked by two guards similar to the ones outside. One had darkly tanned skin, the other a mess of auburn hair.

The king resembled his son, though his skin tone was a shade lighter. His dark hair sported liberal streaks of gray, and wrinkles marred what were still handsome features. But the blue of his eyes, similar in shade to Drystan's, were colder than the icy seas near Teneboure. The smirk on his lips held cruelty instead of playful mirth like Malik's.

How could anyone look at this man and not see him for what he was? Did they see only the title and not the darkness floating just beneath his skin?

The jewels and golden threads of his outfit would dazzle any commoner, but it was the iron brooch shaped like a dragon that caught her attention. A simple piece. And a painful reminder that caused Ceridwen's nails to dig into the skin of her palms.

His attention flew to the door. "And my wayward son." He crossed his arms and drummed his ringed fingers along the fine crimson velvet of his long coat. "How am I not surprised to find you here, Alistair?"

"Father." Malik gave a stiff bow.

"Did you completely forget to check in with your report? Your charge arrived days ago."

Ceridwen swallowed at the mention of Drystan, her throat suddenly dry. He'd made it to the city and the castle. Did the king know he waited for her here even now?

"We'll discuss this later." He waved a bejeweled hand at Malik, a dismissal. Malik moved to the edge of the room but did not leave.

Thank you. Even if not for her benefit, she was glad to have him near, especially as King Rhion stalked her way like a feral cat.

"Lovely concert, my dear. The best I have heard in some time." Despite the inky feeling in her gut, Ceridwen flushed at the praise of her music.

She averted her gaze as he approached, keeping her head respectfully dipped and staring at his polished boots rather than looking the demon in the face.

"Perhaps you'd be willing to play at my castle?"

A trick question. No one could say no to the king, not if they valued their lives. She forced out her reply, careful to keep the bitter edge from her tone. "Of course, Your Majesty. When would you like me to play?"

He paced back and forth as if he were unable to stay still for more than a moment. "Two days from now. I'm hosting a midwinter party of sorts, and your music would be a delightful addition. I assume you can spare her?" This he addressed to Wynnifred. Again, it wasn't truly a question. She couldn't say no without risking the whole of the opera house.

"Yes, Your Majesty. It would be a great honor." She bowed again.

"Very good," he continued. "You may pick the songs. Three or four should be sufficient. I liked the style from today." He waved forward one of the guards attending him. "Jasper, make sure you provide our guest with instructions for her arrival at the event."

"Yes, Your Majesty." Jasper pulled a thick piece of paper from a jacket pocket and passed it to her. They'd prepared for her acceptance before arriving at the show. Only someone used to getting their way would be so arrogant. *Disgusting.* The touch of paper against her palm made her skin crawl.

"That'll be all." He waved his hand at the women this time.

Wynnifred looped her arm through Ceridwen's again as they both bowed to the king. Wynni hustled her from his presence before she'd even fully risen.

On their way out, the king addressed his son. "Alistair, you'll come to me tomorrow and—"

The door shut, muffling whatever else the king said. Outside the room, Ceridwen could finally breathe again. Before they reached the end of the hall, the door opened once more, and Malik emerged, a hard look upon his face. He caught up with them halfway to the dressing room.

"An invitation to play at the castle! That's really quite something." Wynni beamed. From the vacant look on Malik's face, he didn't share her enthusiasm.

Wynni didn't wait for a response before dropping Ceridwen's arm and running off to attend to one of the assistants calling her name.

"What happened?" Ceridwen whispered once she'd left.

"What you'd expect. Criticism and disappointment." He ushered her toward the dressing room. "Come on. At least you have something happy to look forward to."

The weight on her chest lightened. *Drystan, please still be there.*

Bronwyn waited for them outside the room. "Where have you all been?"

"I'll explain," Malik offered. "Go on."

Without hesitation, Ceridwen opened the door and stepped inside.

Chapter 48

Drystan

D<small>RYSTAN WAITED IN THE</small> thin compartment between the two sides of the mirror. He'd have sworn he wasn't claustrophobic, but waiting there in the tight space nearly drove him mad.

A stagehand came in once, depositing fresh red roses in a large vase similar to others dotted around the room, bearing clusters of the long-stemmed flowers. Other more seasonal arrangements stood on the gilded vanity and low table set between a number of cream-colored seats.

She'd amassed quite the number of favors in just a few days, enough that he had to fight the prickle of jealousy trying to worm its way under his skin.

But where was Ceridwen? She should be back by now. Every moment that drew by increased his worry until a sheen of sweat broke out on the back of his neck.

He hadn't failed to notice that the royal box was occupied that night, or who exactly lingered there. The idea of the king that close to Ceridwen set even his beast on edge, all the calm and comfort of her songs fading in the wake of the terrible possibilities his mind wrought.

Finally, the door opened.

Ceridwen entered, even more mesmerizing this close than she was on stage. Though he'd seen her not long ago from above, he almost couldn't fully convince himself she was real. Here, in the capital, in an opera house no less.

"Did you leave already?" she mused aloud, sinking onto a pale settee.

"Ceridwen," he called through the glass.

She leaped to her feet, turning this way and that. "Drystan? Where are you?"

"Come to the mirror." Though he'd tried to open it, the thing held firm from his side. Still, some lock on her side might not keep him from breaking the damnable thing just for the assurance that no one else would ever use it to sneak into her dressing room.

Ceridwen crossed the distance and placed her hand upon the glass. Drystan mirrored it, his larger hand dwarfing hers through the blurry, aged surface.

She gasped, her gaze focusing on his hand against hers, barely separated. "It is you."

"Yes, I'm here," he promised, savoring the look of wild relief that crossed her face. "There must be some kind of lock on your side. Check the frame."

Leave it to Malik to give incomplete instructions.

In haste, Ceridwen ran her palms around the edge of the frame, searching for a release. After a moment, something clicked, and Drystan found that he could move the glass frame.

Ceridwen jumped back as the frame swung wide, and Drystan stepped into the room.

"Ceridwen," he gasped, seeing her before him, no barrier, no stage in the way.

He expected her to run to him, to hug him, or perhaps to weep. He did not expect her to glance away. A tingle of doubt anchored him to the ground, unease wrenching him harder than when he'd spoke with Lord Stellan earlier that day, sharing his secrets and possibly sealing his doom.

"You left me," she whispered.

He dropped his head and slumped his shoulders. *Ah...* "It was the hardest thing I've ever done." He gripped the mirror frame to steady himself in the wake of her rejection. "I only wanted to keep you safe."

That and far, far away from the king and the capital. Yet on that score, he'd failed. He feared the headstrong beauty might beg to join him if he'd stayed. But venturing here on her own, albeit with Malik and Bronwyn, was something he never expected.

"And you really thought running away was the best option?" She sniffled, on the edge of tears.

"If it kept you away from here, far from harm, then yes." The mirror frame cracked in his grip.

"Well, I'm here now." She stared him down.

Damn him, she was. Yet there he stood, like a scolded boy, instead of showing her just how much she meant.

Drystan rushed forward, wrapping her in a crushing embrace. She sniffled again but did not pull away or struggle. Tears dripped onto his dark shirt as he pressed a soft kiss to her hair. Holding her, feeling her in his arms, her scent in every breath he took was a fantasy, one he'd longed for since the moment he left her lying in his bed. "I love you, Ceridwen. I'm so proud of all you've done and accomplished here." It wasn't lost on him that she'd taken the reins of her life into hand and made her dreams come true. His brave, strong woman. "The people love you, and I'm so glad I got to hear you play from the shadows tonight, to see you one last time, but now you have to leave this place."

"No," she mumbled into his chest.

"Go back to Teneboure," he continued, ignoring her. "Forget all this. Live a good life with your family."

She had to be safe and far from here. He could accept whatever fate awaited him. After the harm he'd caused and the fool he'd been as a youth, he deserved whatever future the Goddess dealt. But if the worst happened, if only death and despair awaited him, he could face it if he knew she was out of harm's way first.

Ceridwen slammed a fist against his shoulder. "No, do you not listen?" She shoved him hard and stepped away. "I'm already here, and I'm not leaving. I cannot now anyway."

His heart skipped a beat. "What? Why not?"

"The king..." She swallowed, pausing and weighing her words. But Drystan only saw red. If he hurt her, if he'd found out what she meant to him and had done something... His beast growled within him, a bit of the sound slipping through and causing Ceridwen's eyes to fly wide.

"He asked me to play at a midwinter party in two days," she hurried on. "My absence would not go unnoticed."

Drystan's jaw clenched. "When?"

"Moments ago."

Drystan turned and slammed his fist into a nearby wall, cracking the plaster. "Damn it!"

If only he'd gotten there sooner, or better yet, had just killed the bastard when he first arrived.

"Shhh, someone will hear." Ceridwen rushed to calm him down.

"I'll kill him then. Or before. Somehow. Then you'll be free, and he nor anyone else—"

She pressed her fingers lightly over his lips, silencing the spew of his thoughts. "No." He held silent until she dropped her arm to her side.

"Is that all you know how to say?" A grin twitched at the corner of his mouth.

A blush creeped to her cheeks as she pursed her lips. Somewhere along the way, their roles had switched. "No," she teased, mocking his line from weeks ago.

Drystan trailed a gloved hand across her cheek and down her neck, savoring the goose-flesh rising in its wake and the shiver that rolled down her body. He cupped the back of her neck, just under her elaborate updo, and this time, she did not look away or pull back.

"Ceridwen."

He met her lips with his in a show of all the pent-up desire surging within him. She wrapped her arms around his neck, leaning into him as if he might vanish and she could somehow hold him there. Though he'd long enjoyed music, he'd never made a study of it himself. Though there, locked in an embrace with the woman he loved, he suddenly understood how two distinct melodies could come together to form something even more magical.

Long after their kiss ended, she remained in his embrace, her cheek against his chest and her body pressed against his. She fit there. She belonged there. Every second he could hold her in his arms was a gift.

"What do you plan to do?" she asked eventually.

"Kill him. Avenge my family as well as your mother. Clear my name and escape if I can, though that may be too grand a dream."

A soft smile pulled at her lips as she stared up at him. "Grand dreams are the best kind. The ones most likely to succeed."

He tried to smile in return, but it faltered. "I don't deserve it. The things I've done..."

"Because of your uncle. Because of the darkness he lured you into."

"The blood is still on my hands. I committed the action, no matter the reason." No amount vengeance could wipe that clean.

"We cannot change that. The past is done, even if we wish it otherwise. But we can build a better future," she said. "You taught me that. I cannot bring Mother back, but I can move forward. I have, however hard."

Whatever trials of the darkness she stared down, this woman persisted in spite of them. The wonder of it, the resilience of her spirit, was enviable, and so much stronger than his own.

"When you talk like that, I want to believe everything is possible," he whispered.

"Then do. But we'll need some help. Stay here a moment."

"Wait." He grabbed her arm. "I can't involve you. It's too dangerous. Nor anyone else. I've come this far alone. I'll—"

"Not alone," she interjected. "You trusted Malik and me to help you. You trusted Jackoby and the others to keep your secret even before then."

He frowned. "Trusting others got me into this mess. It's best I go alone."

"We're not your uncle." She took his hand in hers. "Misplaced trust may have gotten you into this, but properly placed trust can get you out." Drystan opened his mouth, but Ceridwen rushed on before he could protest. "Trust me, if no one else."

"Ceridwen..." His shoulders slumped.

"You can't hide from the world forever. We'll do this. Together."

A brief nod was all he had the time to give before she rushed to the door.

Ceridwen showed Malik and Bronwyn into the room, the latter of which did not appear surprised by his appearance. Apparently, Malik had filled her in.

"The midwinter party the king is hosting is going to be our chance," Ceridwen said, keeping her voice in a low whisper as they settled in close within the seating area.

In anyone else, such confidence and fervor would have delighted him, but coming from her, it only made him anxious. The more he tried to keep her from harm, the further she threw herself into it.

"I'm going to play for the king at the party, just as he asked. He requested a few songs, but perhaps I'll make the last one a vocal performance." Her gaze drifted to Drystan, every word out of her mouth sending his spine straightening until it hurt. "I'll write my own, one to tell your tale and reveal the deceptions of the king."

And get herself killed in the process. "No. You can't—"

But she kept going. "Drystan, you can reveal your true identity, proof that the king lied to the people. Once the people see the truth, you can kill him with the blade."

He bared his teeth, a snarl slipping through. "This is—"

Malik crossed his legs on the sofa, ignoring him. "Interesting, but you're missing some important details. For one, my father is incredibly powerful. He's honed the darkness for years. And secondly, there will undoubtedly be guards to contend with."

"We'll knock them out. Distract them..."

Drystan rose, raking a hand through his hair. *It will never work.*

"All of them?" Bronwyn asked skeptically. "And if some are innocent and get hurt?"

Drystan halted his pacing. At least one of them saw reason.

"A barrier spell might help. Or rather, several of them," Malik supplied. "One to keep dark wielders, like my father, contained. Another to halt the advance of the guards."

"As if we can work such a spell on the spot," Drystan snapped.

Malik shrugged. "I have a suspicion where within the palace he'll host the party, one I can easily confirm. We'll work the spells in advance and be strategic in their placement to make sure they don't get triggered early and raise suspicion. The trick will be finding a time to place them when no one's looking."

That part seemed plausible. "I could work some," Drystan said, "under the guise of carrying out the orders of the king." *Goddess, help me, am I agreeing with this nonsense?*

"As could I, now that you mention it," Malik said. "I'm better with barriers anyway, and my father insists I visit the castle first thing in the morning. The area I think they'll use for the party is naturally divided, so it might not be terribly difficult. Father doesn't like to mingle, even with other nobles, but you know how he loves to be seen."

More like worshiped from afar. Seen, praised, the center of their attention, but Goddess forbid he mingle with them as if they were equals. Even before he was king, the man held himself with such arrogance that he should have known he'd be happy with nothing less than the crown, but Drystan wasn't about to start down that path.

"But what about getting the king to confess?" Bronwyn asked, leaping to her feet and staring at them all as if they'd lost it. Perhaps they had.

The pieces Malik laid out made a certain sense that he couldn't fully fault, though involving Ceridwen was another matter. He'd have to discuss it with her and make sure she truly understood the danger they were all in. The thought of her anywhere near the king made his insides hollow out and his monster stir. He'd lost too much to the man already.

"From the sound of him, he'd never admit his own crimes," Bronwyn said.

No, he definitely won't.

"A truth spell?"

Drystan glanced at Malik and shook his head. "It's complex light magic. I don't know it."

"But I do," his cousin responded.

Drystan gaped.

Malik's smile didn't reach his eyes. "My mother was quite proficient. She made sure I memorized that one long before her death."

That poor woman had deserved so much more, as had his own parents. Perhaps she'd realized the true nature of her husband and took steps many years ago to protect her only son from his father's ministrations.

"If we get him in the right area, we might be able to get him to reveal what happened to the king and queen in front of an audience," Ceridwen supplied. "That, combined with my song, would surely sway some minds."

"I have a few nobles on my side already," Drystan confessed.

Malik raised his brows, appraising him in a new light. "So quickly?"

Drystan nodded. "I had to work fast, but those loyal to my parents remain. Maybe, if we're—"

A heavy knock sounded at the door. "Ceridwen," Wynni called through the door. "You have a guest to see you."

Everyone's attention snapped to Drystan. No one knew of his presence there outside those in the room.

He ran for the mirror, slipping into the passage with inhuman speed. No matter who lingered outside that door, it was best they didn't see him.

"Yes, who is it?" Ceridwen called.

Drystan stared through the mirror at the man who entered, squinting and blinking several times to try to make him out through the cloudy glass, but Bronwyn cleared his confusion in a moment.

"Adair?" she asked, rising from the settee. "What in the name of the Goddess are you doing here?"

What in the name of the Goddess indeed...

"Nice to see you too, sis," he replied as Wynni shut the door behind him.

Adair crossed to his sisters, ignoring Malik completely. The young man really was a fool not to pay attention to the people in his midst.

"My regiment has been stationed here for the rest of the season. Training rotation." He shrugged.

"Yes, we know that," Ceridwen said. "But why are you *here*?"

"Why are you here, dear sisters?" he retorted. "I could barely believe it when I saw my youngest sister on a poster. I thought it must be some girl with the same name, but then I asked around, and well, I decided to come check it out for myself. I didn't expect to actually find you here. Either of you. Or you for that matter," Adair said, finally addressing Malik. "What happened to the other one?" he asked Ceridwen. "Lord Winterbourne? Or are you off him now?"

Drystan barely held in a growl, his monster pacing under his skin. If this *boy* ruined all that they worked for...

"Go home, Adair. We're fine," Ceridwen said. "I'll explain later. You should leave."

He scratched the back of his neck. "I know I made a mess of things last time—"

"And the time before," Bronwyn interjected.

"Then too," he said. "But I intend to make up for it. Just...tell me why you're in the capital playing in an opera house?"

"For the money." Ceridwen crossed her arms, staring her brother down with such confidence a trained actress couldn't have done it better.

Adair laughed. "And they what? Heard you play once and decided to give you a major role? I doubt it."

Drystan tightened his hands into fists. He leaned against the ruined frame, ready to spring free.

Malik rose to his feet before he could and said, "Want me to kick him out?"

"Please," Bronwyn snapped.

Malik advanced on Adair, who hastily stepped away, but Ceridwen bolted between them. "Wait." She whirled on her brother. "Adair, how many men do you know in the castle guard here?"

The headstrong fool notched his chin higher. "Quite a few since that's where my regiment is stationed this time. Why?"

Ceridwen... Don't...

Malik spoke the warning racing through his mind. "If word gets out..."

"Trust me," Ceridwen said to Malik, and then stared past him at the mirror, straight at Drystan, where he hovered in the gloom.

Trust you? Certainly. Your brother? Something popped in Drystan's jaw as his teeth ground together.

Ceridwen turned to her brother. "Swear on the Goddess that what we tell you will never leave this room."

Adair stood straighter, his gaze flickering between his sisters. Eventually, he said, "I swear it."

CHAPTER 49

CERIDWEN

CERIDWEN EXPLAINED THE PLAN to Adair, who turned pale and nearly lost his supper on the rug. Drystan's sudden reappearance from the mirror didn't help matters. But at the end of it all, once they laid bare in minutes the truth it had taken her months to uncover, his shock and disbelief transformed into a sullen silence so uncharacteristic of her brother that Ceridwen worried the revelations might have broken something in him. Eventually though, he stared between his sisters in a silence so full of words she could taste the unspoken apology in the air.

"Get me a sash, a mark of the king's guard, and I'll do it," Adair promised. "If I can help at all, I will. For my sisters."

"It's settled then," Malik said, rising to his feet so quickly, Ceridwen would wager he'd been about to do that anyway if Adair had kept quiet a moment longer. "Now I need to find blood. It will take more than my own and my stores for the workings to be wrought."

Adair paled further at the mention of blood. They'd explained a bit of that too—vaguely. He didn't like it, any of it, but where their brother had always been a little carefree and quick, he was the opposite in this, and that, if nothing else, gave Ceridwen the confidence that he was fully on their side.

Bronwyn turned to Malik. "Take mine."

A small gasp slipped from Ceridwen, and she sat a little straighter, gaping wide-eyed at her sister. Malik stared her down as well, perhaps searching for sincerity. His eyes dilated as he watched Bronwyn, emotions Ceridwen couldn't quite place flashing in those green depths.

"It's the best way I can help." Her sister shrugged. "Everyone else has a bigger role than me."

Neither Malik nor Bronwyn looked away from each other. Silence lingered heavy and thick until Adair coughed, rising to his feet. The sound snapped the invisible cord strung taut between them.

"Well, I need to go look up some of my old training buddies if we're going to make this work. Wish me luck. And you two"—he looked between his sisters, his throat bobbing—"stay safe." Adair showed himself out.

Shortly after, Malik and Bronwyn excused themselves, leaving Drystan and Ceridwen alone once again.

He wrapped his arms around her from behind, resting his chin upon her head.

She sighed and eased into his warmth, savoring every fleeting moment.

"I promised to remind you how clever you are." His whispered words drifted over her ear with the warmth of his breath, sending a shiver down her spine.

"Clever. Or very, very foolish." She'd either signed their death warrants or discovered the key to the prison of their lives. Only, she didn't know which. Unfortunately, the first was more likely.

"Either way, you're very, very brave."

His arms loosened ever so slightly. "Don't leave, not yet."

"They'll be wanting to close up the opera house soon, and I need to get back."

Logic did nothing to calm the need humming through her. "A few minutes more. Just like this."

He tilted her chin up and to the side until his face was a breath from hers. "I have a better idea."

Drystan's kiss was far from chaste. He kissed like a man on the way to the gallows, one last taste of sweetness before his doom. Perhaps he was. Perhaps they all were. So Ceridwen kissed him back the same, giving everything she had to the man she loved.

He eased her down onto the settee, their mouths still locked together, sliding his fingers through her hair and ruining the careful updo Wynni's assistants had crafted. Drystan followed her down, his weight settling over her and pressing her into the cushions. His lips left her mouth to trail kisses down her chin, her neck, her collarbone. The barest hint of teeth dug into the skin of her shoulder, causing a little yelp of surprise.

"The door locks?" Drystan asked, lapping at the spot he'd nipped.

"Y-Yes."

"Good." Drystan pushed up on his arms, hovering above her. His gaze hooded as he stared her down. The look alone had Ceridwen's thighs rubbing together in response to the delicious pleasure building there.

"Stay absolutely still, my beauty. I have my own plot to see out before this night is done." And with that, Drystan rose to lock the door, giving them a much-needed moment of peace together.

Bronwyn fiddled with the edge of the bandage wrapped around her wrist. The white cloth barely peeked out between her long sleeves and the dainty gloves on her hands.

"Nervous?" Ceridwen asked, if for no other reason than to distract herself from the monstrosity they approached.

Outside the carriage window, tall stone buildings rose into the sunlit sky, bathing the road they traversed in shade. Only a few more blocks and they'd reach the castle. Already, its towers rose above the high buildings, purple pennants waving in the slight breeze.

"A little." She tugged down her sleeve, covering the bandage. "But my job is easy. I'm just the help after all." She gave a tight smile.

Bronwyn would pose as Ceridwen's attendant rather than her sister today, there to make sure the king's musician had everything she needed for the performance. Ceridwen had hoped she'd stay at Malik's apartments, especially after Chesa volunteered with a little too much enthusiasm to be her assistant, but no such luck. She should have known, given her stubborn will, that she'd insist on coming along.

"The better question is, how are you doing?"

The crimson silk skirts of Ceridwen's dress spilled out around her, and she tried to smooth them down. Anything to calm herself. She attempted a smile but failed.

Someone would die today. Maybe many someones. Whatever the result, she'd be at fault for putting this plan into action. Each bounce of the carriage stirred the tight bundle of knots in her stomach.

Bronwyn reached out across the narrow space between them and covered Ceridwen's hand with hers. "Malik finished his workings, and if things go oddly, we can always make a run for it."

They'd heard nothing from Drystan. She didn't really expect to, but the silence worried her. Had he been successful? Would he be able to let them know if he wasn't? And Adair...

Who knew if they could trust his so-called friends and regiment members. They might have sold them out already.

The carriage rocked to an abrupt halt, sending the women sliding along the velvet seats. Ceridwen's flute case nearly tumbled off her lap and onto the floor.

"Idiot driver," Bronwyn grumbled.

When the driver finally came over to open the door, Bronwyn exited first with the flute case, as expected of an attendant. Ceridwen followed with careful steps. Between the billowing skirts and heeled boots, she surprised herself by not tumbling into the street.

Ceridwen didn't need to shade her eyes as she stared up at the high castle walls looming before them. The setting sun had already dipped beyond their reaches, though evening was still a little way off. Tonight's event would begin as soon as the sun touched the far horizon. She performed third. If they could make it until then without someone discovering the wards or something else going awry, they might have a chance.

Bronwyn passed their papers to the guards stationed at the gated side entrance. Early guests would already be milling around the main gates awaiting entry. Performers had their own entrance.

"Miss Ceridwen Kinsley, as requested by the king."

The man gave the papers a thorough inspection before he nodded to his companion, who opened the gates. "I'll show you to the waiting area."

Numerous performers waited with their attendants in the space provided, occupying the plush chairs that filled of the room just off the central yard. Time passed more slowly than the melt of snow in winter, but eventually the noise outside grew, and excited murmurs tickled her ears, hinting at the many people in attendance at the king's party.

Potential witnesses. If they could keep them here long enough.

The first performer, a dancer wearing layers of thin, flowing silks, was called for. A wall of sound burst inside as she exited to thunderous applause and cheers.

Her performance most likely wouldn't last long, nor would the next, a man who twirled flaming knives. Ceridwen stiffened in the chair. Soon she'd be up.

Each minute stretched like an hour. Her throat grew dry despite the water she sipped. Her boots tapped lightly on the floor. Everything would fall apart if she couldn't play at all.

The door opened again, revealing a middle-aged woman in forest green with two long feathers sticking out of the brown hair pulled back behind her head. "Miss Kinsley, you're up in just a moment."

Outside, cheers rose as the man finished his performance. A mass of colorful bodies filled the space beyond where onlookers crowded toward the front, several holding glasses full of light-amber liquid.

Ornate crystal oil lamps hung from tall posts, bathing the area in light. More torches and lamps clung to the walls and the base of the stage. At the back of the wooden stage, erected before the crowd on one end of the yard, stood the king's box.

The coordinator led the sisters toward the stage. Eyes roved over Ceridwen like spiders in the deep forest, leaving a tingling trail in their wake.

As they neared the stage, she froze. The king sat in the center of his box, draped in an elaborate jacket trimmed in fur that sported his vile dragon brooch, a golden crown upon his head. Malik stood a few people away, resplendent in navy and gray—traditional winter colors. A smaller crown adorned his head. At this formal occasion, he played the role of prince—for now.

A tangle of doubt tripped Ceridwen up as she caught sight of the brooch pinned to his collar. An iron dragon.

Had he turned against them? She thought they could trust him, she was so sure, but that brooch...

Ceridwen looked away, her heart racing as she took in the three men standing behind the king, almost in the shadows. All wore outfits of midnight black, like Drystan had worn the other night, but today their faces were each hidden by dragon masks that concealed their features. Two sported dark hair, one had light brown. Their skin she could not distinguish behind the mask and clothing.

Drystan, which one are you?

One man's attention slid to her and held. Almost as if he'd heard her, though she knew it to be impossible.

"Come along, Miss," the coordinator instructed. Behind her, Bronwyn raised her brows and cocked her head. A question and a reminder.

Ceridwen locked eyes with the young man on the stage one last time, drinking in the support he offered, before she ascended the rest of the way onto the platform.

Bronwyn opened the flute case and passed the precious instrument to her. "You'll be fine. It'll all be fine," she whispered.

If only Ceridwen had her confidence. With a tight smile, she took the flute and crossed the stage. Her heels clicked along the wood, barely audible, as the crowd quieted.

The coordinator followed. Her voice rang loud and clear as she introduced the next act. "Miss Ceridwen Kinsley, playing the three movements of *The Blessings of the Goddess*."

A few heads turned, accompanied by soft murmurs as the song name floated through the crowd.

A familiar tingle traced over Ceridwen's back, igniting a true smile on her face. They could do this. *I can do this.*

Mother, are you watching tonight?

CHAPTER 50

DRYSTAN

A CHANGE CAME OVER the audience as Ceridwen played. They didn't talk to one another, carrying on as if the performer wasn't even there, as many had with the first two. Instead, men and women stood transfixed, listening to her beautiful song spill out into the night. Some of the guards on the upper-level walk relaxed their stances. One of Drystan's fellow dragons almost seemed to nod off, his head sliding forward before quickly snapping upright. But most amazingly, perhaps, the king sat absolutely still, not twitching nor moving as he often did.

There was a power in her music, strong as any magic.

But of all the people present, Drystan was the one who could not relax and enjoy the wondrous tune. Instead, every bit of him was on edge, standing there in the shadows as one of the king's loyal dogs. Guards wouldn't be seen as a threat this night, just a normal precaution. The very present stance of three dragons a bit behind the king? That was a message, a reminder to the nobles—those forced to attend and those who came eagerly—exactly who was in charge and what might await them should they step out of line.

They were lucky the king hadn't decided on more. Drystan could no longer be sure how many the king's dragons numbered. A few identities he knew, but many were a secret or falsified, just like Drystan Winterbourne. Even if they were successful this night, enemies, those loyal to the king, would still lurk in the shadows. Whether they would act out or fall in line, who could say?

Ceridwen drew the song to a close, the familiar last notes of the second movement of *The Blessings of the Goddess* hanging in the quiet evening air. Per the schedule, she should play the third, the rare piece that had commoners and nobles alike flocking to the opera house.

Instead, Ceridwen lowered her flute, stood a little taller, and stepped closer to the edge of the stage, staring out over the crowd. Drystan held his breath as she began to sing.

"Once a king and queen of light ruled the kingdom touched by night. Together they fought back the darkness to bring peace to all who lived within. But darkness grew where light had shone and rose among one of their own. The son of light fell to darkness, tricked by the king's only brother."

Restlessness swept through the crowd. Murmurs rose. The fine hairs on the back of Drystan's neck stood on end.

"The monarchs sought to save their son. Too late. The king's brother had won. The house fell 'til only the son remained. Blamed and accused, his death was faked."

"Enough." The king's voice cut through hers, drawing the song to an abrupt halt. The noise of the crowd continued, building in earnest. Drystan closed his fingers around the hilt of the sword strapped to his side. It was a normal one, refined yet simple. The Gray Blade was sheathed inside his coat, out of sight and awaiting the perfect moment for its use.

Slowly, Ceridwen turned to the king, her chest rising and falling with heavy breaths.

King Rhion jumped to his feet and flung out a hand encrusted with sparkling rings, pointing at the woman Drystan loved. "She sings the truth!"

Gasps rang out through the crowd. Malik leaped from the edge of the royal box and onto the stage. It took everything Drystan had not to join him.

"The girl's songs are nothing but honesty!" the king yelled again before he clamped his hand over his mouth.

Blessed Goddess. Malik's spell struck true. He could not lie.

The king twisted this way and that, his eyes burning with inhuman rage and flickering red in the torchlight. "Alistair, rein that girl in," he snapped.

"With pleasure." Malik sauntered her way. A cruel smirk painted his features. His dragon brooch gleamed in the light.

Drystan edged toward the side of the raised area, aiming for an easy path to leap between the king and Ceridwen should he need to.

Chest heaving, Ceridwen retreated, the perfect picture of terror as Malik grabbed her upper arm. He turned them both to the crowd.

Drystan paused, uncertain. He was supposed to lead her away, get her out of there. They'd agreed.

"The girl has sung an interesting tune." Malik's voice boomed, strong and clear. "You all know me. You've known me all your lives. My mother, Goddess give her peace, was one of your number before she married my father. Believe me when I tell you, every word she sang is true."

A cacophony of sound rose from the crowd, voices drowning out one another until an older man roared, "It's true! Tristram lives! King Rhion killed his brother and the queen!"

Lord Stellan. *Thank you.*

"Stop this!" the king yelled, his eyes flickering an eerie and unnatural red. "Arrest them!"

That was his cue. Drystan advanced with the two other dragons, leaping from the box and onto the stage. But halfway across, his companions halted. The light-haired one slammed a fist against the invisible barrier—light magic to hold back the darkness.

"King Rhion killed King Jesstin and his beloved queen, but there is one royal he missed," Malik yelled to the crowd.

Drystan pulled free his mask.

"Prince Tristram lives." Malik thrust a hand toward him. "He's innocent. Framed!"

The crowd vibrated with tension and sound. Some echoed Malik's claim. Others hastened to the exits.

The snap of crossbows rang out just before bolts crashed into another barrier, falling to the stage in a clatter of wood. Drystan's heart clenched tight in his chest, his monster roaring its fury. They'd aimed at Malik. At Ceridwen.

Other guards rallied against the ones who'd fired. "Listen to the prince!" one called as he knocked a man unconscious. *Adair.* So he held true after all and recruited a number of supporters from the look of things.

It was now or never. He had to act while the distraction held. Without another thought, Drystan pulled his sword, sprinted a few paces, and slammed the tip into one of the dragon's chests.

The man let out a guttural groan and grunt as the blade sank deep. Drystan twisted it for good measure before pulling the blade free. The man fell lifeless to the ground.

The other, the light-haired man, gave a bestial roar. Clothing ripped, warped limbs bursting through seams, as he transformed into a dark beast. Drystan's own echoed the call, the horrible sound ripping from his throat, but he held it back, forced it to stay buried deep inside him. Let the people see the king and his cronies for what they were, but not him, not yet.

Panic rose in the crowd, accompanied by shouts from guards begging for calm and order. Malik grabbed Ceridwen and made for the stairs leading from the stage.

Drystan faced off against the remaining dragon in his beastly form, which prowled back and forth like a wolf waiting to spring. From the corner of his eye, Drystan saw the king rush to the side of the stage, but advancing guards halted his progress. They didn't raise a hand against their king, but neither did they let him through. Wicked claws extended from the king's hand in a flash before they sliced a guard across his face. Screams and blood followed in their wake.

He loathed the loss, the innocents in harm's way, but hopefully the nobles remaining in the yard would finally see their king for the monster he was. The king had submitted to the darkness to the point that there was little separation between man and monster, the man able to summon bits of his beast at will, like the garishly long claws still extended from his hands. There was no king, no beast, just one dark whole that had once been two halves.

The prowling beast sprang at Drystan. He barely had time to get his blade in front of him before the bastard was on him. The impact of the lunge knocked him to floor, his head and back slamming on the wooden stage. Sharp claws dug into his arm. Drystan roared in fury, thrashing against the monster pinning him down and narrowly dodging the snap of its maw. He twisted the blade in his hand, wrenching it up until he caught the beast in the side. It cried out and leaped and away.

Within him, his own beast begged for release, throwing itself painfully against the shell of his human form. Blood and violence beckoned, and he wouldn't be able to hold it back much longer. The other beast sprang again, but this time, Drystan was ready. He met its swiping claws with his blade, the two meeting in a horrible screech of metal. But the beast was clumsy. Drystan's blade sliced a deep gouge along its foreleg before it could retreat. Blood splattered on the ground as it leaped back, putting no weight on the injured limb.

"Father!" Malik's roar carried over the chaos.

The king's attention snapped to his son, bloody claws dripping where he'd disposed of two guards with ease.

Fuck. Run, damn it!

Malik stood little chance against his father. And Ceridwen? He started to turn his head to look for her, but the beast sprang at him again, nearly sinking its teeth into his arm before Drystan bashed it with the hilt of his blade to knock it away.

"Fool boy," the king mocked. "I should have known you had too much of your mother in you."

A heavy wave of air knocked into Drystan, barely letting him keep his feet. The dark cloud rushed across the open space, snuffing out several lanterns in its wake. Red sparks of magic floated down to the stage. The protective barrier was gone—destroyed by the king. Nothing would keep the people or the woman he loved safe from that monster of a man now.

A surge of dark magic floated over him, blurring his vision and tingling across his skin. The beast he faced off against roared, and his own answered. His beast lunged against him from within, sending him to one knee.

Not yet.

He shoved to his feet, facing off against his opponent, just as he heard Ceridwen scream.

CHAPTER 51

CERIDWEN

C ERIDWEN SCREECHED AS KING Rhion's long claws pierced his son's shoulder.

"No!" She reached for Malik, though he was impossibly far away, almost at the center of the stage, where she was far to one side. Malik had ordered her to run, to flee, but how could she just leave him and Drystan in this disaster?

Malik howled in pain as the claws were ripped free in a spray of blood. A few inches to the left and Malik would be dead.

He stumbled and raised his sword to block the incoming blow. Claws screeched against steel before retreating. With each move, the king glided through the air with inhuman speed and grace.

She needed to run. To hide, but Ceridwen couldn't move. Her body refused to obey. The crowd was in turmoil. Some cried. One vomited on the ground. Many more stood frozen in shock or pushed at the gates, trying to flee. "Let them out!" Ceridwen yelled, hoping Adair and his comrades could hear her above the noise. "Get them out of here!"

They'd seen enough. Who could deny the truth of the king now? Unless no one survived to tell of it. Metal groaned as a door near the back gave way under the press of fleeing nobles.

A whimpered wail echoed through the yard as Drystan's sword bit heavily into the side of the monster. It stumbled back as Drystan pulled the blade free. Below them, blood painted the wood in a gruesome pattern of crimson as bright as her dress.

He should have advanced to land the killing blow. Instead, his back hunched. Drystan's head twisted to the side. Ceridwen gasped, catching sight of bright-red eyes.

Goddess, no, not now. Whether from the blood, the fighting, or the nearby use of dark magic, his monster rose to the surface.

"Drystan!" Her voice quaked. "Fight this!" Fear for the man she loved released her frozen limbs. She scrambled to the edge of the stage, cursing her heavy dress and awkward shoes.

He shook his head from side to side as the monster he faced regained its footing, keeping all weight off an injured limb. Drystan adjusted his grip on the blade and advanced.

Nearby, Malik yelped as his father's claws raked his middle. Sweat beaded on the prince's brow. Despite his youthful advantage, he didn't hold the upper hand in this duel.

Ceridwen searched for anything she could use as a weapon, a distraction. Nothing lay close, but if she could get to the dead guard near the edge of the stage...

Growls and wails rang out behind her as Drystan dueled the beast.

Almost there. Almost.

Steel clattered to wood, and she twisted toward the sound. Malik stumbled back, holding his gut, unarmed. She wouldn't make it to him in time. Her whole body shook as she watched the inevitable.

Bloody, raised claws glinted in firelight, prepared to end a life.

A scream that might have been her own split the air.

King Rhion froze with a grunt. The end of a dagger protruded from his side. Thin strips of leather wrapped the hilt of the dull blade.

Not any blade. She recognized it now. The *Gray Blade*.

Drystan panted, arm still extended from where he'd thrown the dagger across the stage. The other beast lay still a few feet from him, head bleeding profusely.

"Idiots, all of you." The king pulled the blade free and tossed it away, ignoring the blood that seeped from his side. "I thought you could be my right hand. My successor!" he yelled at Drystan. "Now I know you're as weak as your father. Unworthy to lead our people."

No... No, it can't be. Ceridwen's legs shook, barely holding her upright. It should have stripped his magic, nullified it. The claws didn't recede. The red in his eyes grew and flickered. *How did we fail?*

In a flash, the king grew in size, his body twisting and transforming until a massive dark beast settled on four legs above a heap of shredded cloth. Golden jewelry clattered to the ground in pieces. With a swift kick of its hind legs, he knocked Malik away. The prince screeched as the beast's foot connected with his wound and sent him sprawling across the wooden stage to where it met a stone wall.

Red eyes flashed as the beast, so much more massive than Drystan's or the one that lay dead, stalked toward the man Ceridwen loved.

Drystan gritted his teeth, a guttural growl of his own slipping free. His jacket ripped as his arms bulged. Red colored his eyes.

A strange calm settled over her. His monster would be with them soon. For once, she was glad. They needed him now, that horrible monster of darkness and death.

The king charged Drystan in a rush of dark, leathery skin and fur. Claws and teeth warred against Drystan's sword.

Ceridwen used the moment to rush to Malik and fell to her knees at his side. He gnashed his teeth, moving his hand in a pattern across his stomach.

"Malik! Can you heal it?" She reached for him without thinking, halting when his gaze slid to hers.

"Trying," he bit out.

She yanked her hand away, unwilling to disrupt his spell further.

Drystan roared as the monster clawed the sword from his hand. Blood dripped onto the ground from his arms before his back hunched. Another cry split the air along with the ripping of dark clothes. Two beats of Ceridwen's racing heart later, the rest of his clothing fell away in shreds as Drystan's monster took form on the stage, facing down the larger one of the king.

He wasn't a man any longer, but the beast who terrorized the city.

The one who attacked her. The one who saved her. The one she loved.

Her teeth bit into her bottom lip. *Please, Goddess, help him.*

Growls rumbled back and forth as they circled each other like rabid wolves.

A set of far doors opened, allowing a stream of uniformed guards to rush into the yard. Some pulled swords free of their scabbards and stepped in front of the remaining nobles. Others stumbled back. None attempted to approach the stage. Would they even know what they witnessed?

The beasts leaped at each other, scratching, snarling, and snapping their teeth.

Pain lanced through her heart as she watched Drystan fight for his life. All their lives. The Gray Blade had failed. He had only his monster's brute strength to aid him now.

The king smashed into Drystan's smaller beast, sending it sliding across the floor, claws leaving deep groves in their wake as he attempted to halt himself.

A woman's cry caught Ceridwen's attention in the yard. Bronwyn cupped her hands over her mouth, Adair at her side. Her attention wasn't focused on the beasts leaping at each other. Instead, it fixed on her and the injured man at her side.

She shook off Adair and ran, climbing the edge of the stair far from the battle taking place on the other side of the stage. Adair rushed up a step behind her, hair disheveled and eyes wide. "Ceridwen, are you—"

"I'm fine."

Bronwyn reached for Malik, but Ceridwen grabbed her hands. "Let him finish." He still traced patterns in his own blood over his skin, trying to heal the wicked wound, which leaked blood onto the floor.

"You'll be fine, you'll be fine," Bronwyn repeated at a near whisper.

None of them would be if the king emerged victorious. Ceridwen turned to the duel.

"Dear Goddess. Where's Drystan?" Adair murmured, following her gaze.

"The small one," Ceridwen's voice cracked out in a rasp.

Claws raked down his side. With a roar, he reared, blood dripping onto the ground, before lunging at the king again.

Despite the dagger wound Drystan inflicted, the king showed no signs of slowing or backing down. Quite the opposite.

Ceridwen's eyes blurred with tears, her heart constricting as Drystan took another blow.

"I'll see if I can rally the guards." Adair rushed to the yard where men had stepped back, watching the spectacle with looks of fear, confusion, and unease. A few more had joined their number. What were they waiting for?

They have to do something. We have to—

In the midst of the chaos and bloodshed, a section from the third movement of *The Blessings of the Goddess* slipped into her head, sung in a musical voice that was not her own.

To test the hearts of man, she gifted darkness too,
A temptation one can only resist if they stay true.
To balance the two, magicless humans remained,
Their gray the counterpoint to the magic strain.
The blade, when wielded with a heart of gray,
Can quench the magic of any gifted this way.

Gray to balance the darkness. Drystan contained both light and dark. They warred within him. *They warred.*

Never could the two blend. Light and dark could not merge to make the gray. But someone who contained neither...

The song strengthened her heart. The shaking in her limbs halted. Resolve gave her strength as she pushed to her feet and stepped away from the wall.

"Ceridwen. Don't," Malik pleaded.

She ignored him. This was her task, hers alone, and she wouldn't fail.

Ceridwen's heart thundered as she closed her hand around the hilt of the Gray Blade, still bloody from where it had pierced the king's side.

Drystan yelped and whined as the king's fangs sank into his leg. The larger beast tossed him across the stage.

Hang on. Just a moment longer.

The king's attention remained on Drystan as he stalked back and forth, looking for another opportunity to pounce on his wounded prey.

With a burst of courage, Ceridwen ran forward and plunged the dagger into the beast's back.

It howled in pain and swung a grotesque arm in her direction. She didn't have the chance to blink, much less move, before it sent her sailing across the stage and crashing into the wood.

Sharp pain roared through her back, arms, and head. Buzzing rang in her ears. Her sight faded until she saw nothing other than blinding white and a pale, blond-haired woman staring at her.

Mother?

Her expression softened into a gentle smile that filled Ceridwen with warmth and comfort.

The world returned in a rush of color and sound.

Bronwyn slid to a stop at her side. "Ceridwen! Where does it hurt? Speak to me!"

Pain radiated through her, but her fingers moved and her toes. She could roll her head side to side.

A deep male voice screamed in pain. The king. Human.

"The king!"

"He *is* a monster!"

Various shouts from the guard rang out.

"He killed King Jesstin and stole his crown! Remember what he's done!" Adair yelled.

"What's going on?" Ceridwen needed to know, to see. "Help me sit up."

Ceridwen winced in pain and held in a whimper as Bronwyn slipped an arm under her shoulders and helped her sit.

The guards still stood in the yard, eyes rapt on the stage. They wouldn't interfere, wouldn't stop it.

Drystan, still a beast, stalked in front of the now human king, who reached for the blade still protruding from his back.

She'd done it. It worked.

A magicless human had to wield the Gray Blade. Only could someone without magic use it to nullify magic—dark or light. And without his magic, the beast that the king released from the prison of his body was no more. He had no more power than any normal human.

As he reached for it, the blade began to crumble. The hilt clattered to the ground. Ash rained down where the blade had been, accompanied by blood from the king's wound. Its purpose fulfilled, the blade ceased to exist. Only one use. At least she'd used it well.

Drystan, still a beast, lunged for the king. With a snap of his fanged jaws, he clamped down on the king's throat and ended his life.

CHAPTER 52
CERIDWEN

D RYSTAN'S MONSTER DIDN'T STOP with the king's last gurgle of life. Ceridwen had known what it could do and seen some of the result, but watching it happen was an entirely different matter.

The monster feasted on blood.

Her vision turned blurry around the edges. The world spun.

Someone, possibly multiple someones in the yard, retched. Others clamored in confusion. One brave soul yelled, "Kill the monster! End this."

Adair tried to hold him back, but it wouldn't last for long. Already two other men pulled free their blades.

Impossibly, they'd done it. But if Drystan were to die now, it would all be for nothing. And if he lived but killed even more innocents... How much could one soul take?

Ceridwen pushed to her feet, ignoring the pain radiating through her body and the dizziness threatening to spill her onto the bloody ground.

"Ceridwen, what are you doing?" Bronwyn asked in a harsh whisper.

"Stay here. No. Go to Malik." If anything went wrong, maybe he could protect her. Though he'd yet to rise himself.

"Don't even—"

Ceridwen's look silenced her. Resignation. Determination. Bronwyn didn't try to talk her down again.

Her voice floated across the stage, clear and strong as she began to sing. "Select children she blessed with the gift of light."

She stepped closer to Drystan, her focus on his pointed ears, the ridge of fur along his back, anywhere but the nauseating mess under his paws and jaws. Bronwyn took the opportunity to slink away, over to Malik.

"Giving them an extra share of speed, grace, and might."

"There's nothing to hold him back. He's just feasted." Malik grunted in pain. "Don't!"

Ceridwen ignored him, too, and continued singing the third movement of *The Blessings of the Goddess*. It was what people had come to hear after all, even though most of the audience had long since fled. The words centered her. They calmed her soul, just as singing had before grief stole her voice. She wouldn't let that happen again. Never.

"From blood they called forth further skill."

The monster raised its head. A long dark tongue licked away the blood on its fangs. She nearly gagged, but a quick shake focused her attention. Adair yelled from the yard, accompanied by other men, but Ceridwen waved them off with a gesture of her hand. At least one called her mad. Others had more creative ideas or warnings.

Not now. Don't interrupt me now.

"Given form through heart, shape, and will."

She stepped over the corpse of the king. Claws clicked on the wood as she neared. A whimpering groan slipped out of its mouth as it sniffed the air.

"Ceridwen, step back. You can't—"

"Don't move yet, you idiot," Bronwyn reprimanded Malik somewhere behind her.

"To test the hearts of man, she gifted darkness too," Ceridwen continued to sing.

Drystan sat on his haunches, a massive wolflike monster whose head was almost as high as hers, though it sat. She reached out her hand as she sang, leaving it to hover between them just a few inches from his snout. The dark tongue flicked out, licking her fingers.

No biting. No clawing.

"A temptation one can only resist if they stay true."

Her whole arm shook as she stepped closer, running her hands along his head over coarse, dark hair. He rubbed against her arm.

One false move, and he could bite her in two. Despite the risk, she slunk closer until she wrapped her arms around his bloodied fur and stained leathery skin.

"To balance the two, magicless humans remained."

His body shook. A sharp whine, like an injured animal, split in the air.

"Drystan," she whispered before the next line. "Their gray the counterpoint to the magic strain."

Limbs shivered in her grip, giving her voice a harsh warble. Bone twisted and shifted. Fur receded. His skin changed.

"I love you. Please come back to us."

Tears leaked down her face, dripping onto the monster slipping back into the form of a man.

"Ceridwen," he gasped.

She smoothed her palm along his face, now more human than beast.

"I'm here. Right here."

Weak human arms slid around Ceridwen's body as Drystan collapsed on top of her, no longer able to maintain his strength in human form. She took his weight, sliding to the floor with him in an embrace of body and soul. Her heart stuttered as she took in the blood marring his bare skin and the wounds that covered him.

Alive, but—

"I love you," he whispered, barely conscious.

"Hold on, Drystan. You did it. You'll be okay." Tears blurred her vision again. The damage to his body undid her where nothing else had.

Malik limped into view at her side, Bronwyn supporting him. In his hand, he held a glittering golden hoop. Ceridwen sniffled and wiped at her tears.

He held a crown. *The* crown.

Malik placed the object on Drystan's head and dropped to one knee. Bronwyn followed.

"All hail King Tristram Ithael, the king who banished darkness once again," he proclaimed.

The men in the yard echoed him. "All hail King Tristram Ithael."

CHAPTER 53

CERIDWEN

IN THE DAYS THAT followed, Drystan managed to mostly recover with the aid of light magic and skilled medical treatment. He still walked with a slight limp—he always might—but he'd lived.

Word of King Rhion's betrayals spread throughout the kingdom, aided by Malik and his many acquaintances throughout the city. Wynni and her troupe of performers provided great help as well, using their fame and talents to support Drystan's rule. Chesa in particular was an avid supporter and used her talents to turn their story into a performance for stages big and small, a way to spread truth through art and music. She even promised to bring other countries to their aid, if needed, though Ceridwen had no idea how an opera assistant would manage such an outlandish thing.

Not everyone supported the dark prince come back to life to reclaim his throne, though. Many were wary, as they should have been, after years of lies, deception, and dark magic. It would take time to bring the court into order and establish a peaceful reign. Change was always difficult. The road ahead might be more challenging than the one he'd walked, but at least Drystan would have the chance to venture it.

And he wouldn't do it alone.

"Are you ready?" Bronwyn asked. Her sister had taken extra time with her hair today, even allowing one of the maids to help her curl the rich brown locks and pull them back in a waterfall that cascaded down her back. A perfect accompaniment to the forest-green dress hugging Bronwyn's chest and swishing about the floor.

Ceridwen took one last look in the mirror and nodded. A braid of hair had been pulled over the top of her head, the end tucked into the updo, which splayed behind her like a sunburst. Nerves stirred in her gut, but the anticipation burning in her heart won out. "If I'm not now, I'll never be."

Bronwyn looped an arm through her sister's. "Father might faint when he sees you," she teased.

A small laugh slipped through Ceridwen's lips. "If our letter didn't leave him bedridden, this shouldn't either."

He'd be there soon with Jaina, Gerard, and all the residents of the manor in Teneboure. Shortly after the battle, when she was confident Drystan would recover, Ceridwen had written them all to let them know what happened and the changes in the capital. Their letters in response contained both joy and disbelief, yet they'd all promised to come on the train, hopefully to stay for quite a while, if not for good. She'd already researched the best physicians in the city. With their skills, perhaps Father could be healed for good. At the least he'd have more help than they could have ever dreamed of before.

Best of all, Mother's death had been avenged. Ceridwen prayed that the years of sorrow her death heralded were finally at an end. She couldn't change the past. She couldn't save her, but maybe, just maybe, they'd saved other innocents by ending the king's reign.

"Ceridwen Kingslayer." Bronwyn's voice held a mix of awe and pride every time she used that nickname.

Ceridwen rolled her eyes. "I didn't kill the king."

"That's not how I saw it." She winked.

A smile pulled at her lips despite herself.

"Sisters." Adair bowed, one arm across the purple-and-gold sash he now wore as a permanent part of his uniform. He'd accepted a position as the head of the household guard with more exuberance than he'd shown in years. To Ceridwen's surprise, he didn't mind being away from Lydia. "Absence makes the heart grow fonder," he reminded her. Perhaps it did. If nothing else, his new position would raise his lot in her family's eyes.

Adair escorted his sisters through the castle halls until they reached the large set of double doors that led to the formal balcony. Ceridwen's heart thundered as she considered who waited outside.

Malik stood nearby, a blinding smile on his face. The rose pin on his chest marked him as Drystan's advisor. He'd tried to refuse...but not for very long. He had a reason to remain near the castle, one that his attention lingered on now despite her feigned indifference.

"He's waiting for you," Malik said, switching his attention to Ceridwen. "They all are."

She released Bronwyn and stepped toward the doors. With one deep breath, she gathered her courage, letting all her love burn bright and fuel each step forward.

Mother, are you watching today?

"I'm ready."

CHAPTER 54

DRYSTAN

THOUSANDS HAD GATHERED IN the streets outside the castle, jostling one another for the chance to see their new king—their former prince come back to life.

Drystan stood alone in the half-moon space overlooking the crowd below. His attire fit his station. A tailored black coat over a crisp gray shirt embroidered with gold. Black breeches and boots adorned with golden designs completed the base of the look. A gold-and-purple sash crossed his chest, shining with medals and emblems of station. He'd donned the attire several times in fittings, but it still didn't feel quite right on him despite the tailor's exceptional work.

Alone, he was incomplete.

Only one thing made him feel better since the gruesome battle during the midwinter party, and he waited for her on the balcony. His future bride, the country's future queen.

It was the first question he'd asked her after he recovered enough from the battle to think clearly. Blessedly, she hadn't kept him waiting long before giving a tearful and joyous acceptance.

Their future might not be easy, his reign presently unstable at best. Dragons still prowled the shadows, and rooting them all out might take a lifetime. Even so, he had reason to hope because he wouldn't be doing it alone.

Drystan's heart leaped into his throat as one of the double doors leading to the grand balcony groaned open. Commotion rose from the crowd as Ceridwen stepped out into the blinding sun.

She'd never been more resplendent than she looked today, though he often thought that, as if her beauty grew with each moment they spent together.

Despite the masses calling her name, she only had eyes for him, and he smiled at her with joy. "Radiant, as always," he said.

"As are you." Ceridwen took Drystan's outstretched hand and curtsied before him, flaring out her navy-blue dress in a grand show.

Malik stepped through the doors and moved to the edge of the balcony. He called for quiet, and the crowd obeyed.

Never releasing Ceridwen's hand, Drystan turned to face the crowd and drew her with him to the balcony's edge. Cheers rang in his ears, wrapping them in a blanket of praise and support, before quieting once more.

Drystan's words were meant for his people, but he looked only at Ceridwen as he gave his proclamation. "Citizens of Castamar, may I formally introduce you to Ceridwen Kinsley, soon to be Ithael, your future queen."

Cheers rose again, louder than before. They loved her, their musician turned brave warrior, tamer of beasts, and now future queen.

Light sparkled off the diamond in the ring about her finger, a sign of their pledge, as Ceridwen curtsied once more for the crowd. She positively glowed at his side, soaking in the support the people offered.

The promise they'd made when Drystan asked her to marry him was twofold. The standard pledge of marriage: to love, honor, and respect. But also, to aid each other. If she lost her song again, he'd help her find it. If his monster resurfaced, she'd be there to sing it into submission.

Together they were balanced—light, dark, and gray.

Just as the Goddess intended.

Thank you for reading *The Musician and the Monster*!

If you enjoyed this book, please consider signing up for my newsletter to stay in the loop
on all major updates and get access to free bonus content!
www.authormeganvandyke.com/newsletter

Also by Megan Van Dyke

<u>The Courts of Faery Series</u>

A Gift for a Fae Warrior (Prequel Novelette) available free to newsletter subscribers
Aine's Day should be a time for celebration with family. But when the Unseelie dark fae
launch a surprise attack, Galen will have to forego the festivities and fight to protect the
Court of the Forest and the woman he loves.

A Bargain with the Fae King (Book 1)
When Lia Ashmore's younger sister is captured by animalistic, dark Fae, Lia will do
anything to save her, even strike a bargain with the seductive King of the Forest Fae. He'll
help Lia save her sister in exchange for what he wants: Lia as his consort.

Bound by the Fae King (Book 2)
Spunky bartender Wren flees a robbery only to end up in another world and the arms of
a stranger—Sigurd, Fae King of Air. Wren longs to return home, but she's the spitting
image of Sigurd's long-lost love, and he's not about to lose her again.

Forgiving a Fae Warrior (Novella – Book 2.5)
Galen is desperate to redeem himself and return to the Court of the Forest and the woman
he loves. But when his plan goes terribly awry and threatens the life of a new friend, the
path to forgiveness may be more treacherous than ever.

Destined for the Fae King (Book 3)
Coming in 2024

The Reimagined Fairy Tale Collection

Second Star to the Left

Banished for doing the unthinkable, selling the hottest drug in Neverland—pixie dust, Tinker Bell wants absolution. Determined to find a way home, Tink doesn't hesitate to follow the one lead she has, even if that means seducing a filthy pirate to steal precious gems out from under his...hook.

The Ugly Stepsister

Only Anna knows the truth about Cinderella: The pauper turned queen wasn't the victim, but the bully. Disguised as a young man and taking the name of Ansel, Anna will do whatever it takes to free her family and set the record straight, even partner with Will, a former royal huntsman, who has a vendetta of his own to settle with the queen.

The Alice Curse

Eliza fled her parent's political maneuverings only to stumble through a rabbit hole and into the arms of a man named Finn, who declares her the next Alice. Ordered to bring Alice to court, for only she can decide if Red or White shall rule, Finn can't fail without losing his head. For Eliza to get home and Finn to stay alive, they'll have to navigate two treacherous courts and their growing feelings for one another. But a path to freedom for them both may be more than the magic of Wonderland can conjure...even for its new Alice.

Stolen Empire Series

Captive of the Stolen Empire

Once a proud heir, Ilya's world changes forever when her homeland is conquered by a tyrannical empire. She refuses to capitulate to Lucien, her handsome captor — but the passion growing between them will change everything...

Acknowledgements

This book was many years in the making and was such a transformative part of my development as an author, so there are many people to thank. But first and foremost, thank you to my children. You both played a special role in bringing this story to life. I wrote the very first draft of this book while pregnant with my son and years later rewrote it for the final time while pregnant with my daughter. I know, writing a book where the mother ends up dying in childbirth seems like a terrible idea to do while pregnant, but we can't always help what stories we are called to tell and when. But I'm blessed that my children arrived safely, and I made it through unscathed as well. You kids are the best part of life, and I'm so grateful for you.

To my husband, thank you so much for your love and support. You make following my dreams possible and show me new ones all the time. I couldn't do this without you, and I'm forever grateful to have you in my life.

To Mom, thank you for all the music lessons. Look, I finally did something with them! But seriously, thank you for always encouraging my creative and artistic pursuits and reading several versions of this tale and all my others. You're always my biggest cheerleader, and I'm so grateful.

There have been many people who have read all or part of this story over the years and given me feedback on it, and I'm grateful for each and every one. A few in particular who helped shape my writing journey and this story include Kat, Jen, Laura, Abby, Christy, Melody, Paulette, Jeni, Carly, and Rebecca. Thank you to my editor, Heather, for helping shape this story into its best self. To my author friends who've been with me through the good times and bad and who've given me invaluable support and feedback, I'm so grateful for you! Especially my fellow Discordant Owl. You all are a treasure. I'm also so incredibly thankful for my Street Team members and early readers who provided feedback on this book and helped shape some key elements, including the cover and series name—special shout out to Sifa for suggesting the latter. I am so grateful for all of you and everything you do to get the word out about my little books.

Finally, my readers. My goodness, I wouldn't be doing this if not for all of you. Seriously. Please know that every time you buy one of my books, leave a review, tell a friend, or simply sit back and enjoy reading it, I am grateful. When I see posts on social media or receive emails and messages from you about my books, it makes my whole day every single time. Without you all, I'd just be sending words out into the void, so thank you so much for helping to make my dreams a reality.

About the Author

Megan Van Dyke is a fantasy romance author with a love for all things that include magic and romance, especially fairy tales and anything with a happily ever after. Many of her stories include themes of family (whether born into or found) and a sense of home and belonging, which are important aspects of her life as well. When not writing, Megan loves to cook, play video games, explore the great outdoors, and spend time with her family. Megan currently lives with her family in Florida.

Connect with Megan

www.authormeganvandyke.com

www.authormeganvandyke.com/newsletter/

facebook.com/AuthorMeganVanDyke
instagram.com/authormeganvandyke
tiktok.com/@authormeganvandyke
bookbub.com/authors/megan-van-dyke